I read of a man who stood to speak
At the funeral of a friend
He referred to the dates on the tombstone
From the beginning...to the end

He noted that first came the date of birth
And spoke the following date with tears,
But he said what mattered most of all
Was the dash between those years

For that dash represents all the time
That they spent alive on earth.
And now only those who loved them
Know what that little line is worth

For it matters not, how much we own,
The cars...the house...the cash.
What matters is how we live and love
And how we spend our dash.

Linda Ellis

PLAYLIST

Can You Feel My Heart by Bring Me The Horizon

Me Against Myself by Wage War

Dark Can Be Beautiful by Alec Chambers

Legends Never Die by Against the Current

Carry On by Falling In Reverse

Going Ghost by Jeris Johnson

Crash and Burn by Maggie Lindemann

Blink-182&u by Cali Rodi

Fall to Pieces by Pale Waves

Only Place I Call Home by Every Avenue

My Happy Ending by Avril Lavigne

Bring Me to Life by Evanescence

Welcome to the Black Parade by My Chemical Romance

Face Down by The Red Jumpsuit Apparatus

Miss Murder by AFI

Bite Me by Avril Lavigne

Street Lightning by The Summer Set

Lately by Future Palace

Dangerous Woman by Ariana Grande

As You Leave by Canaan Cox

Take on the World by You Me at Six

Hell and Back by Self Deception

I'll Be by Edwin McCain

Shivers by Ed Sheeran

Stay by Justin Bieber and The Kid Laroi

scan below to listen

ONE

OCTAVIA

TWO YEARS AGO

"**C**ome on, kiddo. Time to get up," Dad calls out, and I groan into my pillow. We've been on the road for seven weeks, and after leaving Dallas late last night after his show, all I want to do is stay in bed and forget the world.

"Dad, I'm tired. Just let me sleep a little longer."

"We did that already," he says, and I can hear the smile in his words as I pull the duvet up over my head. "In fact, we did that three times already this morning. Come on, we're stopping soon. I thought we might have a day, just us. Like old times."

Guilt and excitement weave together inside my chest. I really would like to stay in bed, but it's been forever since I just *hung out with Dad. Not that that's entirely my fault. He's been so busy prepping for this tour, and then actually being on stage and performing... not that I'm complaining; I love our life. I love our friends and family, love doing home schooling and actually learning about real life shit as I interact with people so different from those I grew up with.*

I just miss him.

Fuck it.

I kick the sheets off as I roll over and climb from the bed. "Where are we? And where are we going?"

He grins wide at my question as I reach for my duffel and pull out a pair of jeans and a t-shirt. "We're in Nashville. You slept for a long time, Bug, we arrived early this morning—the first time I came to get you..." he teases. "I was thinking a walk by the river and then we could go for ice cream?"

"Let me grab a shower, and that sounds great, Dad."

If possible, he smiles wider as he claps his hands together. "Perfect. I'll let Mac know. Panda is fixing you a late breakfast."

"Thanks, Dad," I call out over my shoulder as I head out of the tiny bedroom at the back of the tour bus and make my way to the even smaller bathroom.

I can't fucking wait for a hotel stop, just for a decent shower.

I jump under the tepid stream, trying to scrub away the exhaustion that still clings to me. We've been living like this, on the road, for the last four years. It feels like forever since we were in Echoes Cove, but other than my friends, I can't say I miss it. Even between tours we never go back. We spend the time going to our favorite places around the world.

I love the down time. Even though security comes with us like, everywhere, it's still better than touring. Though, watching women throw themselves at my dad is just plain gross. Admittedly, not as gross as watching the panties thrown on stage being cleared up after the show.

No sixteen year old girl should have to experience that.

I finish up my quick shower, toweling off as fast as I can—because rule number one of using the one bathroom on a tour bus is never be a bathroom hog—and get dressed in my ripped jeans and faded Nirvana t-shirt before heading out to the sitting area up front. The smell of bacon and eggs wafts throughout the bus, and my stomach growls so loud that a flush works its way across my cheeks.

"Morning, V." Panda smiles at me as I grab a mug of coffee before sliding into the booth we use as a dining table, and he drops a plate of bacon, eggs, and toast in front of me.

"Morning, P." I fall on the plate of food like I've been starved for days and basically inhale it while Panda, Dad, and Mac talk about the security for our little trip—because even if Dad goes full Hannah Montana, there's no way Mac's letting us go out alone.

Spoilsport.

It's the only thing about tour life that I don't like. The fact that I can't go anywhere alone. It definitely made getting my first period heaps *of fun. Especially since most of the team are guys.*

I shudder at the memory.

Maybe one day I can go back to being anonymous. Once I'm not on tour with Dad and I open my own studio, the hype around being 'The King's' daughter should die down. I can dream anyway. Normal life seems so far away from this world.

I glance up at my dad as I hear my name whispered among them but shrug it off and finish my breakfast. I check my phone, noticing the time. Maybe I should call this lunch instead. I laugh under my breath to myself, because I'm just that ridiculous, and drop a message to Jenna.

Me:

We're in Nashville. Doesn't your tour cross over with us this week?"

Jenna:

It sure does, Summertime Starlight. We're opening for your dad tomorrow and Friday, then we headline from Sunday. Wanna hang when we get there tomorrow?

I laugh at the nickname she has for me, which just happens to be the title of the song they're about to drop this weekend.

Me:

Hell yes. I miss you guys!

Jenna:

Perfect. Tacos and chill for us.

Me:

It's a date. Let me know when you guys get in.

I smile at the picture she sends me of her and the rest of the Midnight Blue girls pulling faces at me. They toured with my dad a few years back and we've been tight ever since. Even more so since they blew up, because unfortunately, these days it's hard to tell friend from frenemy.

Rinsing off my dishes before I put them in the small dishwasher, I try to dawdle until Dad is ready. Thankfully, he doesn't take much longer, so I just flick through the news app on my phone. Only world news though, because the gossip rags usually make me gag, and social media isn't any better, which is why I ignore its existence. I don't care if Dad's PR manager moans at me every single day about it, it is so not happening.

"Ready, Bug?" Dad calls out, drawing my attention from the headlines of a corporate scandal in New York with Winchester, Duke & Patterson LLC. Some fancy law firm in hot water for something or other. I slip my phone into the front pocket of my jeans and slip my feet into my Chucks.

"Ready." My smile matches his as he waves me to the exit of the bus. Mac heads out first, while Panda hangs behind looking a little pissed. Guess he's not coming. Though, he's not security

11

so that makes sense. Even if he is around most of the time. I grab my leather jacket and aviators from the back of the chair I dropped them on last night and slip them on before skipping down the stairs of the bus.

Damn, it's bright out here. I'm glad for the aves as my long hair blows about in the breeze. Nashville in the height of summer is fucking hot. *I keep my jacket on though, because I burned way too easily when we were here last year.*

My dad drops onto the pavement behind me, draping his arm over my shoulder. "Come on, kiddo, the ice cream is calling my name."

I look around, noticing the chain-link fence running alongside the bus, and realize we're parked at the stadium. As we step clear of the bus, the screams erupt from every direction as fans begin crushing each other to get closer. I groan as Dad chuckles beside me. "We're not going to get time alone are we?"

"'Course we are, that's what Mac and I were discussing while you ate." He squeezes me in closer and I roll my eyes at him.

"Good. Watching women throw themselves at your feet during the shows is enough, thanks." I stick my tongue out at him and he laughs.

"Don't hate the player, hate the game."

I groan at his cheesiness while he continues to laugh at me as we approach the convoy of blacked out Range Rovers. Dad opens the back door for me, taking just a moment to wave to the screaming women before turning his attention back to me. "After you, Bug."

I climb in and he shuts the door, so I buckle up while he walks around to the other side and Mac climbs in the front.

The convoy takes off, then splits up, each car taking a different direction. I look over at Dad, who smirks. "Told you we'd be fine. It's just us today, Bug. Well, and Mac, but we both know he hides in the shadows better than anyone."

I look up and catch Mac grinning at me in the rearview mirror.

"Good." I smile and relax into the soft leather seats as we head through the city. It doesn't take long until Mac pulls the car to a stop in front of an ice cream parlor.

I return my gaze to Dad, raising my eyebrow. "I really wanted that ice cream," he says, laughing. I join him, shaking my head; he's nothing but a big kid sometimes. "Ice cream, then the walk?"

"Sounds good." I smile as I unbuckle and climb from the car, ignoring Mac's grumbling. There's no way he didn't scope the place out as we pulled up. I close the door behind me, looking around and realizing I'm right. The street is almost dead, as is the parlor. Just a few people sitting at the tables in there, and no more than a handful of people walking the streets. When I reach the sidewalk, my dad is climbing from the car, and Mac is already inside.

We head in, and I take in the giant wall board of a menu.

"Holy crap," I utter. How the hell is a girl supposed to make a decision when there are like eleventy billion flavors available?

Dad rubs his flat stomach, sighing. "I'm going to regret this later when I have to hit the gym, but screw it. What's catching your eye, Bug?"

I blink at him before turning back to the menu. "Cherry ice cream scoop, with a dark chocolate scoop, whipped cream, chocolate syrup, and hazelnuts. I think." I pause, glancing at the myriad options, but decide to go for my favorite. Why not? It's not like I eat ice cream all that often anyway.

Dad waits a second until I nod, letting him know I've made my final decision, and he gives my order to the somewhat starstruck girl behind the counter.

"I'll bring those over for you in a minute, Mr. Royal," she stutters before grabbing three sundae glasses. I head to sit at one of the high tables at the back of the store, because sitting up front just isn't a real option, and Dad hops up onto one of the stools while Mac situates himself at the table one over from ours. He sits with his back to us to give us the illusion of privacy while he watches the main entrance of the store.

"I was thinking this might be our last tour for a little while, Bug," Dad says, shocking the hell out of me.

"Really?"

He shrugs as the girl brings over our order, and he waits until she's gone before he speaks again. "We've been on the road for a long time, I thought you might want to settle for a *little while. Senior year is coming up soon and I thought you might want some of those typical teenage experiences."*

"You want to go back to Echoes Cove?"

"Oh, hell no." He scowls just hearing the town name. "We can go anywhere in the world, why would we go back there?"

I shrug and take a bite of my sundae, groaning as the cherry and dark chocolate bursts on my tongue. So freaking good.

"While there is breath in my body, kid, we'll stay far away from there. Too many memories." He scrubs a hand over his face before looking at me again. "Unless you want to go back?"

"I dunno, but I like our life. I like traveling around, experiencing everything the world has to offer. But if you want to stop touring, that's okay too."

He shakes his head as he swallows down a mouthful. "No way, kiddo. I love doing this. The music grounds my soul. I just figured I should be a parent first, but if you're truly happy, then on tour we'll stay."

I grin at him before taking another bite, feeling relieved. Tour life might be sucky sometimes, but the thought of not living like this… just nope.

Life is only going to get better from here. I can feel it.

ONE YEAR LATER

"Where is she?" Dad yells, and I wince as I hear him stumbling around his dressing room. I really thought he'd keep his promise this time. That he'd manage a day without drinking.

It feels like forever since Dad managed to stay sober for a whole day, in reality it's probably only been six months, but watching his descent into this, watching him slowly kill himself... well, it's killing me.

I don't know what happened when we were in Los Angeles for New Years Eve—I didn't want to go to the swanky party he went to—but whatever it was, it fucked him up and he won't tell me what happened or what's wrong.

I've asked him a dozen times, and he just rambles on about protecting me, and ignorance being bliss. I just wish I knew what was wrong with him. He never used to be like this, but it's like he's running from something and using the bottle as his hiding place. It guts me every time I see him stumbling around after one of his shows, but there's nothing I can do about it. Every time I bring it up, he just denies it all and tells me he's the parent.

I miss the man he used to be.

Mac's voice bellows down the corridor before I hear the opening and slamming of a door, knowing he's in my dad's changing room. The amount of coffee and fuck knows what else Mac pours into him before a show so he's able to perform is eye watering, but even that might not cut it tonight.

Erin, Dad's PR manager, might have to dream up a freaking miracle to keep all of this under wraps. I have no idea how she's managed to keep it quiet for this long, but I guess that's why she gets paid the big money from Dad's label.

I should feel bad, hiding from my dad, pretending that none of this is happening, but I can't stomach seeing him like this anymore. I need to wait for his show to be over and catch him while he's coherent. Plead with him to stop drinking. Try to make him see what he's doing to himself. To me.

We can't keep on going like this. He *can't keep going like this. He's going to kill himself, and I can't let that happen.*

The sound of the support band wraps up, and I pray Mac managed to calm dad down enough to get him ready for the show.

We only have two weeks left and then the tour is done. Maybe Mac will help me get him into rehab somewhere. Or maybe we need to actually take a break from life on the road. Give him time to settle his soul and get back to writing *music instead of performing all the time.*

A knock on my door has me groaning internally as Panda appears in the doorway. He looks like he's seen a ghost, but he's never really liked seeing my dad this messed up. "Mac needs you," is all he says before he disappears back down the hall.

Way to be an emotional support right now, P.

I let out a sigh and slip my feet into my Chucks. Should've known I wouldn't be able to hide from this forever. I head down the hall to where Mac is arguing with my dad, who very obviously hasn't sobered up. "Octavia, thank God. He's refusing to drink any of the coffee or anything without talking to you. Can you please just listen to his ramblings for a minute so we don't have to cancel the show? I'm going to get the support act back out for a long encore to give us some time."

"Sure," I sigh, smiling sadly. He squeezes my shoulder and heads toward the main stage to sort out the stall tactic while I take a deep breath and prepare to face my drunk-off-his-ass dad.

Entering the room, I find him slumped on the couch, his head in his hands. He looks up when the door closes behind me. "There's my princess. I need to talk to you."

"You've got a show, Dad, we should talk later." I pour him a mug of coffee from the pot that Mac had brewing. "You should drink the coffee. Eat the food Mac brought down here for you."

"I don't want the damn coffee!" He stands, stumbling as he does, and my heart breaks a little more. I love my dad, but this version of him isn't my dad. "I need you to listen to me. The Knights are looking for us. You're going to be queen if they don't stop, but I don't want that. You're my princess."

I shake my head at his ramblings. He gets like this when he's drunk. Some of the things he says are beyond insane. It's easier to just smile and nod sometimes.

"I'm not going to be queen of anything, Dad. I'll always be

your princess. Just like you're the king. Please, just drink the coffee."

"Fine," he grumbles. "Just never become king. Even if James says it's safe. It will never be safe."

Who the hell is James?

My heart cracks some more at his ramblings.

"I won't become king, Dad. I can't be a king. I'm a princess."

"You better be," he sighs as he starts gulping down the lukewarm coffee and eating the pastries Mac bought for him.

"I'm going to go find Mac," I tell him softly, patting his shoulder. "Promise me you'll eat the food. All of it."

"I promise," he groans, rolling his eyes at me. "I'm sorry, princess."

I close my eyes to stop the tears that prick at them. "It's okay, Dad. We'll talk more later, okay?"

"Okay."

I leave the room, taking a deep breath as I lean my back against the closed door in an effort to compose myself before heading off to find Mac. I need to get my dad some help.

Just two more weeks.

That's what I need to remember.

Two weeks, and then I can get him better help.

TWO

OCTAVIA

Everything since leaving my meeting with Harrison has been a blur.

I really just sold my soul to the devil.

Taking a deep breath, I hold it to try and calm my racing heart. I might have sold my soul, but I saved them; that's all I've wanted since I realized they were shackled. At least now they can be free.

I'm only temporarily restrained.

I hope.

What I'm not too stupid to realize is that I'm going to need some help, so I drop a message to Bentley, the PI I hired to look into my mom. If anyone can hunt down this information, it's likely going to be him.

The part that doesn't sit well with me—that's had my stomach churning since I left that office and slid into the back of this town car—is that I need to keep all of this a secret from the guys. I've yelled at them so often about keeping things from me when they thought they were protecting me, and this makes me such a fucking hypocrite, but it was one of Harrison's terms, so as much as I hate it, I'm not going to ruin the chance I have to free them over something so stupid as my guilty conscience.

The car pulls up to my house and I find Smithy home, collecting the mail.

"Miss Octavia, where have you been?" he asks, eyeing the black car as it drives away.

I try to smile, but it falls flat. He frowns in response and wraps an arm around my shoulders. "How about I fix us some milkshakes and you tell me all about it?"

Pausing, I question whether that's a good idea, but I need to tell *someone*, and Smithy knows about the Knights—he knew my dad—maybe he'll know how to find whatever my dad had buried away that Harrison wants.

I stretch up on tiptoes and peck his cheek. "That sounds perfect, thank you."

He squeezes my shoulders tight before leading me inside and pushing me onto one of the stools at the island counter. The cold granite countertop helps me ground myself and slow my racing thoughts as I try to filter through everything I need to say in order to explain this properly.

Smithy flits around the kitchen, and it's soothing to be back here, just the two of us. It's almost like a flashback to before I realized what a fucking mess my life was. Before secret societies and death threats and stalkers were a part of everyday life. When a school bully was my biggest problem.

And to think I thought I had issues then.

I start to laugh, and Smithy looks at me like I've lost it. Hell, maybe I have, because I laugh until my stomach hurts and tears roll down my face. Each time I try to calm myself by sucking in a breath, I just look up at him and the laughter starts again.

This isn't funny, and that only makes it funnier.

Fuck my actual life.

He makes the chocolatiest shakes I've ever seen; with syrup, whipped cream, chocolate curls, and God knows what else, before sitting down opposite me and sliding one of them over. Once my laughter subsides, I take a sip, sighing at the happy memories the flavor evokes while he watches me.

He lets me procrastinate for a minute while I sip down the thick shake before quirking a brow at me.

I let out a sigh, running a hand through my hair before telling him everything about Panda; what he said while I was gone, having Bentley look into Mom, freaking *everything*. I know he knew some of it already, but I can't tell him the next part without him having the whole picture. Once he's up to date on all of the fucking insanity—and not exactly looking pleased about some of the information I've omitted up to this point—I tell him the part I've been working up to with my ramblings. "I made a deal with Harrison Saint."

He sucks in a breath, frowning at me, but motions for me to continue while he takes a pull on his shake.

"I got the boys free from the Knights. No more strings, no repercussions. Instant access to their trust funds with no stipulations."

"And how, Miss Octavia, did you manage such a feat?"

I pick at the skin by my thumb nail, not exactly enjoying the way he watches me like I'm a naughty toddler. But I suck it up and press on. "Dad set up a contract when he left the Knights. It stipulated that I was free of the Knights, but protected by them. That would be true for me and the rest of my line unless I, or anyone in the future, chooses to join them. It also stated that should I be approached, hurt by, or initiated into the Knights, I instantly take the Regency."

He opens his mouth but I continue, because if I don't get this out now, I never will. "I met with Harrison today, and he gave me the option to stay free." I pause and take a sip of my shake, like the sugar will give me the boost I need to tell him everything. "I could be free if I gave him information Dad has collected on him and the rest of his Sect… or the Knights as a whole, I'm not sure. So I tried to barter the information for everyone's freedom, but he shot me down."

"And then what?" he asks, and I can't read him. His voice is low, like he's pushing down a simmering anger, but I try not to focus on that. Enough people are going to be pissed at me when they realize what I've done, at least to start with.

"Then I told him no deal, that I'd just find the information and release it, so he was fucked either way."

Smithy barks out a laugh and reaches across the counter, taking my hand and squeezing it. "That's my girl."

"Then he offered me their freedom in place of mine. That I would become the Regent heir until my birthday. He gave me two weeks to find the information, which just happens to fall in line with two weeks before my birthday. He also said I couldn't tell the guys of our deal until the deal is done and he has the information."

"Convenient," he huffs, and I smirk at him before continuing.

"Then he admitted to having Dad killed for the information. That Edward Riley was responsible for it. He didn't say outright that I would suffer the same fate if I didn't comply, but it was implied."

His face turns a mottled red as his anger bubbles up to the surface and he takes a few breaths, muttering incoherently under his breath.

"I had suspected as much. Evan said something along those lines when he held me captive, and he had no reason to lie about it. Not really. I just wish Dad would have told me about all of this when I was younger. There might've been something I could have done to save him."

"Absolutely not," Smithy shouts before taking a deep breath. "Miss Octavia, anything your father kept from you was to keep *you* safe. I am positive that he wouldn't have wanted you wrapped up in all of this darkness, and kept it from you as his way to ensure that stayed the case."

"If that was the case, then why would his will require that I come back here? Why not keep me away?"

The corners of Smithy's mouth turn up as he thinks over my question. "I think *that*, my beautiful girl, is likely because of me. Your father knew I was here and alone; I can only assume that he thought if you and I were both alone, better that we be alone together."

I squeeze his hand back, hating to think of him being lonely. It's one of the few reasons I'm glad my dad sent me back here. The thought of not having Smithy in my life now isn't one I want to dwell on.

"Regardless of the why, this is where we are now, and we need to work out how to make the best of it. I do wish you'd come to me before you made a deal with that scoundrel, but if there is anything I can do to assist with your search, please let me know. As for what you did for the boys… while I'm sure they won't be pleased about your sacrifice, in time I'm sure they'll come to see it for what it was."

"Thank you, Smithy." I finish my milkshake, nervous energy gripping my muscles. "At least now we know I'm somewhat safe. The Knights want something from me, so they kind of need me alive; my stalker situation is done with, so I can breathe a little easier; there are still threats, but I know what they are now. That has to be a bonus."

"Hmmmm." He raises an eyebrow at me, his skepticism noted. "We can hope at least."

"Exactly," I say, smiling wide as I jump from my seat. "I need to run, so I'm going to go and get changed, then head out for an hour or so."

"Okay, I'll ensure dinner is ready for you upon your return."

I move around the island and hug him tight. "Thank you, Smithy. For everything."

With a peck on the cheek, I dart upstairs and get changed out of the stuffy clothing I had on for the meeting and change into my leggings, sports bra, and pull a tank over the top.

Definitely wasn't how I pictured my Saturday going, but I can't help but smile.

I bought their freedom, and even if they hate me for it, at least I'll know they're free.

After running until my legs turned to jelly—because running from my problems is obviously how I'm going to get things done—and Smithy making me taco boats, because he loves me just that much, I stare at Bentley's name on my phone.

I haven't reached out to any of my guys all day, and I haven't heard from them either, but I know I need to get the ball rolling on this shit that Harrison wants before I chicken out. The only way to get their freedom, and make sure I don't end up buried next to my dad, is to find the information.

I dial Bentley's number and the ringing seems to go on forever, but when he finally answers the phone, his surprise is audible. "Miss Royal? Is everything okay?"

I can't help but smile. I only met him twice, but he almost sounds concerned. "Hey, Bentley. Yeah, everything is okay. I just wondered if you had some time for me this week? I have some more work for you."

The sound of rustling papers and the closing of a drawer sound through the line before he answers. "I absolutely can. In fact, I'm free this evening if you don't mind a late one? I'm about half an hour away from Echoes Cove."

"That's perfect, thank you. I'll drop you my address if you're okay coming to the house?"

"No need, I still have it. But yes, coming to the house is fine. I'll see you soon." The line drops, and I bite the inside of my lip.

At least I'm getting this out of the way sooner rather than later.

I pad back into the kitchen and find Smithy making himself a cup of Earl Grey. "Miss Octavia, is everything okay?"

"Yeah." I smile at him as I grab a bottle of water from the refrigerator before jumping onto the counter, the cold from the stone surface penetrating my leggings. "My private investigator is heading over; I figure he's going to be a good bet to help me with finding the info Harrison wants."

He looks at me skeptically. "Are you sure you can trust this man?"

I nod at him and smile. "I'm sure. He was recommended by a friend, and he helped me look into Mom to see if we could find her. He's discreet, and I trust him to be professional."

"Who is he?"

"His name is Bentley... that's actually all I know about him," I say, laughing while I shake my head. "Should probably know more, but my gut tells me I can trust him."

"You're a good judge of character, so I'll take your word for it, but how about we get to know him a little if he's coming over this evening?" Smithy's suggestion isn't wildly out there, so I nod my agreement.

"Can't hurt anything."

We talk through the possibilities of where my dad would've hidden something he'd deemed so important, making a list on my phone, and it occurs to me that I should probably speak to Mac too. Nobody on the tour has reached out about Panda, so I have no idea if they know about the stalking or even that he's dead.

Too much has been falling through the cracks lately, but I vow to be a better friend now that some of the chaos in my life should start to settle. Not just to those who were basically my family the last few years, but to everyone around me. Speaking of which…

"How are things with you and Matthew?" I ask Smithy, and he smiles in that lovey dovey way that you just can't help when you're head over heels.

"We are doing just fine. Thank you, Miss Octavia."

I grin at him, my heart soaring that he's so happy. "I'd like to get to know him better, if you'd like that? I know we did dinner, but you might've noticed I've been a little distracted lately."

He barks out a laugh, nearly choking on his tea. "No, it had escaped my notice."

I stick my tongue out at him, and his smile grows. "Well, hopefully things should quiet down a little, so if you're both open to it, we should do something. Even if it's just another dinner. You're family, so if he's important to you, then he's important to me."

"I would like that very much." His smile is contagious and warms my heart.

"Perfect. Well, work out when is best for you guys and I'll make myself free. I know I've got finals and stuff coming, but I'm sure we'll pin down some time."

"Are you ready for your exams? Are your grades where you need them to be?" His fatherly tone isn't lost on me, but instead of coming off as condescending, it just makes me feel loved.

"My grades are fine, I'm just about scraping by, and a few teachers have given me extra credit assignments since I missed those few weeks, but I think it's going to be okay." He pats my shoulder reassuringly just as the buzzer to the gate sounds. I check my phone and see Bentley's smiling face on the screen. I hit the entry button as Smithy strides out of the kitchen to get the door.

It doesn't take long for Smithy to reappear with Bentley, the two of them talking as they enter the room. "Glad to see you guys are fast friends." I laugh as Bentley grins at me.

"You certainly surround yourself with some interesting characters, Miss Royal."

"Please, just call me Octavia," I say, waving for him to sit. "Coffee?"

He nods as he sits. "I'd love some."

I move to make it, but Smithy tuts as he bustles around the kitchen to fix the drink before he places the steaming mug in front of our visitor and takes a seat beside me.

"So, what can I do for you, Octavia?" Bentley asks before taking a sip of the coffee. His eyebrows rise as he sips it. "This is possibly the best coffee I've ever had."

"Miss Octavia is something of a coffee snob," Smithy snorts. "Only the best here."

Bentley grins, his eyes crinkling at the edge as I try to look put out, but I know it misses the mark because I can't help but laugh. He isn't wrong. I love coffee.

"A girl needs the good things in life," I say with a shrug. "As for what I need you for, it's… a little sensitive."

His forehead furrows as he nods. "Ruin people sensitive or

get me dead sensitive?"

"Both?" The word comes out as more of a question than a statement as a blanket of tension settles over us all.

"What exactly are you mixed up in?" Bentley asks skeptically. I open my mouth to answer, but Smithy interrupts me.

"Before we tell you that, why don't you tell us a little about you?"

Bentley seems taken back by Smithy's question but composes himself quickly. "My name is Bentley Kensington. I grew up on the East Coast, living among the rich and famous, where I learned that secrets are as good a currency as money itself. My older brother took over the family business, which I was glad for, because it had never interested me, and I joined the Marine Corps. I can't tell you much about my time with the forces because it's classified, but if you have the access I assume you do, it shouldn't be too hard for you to uncover if you want to look." He pauses, taking another sip as I process everything he's saying. "When I decided enough was enough with ops, I came home and realized I had a skillset that I could mix with what I had learned about secrets when I was younger. I've been doing this for about six years now, and the connections my family has meant I've had some very upscale and high risk clients. Which is exactly how Octavia found me."

Smithy nods, like he believes every word. Not that we have any reason not to, and my instincts still tell me I can trust him.

"Kensington as in Kensington Enterprises?" Bentley smiles at Smithy's question and nods.

"The one and the same."

Smithy stands and pats my shoulder. "Ice cream anyone? I think the rest of this conversation is going to require comfort food."

Bentley looks a little shocked, but nods. "Glad I passed the test."

Smithy chuckles while I nod, agreeing to ice cream, because I'm not an idiot. "You start filling in our friend, Miss Octavia, while I sort the snacks."

I grin at him before turning back to Bentley. "This might take a while, so buckle in."

After Bentley leaves, I feel a lot better than I did after I finished my meeting with Harrison. To say he was a little taken aback by everything I told him would be an understatement of epic proportions. I gave him the option to back out after I laid all my cards on the table, but he laughed at me and told me he's faced scarier people than rich white guys.

He left about an hour ago, and I've been staring up at my ceiling for the last forty minutes, trying to will sleep to come to me. I texted the guys in our group chat, but no one responded. Not that I'm all that shocked, it's nearly one in the morning and most people are sleeping. If they're sane, anyway. And while my guys might not always fall into that category, they're not exactly party animals either.

I'm just hoping Harrison has kept his word and doesn't have them out doing something for him.

I toss and turn, wishing for sleep, and after another twenty minutes, give up.

Late night swim it is. Maybe I just need more exhaustion to shut my brain down.

I kick off the covers and stomp to my closet, slipping out of my pj's and pulling on my swimsuit, wrapping my robe around myself before heading downstairs.

I hit the button to uncover the pool, steam rising from the surface of the water into the cold night air as I flick the lights on so I can actually see.

Dropping the robe onto one of the patio chairs, I break into a run as the cold air hits my skin and dive into the heated water. I push to swim under the surface until my lungs burn and surface to finish my lap before pushing and doing laps until my muscles quiver.

When a shrill ring cuts through the silence of the night, I pull myself from the water and sprint to my phone.

Dread slams through me when I see Finn's name on the screen.

I quickly dry my hands on the robe before answering. "What's wrong?"

My heart pounds in my ears, so loud I almost don't hear him through my panic. "It's Mav. You need to get to the hospital. Now."

THREE

MAVERICK

"**M**av!" The shouts of my name stir me, but I feel like I've been hit by a fucking truck and my eyes feel like they've had sand poured into them as they open. Everything is blurry.

I blink a few times to clear my vision as the memory of what happened comes back to me, just as pain roars in my lower back. That's what I get for dropping the knife I guess, my own fucking knife in the back.

Fuck me.

My dad's dead weight is crushing and my head pounds as I try to bring my arms up to push him off of me. The weakness from the blood loss makes it a lot fucking harder than it should be. The girls in the cages just stare at me with wide eyes, silently. It's not like they can help me; they're literally locked away.

"Down here," I try to shout, but it doesn't feel loud enough, so I try again, barely able to breathe under the dead weight above me, too weak to roll him off.

Please, fuck, don't let me die like this.

I take a few breaths to try and replenish the energy I don't have. I'm covered in fucking blood and I don't know how much of it is mine, but the fact that I can barely focus isn't good. I've been trained for this situation, so I don't freak out, I just need to get some help.

I hear them calling my name above me and realize the door must have been left open a little. That's when I feel my phone start to ring in my pocket. It's set to loud and the ring is so fucking shrill that I can only hope the boys hear it all the way down here.

The sound of the door slamming open followed by footsteps banging down the stairs brings me so much Marie-fucking-Kondo-level joy.

I am not ready to die. I have too many things I want to do with my girl before I die.

"Fuck, Mav!" Finn's voice sounds more panicked than I'd like.

"Help me," I groan as he and Linc pull my dad's dead body off of me. "Knife... in my back."

Lincoln hisses as he rolls me over. "Go grab a towel or

three so we can secure this," he barks at Finn, who nods and disappears.

"We've got you, man. Just hold on." He scrubs a hand down his face and I nod, letting my eyes flutter closed.

Fuck it's cold on the stone ground.

"Is that…?" Linc asks, and I look up at him and nod. "Fuck."

Finn reappears and I bite down as they wrap the knife with the towels to make sure it doesn't move before lifting me from the ground.

"We need to get you to the hospital. We'll come back and deal with… whatever all of this is once you're there," Linc says before they drag me up the stairs and through the house. Finn opens the back door of the Cayenne and they lay me down face-first on the back seat before climbing up front.

The Porsche grumbles to life, and I let my eyes close again.

"Wake up, man." Finn's words just about rouse me as he pulls me from the car. Linc strides toward us, a team of doctors and nurses behind him with a stretcher.

The voices all merge together as my knees give out and the world fades to black again.

The sounds of voices and beeping greet me as I wake, wondering exactly why it is I feel like I took the worst beating of my life. It takes way too much energy to open my eyes, but I find Finn sitting in the chair beside my bed, asleep, and Lincoln murmuring in the doorway with what looks like a nurse.

"S'up, boys," I croak, trying to smile as Finn's eyes open and Linc turns to face me. The relief that washes over them both is palpable.

"Oh good, you're awake." The woman I recognize as Dr. Stanton from when Easton was in here pushes past Lincoln as she approaches me. "I've seen too much of your friends lately, Mr. Riley. I suggest no more run-ins with knives."

I grin at her, trying not to look as lousy as I feel. "Come on Dr. Stanton, you know I can't make promises like that."

I look back toward the door, looking for my girl, but don't want to say anything until the doc is gone.

"Indeed, Mr. Riley." She quirks a brow at me before letting out a sigh. "You are extremely lucky. Other than blood loss, your injury was fairly minimal. By that, I mean the blade didn't hit anything too vital. But it did go fairly deep, so you're going to be sore and healing for a few weeks. We had to repair your kidney, which was damaged by the blade, but not so bad that it had to be removed. Your CT scan showed no brain bleed, but it's likely you have a concussion. We've stitched you up, and you're going to need to take it easy, but no major damage. You'll be out of here in a day or two as long as you remain stable and feel well enough."

"Doc, it almost sounds like you care."

She twists her lips as she rolls her eyes. "I'd just really

rather not see you boys again. Now there's a Foley catheter in place to measure your urine output due to your injury. I'll have someone come and remove it now you're awake."

"There's a tube in my dick?" I ask, and now the discomfort makes sense.

"Yes, Mr. Riley, there is a tube in your penis. Please try to refrain from playing with it until the nurse arrives."

Finn barks out a laugh as I groan before the doc turns and leaves the room. That's some bedside manner she has. I turn to face Linc once the door is closed and drop the bravado about how much I fucking hurt. "My dad?"

"The house is locked down, but we haven't been back there to deal with it yet." He looks at Finn then back at me. "Was that Emily Royal in the corner?"

"Yeah, apparently she's my dad's favorite pet. *Was* my dad's favorite pet." I run a hand down my face, trying to think of how the fuck we're going to break this to my girl. "Where is V?"

"We called her, and she was here, but you were in surgery for a while, so I made East take her home, despite her arguments to stay. I'll call her in a minute now that you're awake." I nod at Linc's answer, I bet that argument wasn't fun.

"Did you tell her?"

Finn shakes his head. "No, we didn't get a good look at her so we didn't want to say anything until we spoke to you. Did your mom know?"

"No fucking clue, but I doubt it. Dad didn't let her anywhere near the basement. What the fuck are we going to tell the Conclave?"

Linc quirks a brow at me. "You don't think Harrison knew she was down there?"

"Oh no, I have no doubt he did. I meant about the fact that my dad is dead." I let out a deep sigh. I'm fucking exhausted, but I want to see my girl before I go back to sleep.

"We'll deal with that later. First, let me call V and get her here. Then Finn and I will head to the house and deal with the clean up. And the girls down there."

I nod, leaning back and closing my eyes when he finishes speaking. "Get my girl here."

Finn laughs softly. "I'm on it." He stands and grabs his jacket from the back of the chair, leaving without another word, while Linc pulls his phone from his pocket.

"We're going to need some help with your dad and this bullshit."

"Who are you calling?"

He glances up at me before speaking. "East first. I figure Chase is as good a guy as any to have on our side right now as well. Then I'm going to call Alex and see if Luc is back in the country."

"Wait, what?"

"Yeah, that's why he disappeared on us. Classified something or other. So I'll ask if Alex knows anything." He puts the phone to his ear and paces the room. Fuck me, this getting stabbed shit is draining. I've been stabbed before, but never lost as much blood as I did this time. I guess that'll teach me.

Some people might find it weird that I have absolutely zero regret or remorse for killing my dad, but I don't. I won't dwell on it. He tried to kill me, and the one thing he taught me is that you don't need to be the strongest to survive this world. Just the deadliest.

I'm also not worried about the repercussions, because one, I have my boys, and two, there's no way the Knights will let my dad's proclivities get out. Which means they'll cover it up, even if we don't.

My biggest worry is what this means for me regarding the fucking business bullshit. I am not made for that shit. Also, I am so not ready to be declared a fucking responsible adult. But it's not like my mom is in any better shape than I am. She's been away, sunning it up on a beach since she got out of the hospital a few weeks ago to try and sort her own mental state out.

Fuck my life.

Edward being gone is definitely an advantage, but it's also a total pain in the dick.

Lincoln circles back to the bed and drops into the chair Finn vacated. "Luc is not back, but Finn just picked up V and East is on his way to get Chase. You should probably rest until they get here."

I snort a laugh. "Yeah, 'cause with the way Finn drives, I'll manage to get my eyes closed for all of five minutes."

"I made him take her to get food." Linc smirks. "We both know she won't have eaten, and she's still not eating properly after the bullshit with Evan."

I frown, mulling over his words. It's not like I hadn't noticed, but I thought she was getting better.

A nurse enters the room, interrupting me as I open my mouth to respond. "Mr. Riley, I'm here to remove your catheter."

I wince, and Linc stands pretty quickly. "I'll be outside," he says with a smirk before dashing out of the door.

I groan as I lie back. "Let's get this over with. And if I get a hard on, it's not my fault. My dick has a mind of its own."

FOUR

OCTAVIA

My heart has been like a hummingbird since Finn called me in the middle of the night. Seeing Maverick hooked up to all those machines just gave me flashbacks of East.

Too many of us have been in the hospital lately, and I'm sick of it.

I'm furious that Edward tried to kill him, that Harrison obviously fucked up somewhere because why else would he try to kill him other than Harrison releasing him from the Knights. Guilt is eating me alive. I can't tell them about it either, so it's stewing inside of me, threatening to make me vomit with every breath I take.

When Linc ordered East to bring me home after we knew

Mav would be okay, I was pissed, but I was also relieved. I was exhausted, and being in the hospital just brings back stuff I don't want to relive any time soon.

That being said, I'm on my way back there with Finn now, and my hands won't stop fucking shaking.

"He's okay," Finn says softly, gripping my hand in his. "I saw him, awake, joking around. Typical Mav. Probably wasn't even really that hurt. Just fucking around with us."

I smile at him, appreciating the reassurance, but until I speak to him myself, the worry is going to gnaw at me. I'm not sure the guilt will ever disappear.

Especially while I'm keeping secrets.

I just have to hope they forgive me eventually.

We pull up at the hospital, and I drop East a message to let him know we got here. He said he was going to see Chase, and I didn't question it. There's so much going on right now, and with Edward being dead, we're going to need a Conclave member on our side.

Maybe more than one.

But that's a future me problem. Right now, I want to focus on Maverick and make sure he's actually okay, and not just pretending to be, because… well, trauma.

I climb from Lincoln's Porsche that Finley picked me up in and round the SUV to where he's waiting for me, his arm outstretched. I take the offered hand and let him lead me back into the hospital. An emergency follows us through the doors, so it's chaos. Finn pulls me back against him and presses us against a wall as the paramedics wheel someone past us, one of them on top of the stretcher doing CPR as they rush past.

I stay pressed up against Finn until the swarm of people have moved past, hoping whoever it is is okay, then turn my focus back to Maverick. Stepping forward as soon as Finn's hold loosens a little, I lead him to Mav's room, finding Lincoln sitting in the chair beside the bed, the two of them laughing quietly as I open the door.

Mav's eyes find me the minute I step through the doorway, and something inside of me settles. He's really okay. My eyes flit over him, trying to make sure that what my mind is saying is real.

"I'm okay, princess," Mav says, patting the bed beside him. It breaks me from my trance and I move toward him, taking his hand and kissing him gently when I reach him. He tugs me down onto the bed and I let out a small squeal before he deepens the kiss. "I've been wanting to do that since I woke up."

I press my forehead against his, smiling to myself. I school my smile and pull back, looking down at him. "You scared me, Maverick Riley."

"Sorry, princess. I won't promise not to do it again because, well, occupational hazard, but know I'll always try to come home to you." He looks so serious, and despite wanting to swoon at the last part of his sentence, I can't help but frown.

I wish I could tell him he's not tied to that life anymore.

Just a couple more weeks.

"You should sit," he says, moving a little on the bed, and I scoff.

"I am not getting into that bed with you. I'll hurt you."

His eyes narrow and he tugs on my hand, pulling me against him, laughing at my squeak as I fall. "Wasn't a request. I need to tell you something, and I need you close while I do."

My heart hammers in my chest. "What is it?"

East and Chase enter the room as I finish my question.

"That's timing. Saves me saying this twice," Mav says, letting out a deep breath. I look across the room and find Linc and Finn watching us. I can't make out what's wrong as both of them have their cold masks in place. That on its own tells me I'm not going to like whatever I'm about to hear.

"Good to see you awake, man," East says, before sitting on the uncomfortable looking couch to the right of the room. Chase follows him.

"What else do we need to know?" Chase asks, looking from Maverick to Lincoln.

Mav shudders beside me, and my stomach twists. Not much fazes him, so this must be bad.

"I'm just going to start at the beginning, because some stuff still doesn't make complete sense to me," he says, and my stomach twists. Guilt burns the back of my throat, but I stay silent. I can't be the reason that he doesn't get free. "Tonight, my dad was in a rage, which isn't new. Not sure what pissed him

50

off, but he said something about 'us kids not knowing our place' or some bullshit like that. Then he did something he's never done. He said he was going to teach me a lesson and dragged me into his basement."

He takes a deep breath, but the whole room stays quiet. He grips my hand in his and squeezes tightly. "I've never been into the basement of my house. I've heard the screams, the cries, but going up against my dad was never an option. He told us to stay away, so I did. I had no idea…"

He trails off so I squeeze his hand back, trying to be the support he needs. "There were cages lining the walls. Girls in those cages. His pets, he called them. Octavia…" he pauses and my blood turns cold. He never calls me Octavia. "He had your mom down there. He said she was his favorite pet. It's why he agreed to kill your father. He wanted you down there, too, so he could have the collection."

I think I'm going to be sick.

I sit up and turn to face him, but he won't meet my eyes. "My mom is in your dad's basement?"

"Octavia," Linc says, stepping forward. I glance at him, then Finley, then East.

"You all knew?"

"Only from when Mav woke up while you weren't here. East had no idea," Finn says. The anger inside of me wants to rip at them for keeping secrets. I have my own that I'm keeping and I'm trying not to be a spoiled fucking bitch, but holy shit this is… I have no words.

I turn back to Maverick, wanting to know the whole story. "Then what happened?"

"Then my dad pulled a gun. He told me there was no point in looking to any of his pets for help, because they were loyal to him. We struggled, fell, I landed on the fucking knife I dropped, and the gun went off as I banged my head on the ground. The next thing I remember was these two showing up."

I let out a breath, leaning back on the bed, trying to let it all sink in without overreacting. I can't tell if I'm numb, or just in shock.

My mom was in his dad's basement. I wonder for how long? "Are the girls still down there?"

"Yes, that's why we asked East to bring Chase. We're going to need some help sorting this out," Linc answers as Mav holds me tightly, as if he's scared I'm going to run away.

I have zero intention of running anywhere.

"I want to see my mom."

"Maybe we should assess what sort of state she's in first. If she's been down there a while… well, Edward isn't—wasn't— the nicest guy. They're all very likely going to need some professional help," Chase says softly.

Finn nods. "The Knights facility that my mom's in. We could move the girls there. Get them help, treatment, and then once she's assessed, I can take you to see her."

Lincoln nods, glancing at Mav who hasn't said anything.

"Should we move your mom there too? I know she's been away for a few weeks, but you said she was fragile. This might just tip her over."

"Probably for the best," Mav says with a nod.

The door opens, and Dr. Stanton enters, frowning at me when she sees me on the bed. I try to move, but Mav's hold doesn't relent. "Sorry to break up this party, but visiting hours are over for this ward for a few hours and Mr. Riley needs some rest. You can come back this afternoon if you wish."

"Doc—" Mav starts, but she shakes her head, cutting him off.

"Rest, Mr. Riley, is the only way you're getting out of here." She looks pointedly at him, and he rolls his eyes.

"Fine," he says before kissing the top of my head. "Come back and see me tomorrow?"

"You know I will," I murmur before jumping from the bed, watching as Linc, Finn, East, and Chase talk quietly.

East moves to me and smiles sadly. "Come on, I'll take you home while they deal with everything else."

I nod, taking his hand. "Okay."

He looks a little shocked, I assume at my lack of fight, but I really just need to process. I thought my mom left me, that she *chose* not to come back. But I could've been wrong. Maybe she *couldn't* come back, and that is a whole new mindfuck for me to try and work through.

The drive home is quiet. East lets me lose myself in my head and I'm grateful. The emotions are like a tsunami fighting a hurricane. The guilt at what happened to Maverick, knowing that this is almost definitely linked to the deal I made with Harrison, the shock of discovering my mom was being kept by Edward—Harrison already told me he had killed my dad—it's all a lot to process.

That on top of the deal I made, the fact that I'm still working through what that means for us all from here... I hate keeping secrets, especially from the four of them, but I know I have to if I want them to be free.

Harrison seems like the kind of snake who will get free of anything if there's even the slightest possibility that he can. I'm not going to give him the chance. The guys deserve to be free, I just hadn't considered that Harrison didn't promise they'd be *alive* and free.

Fucking loopholes.

We pull up to the gates, East tapping in the code before we head up the drive and pull to a stop in front of the garages. "Are you okay?"

I look up at him, trying to work out how to answer him without outright lying. Leaning my head back against the seat, I close my eyes for a minute, hoping the pounding in my head might subside. "I will be. I'm just so sick of the shit those three have to put up with."

"I am too. I've been trying for years to find a way to get them out the way Stone got you out. I know Chase helped with the details of your dad's contract, him being a lawyer and all, but he's a little sketchy about the details. Considering I'm not technically a Knight, I get it. Maybe he'll give you more details?"

My heart skips a beat and I try to lock down my reaction. "I'm not a Knight."

"Not officially, but the contract your dad made means it's probably going to happen at some point." He shrugs before unbuckling and climbing from the car.

Keeping this secret is going to be harder than I thought. I need to work on my poker face.

I climb from the car and follow him inside, finding Smithy and Matthew in the kitchen. "Miss Octavia, Master East. How is Master Riley?"

He pulls out one of the stools for me, motioning for me to sit down, and East sits beside me, watching Matthew closely.

"Where are my manners?" Smithy says, flustered. "Master East, I'd like you to officially meet Matthew. Matthew, this is Easton Saint. One of Octavia's suitors."

"Nice to meet you." East eyes Matthew warily, and I subtly nudge him with my elbow.

Matthew laughs, so I guess it wasn't that subtle. "Likewise.

I've heard so much about you all, I feel like I already know you."

"Funny, because I haven't heard anything about you."

"East!" I hiss. "You sound like Lincoln. Stop it."

He looks at me and has the decency to look sheepish before turning back to Matthew. "Sorry, it's been a long few days."

"I get it," Matthew says, waving him off. "How about we have breakfast together, then you can learn I'm not some nefarious monster in the dark."

I press my lips together, trying not to laugh. If only Matthew knew the monsters we usually play with. I can't help but wonder if Smithy has told him about the Knights. I glance over at him and he's busy cooking, not paying any attention to us.

"Sounds good." East smiles, and I leave them to it, listening in as Matthew tells East about his work—something to do with hedge funds. I tune out when they start talking numbers—not my strongest suit. Maverick in the hospital plays on my mind, and I try to think of a way to confront Harrison about it without getting Maverick in deep shit. I have no idea how the Knights will handle this, but my deal called for them to have the same protections as the Knights. I just hope it's enough.

I tune back into East and Matthew talking about a trip Matthew and Smithy took skiing. The conversation drives me over to Smithy at the stove.

"Hey, is there anything I can do to help?" I ask, needing the distraction, even if just to get out of my own head.

Smithy looks down at me, smirking. "Nothing needs burning, Miss Octavia, but if you'd like to pour everyone a drink, I'm sure it would be welcome."

I laugh softly, shaking my head. "I can do that. Maybe you should give me some cooking lessons. If I get to go away to college, I'm going to need to learn how to survive."

"Indeed," he says, frowning. "Or I can just relocate with you."

I haven't given much thought to college lately. I remember when my goals were so set, but this year has been a minefield. It strikes me that none of the guys have talked about college either, not really. I wonder if they'll go now that they're free?

My future is uncertain, I don't even know if college is still in the cards for me thanks to the deal with Harrison, but that isn't for me to worry about right now. "Sounds perfect," I respond to him, smiling. "Though, you might want to settle down with Matthew rather than coming wherever I go."

"Oh, Miss Octavia, I might be fairly certain I'm in love with him," he says quietly, glancing at Matthew and East behind us. "But if you need me, you are, and will always be, my first priority."

I reach up on my tiptoes and kiss his cheek. "I love you, Smithy."

"And I you. Now pour everyone a drink, breakfast is almost ready."

I've never been more glad that I told him my secret. I only

said I wouldn't tell the boys, and I'm certain Smithy will hold the information in confidence. The last thing I want to do is jeopardize anything, but I also needed *someone* to know.

Heading to the coffee pot, I pour everyone a mug, distributing them on the counter before sitting back down next to East, leaning into his side when he drops an arm around my shoulders.

"So, are you two an official couple?" Matthew asks, and I press my lips together, trying not to laugh.

"Something like that," I say, sitting back up straight as Smithy dishes up the bacon, eggs, and biscuits.

"All four of them are her boyfriends," Smithy offers, and my cheeks flame.

Matthew looks at me, eyebrows raised. "How very unconventional."

"And perfect," East adds, squeezing my hand.

"Each of them offers something that I couldn't live without," I tell Matthew, taking a deep breath and catching the scent of peppermint and spice again. I sneeze as the memory of it assaults me. "That's some cologne, Matthew. What is it?"

"It's a Versace cologne that my daughter buys me every year." He smiles fondly.

"I didn't realize you had a daughter."

"Yes, well, being a gay man in my youth wasn't something I admitted to. It wasn't until ten years ago that I told my family the truth about it all. I am very lucky that my children are as open-minded as they are. I was not so lucky as James to find love early in life, but I have it now, and I'm thankful for it every day." He gazes at Smithy with so much love in his eyes, there's no doubt that whatever they have between them is real.

"I'm glad you found each other," I say, before digging into breakfast.

"So what is the word on Master Riley?" Smithy asks, turning the conversation away from him and Matthew, and I leave East to answer while I eat, watching Matthew closely. I don't want to believe he was the one in that basement, but I can see how much Smithy cares for him and I can't risk his heart on this. I think it's time I get in touch with Bentley again.

FIVE

LINCOLN

I enter the Riley basement for the second time in my life, again with Finley beside me, cursing out Edward. Descending the steps fills me with dread, but this needs to be done. Chase follows behind us, already on the phone to the facility where Finley's mom is a resident, preparing them for new arrivals.

We're just not sure how many yet.

The light is still on from where we dragged Maverick out of here earlier, but it's freaking eerily silent. Edward obviously trained them to be quiet. Just the thought makes me feel sick.

When I reach the bottom of the stairs, I look around the white, sterile room, actually paying attention to detail this time. The walls are lined with cages, stacked two high. Not all of contain women, but the ones that do are more than enough. On the far right wall is a bigger cage, and sitting in the back corner is Emily Royal.

She looks broken. They all do; pale skin, ratty hair, dirty, covered in cuts, bruises, and dried blood. The smells make my stomach turn, dried blood, urine, and God only knows what else.

Fuck only knows what Edward put them through.

Edward's dead body is pallid, open eyes staring up at the ceiling, as disgusting in death as he was in life, lying in a pool of his and Maverick's blood. It's not dry yet. I guess that much blood takes a while to dry.

"I've got him," Finn almost whispers, nodding toward Edward. "You guys deal with the girls. I'll put him in the trunk of your sedan, Chase. We can take him to the crematorium before we head out to the facility."

I'm not surprised he chose to deal with Edward. He's seen the mess the man has made more often than I have. Him and Mav have always been closer, so Mav usually calls him first. I know Finn has faced off with Edward more than once, but it's always easier facing someone else's monster.

He bends down, lifting the dead weight like it's nothing, and hoists the body over his shoulder before heading back upstairs.

"There are seven girls here," Chase utters, disbelief clear on his face. "Plus Emily."

I look at him, trying to take his measure. "Surely, being on the Conclave, you knew about most of their extra curriculars?"

"I tried to keep my distance," he says, shaking his head. "I never wanted to be a Knight. So once I was on the Conclave, I did what I had to but no more. My family's businesses are all above board, I don't let the Knights touch them, and I tried to not ask about their extras. I've used my legal skills to help them when it has been demanded, but this... this is—"

"This is nothing compared to what some of them do," I snap at him. "How do you expect to be of any use to us, to East, when you have no idea what's really been happening around you? They kidnap kids, sell them, fuck them, turn them into murderers. That's just scratching the surface. These girls are just more of the helpless fucks the Knights got their claws into. I'm sure there are mass graves of others just like them."

He blinks at me, like he's only just considering what I'm saying.

I don't have time for this. "Get back on the phone, tell the facility how many are coming, then start getting them out. I'll go grab some clothes from upstairs so they're actually fucking dressed. Leave Emily for me."

He nods and I jog back up the stairs, heading to the laundry room through the kitchen. There's a ton of Mav's shit here, and I'm sure he won't mind me using it. I grab as many hoodies and sweatpants as I can find before heading back downstairs. Finn reappears seconds later and takes the clothes from me, moving to help Chase.

I really hope he has more up his sleeve if he intends to help us.

Running a hand over my face and taking a breath, I steel myself before moving to the larger cage that holds a woman who could be Octavia's twin.

"Emily," I say as softly as I can as I reach the door, undoing the bolt that holds it closed. She could've easily reached through the bars to undo this. I guess that was part of Edward's mind fuckery; giving them the illusion of being able to escape, making them believe they chose to stay here.

I open the door, and she scurries backward, pressing against the wall. "Get out, I don't want to go with you. I want Edward."

"Edward is gone." She shakes her head, panicked.

"He can't be gone. She's the one who's gone. He promised…" she continues to ramble under her breath unintelligibly, shaking her head as she wraps her arms around herself. I'm just glad that she's actually clothed.

I have to assume the *she* that she's rambling about is Octavia. "Octavia is safe. She's at home. Edward won't hurt her. Come on, let's get you out of here so you can be safe too."

Offering her my hand, I wait patiently. She has to be the one to take my hand. She smiles wickedly at me, her entire demeanor changing, and my blood turns to ice. In a blink it's gone and she takes my hand, letting me pull her from the cage.

I don't know what the fuck that was, but there is no way in

hell I'm letting Octavia anywhere near her until I work it out.

Glancing back, I notice Finn and Chase have the other cages empty and Finn is the only one left waiting for me. He raises his eyebrows, and I realize he saw it too. I shake my head subtly, passing her over to him and letting him walk her upstairs without another word.

There are too many secrets hidden in this room, and I'm going to find every last one of them.

It took a few hours to get the girls and Emily situated, and they're all now on a 72-hour lock down while the doctors assess them. After checking back in on Maverick, Finn and I came back to the basement of the Riley house to try and work out its secrets while Chase went to collect Mrs. Riley.

After spending the last few days scrubbing the room clean and dismantling the cages, today we started rifling through the rest of the shit in here. So far, we've found nothing.

"We have to be missing something." Finn tugs on his hair as he stares at the blank white walls. "This place has to be more than a torture chamber."

"Maybe, but maybe not," I offer. "Edward was like a cannon. Harrison would point him in a direction and he'd cause destruction. Maybe he didn't keep anything important. Harrison isn't the type to trust anyone with his secrets but himself."

"Yeah, I guess. Fuck, this is frustrating as hell. I was hoping we'd find something that might work as leverage."

"You and me both." I let out a sigh, trying not to let disappointment flood me. I usually try to dispel any hope, but the thought of Edward being dead, and what that could mean for us… it's too big to completely quash.

Except now that hope is like an icy cold grip on my heart as I try to shove it away.

I check my phone and curse. "We should clean up then head to the hospital. It's nearly time to get Mav."

"Are we bringing him back here?" Finn asks.

"That's up to him. I'd rather he stayed with one of us, but the house is empty, and his biggest reason for avoiding this place is dead now." I pull on the strands of my hair, the sting helping to focus. "We should probably check in with Octavia. None of us have spoken to her for a few days."

"Does she even know Mav is getting out of the hospital today?"

I shake my head. "I haven't said anything, so unless he has, I'm going to go with no."

"We really don't deserve her," he mutters, running a hand over his jeans, dusting himself off. "When I spoke to her the other day, she asked for some space to process the Emily thing, but we always end up so wrapped up in Knight bullshit, then days pass…"

"I get it. I do. I don't disagree with you either, but I'm not letting her go. Not now, not ever. She'll have to pull herself from my cold, dead grasp."

He smirks at me, shaking his eyes. "You've got a weird way with words, man."

I bark out a laugh. "We're all a little bit twisted, but you can't tell me you feel any differently."

"Never said I did."

I softly laugh again, sending Alex another message to see if he has any information on Luc's whereabouts. Fucker ignored my last message. Pretty sure he enjoys messing with me. "Come on, let's get this over with."

We climb from the basement, locking it—and the ghosts of its horrors—away, and head upstairs to clean off. After we both shower and redress, I drive us to the hospital where Maverick is already being wheeled toward us. "It's home time! Where's my girl?"

He looks behind us, his smile dropping.

"You can see her later," I tell him, the nurse frowning at me as I do so.

Finn follows her to get his meds and discharge details sorted as I take him out to the car. "Why isn't she here?"

"She asked for a few days after finding out about her mom. I'm sure we'll see her soon enough."

"Fuck that. Where's my phone?" he swears as he pats himself down, pulling it from his pocket. "She's not going to ignore me. Just take me to her place."

I shake my head, almost jealous of his lack of fucks when it comes to smothering her. "Are you going to be staying with her then?"

He frowns, shaking his head. "No, I don't want to be a burden, not if she's dealing with her mom." He scrubs a hand down his face. "Fuck, this whole being considerate thing is bullshit."

I bark out a laugh. "Yes, yes it is. So where are you staying? Home? With me? Finn?"

"I'll stay with you if the offer's open. Keeps me close to her, and Mrs. Potts will make sure I don't starve."

I nod at him as I help him into the car. "Sounds good. I'm going to try to get Finn to relocate to my place, too. Then we're all close. There's too much going on right now, and leaving her alone feels fucking wrong."

I grab my phone and text East to see if he's heard from Octavia, closing the door to the car once Mav's inside, before heading around to the driver's seat. Finn appears moments later, jumping in the back.

"You're moving in with me for a bit," I tell him, and he nods.

"I figured I would be if Mav was staying there, too. Makes sense."

I don't say another word before pulling away from the hospital. I'll get them settled in, then I'm going to hunt down our girl.

SIX

OCTAVIA

After being a zombie at school these last few days, I'm kind of glad that Indi was away with her parents this week. I've been in a state of shock since I learned about my mom, and I'm just not ready to talk to her about it yet. It's like I'm numb and nothing but anger can touch me right now. I hate it.

I want to feel something else. *Anything* else.

But with the guys dealing with the fallout of everything that's been going on the last few days, and Mav being in the hospital, I've been stumbling around in the dark on my own a little.

I still haven't heard anything about my mom, and I haven't pressed it because I'm not even sure if I want to see her. Plus,

I'm the one who asked for space.

It's not like I'd know what the fuck to say anyway.

Do I just jump in with a "why the fuck did you leave us?" Or do I start with, "how did you end up locked in a basement?" Apparently, I have some resentment toward her bubbling under the surface, and now that I know she's not dead, it's all coming to the forefront of my mind... which isn't exactly the greatest way to go meet my mom when I haven't seen her for basically half my life.

Which is exactly how I find myself in the Saints' basement.

Their gym setup is decidedly better than the makeshift one I've got at home, and even if I just feel exhaustion when I'm done, maybe that will kickstart everything else inside of me and rid me of this rage I can feel building so I can work out how the fuck to deal with all the things I've been ignoring.

Maybe I can figure out a way to confront Harrison. But that would also mean acknowledging that Edward is dead, and since I have barely seen the guys, I'm not sure where we even are with that. Since I haven't heard from Harrison, I can only assume our deal is still in place as I can't exactly ask the guys about it.

I fucking hate secrets.

I start on the treadmill. My pace is punishing and sweat runs down my back, the blue sports crop top and matching leggings giving me room to breathe. I increase my speed anyway.

When my legs feel like jelly, I move to the free weights Lincoln has set up, going through every curl, lift, and fuck knows what else I have stored in my memory until my muscles quiver with exhaustion.

But it doesn't seem to change a thing. It's still like there's a barrier between me and the rest of the world. I can't see it, but it's definitely there.

I drop down onto the mats, fisting my hands in my hair, the sting a welcome relief.

"V? What are you doing here? I thought you were with Lincoln." East's voice wraps around me, and finally, I feel something. I need him.

I look up at him and I don't know what he sees on my face, but his smile drops as he strides toward me.

"What's wrong?"

I open my mouth to speak, not knowing which words to string together that will explain the chaos running through my mind.

His eyes darken the longer I stay quiet. I know he knows what happened, but he doesn't know the constant commentary going on in my head. He's the one person I know won't see me as weak if I break in front of him. He's always been my white knight.

He puts one arm beneath my curled knees and another around my shoulders, lifting me so I'm leaning on his chest, and carries me back upstairs to his room. He heads straight for his bathroom and turns the shower on, stepping beneath it with us both fully dressed.

The cold water sends pebbles skittering across my skin before it starts to warm, and I break a little. I've tried to just push it down, stay strong, be who everyone expects me to be.

"You guys have got to stop nearly dying on me," I croak.

He places me on my feet, putting his finger beneath my chin so I'm looking up at him. "We're not going anywhere, V. Not one of us. Did something else happen that I don't know about?" he asks, and I shake my head. "Then why do you look like your world is ending?"

A shiver runs through me again, and he slowly peels off my wet workout gear before stripping out of his own clothes and holding me against his chest. The fading pink line of the scar over his heart is beneath my ear. I listen for that heartbeat like it's the only sound I'll ever hear again and it soothes me a little.

"My mom." The words are little more than a whisper, but he tenses beneath me so I know he heard. "She was in Edward's basement. She saw what happened with Maverick and Edward. She's been down there for years, kept in a cage… and I don't know if I even want to see her. What would I even say to her?"

I trail off and his arms tighten around me. He doesn't say anything, but I get it. What is there to say to that?

Tears stream down my cheeks, masked by the falling stream of water from the shower. "I can't feel anything."

He pulls back from me, his gaze searching my face before leaning down and kissing me softly. I cling to him like he's the oxygen I need as want pierces through me.

"Let me look after you," he murmurs. His lips move down my neck, caressing my skin, leaving a trail of heat as he moves down my chest.

I gasp as he takes my nipple into his mouth, licking, sucking and biting, and my slick grows between my legs.

"More," I gasp, plunging my fingers into his dark hair.

He looks at me, a mischievous grin on his face, his steel eyes molten as he curls my hair around his fist and tugs so I'm looking up at him. "You don't have to beg, Octavia. I'll give you everything until you can't take any more."

Heat rips through me at the unspoken promise of his words. "Yes," is the only word I can find as he releases me before gripping the back of my thighs and lifting me against him, his hard dick pressing against my stomach as he shuts off the shower and walks me back into his room, gently placing me down onto the bed. His heated gaze walks a path of fire starting at my feet and clawing its way up my body until his eyes meet mine.

"Every inch of you…" the words trail off as he sinks his teeth onto his bottom lip, his entire body primed for the taking, his gaze wild with need, "is mine."

A whimper escapes me, but I nod.

"There isn't anything I wouldn't do for you, Octavia. You know that, right?"

"Yes," I breathe.

With one thigh between my legs, East cages me in against the mattress; eyes like liquid desire stare down at me as his forearms are planted on either side of my head. For what feels like hours, I wait for him to move, to talk, to do *something*. Instead, he simply studies me like I'm the only thing that exists in his universe. At first, I'm not sure what to do with myself. Am I supposed to touch him? Should I be kissing him?

It's only when my entire body begins to tremble with the need for him that I understand his intentions.

He's taking the power and control I am oh-so-happy to hand over right now, taking all the responsibility I just cannot handle and making it his. East wants my attention on him and only him, and from the look in his eyes, he is ready to make me feel every single thing I need to.

Slowly, he rubs his thigh up and down on my pussy with just the slightest pressure, just enough to make me push up against him, eliciting a mewl from deep inside me.

I close my eyes and East immediately stops.

My lids fly open and I'm greeted with his sexy-as-sin half smile. "Look at me, Octavia. Look at us."

Our gazes lock and East brings his mouth to my forehead, pressing his lips there for a chaste kiss before he moves to one eyelid then the other. Next, he gifts me with soft kisses across my cheek and down the column of my neck. When he reaches the hollow of my throat, he pushes his thigh a little harder against my core and I can't stop myself from grinding against him, desperate for more.

The tip of his tongue flicks at the indent of my collarbone

and is gone just as quickly as it appeared, tracing a hot path down between my breasts. His eyes dart up, meeting my hungry gaze as he takes one nipple in his mouth and sucks before nipping, then gives my other nipple the same attention.

I can't stop myself from crying out, pleading for more. I try to rub my thighs together to gain some added friction but his thigh between prevents me from having to do anything at all. I know East, he doesn't want me to work for it. He wants to do the work for me. He wants—no, *needs*—to fix it all for me, whatever it is.

The hint of a smile at the corner of his mouth tells me he knows exactly how much he's torturing me, even if it is the sweetest torture I've experienced in a while. He buries his fingers in my hair, tightening his hold on me, and that edge of pain makes everything else feel so much fucking better.

"Stay with me," he demands, not waiting for a response.

Releasing me, he drags his body down the length of mine until he reaches my navel, his lips leisurely dragging down my skin and lighting up every one of my nerve endings as he goes. Yet, with all his good intentions, his slow descent down my body is nothing short of excruciating.

He merely skims his breath over my pussy as he continues mapping out my curves with devilish open-mouthed kisses, going straight for my thigh, behind my knee, my calf, the arch of my foot, before he mimics the same path on my other leg and finally completing the circuit at my core.

I'm panting; every breath ragged from the torment of his slow burning foreplay.

"What do you need, beautiful?"

He pauses, not taking his eyes from mine, but when I don't speak, he flicks his tongue over my clit for a fraction of a second. "This?"

I growl from the deepest parts of my desire, but he chuckles softly, like he knows how impatient I am.

"What about this?" The pad of his finger runs up my slit and it feels so fucking good I almost shed real fucking tears.

"Yes!" I watch him as he throws me a wicked smile filled with dirty promises.

"Hmm, I had a feeling you might."

In one single move, his mouth latches onto my clit—sucking it hard into his mouth—as two fingers plunge into my pussy, curled exactly right and striking that perfect place deep inside me. I cry out from the perfection of it.

My orgasm is right there. I can feel it building in my core and just when I think I can't possibly wait another second, he changes the angle of his fingers and my entire body detonates like a nuclear weapon.

"Oh my God. Fuck!" I'm gasping out every word as East continues to draw out my orgasm with every lick of his tongue and caress of his fingers.

When I can finally breathe without feeling the burn in my lungs from my screams, I look up at East, my gaze still hungry as I take in his beautifully sculpted body. On his haunches, he takes his cock in hand and begins stroking himself, unhurried and calm. Teasing. Taunting. He looks so fucking hot, my need comes crashing back inside me as though I haven't just had a fucking orgasm. How does he do this to me?

"You taste so fucking sweet, V. Like honey. I could lick you up all fucking day long and never tire of it."

He brings a finger back up to my pussy, coating it with my wetness.

I whimper at the touch, the sound of my need echoing off the walls. It's so intense my legs shake with desperation. I look down at him and see he's driving himself just as crazy as I feel. I know what he's doing. This man won't let himself come until he's wrung out every single orgasm he can from me first.

With both of his big hands at the back of my thighs, East pushes my legs back so that I'm balanced on my shoulders and head, my legs folding over his shoulders as his mouth goes straight for my pussy.

I swear to fuck I see stars, full constellations, and the goddamn heavens open up from just the feel of his tongue as it teases my clit before he pushes two fingers back inside of me to the knuckle.

Oh shit.

My body tightens at the intrusion, and his moans as I clamp down around him almost push me over the edge. The fingers on his other hand tighten against my thigh just hard enough that the bite keeps me from falling off the cliff.

I can't catch my breath as my eyes water when another orgasm threatens to take me away again. It's at the base of my spine, tingling up the nerve endings, and just when I fear it's too early to come a second time, East sucks my clit and I lose all control over my body.

I don't have an ounce of control over anything.

"Oh my God, East, it's too much." I'm going to lose my mind.

"It's never too much, V. Let it all go, I promise I'll catch you."

I don't doubt him on this because I know for a fact, he will always be my safe space.

"Well, I don't doubt you'll always catch me but I just don't want to die of orgasm overload." He smiles at my sass, but the devilish glint in his eyes makes me fall in love with him just a little bit more.

I'm so lost in my dreamy post-orgasmic haze that it takes me a second to realize what's happening. East takes me by the hips and flips me over so I'm pressed face down into the pillow. Lifting my hips so that my ass is in the air at the perfect angle for him to plunge his tongue back inside my pussy, eating me like he's starved.

Holy fuck, that's so hot. The cool air from the open window breezes around us, but I barely feel it, my every thought consumed by his touch. When his soaked fingers reach forward for my clit, I have to bite the pillow below me to avoid squirming from the pleasure pain he's causing. My clit is hyper-sensitive to his touch, but my body is still hungry for more.

His free hand reaches up and tweaks my nipple, and I swear to fuck there's no way he can coax another fucking orgasm out of me. It's physically impossible, right?

He must feel it, sense that I'm doubting his prowess, because for the briefest of seconds, his mouth releases me and he flashes a cocksure grin that makes my entire body react in an instant. "I know your body better than you think, Octavia."

His words unleash the tightened coil inside of me and my orgasm rips through me, my throat ravaged as I scream, and I'm gone. Fucking obliterated by this climax that takes my breath away, right along with my ability to speak or move.

I'm frozen, my fingers burning from how hard I'm gripping the sheets, my lower body spasming while East continues to devour my pussy, dragging out my orgasm almost to the point of pain.

Long after the aftershocks fade away, East continues to lick every inch of me until he's lying beside me, kissing my lips for the first time and sharing my taste with me.

"I think you broke my brain." My words are barely a whisper.

"Then my job here is done." He gives me his sexy grin and my world feels right—at least in this moment. "For now at least."

"Maybe I should distract myself from being so broken, and break you too." A smile teases my lips as I swing my leg over him until I'm straddling him, lying forward so my chest is pressed to him. "Then we can be broken together."

"I'll be anything you need me to be," he groans as I rub myself on his still very hard cock. I gasp at the feel of him sliding between my folds, ready to be tortured by him all over again.

After my afternoon lounging in bed with East, we came down to forage for food. Halfway through making the biggest sandwiches I've ever seen in my life, the front door crashes open and in strolls Lincoln, with Mav behind him and Finn bringing up the rear.

Lincoln pauses when he sees me wearing nothing but East's button down, and the man himself standing behind me in just a pair of boxers. "I see you've both been enjoying yourself."

"Damn, man, I might be jealous," Mav groans as he steps past Linc. I rush toward him and wrap my arms around him, pressing my head against his chest, enjoying the sound of his beating heart. "Hey, princess," he murmurs, drawing my attention back to his face. "Miss me?"

"You know I did," I breathe before stretching up on the tips of my toes and kissing him, showing him just how much I missed him; how worried I've been.

"If that's your welcome home, I might get stabbed more often."

I pull back from him, my hands on my hips. "Maverick Riley, don't you fucking dare."

"Damn, you're hot when you're bossy."

Finn nods his agreement before kissing my cheek and heading toward the counter, and I turn to find Linc already sitting at the table. Mav's hands grip my hips and he pulls me back against him. "I'm looking forward to being fully healed, princess."

His low growl in my ear sends a shiver down my spine and I press against him, leaning up to whisper in his ear, "Me too."

His eyes go wide as I smile playfully before sashaying over to the table, making sure to sway my ass extra because I know he's watching. My day with East has helped a little, but I'm still torn up about everything.

For right now though, I'm going to focus on what I have and be thankful for it. These four are here, and they're all alive, despite too many close calls lately.

I slip onto the empty chair between Lincoln and Finn, and East brings my sandwich over. "So, what have I missed the last few days?"

My question hangs in the air as I take a bite, my long, wavy hair falling over one shoulder as I look up at them. All eyes are on me, and I fight the smile that threatens. Apparently, we all need a distraction at the moment. "My eyes are up here, boys."

"Not much," Lincoln says, his gaze meeting mine. "Your mom has settled into the facility along with the others, and everyone seems as okay as can be expected. We've been blessed with a reprieve, in that Edward was supposed to be away for a few weeks, so no one has been asking questions as to his whereabouts. But when he doesn't check in with Harrison, he's likely to start asking questions."

"How much trouble are you in?" I ask Maverick, who scratches the back of his neck.

"Not sure. Usually killing a Conclave member is really bad, but he was trying to kill me, and I'm also Conclave. It seems to be a bit of a gray area."

"So you should be okay?" I ask and he nods, a small weight lifting from my shoulders. I'm not sure how my deal with Harrison is going to affect him here, and worry pools in my gut. "What about my mom and the other girls?"

"As long as they're in the Knights' facility, they'll be fine. The doctors will work with them, make sure that they're okay, but also make sure that they don't say anything once they're ready for release. I'm getting weekly updates on all patients so I can keep track of them too."

I let out a deep breath as I lean back in my chair. "So, we're really okay?"

"It seems that way," Finn says before reaching over and stealing a quarter of my sandwich.

Relief that they'll be okay fills me. That I'll be okay.

Though I still need to speak to Harrison.

My phone buzzes on the counter, so I push back from the table and go to grab it. Bentley's name lights up my screen.

Bentley:

I might have something for you. Coffee?

Me:

Sure, I'll be home tonight if that works for you?

Bentley:

Can't do tonight, but I can do tomorrow. Be there around 9pm.

Me:

Sounds good.

I lock the phone, looking up to find all of them watching me closely.

"Who was that?" Linc asks, and I quirk a brow at him.

"Jealous?"

"Don't answer a question with a question, Octavia," Lincoln grumbles.

I fold my arms over my chest, not wanting to lie to him, but I can't tell him about Bentley either. "You do not own me,

Lincoln Saint. You don't get to know all my secrets. A girl has to have *some* mystery."

SEVEN

OCTAVIA

My stomach churns as I drive to school. Indi is back today, and she's my bestest bitch, so she's going to know something's wrong. I'm not even sure where to begin when she asks me what's up, because I know she will.

It's why I chose to come in alone today. I needed some time to clear my mind, prepare myself to talk about my mom. I can't tell her about the deal I made… but I really need to tell someone other than Smithy, because I'm not sure that keeping it just between us is the best idea. With so much going on around us, if something happens to me, I need someone else to know the truth. Especially when making a deal with the devil feels like a surefire way to end up on the wrong side of alive.

I pull into my usual parking space and take a deep breath as Indi pulls into the space beside me, smiling widely as she shuts off the car. I grab the coffees I picked up on the way in from the cup holders and climb from the car to meet her.

Coffee is always a good distraction.

"Bitch, I missed you!" she squeals, taking the coffee and hugging me. "Never let my parents keep me hostage again. Upside: I'm down from cast to splint so I can finally drive again!"

"I am happy for you, my friend." I smile, looping her splinted arm through mine before taking a sip of my coffee. "How was your trip back east?"

"It was sucky, and wet. I never thought I'd prefer the west coast, but apparently the sunshine grew on me. Could also have something to do with my parents trying to set me up with their friend's kid. Like, I might have a thing for twins, but I'm taken."

"They did *what*?" I screech as we enter the school. "How did the guys take that?"

She looks at me, wincing. "About as well as you'd imagine. Apparently my parents don't approve of my current relationships." She rolls her eyes as we head to my locker. "But fuck them. Like I told them, Sawyer St.Vincent is lovely, he's a little older, cute in a labrador puppy kind of way, but he's not for me. I'm in love and I'm happy. Plus, I'm pretty sure he has a girlfriend and his mom just hates her."

"Ouch. I'm sorry, dude. That sucks." Dropping her arm, I

grab my books for class before heading to her locker.

"It's all good. What did I miss?" she asks as she sorts herself out. "Shit, I forgot to grab a book from the library. Detour there before class?"

"Sure," I say, smiling tightly. She seems to forget her question and tells me all about the people she met back home, including Sawyer, his twin Asher, and his other friends. I smile and nod, *oohing* and *aahing* where expected, trying to ignore the churning in my stomach as we approach the library. At least it's quiet and mostly deserted. I can answer her questions without having to deep dive into everything.

We glide past the librarian as we enter, and she pays us no attention as Indi drags me to wherever it is she can find the book she needs. Once we're in the back of the stacks, she asks again. "So what did I miss? And don't tell me 'nothing'. I saw how your face dropped when I asked before."

Goddamn, she's perceptive.

The warning bell sounds, saving me a little. "Short version?"

"For now," she nods, grabbing a book from the back wall.

"Mav's dad tried to kill him. Mav won, but ended up in the hospital. And my mom was in a cage in their basement."

She looks at me wide-eyed. "What the actual fuck? Stupid bell! Stupid school! Stupid short version! I'm coming over tonight and you're telling me the long version. Don't bother trying to stop me."

I nod, hurrying us back to the main desk so she can check

out her book. We make it to class just as the final bell rings. Miss Summers raises a brow at us as we slide into our desks but doesn't say anything further.

Today is no different than the rest of this week. I go through it in a fog, glad I downloaded the dictation app on my phone for class after seeing a tip online about it, because I'm going to need all of the notes when it comes to trying to catch up.

My classes pass in a blur so by the time I leave music and head toward the cafeteria, not paying much attention to my surroundings, I find Blair at my locker.

Fuck my life. I'd forgotten about the shit I started with her. I'd forgotten about pretty much everything outside of my deal with Harrison, and my mom.

I really need to get my shit together.

"We need to talk," she hisses as I throw my stuff in my locker.

"What do you want, Blair?" I sigh. I know this was my idea, but I don't have the brain space for her right now.

"Not here," she says, rolling her eyes. "I'll come by the house after school."

"Sounds good," I say, nodding, and she flicks her icy blonde hair over her shoulder and struts away from me.

Awesome, another thing to try and remember.

That's when I remember Indi mentioning coming over tonight to discuss what I dropped on her this morning.

I head to the cafeteria and realize I haven't seen any of my guys today. Not that shocking with Mav, he's still healing, but I thought I'd have seen Linc or Finn, so I drop a message in the group chat to ask where they are. East's replacement as Coach was taken on full-time when his injury was as bad as it was, which sucks. It *does* mean we don't have to hide our relationship anymore, but it also means I have fewer places of sanctuary in this hellscape.

Mav:

In bed, could do with some company ;)

Finn:

Mav, fuck off. We're just wrapping some of the shit up with Chase, pretty girl. Sorry we didn't let you know.

East:

I thought someone else was supposed to tell you *glares at Linc*

Linc:

So sue me, I knew she'd try and join us and she has her GPA to worry about.

I smile at that before messaging them back

Me:

As long as you're okay. I'll head to lunch, if you need me let me know

Mav:

I need you. In my bed. On my dick.

I burst out laughing, because of course.

Me:

Maybe later ;)

I pocket my phone and take a deep breath before walking through the doors to the cafeteria, my jaw dropping when I take in the sight before me.

What in the actual fuck?

After avoiding the chaos in the cafeteria with the weird as fuck beat down between the football team and the hockey team, I was glad to escape the wave of insanity that seems to have crashed over ECP this afternoon.

When I get home, I let out a deep breath and climb from the car, preparing myself to speak to Indi about everything that's been going on. I'm just glad Smithy is already in the know.

Bentley is heading over tonight anyway, so if I'm looping people in, this is probably the best way to do it. I feel sick to my stomach at not telling my guys about it.

For some reason, I feel the most guilt about not telling Finn. Probably because he's fought so hard to be transparent with me, but if it buys their freedom, their happiness, I'm just going to have to suck it up.

I'm half hoping that Indi or Smithy will tell me I'm doing the right thing, because doubt fills me every time I let myself think about it. Making a deal with Harrison Saint is the equivalent to selling my soul, but surely one soul for the good of the many is worth it. Especially when it's not forever.

Right?

I rest my forehead on the steering wheel hoping for some sort of sign that I'm doing the right thing. When I sat in that room with Harrison, it was the obvious answer. It was the solution to all of their problems. To their suffering. To giving them the chances and opportunities they deserved. They didn't deserve to live a life of writhing pain and darkness. They'd done enough.

My sacrifice was the least I could do.

It's not the sacrifice I'm second-guessing. I would never.

It's the secrets I have to keep until my birthday. The thought of telling them they're free brings me so much fucking joy, but I know none of them are going to take it very well.

Least of all Linc.

Especially after all of my bitching about secrets being kept 'for the best.' I'm such a fucking hypocrite, but I can finally see why they keep a piece of themselves back. Well, except for East. He's been all in since the beginning.

If I thought he wouldn't tell Lincoln, I'd tell him in a heartbeat, but those two keep very little from each other, and getting them free is more important than alleviating my guilt.

I climb from the car and trudge into the house, smiling when I hear Smithy singing from the kitchen. I'm definitely going to need comfort food for the conversations I need to have tonight.

I round the corner, startling him, but still he smiles at me. "Oh, Miss Octavia. I didn't hear you get home. How was your day?"

"It was a weird one, Smithy," I say as I grab a bottle of water from the refrigerator and climb onto one of the stools at the center island. "Indi is coming over later, as is Bentley."

He raises his eyebrows at me, looking shocked. "Both of them? That's an interesting combination."

"It gets more interesting. Blair is heading over *before* they get here."

He sneers at the mention of my cousin and the corners of my lips tip upward. "What on earth could she want?"

"Bitchy high school queen bee take down plots if I had to guess." He looks at me, thoroughly bewildered. "I know, I know. But Mikayla took her throne after everything that happened with Nate, and she is even fucking worse than Blair was. While

I dislike Blair for the most part, she was better than Mikayla is, and better the devil you know, you know?"

I shrug my shoulders as he pushes up from where he's leaning against the counter. "Well, I've never been one to second guess your judgment, so if you think this is the right path, then I'll follow you down it. Do you need anything from me this evening?"

I rake my teeth against my bottom lip, contemplating my answer. "Not with Indi or Blair, but if you could be here when Bentley comes. Not that I don't trust him or anything, just, I'm not sure what he's going to tell me, and some support might be nice."

"Of course, Miss Octavia," he says, coming to my side and giving me a one-armed hug. "Anything you need, all you need to do is ask."

"Thanks, Smithy."

"Always, Miss Octavia. Now, if your cousin is coming over, I'm going to make you some taco boats. You're going to need some happy food."

I grin widely at him. "You're the best, Smithy."

He winks at me and I bark out a laugh. "I try, Miss Octavia. My only request is you keep Blair in the lounge area. I don't need that negativity in my kitchen."

I nod at him and jump down from my stool as the buzzer for the gate sounds. "Of course. That'll be her now. "

I open the gate from the app on my phone and move to

the front door to let her in, dropping Indi a message to tell her to get her ass here so I'm not alone with the she-devil for too long. Sometimes I miss how close I used to be with Blair, and others... others I remember the shit she did to me when I got back here—how she ruined all of my dad's shit—and those times I couldn't give a fuck.

But this is for the greater good. So I suck up my inner 'I don't wanna' and paste a smile on my face as Blair approaches.

"Good, you're here. Let's get this sorted shall we? Where is your sidekick?" She breezes past me, like the child of privilege that she is, and barely even looks at me as she does. Grinding my teeth together, I close the door, remembering that Blair isn't the big bad in my story.

Even if she does manage to push every single fucking button I have.

"Sure, come on in, Blair. I'm great, thanks. You? Oh, that's awesome. I'm so glad I helped you find legal defense for your dad. Yeah, of course, make yourself at home."

She narrows her eyes at me before rolling them and flicking her blonde hair over her shoulder. "Don't be such a dramatic bitch, Octavia. You came to me, remember? I don't need to be here."

"And I don't need to keep encouraging Chase to help Nate," I counter, and she sighs before dropping onto the couch.

"Fine, fine. Do you want to hear what I have planned or not?"

I move to the couch, sitting on the opposite end and turning to face her. "That depends, do you need my help for any of it?"

"Of course not," she scoffs, looking at me like I'm insane. "I do need the guys' help though. No one can cut a bitch to size in a second quite like they can."

I let out a dry laugh, cause she isn't wrong. "I'll speak to them once you tell me what you have planned."

The buzzer for the gate sounds again and I check my phone. Seeing the Wrangler out there, I let Indi in. "Indi is here."

"Of course she is," Blair huffs as my bestie bounces into the house with a smile on her face. The smile drops when she sees Blair's icy look, and she rolls her eyes as she drops next to me.

"Don't pause on my account. We've all got shit to do."

So Blair tells us her plan to dethrone Mikayla using her boyfriend, who isn't actually her boyfriend. How she'll need the boys there to cut her to pieces in front of everyone, because despite them not being as involved in school politics as they once were, they're still the true kings of the school.

My kings.

"It could be worse," Indi says with a shrug, and I nod.

"I'll talk to the guys."

Blair stands, and brushes down her skirt. "Perfect. I'll get out of here. Just don't let me down."

"Have I ever?" I ask with a raised eyebrow, and after a second she looks a little sheepish.

"I guess not. I'll let myself out. See you at school." She

breezes out of the house as quickly as she appeared, and I let out a deep breath.

One hard conversation down, and an even harder one to go.

"That was surprisingly painless." I look over at my bestie, who seems much less relaxed now that Blair is gone, which I didn't expect. "But you and I still need to have some words, bestie."

"I know," I say before running a hand through my hair. "I wanted to go and see Mav tonight, but there's so much going on, and you only know half of it. But I need you to promise me that what I'm about to tell you goes no further than here. Some of this stuff, only you and Smithy will know."

Her eyes go wide, and she opens her mouth to ask a question, but I shake my head and interrupt. "It'll make sense when you know."

I move to make a start when Smithy appears. "Milkshakes! I figured these would be needed." He drops the drinks onto the coffee table and presses a kiss into my hair before bustling back to the kitchen.

"Damn this must be bad," Indi mutters as she picks up her milkshake and sucks on the straw. "Okay, now I'm ready."

If only I were.

I pick up my drink and take a mouthful, letting the chocolate distract me while I pull myself together, then I tell her everything. What happened with Mav, about my mom, about Edward, and finally, my deal with Harrison.

By the time I'm done, she's just staring at me slack-jawed.

I give her a minute to process, taking another sip of my milkshake. She closes her mouth, then reopens it like she's going to speak before closing it again.

I think I might have broken her.

It takes another full minute before she explodes. "Are you fucking insane? Harrison Saint is the epitome of evil incarnate. He's like the real life Dolores Umbridge. Why in the ever loving fuck would you sign yourself over to him?"

I look over at her, hoping she understands, because I'm going to need my bestie's support to survive this. "To free them."

The answer is as simple as that. I've seen the lengths my kings are willing to go through for me, so now, I'm willing to step up to the plate and sacrifice for them. Like any queen should.

Understanding flitters across her face and she deflates. "I don't like it, but I get it. And now I see why the secrets. They're going to lose their fucking shit when they find out what you did."

"I know," I say, sounding as small as I feel. "But it's worth it."

"I hope you know what you're doing, but you know I'll be at your side no matter what. Ride or die."

I lean forward and wrap my arms around her, squeezing her tight. "Ride or die."

"So how do we get this information the dick supreme

wants?"

I pull back, and clasp my hands in my lap. "I have a plan. I've hired a PI—he'll be here later on if you want to stick around—but I'm also going through all of my dad's old stuff. What Harrison wants isn't something that he'd have just left lying around, so I have to assume it's here or in the personal belongings that were shipped back from the tour."

"I'd love to stick around, but I have to check in with Ryker. He had a major blow out with Ellis earlier. It was really fucking bad. Dylan called me after school and well…" She blows out a breath and shrugs. "I don't even know how the fuck to fix it, but I have to try."

"I get it. I'll let you know what Bentley found, even if it's nothing. And thank you for being here for me."

"Always, bitch. Always."

EIGHT

OCTAVIA

After a weekend of going through my dad's shit and still barely seeing my guys, I'm almost desperate for some time with them. Which is why instead of heading to my garage, I'm hauling ass next door. I know Finn and Mav are staying with the Saints on a somewhat-permanent basis now, so I know everyone will be here, and dammit, I need some time with them.

I push open the back door to the kitchen and find the four of them at the table: East in his t-shirt and sweats, the other three in their school uniforms. Linc looks like perfection, his tie straight, blazer pressed, and hair done. Finn looks a little rumpled, but still put together, and Mav… well, his shirt is half undone with the sleeves rolled up, his ink on display, his tie is loose around his neck, and he has total bed hair.

Yet every single one of them makes my thighs clench and my mouth drool.

Hell fucking yes.

"Morning." The word is more of a purr than an actual word as they all drink me in with their eyes. East is the first one to his feet, and he strides toward me, pulling me into his arms. He doesn't even say a word before he presses his lips to mine and kisses me until I'm breathless. My fingers grip his t-shirt like I'm holding on for dear life. Hell, at this point, I might be doing just that.

"Fuck, I missed you," he murmurs against my lips before pulling me back against him, his arms locked around me tight. It's been almost a week since I saw him, and it's too fucking long. On the one hand, I was grateful, because not seeing him meant not lying to him, but damn I missed him. I tell him as much as he releases me, and I find the other three smirking at me.

Maverick stands and swaggers over to me, capturing my hips in his hand before pressing up against my back, his hard dick pressing into my ass. "Did you miss me too, princess?"

I groan as I lean my head back on his chest, and he peppers kisses down the sensitive skin on my neck. "You know I did."

"Good," he breathes in my ear. "I'm going to find you later, and I'm going to bury my dick so far inside of you that you're going to feel me for days."

I whimper at his words as his hand dips from my hip, under my skirt, and into my panties. His growl in response to how wet I already am makes my knees weak. "Fuck me, she's soaked," he tells the others, whose heated stares are all on me.

Lincoln is the first to break the spell as he stands. "We should get to school." He acts unaffected but the outline of his hard cock in his slacks is blatantly obvious. I grin at him as he looks at me with a promise in his eyes.

I might have missed them, but it's obvious they all missed me too. I don't know if this will last forever, especially because I know they're not going to take the news of my deal with Harrison well, but I push that to the back of my mind for now.

I want to enjoy this—them—while I can.

"Yeah, school," I murmur as Maverick grinds into my ass before pulling back, as if reminding me of his earlier promise.

Finley stands, moving toward Linc, but I look to East. "What are you doing today?"

"I'm doing some more physio. Need to get back in tip top shape so I can make sure I can keep up with you." He winks at me and I laugh softly.

"I'm sure you're already keeping up plenty," I tease, and he grins back at me.

Finley grabs my hand and pulls me along with him through the house, following Linc, with Mav behind us. "You're riding with us today."

I glance up at Finley, who seems as tightly wound as I feel

107

after my welcome from Mav and East already this morning. Just under a week with zero orgasms from them and I'm a wanton mess. Sometimes I don't even recognize the girl I've become, but I'm not sorry about it. Not when the four of them are everything I ever wanted.

Lincoln climbs into the driver's seat, and Mav hops in the front with him, calling shotgun.

"Guess that means I've got you to myself for the ride," Finley growls in my ear, opening the back passenger door for me. He grabs my waist and lifts me into the seat, buckling me in before moving around the car and climbing in himself. He moves to grab his seatbelt before looking over at me. "On second thought..."

He trails off before reaching over and unbuckling me. I squeak as he pulls me across the backseat and situates me on his lap. "Much better."

"Knew I should've sat in the back," Mav grumbles as Linc starts the car. He catches my eye in the rearview mirror now that I'm sitting on Finn's lap behind him, and the heat in that look is enough to leave me scorched.

"You like how he watches you, pretty girl?" Finn's words are no more than a whisper in my ear as he trails his fingers along the inside of my thigh, making me squirm in his lap. His fingers never move to where I want them and he uses his other hand to clamp me in place so I can't grind down on him either. "Patience is a virtue."

His breath against my neck sends shivers skittering over my skin, and I only realize the journey is over when Lincoln climbs out of the car.

Holy fuck, if this is how they're starting my day, I know I'm going to combust before it's over. And how beautiful it'll be to burn.

The bell rings for lunch, but this day just feels bizarre. We're trying to get back to what should be 'normal' for the God-knows-which-number time this year and it still feels weird. Like, how the hell am I supposed to just keep going with the mundane of everyday with everything else I've got going on.

That's on top of how the guys have spent every opportunity today riling me up. Touches here, glances there, kissing me until my lips are swollen between classes. I knew they were going to tease me today, but I'm not sure how much more I can take.

A door opens to my right as I pass by and Maverick's grinning face fills my vision before he drags me into the empty classroom. He locks the door behind him and pushes me up against the wall.

"I've missed you, princess." He claims my lips like they were made for no one but him and kisses me until my lungs burn.

When he releases me, I let out a soft laugh. "I missed you

too. How is your back? Are you healing okay?"

His eyes narrow as he watches me. "I've been fine for days, but you've been avoiding me. All of us. We don't run from each other."

"I wasn't…" I trail off and stop because I don't want to lie to him. I spent most of the weekend with Indi or holed up at home looking for answers for Harrison, and I haven't paid much attention to my phone. "I didn't mean to. I've just been trying to give you space to heal."

"I never need space from you." His words are fierce, but the flicker in his eyes tells me that he's hurting.

"Is that why you've all been driving me insane today? Because I've been avoiding you?"

He smirks at me. "That's one reason."

It's not hard to read between the lines: he's been avoiding me too. He was only next door, but I know this whole thing with Edward and my mom has been eating at him. It's written all over his face. I reach up and cup his cheek in my hand. "You know none of this is your fault, right?"

His eyes flash and I know, without a doubt, he's blaming himself entirely.

"None of this is your fault, Maverick Riley," I say, bringing his hand to my heart.

He takes his hand from my chest and runs it through his overgrown hair. "Then why are you avoiding me?"

"I'm not avoiding you."

"Yes, you were," he bites. "Now I'm going to show you what happens to bad girls when they avoid me."

He spins me around and pushes me against the wall, my wrists clamped in one of his hands at the small of my back while he uses the other to pull down my panties. He taps my ankle and I lift each foot so he can take them off. "These are mine."

I look over my shoulder at him and his wolfish smile as he pockets them. I open my mouth to object but he kisses me again, reaching around with one hand and teasing my clit.

"What if someone comes in?" My eyes dart to the door, and I'm grateful that he had the wherewithal to lock it.

"Someone will come in, princess." His words are at my ear, a whispered sin that lights me up every time. "I'm going to come in your pretty, tight, fucking voodoo pussy."

"Well, that's not much of a punishment." My sass will get me into a fuckload of trouble one day, but getting into trouble with them is too much fun for me to worry.

Mav doesn't answer and with no time to analyze the devious mind that belongs to Maverick Riley, I gasp as he plunges two fingers inside me and bites down on my earlobe.

"Fuck." We both curse at the same time, me from the feel of him inside of me after a day of teasing, and him at how ready for him I am.

"I love how wet you get. Your body is always primed for me."

He's not wrong. And right now, I'm not beneath begging for

him to satiate the need that's been building in me all day.

Taking his fingers out of my pussy, he coats my lips with my juices, painting them on like lipstick as he lines up the head of his cock at my entrance.

The anticipation is killing me, reminding me of how much I've missed him.

Just as I open my mouth to suck on his fingers, he thrusts both in my mouth and his dick deep inside my pussy.

He freezes once he's buried as deep as he can get, the fullness that is Maverick Riley making my insides burn with need, and my arms scream with pain as he holds them tight behind me. "Fuck, I needed this. I needed to feel you, princess. You don't get to hide from me ever again."

Shoving his fingers practically down my throat, he fucks me against that wall like a man possessed. I've never been so willing to hand myself over to him.

Once his fingers are sucked clean, he places his hand at my throat and uses that pressure to hold me in place as he fucks me so hard that I see stars. He did promise I'd feel him for days, and holy fuck is he delivering. The only thing that keeps me from screaming is the knowledge that anyone could open that door if they hear us.

"Think anyone will notice if I leave my fingerprints on your throat? Think they'll walk away from you knowing that you belong to me?" His movements are erratic, his thrusts desperate and hard, his voice rough around the edges, his fear of losing me clear in each of his words.

He shows me just how much I belong to him, mixing my pleasure with pain as he bites down on my shoulder when I don't answer him. His brand of pain never felt so good.

"I'm yours, Mav. With or without your mark, I'm yours."

"Damn fucking straight you are. *Mine.*" He continues to slam me against the wall until his fingers tighten on my throat and he orders, "Rub your clit, princess. Do it fast because Mrs. Banks will be coming back to this classroom in about three minutes."

Fuck.

He releases my trapped wrists, moving his hand to my hip while keeping his other at my throat, and I make quick work of placing two fingers on my clit and rubbing furiously as he pounds into me.

Once. Twice. On the third drive against the wall, I bite down on my lip—the taste of copper exploding on my tongue—to avoid screaming and letting the entire school know I'm being fucked within an inch of my life in the middle of the fucking day.

"That's right, fuck yeah!" Squeezing his cock with my pussy as he squeezes my throat, my orgasm seizes my entire body, making me clamp down on him harder and push him over the edge. I revel in the feel of him unraveling, knowing that it's all because of me.

"Fuck, I needed that." His words make me feel alive as I

suck in air when he releases his hold on my neck.

"Me too, Mav, but seriously, I still don't know how that's a punishment."

Turning me around, he takes my wet fingers, pushes them between my legs, and coats them with us both before guiding them back in my mouth where I suck them dry.

That's when he kisses me, tasting us both on my tongue.

"Good luck avoiding me now, princess." And then he's gone.

He took my panties.

As if on cue, his cum trickles down my thigh, leaving a sticky mess behind.

That's my punishment: spending the rest of the day without panties and sticky from him.

Asshole.

I haul ass out of the room after him and dive into the nearest bathroom to clean myself up as best I can. Thank fuck my next class is music. Miss Celine isn't such a stickler for time keeping. Once I'm no longer sticky, and I put myself back together as best I can, I rush through the halls, darting into class just as the final bell rings.

My phone buzzes in my pocket and I risk a glance at it since Miss Celine isn't here yet.

I regret it instantly.

NINE

EAST

I wait until the four of them have left for school—half wishing I was still teaching, just so I could be with them, but not hiding my relationship with Octavia is a definite upside that I'm not willing to give up—before I head down to the gym in the basement.

As much as I try not to feel removed from the unit that we all make up, it's harder, being older than them. Especially when my injury has sidelined me so much the last few months. But I'm finally getting back to fighting fit and I intend on being able to keep up with her, with all of them, for a long time.

I've spent most of my life being miserable, trying to find a way to defeat Harrison, and while that's still definitely a focus of mine, it's no longer the only thing I'm living for.

Now, I have her.

She lights up my world and shines on all of the darkest parts of it, bringing me back to life. I never really let anyone see the darkest parts of me; I wasn't a Knight, and I knew the boys had much harder shit to deal with, so I tried to be the light and breezy one.

That didn't mean that I wasn't my own version of broken. Harrison saw to that. With every dig, every bruise, the cracks inside of me grew. And now Octavia is helping me see that being broken can be a good thing. That I don't need to hide those parts of myself.

At least not from her.

Or from them.

It's because of her that I've been so willing to try and get to know Chase.

I peel off my t-shirt as I climb onto the treadmill and start my warm-up. My heart is healed, but the scar on my body is a reminder of how close I came to losing everything. Those moments of pain, when the bullet entered my body and ripped through me as I dove in front of Lincoln, it was like all I saw was her.

The happiness that I'd finally had the chance to love her, and the devastation that our time was over, that I couldn't regret saving Linc. But sacrificing any more time with her would be something that would cling to me in my final moments.

As I push my body past its limits, running until my lungs scream and my muscles burn, I focus on that feeling. It's what keeps me going, fighting for a better outcome for us all.

When my heart feels like it's going to explode in my chest, I slow the treadmill before starting on the free weights. I don't have a job anymore, so this is how I've been focusing on not losing my mind with everything that's been going on.

After punishing my body for a few hours, I decide to get ready to meet with Chase. I need to speak to him about this whole Edward thing and check in on how things are going with Uncle Nate. While we were all happy for Nate to rot after what he'd done—not only to those he'd stolen from, but to Octavia—I was reluctant to ask Chase to help him, but it turns out I can't deny her anything. Not that I'm going to admit that to *her*.

Well, maybe.

I pull on a shirt and a pair of jeans after my shower then step into my favorite sneakers. Smart but casual, and where we're going isn't exclusive enough to require any more than that. I check the time on my Breitling watch before pocketing my phone and grabbing the keys to my Mustang. We agreed to meet at Tucci's in the city. His work keeps him there a lot, and it's not like I have anything pressing to stop me making the drive.

I hook up my phone, putting on the playlist Octavia shared with me, the corners of my lips tipping up when *Carry On* by Falling In Reverse blasts through the speakers. I'm pretty sure music is her love language, so her playlists always make me feel closer to her—even if the music isn't what I'd typically listen to. Thankfully, my taste in music is pretty eclectic.

I put the car in gear and pull out of the garage, the car gliding through the gate and opening up as I leave Echoes Cove.

The drive is reasonably long, but it affords me time to think over what I want to cover with Chase today. While I know he'd like a relationship that is more than just helping us deal with the Knights, it's not all that easy to bridge the gap from where we are to where I know he'd like us to be.

He's proven himself to be an ally, that we can trust him—to a point anyway. Outside of the five of us, we don't trust very easily. Though lately we haven't had much choice but to reach beyond the limitations of our group. There's been too much shit going on.

I also want to speak to Chase about what he thinks is going to happen with Octavia now that the contract Stone made has been uncovered. None of the Knights have approached her again as of yet, and I can see how much it's weighing on everyone. Hell, I can feel it hovering in the background of every day, like we're all just waiting for the ax to fall.

Once I've pulled up to the front of Tucci's, I hand the valet my keys and head inside.

"East!" I look to the back of the room when I hear my name called and find Chase already seated. I smile at the hostess and make my way past her toward where Chase is waiting. He stands as I approach, offering me his hand paired with a big smile when

I reach him. "Glad you could make it."

I take my seat, and the server brings me a glass of amber liquid to match the one already in front of Chase. "Could I get a water as well?"

She looks shocked, but nods and rushes away, leaving me to turn my attention back to Chase.

"This still just as awkward for you as it is for me?" he asks and I laugh, nodding. "Oh good, at least we're both in the same boat, I guess. After the tongue lashing I got from Lincoln at the Riley place, I didn't know that I'd hear from you again anytime soon. It would appear that keeping myself as removed as possible from the Knights puts me at a disadvantage."

I shake my head, mentally rolling my eyes at Lincoln. "Don't take it personally; that's just Lincoln's way. He's cold, calculating, and absolutely the guy to get shit done. He also doesn't have much tolerance for people who don't operate the way the three of them do."

"Oh, I noticed," he says before taking a sip of his drink. "I can't imagine what it was like for the two of you growing up with Harrison, knowing about the Knights. My father was an asshole, but Harrison makes him look like a fucking angel."

"Harrison is so far beyond an asshole," I say with a shrug. "But we've survived him thus far, and we'll continue to do so to the best of our ability. Speaking of… does you finding out that I'm your son mean I'm going to have to go through induction? I know you never brought in a second because you didn't have anyone else, and I know how the Knights work."

He frowns as he leans forward. "No one has said anything yet, but I'm sure Harrison is biding his time. As much as he hates that I didn't have an heir, I think he was looking forward to my line being over so he could replace me with someone he deemed more worthy. But I'd expect the nod, better that than not being prepared."

My heart sinks. I knew it was a possibility now that we know the truth of my bloodline, but I was still hoping it would be different. I've been trying to find a way to get Lincoln out, not end up in myself.

The server reappears with my water and takes our order. I go with steak without even glancing at the menu. Steak is good everywhere, and I'm not really here for the food. Once she disappears we make small talk, learning things about each other, like how he got into Law because his father forced him, but as soon as he was able, he changed his style of practice and started to work as a prosecutor rather than defense attorney, and only helps the Knights when absolutely necessary. He's still the best in the state though, which is no small accolade. I learn about the family I should have had, though they don't sound much better than the Saints.

Once the food is brought out to us, we eat in a somewhat comfortable silence, but there are still answers I need, and as amenable as this has been, my family—my real family—comes first. "Is there any news about what's going to happen to Octavia since she was attacked by a Knight?"

Chase's eyes flare as my question sinks in, and he wipes at his mouth with the napkin before he answers. "Not yet. Though there have been several heated debates within the Conclave about it. I helped draw up the contract for Stone, but I was never privy to who it was that got it pushed through. Now that we know it was the Archon, people are hesitant to try and bring her back into the fold. Except for Harrison. He seems almost eager to bring her back. Of course, Edward and Charles were on his side, but now that Edward is no longer a player, he's going to have issues forcing the matter if it isn't something she wants."

"That surprises me." I lean back, letting all of that process. "The agreement stated that she would become Regent, I can't imagine Harrison agreeing to just step down."

"Neither can I. He obviously has something in mind, but he's not sharing it. I know he met with her, but as far as we were told, it was just the two of them discussing the contract Stone put in place. No offers have been made in either respect."

I frown at his words. Harrison never does anything without being four steps ahead. Chase's words mirror what V told us about her summons to him, but something still doesn't feel right.

"You should also know I'm doing what I can for Nate, but without the Knights officially greasing the wheels on his behalf, the case against him is pretty solid. The only thing I've been able to ensure is that Blair's trust, and the apartment that was in her name in the city, is still hers and completely untouchable by the IRS."

I nod, letting it all sink in. What a fucking shit show this has all become. "Thank you for helping with him. I'll give Octavia the update, though I'm not sure how well that'll go down either."

He watches me closely, leaning forward before asking, "Are you happy?"

I startle at the question and he must see it, because he continues. "With her, I mean. It's no secret that she is involved with the four of you. I'm not a jealous man, but even *I* can't imagine sharing her."

"Then you've obviously never loved someone the way we love her," I tell him with a shrug. "She needs each of us. There are so many different sides to her that no one of us could meet every single need she has. This way, we can. And as long as she's happy, so are we."

His eyes sparkle at my answer and he takes another bite of his meal. "I can't say I'd ever thought of it that way, but as long as you are happy, then I'll do my best to ensure that no one interferes with it. My reach is limited, despite being on the Conclave, because I've kept myself so removed, but I will do what I can."

After my meeting with Chase, I'm glad to be home. When Lincoln got back from school, I suggested watching the football game together, and to my surprise, he agreed.

"Oh come on!" I yell at the TV, while Linc groans beside me. It's been forever since we just sat and watched a game. It might be a game we missed from last season, but fuck it. This year has been a lot and we haven't exactly had time to just sit and chill the fuck out.

We've had a heavy few months, but I think there might finally be some light at the end of the tunnel.

A knock at the door draws my attention and I turn to find V standing there, looking almost unsure as she enters the room.

"What's wrong?" I ask, because she looks like something's on her mind, but then she grins, and I swear, it goes straight to my fucking dick.

"Octavia?" Lincoln says her name as more of a question when she locks the door behind her.

"I thought we could blow off some steam," she says to me before glancing at Lincoln. "I didn't know you'd be here, but you can join us if you want to…"

I glance at him, wondering what she has in mind when she starts to unbutton her coat. I groan as her bare skin peeks through until she drops it to the floor, standing before us in just a black lace and silk bra and thong, with black stilettos a mile high.

"Holy shit," I mutter as my dick stands to full fucking attention and I drink her in.

Glancing over at Lincoln, I can tell he's as enchanted by her as I am.

"So, want to play?" she says, her laugh twinkling as she stands with her hands on her hips.

I jump over the back of the couch, glancing at my bed. "Hell fucking yes."

As I stride toward her, she giggles, and once I capture her, she whimpers in my arms as I steal her breath with my lips. She tastes like cherries and fucking sunshine.

If there's one thing I know about my brother, it's that his entire life revolves around control. Especially during sex, which is why I turn to him, a smirk firmly planted on my lips, and raise a questioning eyebrow.

With a subtle tilt of his chin, he tells me to lie down and have her straddle me. But it's only when I see him sitting on the oversized chair facing the bed that I realize he wants to watch first.

So, watch he will.

I take V to my bed—propping myself up against the headboard—then capture her mouth once again, reveling in the feel of her melting beneath my touch. Our tongues dance as she straddles me and lets her hair fall around us in a silky curtain. There are no sounds—Linc having turned off the television as soon as we realized exactly what game V wanted to play.

I'm pulled from drowning in her by the sound of a zipper sliding down. Realization dawns on me that my brother is enjoying the show as much as I am. Though, as much as he loves V's luscious ass, I'm guessing he's jonesing to see her pussy—open wide and wet for us. Not just wet, she's fucking soaked. I can feel her need as she rubs herself on me, her heat destroying the barrier of my sweatpants.

Reluctantly, I break our kiss and turn her around. She's still straddling me, but now she's facing Lincoln. If the dark pupils that have obliterated his gray irises tell me anything, it's that he's so fucking turned on he might not let me play with her alone for long. Not that I mind sharing, but I'm going to revel in having her to myself while I can.

V places the palms of her hands between my legs and starts rubbing her panty-clad pussy on my rock-hard cock—it almost hurts, it feels so good—giving Linc a fantastic view of her rack, which gives me a prime view of her ass. Fuck, I love her body.

She's getting herself off, teasing us both as she moves slowly and seductively, and it's hot as fuck.

With my back to the headboard, I watch—ensnared in her sexy little private show—as Linc's intense stare moves from her eyes to her mouth to her tits to her pussy and then back again. Over and over, his eyes scan her body as if trying to decide which part of her he's going to mark first.

I know he's reeling himself in, trying to drag all of this out as long as possible. To anyone watching, he looks almost bored. But I know better and so does V. The too-tight hold on his now exposed cock. The tic in his jaw like he can't wait to bite the softness of her flesh. The intensity of his stare, the way his attention is focused solely on her. They're all signs that what he really wants is to be buried deep inside her and fucking her within an inch of her sanity.

As his older brother, it is my duty to push him to his own limits, so I do what I must.

Raising one hand, I snap off her bra and let the soft fabric fall on the mattress between her spread legs. Linc's eyes follow the bra down and slowly trace their way back to her tits—all swollen and plump with desire. And just to fuck with him, I place my right hand on her tit and pinch her nipple, eliciting a mewling sound that I can feel straight in my balls. With my other hand, I reach up and wrap her long, silky hair around my fist and pull her head back enough to expose her slender neck.

Then I lick her exposed skin and watch my brother as his restraint tumbles away every time my tongue teases her flesh.

"Touch yourself, V. Show us just how fucking wet you are." My voice is low but we can all hear my words, and by the slight jolt of Linc's cock, I know he's going to kick my ass later for pushing his control, but I don't care. This is what V loves—driving us fucking crazy—and I will always do whatever she wants.

V slides her hand inside her panties and begins fucking herself slowly, rubbing up and down my cock, all the while teasing her own clit.

I'm torturing myself as well as my brother. This feeling of almost being inside her is one of Dante's circles of Hell, I'm sure of it.

"Look at him while you get yourself off. He's so fucking hard for you, V. What he really wants to do right now is come over here and take complete control. He wants to mark you. Bruise you. Come all over you." With every one of my words, V's hand picks up speed, rubbing herself into orgasm while Linc tightens his hold at the root of his dick to keep himself in check.

"Enough." One word and we both freeze.

Rising to his full height, his cock exposed through the zipper of his jeans, he brings his hands to his shirt and takes his fucking time unbuttoning every one of his buttons before letting it fall off his arms. Without looking, he throws it on his recently vacated chair—his eyes only on V.

"Rise up, Octavia. Show me your cunt."

She obeys without a second's hesitation, forcing me to let her go—my hands falling to her waist.

Linc's right hand returns to his cock, leisurely stroking himself like he has all the time in the world when, in truth, he's probably seconds away from ripping shit up like a savage.

Kneeling in front of her, he reaches up with his free hand and places one of hers on his cock, silently telling her to continue what he's started. Meanwhile, he latches onto the thin straps of her panties and with one flick of his wrists, the material snaps—her panties falling between her legs on top of her discarded bra.

"Much better," he praises, his mouth now just an inch from her lips. Her body is vibrating beneath my fingers, her anticipation of Linc's next move palpable.

"If I had my way, you'd be naked for me all day and all night."

I couldn't agree more.

Clutching the back of her head, Linc takes possession of her mouth, kissing her hard and fast like he just can't help himself—the need for her too strong to resist. His fingers are inside her, fucking her with abandon.

Leaning in, I pepper soft kisses to her neck and back, reveling in the goosebumps that pop up along her skin.

We do this to her. *We* make her body react like this. It's heady and I never want it to end.

V's sudden cry shakes me from my kissing trance—her body freezing, her breath caught in her lungs—as Linc pushes two fingers inside her pussy again, his eyes flashing with the feel of her. Or maybe because of her reaction to his touch. It's addicting the way she responds to us.

Bringing her to her first orgasm, her cries are swallowed up by his mouth, her body convulsing in my hands. I can't help myself as I lick a path across her shoulder blades, from one side to the other, as she shakes and moans for us.

"Now, be a good girl, Octavia, and turn around so I can fuck your ass while East destroys your pussy." She whimpers in response, and my cock jumps in my sweats.

Turning around, she looks up at me, her drunken gaze taking a stroll down my chest and I know instantly that she doesn't approve of my still-clothed body. Reaching behind me, I fist my shirt and immediately rip it off, exposing my naked chest for her.

Linc makes his way to the drawer of toys where he digs around for the lube. I take this as my cue to push my sweats and boxers off, all without displacing my girl. Her hands are splayed across my chest, her mouth following them, her lips sucking on one nipple before making her way to the other—her wet, naked pussy rubbing along my hard shaft. It's torture. Beautiful, magnificent torture.

My gaze flicks to Linc where he's lubing up his cock, his breathing running wild yet controlled. Only he could make those things happen at the same time.

"Up, Octavia," he commands, and she moves instinctively. Rising on her haunches, she aligns my cock with her entrance and slowly—oh-so-fucking-slowly—the little vixen sinks down, engulfing my entire dick deep inside her tight little pussy.

A groan falls from my lips at the feel of her sheath around me, and I don't care to control it. I kiss her with abandon as she moves on my dick.

I won't ever get tired of this.

Of her.

She pulls back from me, glancing over her shoulder to watch Linc, and I can't help but follow suit.

His jaw tics with anticipation as he watches her ride my dick before he moves in behind her. He grabs onto her hair, pulling her head back and claiming her mouth like a fucking beast, before he leaves a hot trail of open mouth kisses down the nape of her neck. Her moans are breathy as I move my hand to cup her cheek, bringing her lips back to mine while Linc feasts on her.

She devours me, moaning every time she feels Linc's touch as he rubs the lube across her tight little ass.

I can't fuck her hard or I'll never last, so I keep her rhythm slow with my hand on her hip as she rises and falls on my dick. She gasps as one of Linc's fingers, maybe two, plunges into her ass. I can feel it along my shaft through the thin layer between her holes. The noises she makes are like gasoline to the fire already stoked within me, and I have to hold her still on top of me for a moment while Linc opens her up.

Behind her, Linc fucks her harder and harder with his fingers, the movement pushing her more and more onto me—her kisses becoming more and more aggressive as I feel him reach around her with his other hand and stroke her clit. She clamps down, coming apart all over my cock, and it takes all of my restraint not to fuck her through it.

My hands are all over her—her tits, her waist, her face—until she comes back down and grins at me. I end up digging my fingers into her wild mane and start to fuck her again, pushing my cock deeper and deeper inside her as Linc withdraws.

"Stop."

I do as he commands, which earns me a bite on my bottom lip. My impatient little vixen is not happy about having to wait, despite the fact that she's already come once.

"Fuck," she breathes, gripping my shoulders as Linc pushes inside of her. He curses as I feel him enter her, and V's closed eyes and open-mouthed expression show me just how good she feels.

"Breathe, baby. Relax and let Linc in." Biting her bottom lip, V exhales slowly, allowing him to push in deeper. It takes him a minute to settle in but once he does, her pussy gets so damn tight I struggle to keep myself under control.

We're both inside her, her mouth on me again briefly before Linc wraps his fist around her hair and pulls her head back so he, too, can kiss her already swollen lips.

We get into rhythm, him pulling out every time I bottom out. Me sucking her nipple, biting at her exposed skin while he ravages her neck and jaw and lips.

We push her past her limits, burying ourselves in her, working to a rhythm that means she's full of one of us at all times. We take turns burying our cocks inside her until Linc's gaze flicks to mine in a silent order to make her come again.

My mouth latches onto her nipple and my fingers seek out her clit as I expertly ravage her body, loving the way she responds to me. To us.

Her cries get louder and louder as I increase my strokes across her clit while we pound into her. Between us, she's losing her fucking mind and I love every second of her falling apart in our arms.

"Fuck! Yes, God, yes, please." She's barely coherent as I fuck into her pussy, Linc setting the speed and me just keeping up.

At this pace, we won't last much longer.

No sooner does the thought come to me before V begins to move erratically, her orgasm building again right in front of my eyes. I watch as it takes over her entire body and when her cries erupt between us, we all freeze for the briefest of seconds as she clamps down around us both.

It's all too much for me.

The tingling at the base of my cock is my only warning that I'm about to explode inside her.

Linc nods, and at the same exact time, we bury ourselves inside her all at once, coming together as she rides out her orgasm.

I pant as I come back down to earth, her forehead resting on my shoulder while she shivers as Linc withdraws from her.

Fucking hell.

Best impromptu visit ever.

I lift her from me, tucking her against my side when Linc disappears into my bathroom and returns with a washcloth to help clean her up. I take care of her before cleaning myself up, leaving her tucked into my side.

Lincoln climbs up behind her as she practically purrs between us, one hand on my chest, and the other on his thigh as he wraps himself around her.

We might have to fight to keep this bliss we've found, but I already know we'll all fight with everything we have to ensure she is the one that remains happy.

No fucking matter what.

TEN

OCTAVIA

Having made Indi my alibi for the night, I check the message from earlier as I climb into my car. I hate to do it, and I'm lucky she loves me, but there's no avoiding tonight.

Harrison:

Your training starts Wednesday evening. Do not be late. 8pm sharp. <Pin drop>

I double check the address as I put it into my maps, trying not to freak out that I'm being taken out into the middle of nowhere. I wasn't stupid enough to follow Harrison's directions without telling Smithy where I was going, and Indi knows as much she needs to know to cover for me, but I don't want to drag her into this any more than needed.

It's enough that I'm tangling myself up in this; I don't need to drag her down with me.

I take a deep breath and start the car. *Going Ghost* by Jeris Johnson blasts through the speakers, helping to calm my frayed nerves. I have no idea what training consists of, but I took Smithy's advice and wore something ultra comfortable just in case. So I have black leggings, combat boots with thick socks, a crop top, and hoodie on. My leather jacket is along for the ride, just in case.

I look way more badass than I feel. My heart pounds wildly as I pull out of the driveway and make my way toward wherever the fuck it is that Harrison's leading me to. I try not to think about what could be waiting for me in the middle of nowhere, or what the Knights' version of "training" could consist of. With what I know about them, it could be anything.

I guess I should be thankful Harrison didn't mention an initiation. The thought of having to kill someone, just because, doesn't sit right with me. Not that I judge my guys for doing what they had to in order to survive—I'm all for fighting to survive—but I made this deal, and the thought that I may have agreed to just kill someone makes me want to vomit.

If someone came at my family and they needed to die in order for them to stop, then I'm all for it, but just because a jumped-up guy in a suit says so? Yeah, no.

I leave Echoes Cove in my rearview with *blink-182&u* by

Cali Rodi as my theme song. I sing along with her at the top of my lungs, trying to pump myself up for whatever is going to happen tonight.

My phone buzzes in its holder, and Linc's name pops up on my screen.

Linc:

You sure you can't hang out with us tonight?

I tap my apple watch and speak my response into it.

Me:

I can't, girl time is required. Tomorrow?

I wait, hating that I'm lying to him, as those three dots bop up and down as he types his response.

Linc:

That's too far away. Come and climb in my bed when you're done. Doesn't matter what time.

Me:

Are you okay?

Linc:

I will be when you're here in my arms.

God he makes my heart hurt sometimes. If tonight wasn't part of holding up my end of the deal, then I'd turn this goddamn car around and head straight back to him. Something is obviously wrong, but I also know he hates talking about shit over text.

I chew on the inside of my lip, wondering if he's found out the truth somehow. If Harrison told him as a fuck you, but I shake that thought off. If he knew, he'd be less wanting to hold me and far more shouty.

I have between now and my deadline to work out how to break the news to him. Thankfully, I still have about a week until then. It doesn't seem like that much time when I think I still have to find the information Harrison wants, to learn as much as I can to take my seat as Regent and lose a part of myself so that they can be free.

I've totally got this.

At least I fucking hope so.

The map directs me off the main road, and the night grows darker as I approach my destination. My stomach churns when I notice that the screen says I'm only ten minutes away from where I'm heading. I drive through what looks and feels like a ghost town, my phone directing me to weave through the streets, bringing me to an abandoned warehouse. Well, warehouses. I'm in the middle of an abandoned industrial park.

Totally not creepy. Nope. Not at all.

I shut off the car and take a deep breath before pocketing my phone and climbing out.

"I wondered how long till you arrived." I spin on my heel at the voice, trying not to scream. When the figure steps from the shadows, relief floods me. "Good to see you again, Octavia."

"Alex? What are you doing here?"

He barks out a laugh as he steps toward me, hands in his pockets. "It seems the deal you made with my Uncle left some holes. So I've been dragged in."

My jaw drops as my heart sinks. That was never meant to happen. That wasn't what I arranged. I didn't think I needed to protect Alex too.

Fuck.

"Alex—" I start, but he cuts me off.

"Nothing to be sorry about, baby Royal. This was a seat I wanted anyway, there was just no way in for me. Now there is. But don't worry, your secret is safe with me. That being said, *you* need to keep this secret too." His eyes narrow as he watches me. It takes me a second to understand, but then it clicks.

I nod, not having any other choice. "Okay. I can do that."

"Good, that means you pass the first test. Now come on, Dad's waiting for us inside. It seems the Knights want to assess our skills before we start our training." He rolls his eyes as he steps toward me and puts his arm over his shoulder. As much as I shouldn't be, I'm relieved I'm not going through this alone.

"Wait, your dad? Luc is the one training us?"

"I am," Luc's voice cuts through the night, just as light spills from an open door. "Now get in here. We don't have all night."

Alex squeezes my shoulder and leads me inside.

Whatever happens from here, I can't regret it. Not when I know what this means.

Not when it's for them.

"Good to see you again, Octavia."

I startle as my name echoes in the giant empty room. Looking around, shock floods me when I see the blonde on the opposite side of the room. "Artemis?"

"The one and only. You're looking beautiful as ever." Her grin is wide as she sashays toward me, and Alex laughs beside me. She wraps me up in a quick hug, kissing both my cheeks, leaving me beyond shocked. I jolt back to reality and hug her back before she pulls away.

"What, no love for me?" Alex grins at her, and she snarls at him. "I guess not."

"Enough fucking chit-chat. Let's get this show on the road shall we? Power off your phones and get your shit together." Luc's orders make me stand straighter as he storms across the room. I do as he asks, quickly pocketing my phone once it's off, waiting for whatever's coming next. The lights go down in the room, and green neons illuminate the space.

Artemis hands both Alex and me a gun. "Let's see what you've got, shall we?"

She walks away from us as Alex steps up beside me, excitement rolling from him. "It's like extreme laser tag."

I roll my eyes at him and look over the gun. I expel the clip and check the ammunition. Blank rounds.

What the actual fuck?

"Well, that's no fun." Alex pouts, but then grins again. "Good luck, baby Royal. Let the hunt begin."

Smoke starts to fill the room, making it even harder to see, and Alex disappears around one of the temporary walls.

I guess I better get started. Becoming the hunted doesn't sound like much fun at all. The only problem is I have no idea what my target even is.

Stupid fucking disadvantages. Knowledge really is power.

I duck in the opposite direction to where Alex went, trying to focus on the sounds around me since the visual space in here is basically zero. And then music starts up, along with strobe lights.

Is this a fucking rave?

A rave with firearms. How the fuck is this training?

I move through the space, pistol raised, trying to clear the space. I don't even know what I'm looking for and I feel fucking ridiculous.

The next thing I know my feet are being swept out from underneath me. I fall backward, my back slamming onto the concrete, and the breath whooshes out of my body.

Mother of fuck.

Artemis' face appears above me and she blows me a kiss. "No hard feelings, but do better." Then she flits away, disappearing into the smoke.

Okay, so goal one: don't get knocked on my ass again.

I groan as I push myself to my feet and pull my hair up into a ponytail. I need it out of my face if I'm going to get through this. Especially if I don't want to get my ass handed to me again.

Dusting myself off, I crouch down and try to get my bearings.

Knowing that Artemis is the hunter, it's probably safe to assume Luc is as well. Which means Alex and I are the hunted.

At least now I have a semblance of an idea of the game.

Taking a deep breath, I head in the direction Artemis went when I hear a cackle of laughter that has me spinning around.

There's no one there.

Fuck these Jedi mind tricks.

I blow a loose tendril of hair out of my face and spin back around, trying to get my bearings. This is the weirdest fucking training I've ever experienced. I hear a yelp followed by a crash somewhere in the distance.

I guess someone got Alex.

At least if they did we're one for one. Petty as it is, that makes me feel better.

Just as I get my head on straight, the music cuts out, the lights stop flashing, and the fluorescent lights above me flicker on.

"That was pathetic!" Luc roars, I can't see him, but that doesn't stop me wincing at the dressing down. He stomps into view, motioning for me to follow him, and I pick up the pace to make sure I don't lose him. He comes to a stop where Alex is face down with Artemis sitting on his back. It takes everything in me not to laugh as I clamp my lips together.

Her eyes dance with laughter when she sees me and jumps to her feet, letting a grumbling Alex up. I'm a little surprised she bested him, considering who he is and where he's risen to, but apparently there is more to Artemis than I realized. Maybe she does live up to her namesake.

Luc shakes his head at Alex. "Let's see how you do working in pairs, shall we?"

He stalks away and Artemis gives me a delicate finger wave before rushing off behind him. I turn to Alex, who looks pissed, and shrug when he raises his eyebrow. I'm guessing because of the giant smile still on my face. "I'm glad I'm not the only one she took down."

"Yeah well, she's fucking psycho."

"All the best girls are," I tell him with a wink.

"Uh-huh. There's nothing quite like being beaten to make me work harder though. You ready for this? Now that I have an idea of the rules, I refuse to be the prey in their game of cat and mouse."

"I'm ready. What did you have in mind?"

After a few hours of being assessed and then reamed for everything we did wrong, Luc dismissed us, muttering to himself about unskilled wannabes. I didn't bother to correct him because tonight showed me that I have a lot to fucking learn if I want to survive this world. My dad might have given me a fuck ton of skills, but he never intended for me to end up in this cesspit. So while they might help me in the life of a 'normal' person, I'm barely treading water over here.

"Hey, Octavia! Wait up!" I pause at Artemis' request, waving to Alex as he heads back to his car, exhaustion painted all over his face. I get it. I'm looking forward to curling up next to Lincoln just as soon as I'm back.

Artemis reaches my side just as Alex climbs into his car, and a yawn rips through me that I have to stifle. "What's up?"

"You did good tonight," she starts, and I snort a laugh, looking at her sideways. She just shrugs. "Okay, well maybe not good, but okay. There's definitely potential. It's harder, as a woman, to do what these guys do with such ease. Typically, anyway. Luc is going to be handling most of your tactical training, but I wanted to offer myself up to help you too, if you'd like. I've had to learn a lot of shit the hard way."

I watch her closely, trying to work out why she's being so nice, and she must read it all over me because the corners of her lips tilt upward. "No ulterior motives here, Octavia. Just a helping hand. I've seen what your guys are capable of and I'm not about to cross them if I don't have to. Plus, I like you." She shrugs, her gaze raking over me again.

It could be a really bad idea, but fuck it. "Sure, that'd be good, thank you."

"Perfect. I know you run with Lincoln every morning, but try and hit some free weights to work on your upper body strength. That shit will help. Luc will have you training with him three out of seven nights, I'll claim two others, then you've got two for other shit. We'll have you turned into a lean, mean killing machine in no time."

I bark out a laugh at her. "Sounds totally reassuring."

"Better to kill than be killed." Her voice has lost any lightness from before, and I nod solemnly as we reach my car. "I'll be in touch. Night, Octavia."

I climb into my car, aware that she's watching me. She stays there, watching, as I drive away, blurring into a shadowy figure in my rearview.

I groan when I see the time. Maybe climbing into bed with Lincoln right now isn't a good idea. I can't decide if he'll ask more questions about the time or if I just don't go to him at all. When I leave the ghost town, I let the car idle as I power my phone back up. It buzzes in my hand as a few messages come through.

Indi:

*Hope everything went okay. Please let me know you're alive. I
don't want your guys to skin me if you're not.*

I laugh at her and drop her one back.

Me:

I'm alive, a little bruised, but alive. I'll catch you up tomorrow.

Then I check the other.

Lincoln:

*I don't know what you two are up to, but come home. I'm in
your bed. I didn't want to be without you tonight.*

I guess that answers that question. I put the phone on the
holder, hitting play on my playlist and turning the volume down
as *Crash and Burn* by Maggie Lindemann starts playing. The
drive back doesn't take as long, mostly because of how late it is,
but my lead foot might've played a part in it, too.

I'm so ready for bed.

When I get home, I park the car in the garage and head
inside. It's so freaking dark, so I use the flashlight on my phone
as I tiptoe up the stairs to my room. I open the door as quietly as
I can and find a sleeping Lincoln Saint in my bed, the sheets just
barely covering him, bunched at his hips.

Damn he's so freaking beautiful. It's rare that he looks so peaceful, but when he sleeps, it's the only way to describe him. He murmurs softly as I close the door and I head into my bathroom. I need to rinse the night off of me, so I strip out of my clothes and grab the fastest shower of my life before drying off and slipping into shorts and a tank. I sneak back into the room, finding him still asleep. Which is surprising, considering he's usually so guarded.

He must be exhausted.

Slipping between the sheets, his heat calls to me, but I don't want to disturb him.

"Octavia," he murmurs as I settle, his eyes fluttering open, still blurry with sleep. "Good."

He doesn't say anything more, just pulls me into his arms so I'm splayed against his chest, wrapped up in his warmth. I press my lips softly to his shoulder, and he purrs softly, already asleep again, so I close my eyes and lose myself in his warmth.

I could get used to coming home to him.

ELEVEN

OCTAVIA

Waking wrapped in the heat of Lincoln and the smell that is just so thoroughly him brings a smile to my face. It feels like too long since I've had any alone time with him. With any of them—except for East.

My smirk grows thinking about the last time I was alone with East, and Lincoln stirs as his alarm goes off on my bedside table. I run my hands up his bare chest, enjoying how he squirms beneath my touch as goosebumps rise on my skin. "Keep teasing me and see where it gets you."

His voice is gravelly and full of sleep, yet the promise in his words zips straight between my legs. "That doesn't really sound like a deterrent."

His hands reach down and circle my hips, pulling me on top of him, and I groan at the feel of his hard dick pressed against me.

Goddamn clothing in the way. He arches up to grind against me, pulling another gasp from my lips. I look down at him, my hands on his chest, and he looks like some sort of dark god. His dark hair messy and bed mussed, his gray irises so light that they almost shine like silver. His eyes narrow as I grind down on him again and I whimper at the feel of him beneath me.

Going on top isn't something that we've done just the two of us. He's more prone to domination when it comes to me. Not that I'm complaining, but the thought of bringing someone as powerful as Lincoln Saint to his knees beneath me is heady as fuck.

I lean forward, pressing my lips against his and his arms clamp around me, crushing my chest to his as he devours me, rolling us without breaking our kiss until I'm caged beneath him. He pulls back just as my lungs start to burn and lifts my tank. I arch my back and raise my arms to help him remove it before he throws it across the room.

He sits back, perched between my legs, and stares at me. Using the pad of his thumb, he pulls my lip from between my teeth, then drags his hand down my throat, between my breasts, across my navel and to the hem of my shorts.

My entire body tingles in anticipation of him as my eyes rake over his bare chest and the outline of his huge cock in his boxers. I lick my lips, pressing them together as I feast on the sight of him. He pulls my shorts down and I lift my hips, impatient to feel him.

When he throws them behind him, he slides backward and lowers himself to my core. "Linc," I gasp when his hands press down on my thighs as he drinks in the sight of me. I writhe with anticipation, his breath dancing erotically across the lips of my pussy.

"Please."

I have no issues begging him if that's what it takes.

"Quiet, Octavia." His rumbled words send shivers down my spine, and I grasp at the sheets to stop from tangling my fingers in his hair and riding his goddamn face. His tongue flat against my clit earns him a guttural cry just before he pulls back, the cool air caressing my pussy where his hot touch used to be. "I said *quiet*."

Holy fuck. I can't do quiet. But the way he's looking up at me from between my thighs makes me want to do whatever he asks.

I press my lips together, desperate to feel him.

"Eyes on me, Octavia."

I swallow the whimper at his command, but do as I'm told, watching as he moves back to my pussy and swipes his tongue, slowly, up my slit to my aching clit then back down again.

Mother of fucking God, yes.

He teases me lazily, taking his sweet-ass time, his gaze

on me as I drink him in. I'm enraptured by him, by his every fucking move. Every touch and every word sends a bolt of electric energy straight to my clit.

My back arches off the bed as he sucks my clit between his teeth. It's getting harder and harder to keep my eyes on him, the need to close them nearly impossible to ignore. Around and around, his tongue circles my bud of nerves, driving me to the point of insanity. All I want to do is latch on to his hair and keep his mouth at my pussy for hours. Or forever.

I crawl closer to the edge, my toes tingling as he licks and sucks every last inch of my soaked lips, his hands splayed across my thighs, fingers indenting my flesh with the force of his need.

Just when I think I'm about to fall into oblivion, he pulls back, eyes sparkling. It takes everything I have not to scream at him for stopping. He told me to be quiet, so that's what I'm going to do.

"Such a good girl," he purrs before thrusting two fingers deep inside me. I clamp down around him. "Be a good girl, Octavia, and come all over my fingers."

The digits slide almost all the way out before plunging back inside me, curling as they hit that perfect spot before he teases my clit again with his tongue. He adds a third finger just when I think I can't take any more, and that extra bit of sensation is all it takes to push me over the edge. My body screams in the way my voice wants to as it loses all control to the ministrations of his mouth, his fingers, his fucking talent at making me come like a savage. All the while he keeps on finger fucking me until I lose my fucking mind.

"You come so pretty for me." He sits up, his fingers still inside me, leisurely fucking me, in and out like he's got all the fucking time in the world. I preen under his words, wanting to please him further. Pushing up, I rub my hand over his still covered dick, desperate to have him in my greedy little mouth.

Our gazes crash and there's no doubt he knows exactly what I want. In seconds, he brings his fingers from my pussy and pushes them into my mouth, making me taste myself. "Suck."

I lick and suck them clean, the way I want to suck on him. He pushes them further in, making me gag, his eyes widening a little as I do. "Kneel."

Scrambling from the bed, I do as he asks, sitting back on my haunches, waiting for his next command.

"I do like it when you're this pliant." I glance up at him, and his gaze screams power. It sends a jolt through me, and I know that right now, I'd do pretty much anything he asked of me. He approaches me slowly, as if he's stalking prey, pushing down his boxers when he reaches me, and I gulp as his dick bobs freely in front of my face.

Licking my lips, I cast my eyes up to his as he grips his cock at the base, stealing my attention with each stroke of his palm. "Open your mouth and stick out your tongue. Keep your hands on your thighs."

My heart races with his every command, feeling strangely

empowered when I follow his instructions. Hands on my thighs and mouth open like his dirty little toy. With my tongue waiting for him, he rubs the tip of his cock against it, groaning as he smears the bead of precum all over it. I dig my nails into my thighs as the need to wrap my lips around him, to drive him as insane as he makes me feel, grows, but when he calls me his good girl it stirs something deep within me and that keeps me planted where I am.

Two fingers grip my chin, tipping my head back until our gazes meet, and he pushes his dick in further, slowly, until I gag around the tip of him, saliva pooling at the back of my throat as he holds his dick there.

Tears slide down my cheeks, his eyes glinting as he watches them fall. Pushing his dick as far down my throat as he can, he pulls out just before I'm at my limit and tilts my head further so he can start the process all over again. I groan around his cock, making sure to keep my mouth wide open and tongue out as he instructed.

His hand leaves my chin, fingers curling around the long strands of my hair before he pulls down hard, the lick of pain making my eyes water. "I'm going to fuck this pretty little mouth, Octavia, and you're going to take it without complaint. And the next time I tell you to be quiet, remember my favorite way to make that happen."

I whimper around his dick, my heart racing as he pulls out again, his hand in my hair keeping my head where he wants it before he does as he promised. Drool runs down my chin and onto my bare chest as he fucks my face with abandon; my wetness pooling between my thighs tells me just how much I don't hate it.

"Fuck, Octavia. You feel so fucking good." His groans make my pussy pulse and I desperately want to touch myself, get myself off while he uses me to do the same.

He pulls out, my throat raw from taking him as roughly as it did, and he pulls me to my feet by my hair. I scramble to stand at his will. "Bend over and hold your ankles."

I reach forward when he releases me, wrapping my hands around my ankles, my thighs burning at the pull. He glides his fingers through my wetness from behind, pulling a moan from me as he gathers my juices and stretches me open again. "So ready for me." I barely feel the head of his dick against my entrance before he takes me in one hard, powerful thrust. "Use that filthy mouth of yours to tell me how good this feels."

Thank fuck.

He grips my hips and drills into me, eliciting cries from deep within me with each and every thrust. I was already so close from being his toy, but the thick feel of him dominating every inch of me threatens to push me over the edge of sanity.

"Please," I beg, and he responds by running two of his fingers over my painfully engorged clit, gathering ample amounts of my slick before moving them to my asshole. Cries fall from my lips as he coaxes me open with the pad of his finger while increasing the tempo of his thrusts. In and out, he alternates his rhythm. Fucking my pussy with his dick while his fingers fill my ass. I am so fucking full, and it's delicious. Linc is everywhere, everything. All over me and inside me. The dual sensation makes me lose my fucking my mind. I gasp and I moan, sounds coming from somewhere inside me I didn't even know existed. He changes up his speed, alternating between filling me with his dick and his fingers, and I feel like his ragdoll. Taking everything that he's willing to give as I hurtle toward my orgasm.

"Come for me, Octavia."

With his permission, I come savagely all over his dick, my breath hitching with the force of it. His hand at my hip keeps me upright as my knees go weak. He thrusts into me one final time with a roar, his body shaking with the power of his climax as his dick pulses inside of me.

Holy fuck.

Pulling out of me slowly, he uses the hand that was on my ass to keep me steady as the other moves to my pussy, pushing his cum back into me.

Fuck, that's hotter than it should be.

"You can let go of your ankles now, Octavia," he says before wrapping his arm beneath me and lifting me, bridal style, into the bathroom. "Let's get you cleaned up, shall we?"

He sits me on the counter before turning on the shower. Once the water is heating, he comes back and cleans me up with a washcloth, and I'm thankful he's taking charge once again because he fucked me boneless. When steam starts to build in the room, he takes my hand, pulling me from the counter into his arms, and walks me into the shower.

"I love you," he whispers, capturing my lips with his as we move under the water. "And I'll do whatever it takes to keep you."

After a draining day of school and exam prep, my brain is fucking mush. It might have something to do with the mind-blowing way I started my day, but I am not about to complain about that.

Upside, I haven't had a moment to worry about my fuck fest of a training session last night, even if it felt like more of a test than training.

My head rests on my folded arms atop the counter, where I've been sitting for the last hour trying to understand the sample exam question that the business substitute gave us and failing. My phone buzzes beside me, and the voice in my head that begs for sleep tells me to ignore it, but it could be Indi or one of the guys, so I lift my heavy head and glance at it.

Fuck my actual life, should've just gone to sleep.

Harrison:

Conclave Meeting in two hours. Do not be late, Miss Royal.

<Pin drop>

Ughhh!

Just what I need. As if last night wasn't enough. My phone buzzes again and I want to bang my head on the counter.

Luc:

Training's rescheduled. See you Saturday, kid.

Then I notice an earlier message from Alex sitting in my inbox

Alex:

Did you get summons this morning, Baby Royal. I'm still in EC. Grab me on your way?

Me:

Got it just now. But sure, I'll text you when I leave.

Since Luc's message requires no response, I close the message threads just as Smithy enters the kitchen. "Why so glum, Miss Octavia?"

"I'm tired, and I just got summoned to my first Conclave meeting. I'm sure Harrison did it on purpose so I don't have my wits about me, but that doesn't exactly make me feel any better."

His lips twist as his frow burrows. "That man… well… I won't speak my true thoughts in front of you, Miss Royal. Now then, why don't you run and grab a shower, it might perk you up. I'll sort out a light dinner for you and make an extra strong coffee to help too."

I slide from the stool and wrap my arms around him. "You're the best, Smithy. Thank you for everything. I don't know what I'd do without you."

"Well, let's hope you don't have to find out for quite some time." He quickly squeezes me back, and when he releases me, I grab my textbooks from the counter and drag them up to my room with me. I rush through a cold shower, the icy chill of the water doing what I hoped it would and waking me up a bit. I dress in skinny jeans, a pair of red-bottomed heels, a white shirt, and a blush blazer before running my fingers through my wavy hair.

It's not the best, but it's a major improvement on how I looked before. Once I'm back in the kitchen, I rush through my food and chug down the coffee, realizing I have to leave if I'm going to grab Alex and get to this fucking meeting on time.

"I'll see you later, Smithy!" I call out as I dial Alex's number and put the phone to my ear, grabbing my keys and heading to the garage.

Alex picks up as I slam the car door closed. "S'up Baby Royal?"

"Your ass better be ready, Alex. Where am I picking you

up?" I ask, hitting the speaker as I put the phone in its holder and start the car. I reverse out of the garage as he laughs.

"Look behind you, Baby Royal."

I glance up at the gates and hit the brakes. I open them and Alex strides toward the car as I end the call and set up the map to the pin drop Harrison sent me. Once he's in, I pull away as quickly as I can. The last thing I need is one of my guys spotting us together. Not that I've heard from them since school, but that isn't the point. If they saw me driving off with Alex, they'd ask questions I can't answer.

Escaping their notice, all of their notice, is the first downside I've discovered to being with all of them. Go figure.

We drive in silence for a while until Alex's bouncing leg starts to grind on me as much as his tapping on the dash. "Will you stop?"

He grins sheepishly at me, running a hand through his blond hair. "Sorry, Baby Royal. It's the first time I'm coming face to face with the big, bad Masters of the Universe. Has me full of nervous energy."

I scoff at him, rolling my eyes. "They're not Masters of the Universe. Just jumped up assholes with more power than anyone should have."

"Exactly. Which is precisely why you made your deal with them. You knew it was the only way *because* they're Masters of the Universe, or at least our sect. They command the way the world works, even for those who have no idea of their existence.

That is power. Being the puppet master."

"They're not even the top of the food chain," I sigh, tucking my hair behind my ear. "They just think they're the puppet masters, but even they answer to someone."

"You mean the Prism?" he asks, and I nod.

"Them, and then the Archon. He's the one that made the deal with my dad, which is how I ended up here."

"Yeah, I heard."

I side-eye him, wondering how exactly he heard about that, but that's not really important. Especially since he's joining the Conclave.

My eyes go wide as one thing occurs to me. "Do you think the guys have any idea *why* they're not at this meeting tonight?"

"They haven't been told there's a meeting. Juniors don't have to go to *every* meeting." I glance over at him, eyebrows raised in question. "I met with Harrison this morning and asked the same question."

I grumble under my breath about fucking secrets, feeling like a hypocrite, when he sighs. "It's that building ahead."

I look up at the behemoth building that I met Harrison in before and take a deep breath.

Time to face the music and see just what my deal with the devil looks like.

I slide into a seat one down from the right of the head of the table, giving the Mitchell pair a quick once over as I do. They might be as useless as Artemis said they were if I'm going on sight alone. They really don't seem like they want to be here, like they're so disinterested they might just fall asleep, so I wonder why, or even how they managed to keep their positions in the conclave. Pretty sure that Harrison isn't one to tolerate incompetence.

Artemis grins coyly at me across the table, a subtle nod of hello before her bitch mask falls into place. I let my own slide over my features, waiting for the rest of the Conclave to enter the room.

Chase enters next; he pauses when he sees me, but it's so brief that it would've been hard to notice if I hadn't been watching so closely. He sits next to Artemis, whose dad enters moments later, followed by Alex who sits between me and what I'm sure is Harrison's seat. He salutes me with a cocky grin on his face, and I can't help the upwards tug at the corners of my mouth.

Finally, Harrison and Charles enter the room, meaning that everyone is here and my first Conclave meeting is about to begin.

This doesn't seem as terrifying as everyone makes it out to be. It feels more like a dick measuring contest about who can do what, but what do I know? We haven't even started yet.

Charles takes his seat opposite me, his distasteful sneer

growing as his gaze roams over me before Harrison takes his seat beside me.

He glances at me before turning his attention to the rest of the room, and an icy drop of dread runs down my spine.

Yeah, this isn't going to be fun.

I try to pay attention as he makes a quick introduction of Alex and I to the rest of the Conclave, then jumps into talking about business that I have no fucking idea about. I slip my hand into my pocket, hitting the record button, so I can at least try to decipher some of this later with Smithy and hopefully have it make more sense.

"We have another pressing issue. The Kings are pushing back against our previous agreement. I need someone to take care of that." My head spins toward Harrison, gaining my attention instantly. "Alex, I think with your position within the Rebels, you are the best suited to deal with the Donovans. Do not disappoint me."

Alex nods once, squeezing my thigh reassuringly under the table. I don't dare show my panic on my face, or my palpable relief knowing that Alex won't hurt Indi's guys.

Harrison turns his gaze to me, pinning me with his unrelenting stare. "As for you, Octavia, you are already aware of what we need from you. The clock is ticking."

I dip my chin, acknowledging the thinly veiled threat for what it is. Artemis raises a brow at me, but I don't react.

"If that is all, I have to head to the Pit. We have some new recruits ready for initiation. This is one of my favorite parts. Helping mold our new members into who, or shall I say *what*, we need them to be."

No one says a word, though the look of disdain on Chase's face is unmissable. After a beat of silence, Harrison claps his hands once and stands. "Good. I'll see you all in a week. Alex, if you'll walk out with me, I'll run you through the King issue."

Alex stands and leaves with Harrison, Charles filtering out quickly after them. The Mitchells leave next with Artemis' dad, leaving me with Chase and Artemis in the room.

"I assume that East does not know about this... latest development." Chase frowns at me like I've committed the worst sin possible, and maybe I have, but fuck him. He doesn't get to judge me.

I quirk a brow, giving him my best ice bitch glare. "He does not. None of them do. And it's going to remain that way, as per my agreement with the Regent."

He just looks disappointed as he shakes his head. "Be careful playing with fire, Octavia. You will get burned."

Without waiting for a response, he stands and exits the room, leaving me alone with Artemis, who just smiles at me salaciously from across the table. "And then there were two."

TWELVE

OCTAVIA

This week is kicking my fucking ass. Between the 'assessment,' running with Linc, the start of prepping for finals, and dealing with Harrison, I'm about at my limit. Which is why my text reminder from Luc at four this morning was grossly unappreciated.

Luckily, Maverick slept straight through me leaving, and he'll likely still be asleep when I'm done here.

"Octavia, your stances are just fucking sloppy," Luc barks again, and I lose my shit.

"Maybe if I wasn't woken up at four in the fucking morning and dragged here by half-past, I'd be a little more coherent. But it's now barely five, I've had no coffee, and I'm fucking tired."

His eyes narrow at me before he drops his stance and stalks toward me. "You think the Knights are going to make sure you're in tip top form everytime they send you out? You think the ones who will come for you once they know who and what you are now will care if you're half asleep when they attack you? You need to be prepared for *anything.*"

I deflate at his words. He's right. I know he is. He softens when he realizes his blows hit their mark. "I'm trying to prepare you, Octavia. Trust me, I'd much rather none of us be in this mess, but we don't have the luxury of being able to go through life with rose-colored glasses on. Now, let's go again."

I tighten my ponytail and drop into the stance he's showing me. Thankfully, my somewhat casual training with Maverick, and the training my dad and Mac put me through on tour, gave me a peek into what I need to know, but my time with Luc, albeit short, has shown me I am woefully unprepared for the hellscape I've stepped into.

My bruises are going to have bruises.

He comes at me again, attacking me, quick as fuck and deadly as a viper. I know he's pulling his punches, but not so much that they won't leave marks.

Hiding those is going to be fun.

We spar for the next hour until I'm panting and broken. "You did good, kid. We'll get you to where you need to be, just try to stay alive in the meantime. We'll go again Monday. Hoping to have you fighting with blades by the end of next week. Make sure to hit the gym daily to help your conditioning. And eat right, none of that starving yourself to be thin bullshit. Give your body what it needs."

I stare at him slack-jawed as he throws me a towel, and I drop back onto the mats of the gym we're in. Though "gym" is me being generous. I don't recognize the place and Luc assured me the guys wouldn't find me here.

That's all the reassurance I needed.

I suck in air, groaning as I lie back and close my eyes. He just said fighting with blades. I am not Maverick, and as much as his blades fascinate me, the thought of using them... nope. Give me a gun over a blade any day. Though I get the feeling my preference isn't going to make any fucking difference to Luc. He's following orders as much as I am, so my opinion on it is worth fuck all.

Pulling myself back up, I move to the side of the room, grab my keys, phone, and water bottle and hightail it out of there back to my car. Thankfully this place isn't far from home and Maverick should hopefully still be fast asleep.

I make the drive home quickly, stashing the car away in the garage before rushing upstairs. Maverick is still very much asleep, and I loosen the breath in my chest, the weight that's been sitting there since I woke up lifting a little.

I need to shower. I'm fucking gross right now.

Moving into my bathroom, I turn on the water and undress while it heats. We have no plans today, and I'm kind of looking forward to having a chill weekend. We've all been full speed ahead with everything lately and I feel like none of us have had any time to breathe.

I've also barely seen Indi, and that's pissing me off too. Once upon a time, I didn't have anyone, but I also had no one dictating my actions to me. Of course, now that I have people I want to spend time with, someone is trying to pull me away from it all.

I'm not sure what I did in a past life to deserve all this, but apparently karma is a bitch and she's enjoying herself.

I start showering, groaning as my fingers run over the soreness of my body, when I hear movement in the room. I open my eyes and find Maverick's eyes on me, devouring me as his heated gaze takes in every inch of me.

"Now this is a wake up call." He grins salaciously as he stalks toward me—obviously ignoring my bruised skin, not that I'm complaining—pushing his boxers down as he does. "And I could get very used to having you as my breakfast every morning."

Sitting next to Finley in the Lamborghini, my anxiety is skyrocketing as we hurtle down the highway toward the facility where my mom is being looked after. After the insanity of training with Luc this morning, and then my second wakeup call with Mav, when Finn asked if I wanted to spend some time with him, I jumped at it. His calm usually helps to center me. But when I got in the car and he told me where we were heading... well, I've felt sick ever since.

I could have said no, told him I didn't want to, but I've also vowed to try to stop running from my problems. It hasn't gotten me anywhere, but I'm trying. Having made my deal with Harrison, while it's got me tied up in knots, I don't feel as shitty as I should about it because it was *my* choice. Not a reaction to something happening to me.

There's something freeing about it.

So... here I am, shitting my pants about facing the woman who birthed me. Sure, we had some good memories before she left, and of course now I understand her fear and why she wanted to leave, but I still don't forgive her for leaving Dad and me behind. Who knows what we could have survived together?

Finn reaches over and twines his fingers with mine, squeezing my hand once. He doesn't say anything, because we both know he doesn't have to. There isn't anything *to* say.

He's going to check up on the others who were prisoners of Edward's, ensuring that the staff are giving Linc all of the information on them. As for me... well... I'm going to try and not vomit before I see my mom.

I still have exactly zero idea of what the fuck it is I'm supposed to say to her. I don't know, and could likely never understand what she's been through at Edward's hands, but she doesn't know me either. I don't know if she even *wants* to know me.

And that, right there, are where my mommy issues come to a head. All I ever wanted was for her to love and want me. But she left. Dad was amazing up until he wasn't, but at least he was always there. And I can't help but blame her, at least a little, for how he ended up. If she hadn't left, things might have been different. He might have been able to stand the pressure and bullshit that came with his fame along with the demands of being a Knight.

But now we'll never know. All because she wasn't strong enough to stick it out.

There's also the chance I'm wrong, and that she didn't want to leave. She just wasn't brave enough to stay. While I can understand that, it makes me sick. It doesn't matter how afraid I was, if I had a child, I would never leave them behind.

Never.

"Your thoughts are so loud, pretty girl. Is there anything I can do?"

I glance over at the blond, tortured god beside me, both loving and hating that he sees the darkness in me but doesn't shy from it because he has the same darkness in him. His might run deeper than mine, but we're all a little broken, and that's why we fit together.

"No, I'm just nervous. And angry. And conflicted about being angry. I'm a mess." I let out a breath, blowing a few strands of hair off of my face, wishing I could make sense of everything in my head.

"I'm sure your mom is just as nervous."

"Does she know I'm coming?" I hadn't even considered that. Chewing the inside of my lip, the butterflies in my stomach start freaking raving, even as he shakes his head. "No, I asked them not to tell her, in case you weren't ready. But she has to know you'll be coming to see her sooner or later. Though, considering how long she's been with Edward, she might not have thought about it at all."

I don't know how to feel about that. What if she doesn't want to see me? She did leave after all. Even if she ended up ensnared by Edward, I know she was free for a few years before he took her. Though I still don't know *why* he took her and probably never will.

I focus on the passing scenery as we finish the journey in a comfortable silence while I get lost in my head again. When we pull up to the entrance of the facility, I'm shocked by what I see.

The beach in the background, the sleek, white, modern building that almost looks like a hotel. It emits a feeling of calm that I hadn't expected. Apparently Ocean Falls Wellness center is nothing like I imagined, even though I had no idea what to expect. Finley pulls the car into the parking lot, not moving once he kills the engine.

He gives me a minute to try and settle the nerves inside of me, but I'm not sure they're going anywhere. This is fully going to be a 'fake it till you make it' moment.

I squeeze his hand before releasing it, unbuckling myself and climbing from the crazy low car. I'm glad I wore jeans, 'cause climbing from this thing in a skirt is asking for me to flash my panties. I straighten my leather jacket and smooth down my hair, nerves getting the best of me before Finn rounds the car and pulls me into his arms.

"If you're not ready, we can just head home." He squeezes me against him, and I swear the storm-ridden waves inside of me calm as his heartbeat fills my mind. I take a few deep breaths, matching my breathing to his as I sink into him.

He stands there with me for a few minutes, just holding me, giving me the space to be anything and everything I need to be, while he fills the role of life jacket. With a final squeeze, I pull back from him. He doesn't release me right away, his gaze on mine, watching me intently as he brings his hand to cup my nape, a thumb swiping over my cheek. "You are all that matters to me, if you don't want to do this, you don't have to."

I shake my head as my heart swells. "I need to do this. I need some answers that only she has. But thank you." Stretching up on my tiptoes, I softly press my lips to his, and he kisses me like I'm the only thing he'll ever need.

"Whatever you need, I've got you."

"Then let's do this." He watches as my resolve takes over my expression and nods, taking my hand back in his.

"Let's do this."

He leads me inside and I follow willingly, despite my erratic heart beating wildly in my chest. He speaks to a woman at the front desk like he's known her forever. Considering when he put his mom in here, he probably has.

"If you'll just wait here, I'll go and see if they're ready for visitors," the older woman says to Finn with a kind smile, and he leads me over to the couches in the bright space.

"This is a Knights place?" I ask him quietly and he nods. I have so much to learn, and I wish they could help me, but I'm pretty sure if I ask too many questions, they'll start to wonder why.

"The franchise is owned by Aretmis' dad. The sects across the country use them when needed. There are dozens across the Americas. Not really surprising that they're required with what the Knights are responsible for, but they're also open to the general population. The whole world is fucked up." I clamp my lips together and nod. He isn't wrong, the world is fucked, but I'm glad that this place is open to everyone. The Knights would only have the best of the best here, and people deserve access to that.

I can't help but wonder if they target people, vulnerable people, that come here. It seems like something Harrison would do. Though it occurs to me I don't even know how far this sect reaches. That's probably something I should learn if I'm going to take my mantle as Regent.

I need to start writing questions down in a notebook or

something.

The woman from the front desk reappears, looking a little frazzled. "I'm very sorry, Finley, but Mrs. Royal has denied visitor access."

My heart sinks at her words, but it also pisses me off.

"It's fine," I say, reining in my anger, because it's not her fault and there's no point in shooting the messenger, though Finn's frown looks anything but fine. I turn to him and squeeze his thigh. "You do what you need to do, I'll wait here for you."

I try not to let him see the churning waves inside of me picking up force once again. I'm not sure why I'm surprised she doesn't want to see me. She left. She didn't want me, want us. It makes more sense that she wouldn't want to see me.

So I swallow down the disappointment that I hadn't expected and keep my head held high.

This is just a bump in the road, and I'll get the answers I want some other way. It might just take a little longer than I thought. With that in mind, and my deadline with Harrison imminent, I pull out my phone, and ask the devil for an extension on our deal. I need more time, there's been so much going on, I've barely had time to start searching for what he wants.

He doesn't keep me waiting for long. And while I get what I want, it doesn't make me feel any better.

Harrison:

Two more weeks, Miss Royal. I'm being overly generous here, it won't happen again. Ensure I have those documents by your birthday, otherwise our deal is done. The boys will stay exactly as they are, and you... well, you will be right alongside them with no hand to play.

I let out a deep sigh as I step into the hot tub. This day has been draining as fuck, so when Finn suggested chilling out in the Saints' hot tub, I was not about to pass it up. Especially when he offered up a back massage too. Those hands of his are big and strong; they're too fucking good against my skin.

I close my eyes and rest my head back against the rest, waiting for him to join me as the hot water starts to loosen my muscles. I'm exhausted, mentally more than physically, and I really need some down time.

I wonder if Indi is up for a girls' weekend.

Not that I don't have enough shit to be juggling right now, but escaping sounds like fun, and after the storms in the East, I know the slopes are thick with snow and calling my name.

God, I miss not having any ties to my time or destination.

I hear footsteps approach, and a smile plays on my lips at the thought of Finley unwinding with me. Fuck knows he needs it too.

They still don't know my secrets, and it's killing me to keep it from them, but knowing that their suffering is nearly over brings so much joy to my heart that I can handle the fact that they're going to be mad as fuck when they do find out.

"How you feeling, pretty girl?" I open my eyes at Finley's low, smooth voice and lean on his shoulder. "Better now?"

"Much," I sigh as I hear a second set of footsteps before Lincoln comes into view and climbs into the tub with us. His eyes are hooded as he watches us. "I didn't realize you were home."

"You didn't ask," he says, his voice so low that shivers break out over my skin. I'll never know how I got so lucky as to have all four of these guys look at me and love me the way they do, but I'm not about to question it.

"Come here," Finn says, pulling on my hand until I'm sitting in his lap. His hands move to my shoulders where his strong fingers start to massage at the knots in my muscles there.

My eyes drift closed as I let out a moan. "Fuck, that feels good."

His lips feather against the skin where my neck meets my shoulder, but his hands continue to work me, making me boneless beneath his touch.

Behind me, the unmistakable hardening of Finn's cock doesn't escape my notice. Knowing that I do this to him makes me immediately wet for him. For them. Reaching back, I gather my hair to one side and bow my head as Finn massages a particularly hard knot.

The slight splashing of water gets my immediate attention—

I'm hyper aware of Lincoln's every move—prompting me to open my eyes. My gaze lands directly on his hand wrapped around his rock-hard cock, making my tongue dart out and lick a wet path across my lips.

Anticipation skitters over my skin like lightning, my mouth watering for the taste of him as he rises from his seat and makes his way to me in less than three steps.

Finn's hands never falter as Linc buries his fingers in my hair at my temple, dragging them down until his entire hand is cradling my nape, pulling my head back until I'm forced to look at his stormy, gray stare.

"Think you can suck my cock while Finn pummels your pussy?" His words are crude but his eyes—those deep slate-colored eyes—are heated.

I don't answer right away, licking my lips provocatively just to fuck with him a little, but watch him as he follows the deliberate stroke of my tongue.

"You know I can."

He smirks at me as his hand tightens against me. "Yeah, I do. Open your mouth."

I don't hesitate. My mouth drops open and behind me Finn grips my hips hard enough to position me right over his rock-solid cock—my knees now straddling Finn's thighs as I kneel on the bench. My eyes fix on Linc as I wait for Finn to pull me down over his dick, but he doesn't. He just rubs the head of his cock through my slit, gathering my juices as they mix with the water in the hot tub.

Linc smirks and I swear just the power of him makes me shake with anticipation.

"Eager little vixen, aren't you, Octavia?" His words are soft, the head of his cock gliding over my top lip, then my bottom, tracing the "o" of my open mouth.

Slowly, he pushes his cock inside my mouth as Finn teases my clit with the head of his cock. Around and around, he teases, earning them a moan around the length of Linc's dick as it slides all the way to the back of my throat.

"Such a good girl. Swallow, let me feel it." I do. I work the muscles of my throat and my reward is the curse that escapes Linc's delicious lips.

Finn applies more pressure on my clit, making me squirm in his arms. Afraid to fall forward, I latch onto Finn's forearms, taking advantage of the move to try and slide down his cock

Linc *tsks* at me, but I can't speak, my mouth being full of his cock, yet I feel so much.

Finn's entire length gliding, slipping inside of me briefly but pulling right back out makes me whimper.

Linc's grip on my hair tightens as he begins to fuck my mouth until tears stream down my face. Pushing in and out at a steady rhythm, my gaze never leaving his. Linc bites his bottom lip as he tells me everything he never says with a look alone.

"Take it." His order is full of lust, desire so strong I can taste it in the pearl of precum that coats the back of my throat.

I do as he commands, preening at his string of curses as I do.

His gaze flicks behind me to Finn and not a second later, I'm full of cock. My pussy and my mouth both full to the hilt. I'm choking on Linc, my eyes watering deliciously with the force of his thrusts. When he pulls out, Finn stays buried inside me, cursing and telling me how tight I feel. How warm I feel. His mouth at my ear, he tells me he loves me. How he wants his dick buried in my pussy all fucking day. All the fucking time.

I don't have time to register everything Finn says because in the following second, he's pulling out as Linc is pushing his cock back inside my mouth.

"Play with your clit, Octavia. Make yourself come while we fuck you." God, his dirty mouth will be the death of me. I used to think there was something deeply wrong with me because I loved this so much, but now? Fuck it. It's who I am.

Reaching down, I bring two fingers to my clit and rub in time with their thrusts. One in, the other out and on and on they fuck me. Deep, hard, precise plunges inside me. It's like they've been practicing their moves. Or maybe we're just made to be together like this.

"Such a filthy girl, Octavia. Sucking my cock and fucking Finn in this hot tub. Such a good girl."

His words ignite my orgasm like a small ember that starts at the base of my stomach and explodes into a million licks of fire throughout my entire body. I can't even continue rubbing myself, afraid I'll fall into the water. Linc holds my head hostage as he slams his dick in and out of my mouth—coating himself with my dripping saliva.

"That's right, V. Fuck, you feel so fucking good all over my dick." Finn fucks me almost punishingly, when Linc pulls out and comes all over my mouth, my lips, my chin. His grunts and moans are fuel to my fire as my orgasm continues to ravage my body.

Finn roars as he comes inside me, pumping quick hard thrusts to the hilt right before he freezes and groans in my ear.

A shiver courses over my body as he empties inside of me, and I lick Linc's cum from my lips and chin, his eyes heating again as I do. His control snaps and he kisses me, tasting himself on me as my pussy quivers around Finn's dick.

"Fuck," he groans from behind me as his fingers dance up my spine.

The door to the room slams open, startling us all, and Linc spins to face whoever is coming toward us, hiding me from them. I peek around him when his shoulders relax and see Maverick striding toward us as he reaches behind him and pulls off his t-shirt. Pretty sure he shouldn't look so fucking hot doing that one action but, fuck, he does.

"Looks like I missed the fun. Guess I'll just have to tap in now."

THIRTEEN

LINCOLN

These last few weeks have been more bleak than light, but I am desperately fighting against the waves that keep threatening to suck me under and drown me. My father might think he's a God, but Poseidon he isn't, so these murky waters are not going to steal me and the things I love.

I fucking refuse.

Trying to keep V happy while dancing around the minefield my father has dropped me in the middle of is proving more work than I ever expected, but for her, I'd happily do the dance a thousand lifetimes over.

What I'd rather not do, is deal with the red-headed succubus that supposedly wears a ring that is meant to bind us together.

Over my dead and cold body.

I just need to find an alternate way to keep Harrison happy so that he doesn't follow through on his threats to rip Octavia away from me if I don't do what he asks. I knew when she came back here that if I let myself fall for her, claimed her as my own, she would become my weakness. I knew it would hurt her—hurt us both—and yet, I was her captive the minute her hazel eyes met mine her first day back.

Even if I fought it, I knew we were inevitable. I knew that once I gave in, I'd never let her go, no matter what.

Unfortunately, Harrison seems to have his own fucking plans for my life, but like I've told him before, I'm not a whore, and it's my fucking dick. If he wants the union so bad, he can fuck her. It's not like he's opposed to younger women or devoted to monogamy. God knows he's cheated on my mom their entire marriage, even if he does demean her for doing the same damn thing.

I finish my reps on the chest press, dropping the lift with a thunk before grabbing my towel and swiping it over my face. I've been in the gym all morning trying to clear my mind of the bullshit so I can focus on this afternoon.

Date day with my girl.

I haven't been able to snag much alone time with her lately and it's pissing me off. Between the Knights bullshit, dealing with the guys and everything else we have going on, and keeping that succubus away from me, I've barely had time to breathe, let alone spend time with Octavia. I mean, I got quality time with her yesterday, but I still had to share her. While sharing with my brothers isn't a hardship, I just want to be selfish for a night. Which is why I made her promise me her afternoon today.

I am going to distract her from all of the darkness around us, even if it kills me.

She shone so bright when she first got back, and it's impossible not to see how being around us has started to dim that light. Not that there's anything wrong with her being dark, but we never meant to break her.

Fuck me, my head is a mess.

I jump in the shower, freshening up before drying off and shucking into a pair of jeans and a t-shirt, running my hands through my damp hair. What I have planned for today doesn't require anything but comfort.

Once I make it back to the kitchen, Mrs. Potts is already waiting for me. "Oh, Lincoln, dear. Good, you're here before I take off. Are you sure you're ready to make this on your own?"

Her smile is warm and loving, the surrogate mother who basically raised me, and I feel nothing but kindness for her. Even if she is doubting me.

"We've been practicing this meal in pieces for years. I can do this." I grin wide at her, and she rolls her eyes.

"Well, it's true you've always been able to do anything you set your mind to." She huffs out a breath and finishes wiping down the already-spotless counters. "Just remember to clean as you cook so you don't destroy the kitchen, and do not open the oven until the souffles are fully risen. I've stocked everything, it's either in the refrigerator or the pantry, so you should have everything you need."

She saunters over to me and presses her hands against my cheeks. "And if you break my kitchen, I will make you repair it by hand. None of this hiring someone else to fix your mess bother."

Winking at me, she releases me and I laugh softly. "I promise not to break anything, though if I do, you'll never know because it will be repaired before you can find out."

"A woman always knows, Lincoln Saint. You'd be wise to remember that."

I shake my head with a smile as she leaves. She might be the only adult in my life that has always treated me as a human, with love and kindness, rather than wondering what it is I can do for her.

Once she's gone, I hook my phone up to the speakers, putting on *Fall to Pieces* by Pale Waves

, and get started on the prep work for my plans with Octavia.

I intend to take her on a sensory rollercoaster that she'll never want to get off of. I start by melting the chocolate before dipping the strawberries and putting them in the fridge to set. Could I buy them? Of course, I could buy every single thing I have planned, but that's too easy, and I'm not about taking the easy way out.

Not when it comes to her.

I pick up my phone and pull up my thread with her.

Me:

T-minus two hours.

Octavia:

I'm both excited and afraid. Are you sure you won't tell me what you have planned?

Me:

Oh I am absolutely sure I won't. Just come comfortable ;)

Octavia:

Hmmmm, if you say so. The anticipation is killing me.

Me:

That's the best part.

I grin as I pocket my phone again and deep-dive into this prep. I'm looking forward to this date afternoon more than I'm willing to admit.

Losing myself to the prep, the time flies by, and by the time the back door is opening, I'm just wiping down the last of the counters from my clean up. She breezes into the room, her long hair cascading down her back in waves, in no more than a pair of cutoffs and a crop top.

"Goddamn you are beautiful," I groan. This girl makes me fucking weak, and I'm useless to stop it.

A blush spreads across her cheeks as she smiles bashfully at me while she toes off her Converse by the back door before skipping over to me and wrapping her arms around my neck. "You look pretty fucking edible yourself."

Oh, she's going to be eating me... she just doesn't know it yet. I smile down at her as I grasp her hips. She stands on her tiptoes, fingers intertwined behind my neck, so I lift her to sit on the counter. She squeaks as her feet leave the ground and the sound goes straight to my fucking dick.

Once she's perched and I stand between her legs, I capture her rosy lips and take from her. She nips at my lip, stirring a growl within me, and I tighten my hold on her. When I pull back, her chest rises and falls as she pants, eyes closed, before fluttering her lashes open to look at me. "I could get used to that kind of hello."

I grin coyly at her. If she had any idea the things I'd happily do to her, as a hello or anything else, that blush of hers would spread. I've only just barely skimmed the surface of the things I want to do with her, but I figure we have forever, so why rush? Long gone are the notions that I'll ever give her up.

"So, what exactly do you have planned for this date of ours?" she asks, trying to look innocent. But I know better than most that there is nothing innocent about Octavia Royal.

Not anymore.

I feather my fingertips across the bare skin of her waist, moving down until I grip her thighs. "It's a surprise."

She pouts at me and I let out a soft laugh before pulling down on her lip with my thumb. She nips the pad of it, and my eyes go wide as my heart picks up its pace. "You're playing with fire, Octavia."

"Maybe." She shrugs before sucking my thumb into her mouth. "But maybe I want to get burned."

Having my girl tied, blindfolded, and naked is fucking exquisite. Watching the way her body writhes in anticipation, especially now that her eyes are covered, is enough to push me to rush, but there is no way in hell I'm rushing through this time with her. There is something freeing about being bound, giving up the control and responsibilities of anything and everything. I love that I can give this to her—the freedom in my control—and so much more.

"Lincoln." She calls my name, almost breathless, tugging at her bindings. "I thought this was supposed to be us hanging out."

"Are you complaining?"

She bites her lip at my question before shaking her head.

"Good girl. Now, be patient and you will be rewarded for

it." She whimpers as she tries to rub her thighs together, the anticipation making her fucking wet already. Little does she know, I intend on dragging this out all fucking day.

She is mine to feast on, but half the fun is in the build up. I've toyed with edging and denial with her a little, but I haven't dragged it out like this. Not that I intend on denying her anything, just letting her think that I am.

I adjust myself in my jeans, my dick rock fucking solid already, and I haven't even started.

Leaving her tied to my bed, I leave the room, making sure the door is locked, and head downstairs to get everything I prepared for today. Everyone else is out, with strict instructions to stay the fuck gone until later.

This is my time with her, and I intend to enjoy it.

Grabbing everything I need, I put it in the basket Mrs. Potts tucked away for me and head back upstairs. I open my door quietly, padding into the room, barefoot on the carpet. "Are you there?"

Her voice is quiet, but already dripping with need. She is enough to test any man's patience.

"I'm here," I call out as I close the door, before slowly making my way over to where she's bound. I open the basket and lay out the sensory feast I prepared earlier, before heading to my closet and grabbing a few other goodies I'm going to need. I watch her from the bottom of the bed, spread open for me, and swallow a groan. This is about her. Everything she doesn't even realize she wants. But the way she reacts when I call her a good girl tells me everything I need to know about how much she's going to enjoy all of this. "Open your mouth for me."

Her tongue swipes across her lips before she parts them, her hands clasping at the ropes that tie her to the bed frame. Moving closer, I grab one of the chocolate-covered strawberries and press it between her lips, her breath hitching as she tastes the sweetness. "Bite."

A moan reverberates through her as she does as she's told, and a smile plays on my lips. She follows orders so fucking well. I can't wait to test her limits.

Once she swallows, she smiles softly. "That was… unexpected. And delicious."

Leaning forward, my lips brush against her ear, "I like unexpected." A shiver runs through her, dragging my smile wider as goosebumps appear on her skin when I press my lips against the sensitive skin on the column of her throat. "Want to keep playing?"

She nods, and I clasp her throat, giving just the right amount of pressure for her to feel like she's being deprived of air, without actually taking anything from her. "Words, Octavia."

"Yes," she pants, and my cock twitches again.

"Better."

I pull an ice cube from the bag in the basket and move to place it against her ankle. She squeals at the cold, trying to pull her leg away as I trace the cube up her calf, tracing it with my tongue before moving it up her thigh to the apex of her legs. She whimpers when I run it across the lips of her pussy, and I feel my inner caveman beating on my chest.

Mine.

All fucking mine.

To do with what I please.

I pick up the feather from the floor and trace it down the other side of her neck, moving to the curve of her breast, trailing between them and down to her navel as she mewls at the light touch.

"Please."

Her pleas as she writhes beneath me make me shake my head, even though she can't see. "Soon."

The slam of a door shakes the foundations of the house, and I whip my head toward the sound, even though I can't see anything.

"Lincoln!" I wince at the roar of my name.

Fuck my life.

The one person I couldn't control coming and ruining this did exactly fucking that.

"Lincoln?" She says my name like it's a question, and I let out a sigh as I lift her blindfold.

"Sorry, baby, the monster calls. I'm going to untie your hands, then run down to see what the fuck he wants. Get dressed. The last thing I want is you vulnerable up here while he's this pissed."

She nods her head and I kiss her, putting every fucking flame inside of me into it before I untie her.

"Hopefully, I won't be long."

She nods at me, a frown marring those beautiful lips as she looks up at me with her big doe eyes.

I could fucking kill Harrison right now.

Maybe I will.

I clench my hands as I fold my arms over my chest. After being yelled at about fuck knows what for an hour, I texted Octavia and told her she should probably head home because I had no idea how long Harrison was going to go at it.

She texted me back to let me know she'd snuck out the back. Thankfully, she didn't have to pass Harrison's office.

He's been sitting, seething quietly with a glass of scotch, for the last half hour. I tried to leave before texting Octavia again, but he threw a glass at my head, so I ground my teeth together and put my phone away. I've been waiting here for Harrison to actually let me know what the fuck it is he wants since, but my patience is running thin.

I thin my lips, and he raises an eyebrow at me, like he's waiting for me to lose my shit. Luckily, I'd dropped a message to the boys to let them know to avoid the house until I gave them the all clear. I'm half hoping they're over at Octavia's, because the thought of her there alone when Harrison is in this mood is enough to put my teeth on edge.

"So, when were you and your little friends going to tell me about Edward?"

I keep my face straight, maintain my posture and give absolutely nothing away. Just like the monster himself taught me. I don't know what he knows, but I knew this was coming. My biggest worry is what this means for Maverick.

He leans forward, his elbows on his knees, glass cradled in his hands, eyes never leaving me. I know what he's waiting for, but unfortunately for him, he trained me himself to not bend. I don't bend, I don't break; not for him, not for anyone.

After watching me for two full minutes, he smirks. "Well, at least I trained you right." He pauses, finishing his glass before he stands. "I already know what happened, and I understand why you didn't say anything. It's being dealt with, but this leaves a hole. Maverick will have to step up."

I keep still, refusing to give away just how much his words piss me off.

"As long as he does that, he can remain a solo chair, like Chase has done up until now. I'm sure you'll be glad your brother will finally be a brother-in-arms. I assume he's told you all about that?" His smirk grows as my jaw tics. "Oh dear, I guess not all is well in your little circle like you thought. No matter. You don't need them. You're the Regent Heir. Your path is already forged. Speaking of…"

He trails off, moving to pour himself another drink as I take a deep breath, trying to reinforce my walls against him. No one else has the power to cut me down like he does, and I fucking hate it.

"You have a date with Georgia the weekend after next." He turns to face me and I grind my teeth. It's Octavia's birthday that weekend and he fucking knows it. Despite my denial of being with her, I'm not stupid enough to think he doesn't know. "Seal the fucking deal already. I told you, if you don't secure this, it will be your little girlfriend who pays. Keep her on the side once you're married, I don't give a fuck. But you will secure this alliance for me. Otherwise your girlfriend will suffer the same way her mother did."

My stomach drops. There are more than enough Knights with proclivities similar to Edward's. He might've been one of the worst, but there are always other monsters lurking in the shadows waiting for their time to strike. The thought of Octavia, captive to one of them…

"Or I could just be done with her once and for all. Not like there isn't enough Royal blood on my hands already."

"Fuck you," I growl, hating myself for the slip. It'll be worse for us all in the long run, but I have heard too many threats toward her fall from his fucking lips. I'm at my limit. "You leave her the fuck alone, otherwise you'll regret carving me into everything you wished you could be."

He barks out a laugh. "There's the little monster I created.

Good to see you're still in there, that she hasn't turned you soft. But do not push me, boy. Marry the redhead, fuck the Royal, I don't give a shit, but do what I told you to do, otherwise I'll show you what a *real* monster looks like and *she* will pay the price."

FOURTEEN

OCTAVIA

I smile as I bounce down the stairs; Maverick's laughter as he trails behind me is intoxicating. After my morning run with him and Linc, then my afternoon that was cut way too short with Lincoln, Mav has been in a playful but competitive mood since he came over when I got back—even if I was a cranky bitch at first because well... all revved up with nowhere to go. That being said, I love afternoons like this, where we get to just be teenagers. They're few and far between.

Soon, he'll have this every day and I can't wait. I'm excited for him.

"Penny for your thoughts?" he asks as he jumps off the bottom step and lifts me from behind. I let out a squeal as his arms clamp around my waist.

I laugh as he spins me around and when he comes to a stop, I lean my head back on his shoulder so I can look up at him. "Just that I like this. Seeing you like this. It's nice."

"Oh, I can be more than nice," he jokes, wagging his brows at me.

"I'm very aware, now put me down, you brute."

He spins me in his hold and I wrap my arms around his neck and my legs around his waist. "Looks to me like you like where you are."

"Maybe I do," I tease as he strides across the room toward the kitchen.

He puts me down on the counter so he's standing between my legs, a devious grin on his face. "How do you feel about keeping up my joyful spirits?"

I quirk a brow at him, trying not to laugh. "What did you have in mind?"

"A bet."

"A bet?" I ask and he nods, his smile growing.

"A bet," he says, wagging his brows at me again. I laugh loudly as he nuzzles my neck, tickling me until I squirm in his hold.

"What's the bet?"

"I bet that you can't stay quiet enough for me to eat you out right here, right now, without someone finding us."

My heart races in my chest. Smithy and Matthew are here

this weekend, I have no idea where but they didn't tell me they were going out. Regardless, I can't deny that the thought of getting caught is both terrifying and exciting all at once. My skin prickles at the thought, and I lick my lips as I consider it, especially since I'm still coming down from my time tied to Lincoln's bed. "Okay, so if I win, then what?"

His grin is breathtaking as he stands between my legs, his fingers toying with the bare flesh of my thighs. "If I lose, you get to ride my bike with me sitting in the bitch seat."

I gasp quietly. He doesn't let anyone play with his baby. Hell, he fucking adores that bike. I've been itching to play on his pretty, and his territorial hold on it just makes me want it more.

"And if I lose?"

"Well, if you lose," he pauses as my breath hitches, his pupils blowing as he watches me like the predator he is. "If you lose, you choke on my dick, and be my little fuck toy until I can't go anymore."

Knowing how many times he's capable of performing, that's a little daunting, but my pussy clenches as he brushes his fingers up my thigh, under my skirt, and against my panties.

"I don't know," I murmur, worrying about Smithy finding me splayed out on the counter if he is home.

Maverick pushes his fingers past the lace of my panties and pushes through to my clit, making me groan as I tip my head back. "That wasn't very quiet, princess. I guess I can understand you not wanting to lose."

I bring my head back down to glare at him. "I won't lose."

"Does that mean the bet is on?" he asks, his lips whispering against mine as his fingers gently tease my pussy before sliding inside of me. I gasp at the intrusion and bite down to stop my groan spilling from my lips.

"Yes." The word falls from my lips and he kisses me with so much heat, I'm sure they'll bruise.

"Good girl," he whispers when he pulls back. My eyes go wide as he pulls a switchblade from his back pocket. "You like this don't you, princess?"

My eyes stay on the glinting metal as he glides it down my chest, cutting away my crop top, which falls down my arms, and I try not to breathe a sound as the blade slices my skin a little. The cut walking the line of too much as he undoes my shorts and teases my clit through the lace of my panties.

"Tell me you like it," he demands, eyes darting to the thin line of blood that trickles down my chest before bending down and licking it up, kissing the broken skin when he's done.

I groan as the pleasure mixes with the pain in a way that Maverick seems to have perfected. "I like it."

He growls as he rips the knife away. "Hips up," is all the notice I get as he rips my shorts down before dropping to his knees.

Splaying his large hands over my thighs, Mav pushes as far as they'll go and pulls me to the edge of the island.

Bracing myself with one hand behind me and the other on Mav's dark head of hair, I audibly gasp as he takes my panties in his teeth and rips them apart like the savage he is.

Fuck, that's hot.

The look he gives me—a smirk firmly planted on his lips—tells me he knows exactly what he's doing. The whole time he'll be eating me out, he'll do it with the sole purpose of making me scream.

I may have gotten myself into a mess, but I'd walk across burning coals before admitting that to Maverick fucking Riley.

My knuckles ache with the force of my grip in his hair as his mouth kisses my pussy lips and his tongue plunges inside me, licking one side then the other, his fingers digging into my flesh with every move of his mouth.

I moan, the sound stifled by my self-control. Just barely.

Mav looks back up at me, his eyes crinkling with amusement and determination. He knows he's only seconds—maybe a minute or two if I'm lucky—away from winning his ridiculous bet. Actually, what's ridiculous is that I would subject myself to this torture.

Who the fuck am I kidding?

Staying quiet with any of them is so freaking hard. I just tried this game with Lincoln and failed miserably. No idea why I think I'm going to win this time, but I'm not one to back down from a challenge.

My breaths are coming in fast and gaining in fervor with

every lick and suck and bite that he offers my greedy little cunt. I'm riding his face when he plunges two fingers inside me, his mouth closing around my clit and his tongue flicking it with laser sharp precision.

I don't even realize I'm screaming until his mouth is on mine—capturing my screams—sharing my taste with me as our tongues battle in a kiss so hot it makes my orgasm prolong around his fingers still fucking me. Hard. Fast.

"I love winning my bets almost as much as I love hearing you scream my name."

Had I screamed his name?

"Oh yeah, princess. Loud and fucking clear." His answer tells me he's able to read my confused expression. "And now, I'm collecting my winnings."

Goddammit. I knew I wouldn't be able to win this.

Barely aware of my surroundings, I grab Mav by his hair and stare at him with—I'm guessing—horror written all over my features.

"Did Smithy and Matthew hear me?" Oh, fucking hell, I would never be able to look them in the eyes ever again.

Mav's laughter roars out like a dark storm over the ocean. God, I love seeing him freed like this. Happy. Carefree, even.

"No one's home, princess. I made fucking sure of it before I brought you down here."

My eyes narrow on him and I suddenly feel feral. "You fucker!"

"I sure am, princess. But first, you're going to suck my cock just the way I like it." The next thing I know, Mav carries me in a fireman's hold over to the couch and lays me down with my head hanging over the armrest.

Yeah, his favorite way to get sucked is with my head hanging and his access to the back of my throat, so he can grasp my neck in his hands and feel himself as he fucks me.

I love it like this too, but I'm definitely not telling him that or else he'll find some other depraved way of making me come.

Once I'm settled, my mouth eager to taste him, his jeans are down around his ankles and his cock is already in his hand, rock hard as he strokes it, gripping it tightly. He almost looks angry.

When our gazes meet, he looks at me like I'm the center of the Universe, the softness in his eyes so endearing, so honest, it makes me fall in love with him all over again.

"Open that gorgeous mouth of yours, V. Take all of me in." Bracing himself on the back of the couch, he leans in and angles his cock into my mouth, slowly, until he's all the way in the back of my throat. He moans, the sound so fucking sexy it makes me wet and achy all over again.

"Fuck, your mouth is heaven."

Once his groin is pushed against my face, his free hand comes to my throat, squeezing hard enough to make my eyes water and saliva pool at the corners of my mouth.

"Goddamn, you're stunning with my dick buried so deep in your throat I can feel it against my fingers."

I can't answer him, obviously, but I can acknowledge his words. As filthy as they are, for Mav, they are as romantic as can be.

I use my throat muscles to squeeze the head of his dick and revel in the beauty of him throwing his head back and moaning.

Because I do this to him.

He pulls out, looking down at me and when our eyes meet again, determination is written in the depth of his gaze.

His determination to fuck the breath out of me.

Just by the tautness in his shoulders, I can tell he's going to fuck me after this and it's going to be glorious.

Without a word he moves back, tugging me down so I'm on my knees and he grasps my chin, opening my mouth wide. He barely gives me time to suck in a breath before he shoves back inside, his fingers pressing against the sides of my throat.

In and out. Pushing through my gag reflex, using my nose to breathe, I allow him to fuck my face like the animal he thinks he is.

He's my lion. Feral, protective, and dominant to his last breath.

"Fuck, I love your fucking mouth. Play with your clit, princess. Make yourself come for me." His order sends a bolt of lightning up my spine, and I cave to his demands.

My fingers reach down to my clit, two of them rubbing over my hard, swollen nub while I try to concentrate on his accelerating rhythm. Faster, he fucks me with precision, never giving me too much, always careful not to hurt me. Too much.

It takes me less than thirty seconds to get my orgasm building again, my eyes trained on Maverick's beautiful face. He's enraptured as he watches me play with myself, his hand wrapped around my throat as he feels his cock sliding in and out of my mouth. He licks his lips—slowly and deliberately—like he misses tasting me even though it's been no more than minutes since he last had his tongue inside my pussy.

His gaze comes back to mine and I hear his silent words. His silent demand. He wants me to come.

My hips buck up and my fingers quickly gather my juices from my slit and bring them up to my clit where I rub circles—almost frantically—all the while trying not to choke to death on Mav's cock.

He knows exactly when I'm seconds from coming because he buries his cock inside my mouth and grinds down against my face, making my orgasm explode from deep inside me. I can't breathe and that fact makes my climax all the more powerful.

"Holy fucking hell, princess. You've never looked more beautiful than you do right now."

I must look a mess. My eyes watering. My mouth coated with my dripping saliva. My pussy soaked with my second orgasm, yet he calls me beautiful. He might be a monster, but he's my monster.

Mav, who still hasn't come, pulls out of my mouth and adjusts my position, pushing me back onto the couch before burying his cock inside my pussy, my legs hanging over his shoulders as he kneels.

He's not gentle. All semblance of control seems to have left him as he pummels me like he hasn't fucked me in years. The smell of sex and the sounds of skin slapping on skin are all around me. Trying to keep up with his frantic fucking rhythm, one hand clutches the back of the couch while the other grabs the armrest behind my head as I watch him plunge in and out of my hungry pussy—his eyes darting from where our bodies meet to my eyes and back again.

He's like a man possessed, his need for me overwhelming and beautiful.

Mav is a lot of things, but more than anything, he's in love with me and fucking me like this is the best way he knows how to show me.

With his intensity.

His commitment to bringing me pleasure.

And fucking hell, does he ever bring me pleasure.

"Your pussy is so desperate for my cock, princess. It's soaked, your cum is coating my cock like a fucking waterfall." He's close. So fucking close I can feel him growing inside me. Then he stills—his dick so deep inside me I can practically feel him in my belly.

I catch my breath as one of his hands comes to my clit— his thumb working my sensitive nub into another orgasm. How does he do that? "Come for me again, princess."

I am captive to his hold on me. He looks at me and every one of his feelings are written in his eyes. I am powerless to his demands and I come once more, clamping down on his dick, dragging him over the edge with me.

He rests his forehead on mine, his heaving breaths in perfect time with my own as he rests while I try to pick up my broken psyche from the ground around me. It's useless. I am his, and I have zero regrets about that.

"Holy fuck, princess." His words are little more than a murmur as he kisses me once more, his dick hardening again without having even left me.

He pulls back, rocking his hips and making me gasp as I meet his gaze, his eyes sparkling. "Oh, I'm not done with you yet, princess."

After the rollercoaster of the weekend, I'm almost glad it's Monday morning and that I'm pulling on my uniform for school. My workout with Luc this morning was fucking brutal, followed by my run with Linc, and I swear I could sleep for four days. Pretty sure Lincoln could tell I was flagging, but there's nothing I can do about it other than push harder.

Which is exactly what I intend to do.

My phone buzzes on the dressing table, Artemis' name flashing on the screen.

Artemis:

Don't forget that you're with me tomorrow, girlie. See you bright and early, sweet cheeks. And yes I mean your ass ;)

I laugh out loud, dropping her a message to say I haven't forgotten. It should probably be weird that she kind of hits on me every time we talk, but it's not. I'm all about accepting people for who they are, and this is apparently who she is. Plus, she makes it funny every time, so I know she's harmless. It might be nice to have a friend who understands this crazy world. At least she knows my secret, and has zero judgment for me handling my shit.

Blowing out a breath, I run a hand through the waves of my hair before grabbing my bag and going downstairs.

When I reach the kitchen, I find Smithy and Matthew dancing to the music filtering through the speakers. They look so freaking happy, so I keep my mouth shut and just let them be until the music stops and Smithy notices me leaning against the wall. "Oh, Miss Octavia. You're awake."

It's cute how flustered he still gets when I catch him with Matthew.

"I am, I've been up and out already. Just wanted to grab a protein bar before I go get Indi."

"Protein bars are not breakfast," he huffs, rolling his eyes.

"James, leave the poor girl alone. We can't all eat organic, GMO-free foods all day." Matthew winks at me as he teases

Smithy. It's still weird to hear him called James. I don't think I've ever heard anyone else call him James.

"At least take a tumbler of the smoothie I made this morning." He doesn't wait for me to say anything before he grabs my matte black cup and straw and starts pouring the pink smoothie into it. I shake my head, smiling, and take it from him once I grab a protein bar from the cupboard.

"Thank you." I peck his cheek as I take the cup. "I'm going to be out tonight, so don't worry about dinner."

"You say that like he won't just leave leftovers out for you," Matthew teases, his eyes crinkling at the sides.

This, all of this right here, is how I know the cologne from the basement wasn't his. He freaking adores Smithy, and while I might not always be the best judge of character, now that I have gotten the chance to know him, he just gives off good vibes. I'm sure that he wouldn't hurt Smithy, and hurting me would hurt the old man.

"Well, if you do, I'll make sure not to blow up the kitchen when I heat them." I stick my tongue out at Smithy as he flicks a tea towel at me.

"Get on with you. You'll be late to school if you don't leave soon."

I check the time and realize he's right. "I'll see you later!"

"Drive safe!" he calls out as I run to the garage. Once I'm on the road, I relax a little. At least there's only another two weeks until my birthday, and then there won't be any more secrets.

I just have to hope that they're not so pissed at me that they don't just bank it and drop me anyway. Not that I think they will, but the possibility is still there.

Pulling up in front of Indi's house, I beep my horn twice and slam down the protein bar, taking a sip of the fruity smoothie Smithy gave me. My little ray of sunshine bounces up the sidewalk before diving into the passenger seat of my car, all smiles. "Morning!"

Her grin is infectious as she pulls on her seatbelt then swipes my smoothie. "Oohhhh this is good! Smithy is a freaking God. I'm going to steal him. Or better yet, let's go to the same college, and we can room with him."

She looks so hopeful at the prospect that I can't help but laugh. "Maybe. I really need to send in my applications. I'm so fucking behind."

"Pfft, you'll be fine. You're Octavia freaking Royal. Even if you weren't richer than God, I'm pretty sure the Knights could pull whatever strings needed to get you into whatever school your heart desires." I glance at her as I pull away from the curb, and there's not an ounce of resentment on her face. She's just speaking the truth as she sees it.

"Yeah, maybe. Though I'd rather not use the Knights. I just need to get my shit together. Too much has fallen by the wayside lately. Speaking of which, we need some girl time before exam season kicks in. Spa weekend again soon?"

She slurps down the last of my smoothie before nodding. "I

am so down for that. I loved our last weekend away. Have you thought much about prom? 'Cause we're going to need to start shopping and preparing for that soon too."

I clench my hands on the steering wheel. I haven't thought about any of it. My senior year has not gone how I thought it would. Stalkers and secret societies will do that to you. "I don't even know if we're going."

"You have to go! It's our prom! And after homecoming, we deserve a good fucking prom. Please?" She turns her big puppy dog eyes on me, and I already know I'm not going to be able to say no.

Letting out a breath, I nod. "Sure, I'll try and talk the guys into it if yours are coming…"

"Yes!" she exclaims with a fist pump. "They're coming, but if yours won't, then we can just go together. Pretty sure Ryker would rather rip off his fingernails than go to another dance at ECP, but he has a problem saying no to me when it comes to stuff like that."

Her salacious grin makes me chuckle. "Oh, I bet he does."

We pull into the school lot, finding the boys standing around Lincoln's Porsche, and I maneuver the Range Rover into the space beside it. I know I said I should get another car, but there's something about driving my dad's that just makes me feel close to him when I'm in here. It's weird, but I'm not about to question it. There's enough crazy in my life that I've stopped questioning the things that bring me some semblance of comfort.

Indi bounces out of the car and I follow suit, moving over to where my guys are standing, their conversation stopping once we reach them. I raise an eyebrow at them. Not suspicious at all. "Everything okay?"

Maverick swaggers over to me, all showy, and wraps himself around me before planting his lips on mine. "Better now that you're here."

Indi rolls her eyes, and I smirk as he sees. "Don't be jealous, Pixie Spice, just cause there's no D here for you."

"I've got plenty of dick, thanks," she snaps at him playfully. "At least mine don't paw all over me like barbarians every time we're in public.

"Sounds like you're jealous to me, Pix."

"You're such an ass," she hisses at him while Finn rolls his eyes. I look over to Lincoln, whom I haven't heard from since escaping his house yesterday thanks to Harrison's interruptions. I ask him with my eyes if he's okay, and he nods subtly. Doesn't exactly fill me with hope, but until I can get him alone, it'll have to be enough.

The bell rings, jolting me from my thoughts, and putting a stop to Indi and Mav's bickering. "Come on, let's head in. We don't want to be late."

I loop my arm through Indi's and wink at Mav as I do before sashaying away from them, feeling their heated stares on my back. A girl could get used to this sort of attention on a permanent basis.

Now I just have to hope that they won't hate me once they have their freedom.

The morning has been a blur of exam prep, final assignments being set, and of course, Miss Celine reminding us all of our performance in front of the entire damn school for music—something that had entirely slipped my mind. Originally I'd been paired with Raleigh. Obviously, that isn't the case anymore, so now I need to compose my own piece to perform.

The thought of singing in front of the school makes me want to be a little sick, so I'm thinking maybe a piano piece, but I'm not sure that Miss Celine is going to let me get away with that.

I'm so lost in my thoughts that I'm not paying any attention to my surroundings until I walk into something hard and end up sprawled on my ass on the floor.

Fuck me, that's going to bruise.

I look up and find Raleigh glaring down at me, like I summoned him with my thoughts. "If you wanted another run at me, Octavia, all you had to do was ask."

"Suck my dick, Raleigh," I hiss as I push myself up, grabbing my backpack once I've brushed myself off.

He barks out a laugh, running a hand down his face. "I knew there was a reason I was so drawn to you when you came here. I also know I fucked up, a lot. Any chance you're ever going to forgive me?"

"Maybe when it snows in hell." I shrug, folding my arms across my chest. "Is there any reason you were in my path, or did you want to shove me down again?"

"I wanted to talk. Privately." He looks hopeful as he watches me, but fool me once and all that.

"Raleigh, there isn't anything left to say between us."

I make a move to step around him, but he moves back into my path. "Come on, Octavia. We're going to be family soon. I'm a Knight now, even if I'm not sitting on the Conclave yet, it's going to happen. We'd be better as friends."

"What do you want, Raleigh?" I sigh, realizing he's not going to let this go until he says whatever it is he wants to say.

He glances around, face paling a little as he does. "Not here. I'll text you."

He turns on his heel and strides away from me, leaving me slack-jawed. Fucking Raleigh. I glance around to see what or who could have made him react like that, but I don't see anyone. Pretty sure everyone else is already outside on the quad enjoying the sun or in the cafeteria.

Weird.

I head to my locker and put my bag inside along with my books, just keeping a hold of my card purse and my phone before heading to the cafeteria. Pushing through the doors, I walk in and suck in a gasp as the cheers and shouts echo around the room. Mikayla is sprawled on the ground at Blair's feet, shrieking, while Blair glowers down at her.

I guess the plan she had in place either didn't work, or she had enough of Mikayla's bullshit. Glancing over to our usual table,

I see my guys, sitting with Indi, watching everything unfold. I nod at Lincoln, because while this isn't what we discussed, he can play his part now. He grins before his icy mask drops into place and he stands, strolling over to the two disgraced queens, who are now engaged in a silent standoff, with his hands in his pockets.

The cafeteria grows quiet as the king approaches and the crowd parts as he reaches them. "This is over. Mikayla, you've had your fun, but you're obviously not fit to wear a crown if you can't keep it." He glances over at me and I suck in a breath.

Don't you fucking do it, Lincoln Saint.

I glare at him, but the slight tipping up at the corner of his lips is all I need to know that he's going to fucking do it anyway.

"Neither of you are fit to be queen. The only true queen here is the Royal herself. My queen." He tips his head in my direction and everyone's gaze swivels to me.

Fuck you, Lincoln. I never wanted the goddamn crown.

There isn't anything I can do here but nod, undermining his power isn't going to look great, but Blair is going to fucking kill me. If the blazing look in her eyes is anything to go by, she's already picturing me writhing on the ground in pain.

Just awesome.

"So be it," is all Lincoln says before moving to stand beside me and claiming my lips in front of everyone. My mind goes fuzzy from the intensity of his kiss, and I clasp the lapel of his blazer in my fingers as the rest of the room fades to nothing.

Goddamn can he kiss. He pulls back, that secret smirk he has just for me on his face disappearing quickly before he leads me back to our table. So much for keeping our relationship under wraps.

The crowd disperses now that he's spoken, murmurs and glances follow us as we sit down and Indi's eyes dance with delight as I slide into the chair beside her.

"Long live the Queen."

FIFTEEN

OCTAVIA

I drop onto the couch and turn on the TV. Smithy left me a note to say he and Matthew are going away for a few days to see Matthew's family, so I have the place to myself. I can't help but smile, happy for him, because if anyone on the planet deserves some happy, it's Smithy.

After Lincoln's declaration at lunch today, everyone seemed to decide that being my friend was top of their to-do list. My cheeks ache from the fake smile I've had plastered on for most of the day. Indi thought it was a riot and gave me all the shit about it the entire drive home. I swear, if she calls me queen one more time, I'mma lose my goddamn mind.

Once I dropped her off, Mav and Finn took me to the

fighting gym again, helping me work through some self-defense techniques with them. Picturing Lincoln's face on the punching bag as they walked me through combinations during my warmup helped deal with some issues, especially since he disappeared to God only knows where after school.

I know the guys saw my bruises from my Knights training, but neither of them questioned it. And I'm eternally thankful for that because between self-defense with them, training with Luc, and running with Linc, I'm freaking exhausted. That's on top of the fanfare at school.

Mav strolls in from the kitchen, bowl of popcorn in his hands, before he drops down beside me. He grins at me and shoves a handful of popcorn in his mouth like an animal. I chuckle at him, shaking my head as I put on one of the crime documentaries I have on my watch list. "You good with this?"

"princess, as long as I'm with you, I'm good with whatever." He passes me the bowl of popcorn and pulls my feet into his lap. I groan as he rubs circles into them with his thumbs and starts the show. It feels so freaking normal, and just, good.

I try to focus on the TV, but I get lost to the rhythm of his touch and drift off to sleep. I only realize I've dropped off when I wake as he lifts me into his arms, tucking me against his chest. "Sleep, princess. I've got you."

I nuzzle into his neck as he holds me in his strong arms, enjoying the warmth of him, but a pang of guilt wakes me further. "We were supposed to hang out."

"We did, and now we're going to go and sleep. I'm just going to have to make sure you have a good breakfast since you missed dinner. But you're obviously tired. It's been a heavy few months, we're all tired."

"Should you even be carrying me? How are your stitches healing? You probably shouldn't be carrying me." My thoughts aren't exactly coherent, but he just laughs.

"There is nothing in the world that's going to make me put you down right now. My wound is practically healed; I've had worse. Trust me, carrying you isn't exactly a hardship." He kisses the top of my head and I trust that he'd tell me if he was in pain, so I snuggle back into him as he starts up the stairs.

He sits me on the end of the bed once we reach my room. "Arms up." I follow his instructions and he peels my hoodie and t-shirt off of me, leaving me in my bralette. He taps my hips and I push up, letting him drag my leggings down.

"Goddamn you're beautiful," he breathes, his gaze raking over me. He lifts me again and pulls back the sheets, sliding me onto the bed once he has, and tucks me in. He strips down quickly after and dives in on the other side, pulling me onto his chest. "Sleep, princess. I got you."

"Not going to check for monsters under the bed?" I tease as I roll toward him, throwing my leg over his hip and snuggling in.

"There's no monsters in here but me," he murmurs as he wraps an arm around my waist, holding me tight against his chest. "Even if there were, we both know I'd be the bigger monster."

"You're not a monster," I murmur as my eyes flutter closed, pressing my lips against the warm skin of his chest. "But even if you were, you'd be my monster."

His monster is just part of who he is, but I know he wouldn't hurt me. Not again. He wants to keep me safe, but he wouldn't cage me or break me. "I'll be whatever you want me to be, princess."

"I love you, Mav." The words are little more than a whisper, but I feel him relax beneath me as I say them. He runs his hand down my hair, twisting it around his fingers.

"I love you too, princess. Now sleep."

Like his words command me, I drift off, wrapped in his warmth, feeling safer and more content than I remember feeling in a while.

"Again!" Artemis shouts as she comes at me once more and I try to fight her off. Goddamn she is quick. Fucking lethal, too. She grabs my arms, twists and pulls, using my momentum against me, and the next thing I know, I'm on my back, winded, with her above me. "You really need to focus."

She climbs off of me and offers me a hand, pulling me up from the ground once I manage to pull air back into my lungs.

"I'm trying," I wheeze. "You are just wicked fast."

She nods. "The men in our world underestimate women. They see us as feeble, weak, slow. Not someone to be feared. You can use all of that to your advantage. We are smaller, typically weaker, but with the right knowledge, you can use it against them. We can be faster, because we're smaller. You can use their momentum and strength against them. You just need to know how to do it. You've got some instincts, and it's obvious you've been trained, but it's been sloppy. That, or you've forgotten most of it, gotten complacent."

I can't deny that. Other than my occasional sessions with Maverick, I haven't done anything to keep my self-defense skills up since Dad died. I probably should have, but it's not like I've not been busy. "Complacency is my weakness."

"It's the downfall of most. But not on my watch, girlie. Tonight, you, me, and Luc. I'll fight him, you can watch, and then I'll walk you through how I beat his ass."

I bark out a laugh. "You think you can take him?"

"Oh, I know I can." She grins as she sashays away from me, grabbing two bottles of water and throwing one to me. "I also know I can teach you how too—if you'll pay attention. Now hydrate, and show me what you've really got."

I roll my eyes at the mirth on her face and drink the water. We've already been here for forty-five minutes, and I need to be going soon if I'm going to make it back in time to run with Linc. I hope Mav didn't wake up while I was gone, cause I have no idea how I'd explain to him why I wasn't there.

Maybe I should stop letting them sleep over.

Nope, don't like that.

"Let's go!" I flinch at her bark, swallowing down the last of the water, and try to remember everything I've learned about fighting. Stamina isn't a problem, my issues are all down to technique, so that's what I need to focus on. Maybe watching her and Luc later will help.

She runs me through a few test throws, showing me how to use her speed against her, the same way I would a guy. To use their momentum to incapacitate them. "With the Knights, if you need these skills, your options will be fight or kill. Ensuring they're on the ground is the easiest way to do either. Throat, eyes, knees, and balls are your go-to zones. Soft, fleshy, and easy to damage. The knee is harder, but if you can kick at the right angle, with enough force, you can make it so they can't chase you if you need to run."

I nod, trying to soak it all up. I check my watch and balk. "I need to go."

She nods once and wipes her brow. "Go, just be back here later. I'll text you a time once I've spoken to Luc. No excuses."

"I wouldn't dream of it." I smile at her playfully and she swats my ass with her towel, causing me to let out a yelp.

Her responding grin is almost feral. "Make sure you don't."

The masseuse rubs at the knots in my shoulders while Indi groans from the table beside mine. "Enjoying yourself?"

Her eyes flutter open as she turns her head to face me. "We should do this more often. Like, I am totally down to be your wingman when you are stressed and need this as an outlet. As your best friend, I'll sacrifice to help you. Especially when it means missing class."

I cackle at her as the guy rubbing her back smirks. "I'm so glad you're so willing to be on hand for me."

She closes her eyes and sticks her tongue out at me. "What can I say, I'm selfless as fuck."

"Oh yeah, totally," I murmur as I drop my head back down onto the rest as my masseuse moves to my head. "Hot tub after this?"

"Whatever you want, bestie. Selfless, remember?" I snort a laugh and she flips me the bird, making me laugh harder.

The soft music spills out over the quiet of the room, the scented oils filling my senses; every possible trick and toy to help trick the body into utter relaxation. I'm glad for it, because I really need this. After Gracie refitted our extensions and colored her hair, we decided a spa evening was the best way to continue our day.

Obviously.

The soft chimes ring out, signaling the end of our session, and I let out a deep breath. I've basically melted into the bed, become one with it, and I don't want to reject it by getting up, but I also know that there's someone booked in here after us.

Indi groans beside me, obviously feeling the same way I do. "Come on, oh selfless one. Let's go dip in the hot tub before our facials."

"Fine," she sighs as I push myself up and swing my legs around. My masseuse hands me my robe and I slip it on, Indi doing the same before they leave us to redress. Once the door is closed, I drop my robe and pull on my bikini top, my panties still in place under the towel. Once it's on, I pull the robe back on, noticing Indi is already done and waiting for me.

"All joking aside, thank you for this. I know you're dealing with a ton of stuff at the moment; I know you're busy."

I quirk a brow at her, then frown. "What's wrong?"

"It's nothing." she says, looking down at her feet.

"I know I've been busy and wrapped up in my own drama, but that doesn't mean I don't have time for you. Now, spill it, sunshine."

She sucks in a deep breath and shudders as she expels it. "Alex… he kissed me. Again."

My eyes go wide as I reach for the door handle. "I'm sorry, what? You've seen Alex again?" Wow, I really have been a shitty friend lately if I didn't even know that. I open the door and she hurries through it. I follow her out then loop my arm through hers, pulling her through the spa to where the hot tub and pool area is. Since it's mid-week, the place is a ghost town, so I encourage her into the tub, following closely behind.

"Okay, spill it," I say once we're both seated in the hot water and the jets are going.

She bites at her lip and I stay quiet, letting her start in her own time. "He came by the house to talk to Ryker. About whatever issue it is that they have. I answered the door, and he looked shocked to see me, but I didn't think anything of it. After he was finished with Ryker, I was heading home, so I walked him out and he kissed me. Again. Dylan saw."

Her last words are little more than a whisper, but holy shit. "What did he say?"

She shrugs, and wrings her hands out. I could kill Alex for making her feel like this. Fucking asshole. "Dylan is... Dylan enjoys watching me with others. Usually just the twins, but well, he didn't seem to have an issue with Alex. But you know how he is. Dylan would raze the world if it made me happy. He said he saw how I kissed Alex back, and if I wanted him too, then he was good with that."

"And do you? Want Alex like that, I mean?"

She looks up at me through her lashes, obviously torn up about it. "I don't know. Sometimes I think I do, but the thought of speaking those words to Ryker or Ellis... I don't know if I can do that. Surely that means I don't want him. Not enough. And it's greedy, right? To want someone else as well."

"I think if it's what you want, and you're already in a poly relationship, then these things evolve and adding to it could be as natural as breathing." She nods at my words. "But the real question is, what do you think you want? Once you have the answer to that, the rest should fall into place. Especially if Dylan is on board. If you want Alex too, I'm sure he and Dylan will help you when it comes to the twins."

"Yeah, maybe." She drops her gaze, tucking a strand of her hair behind her ear. "Could you imagine telling Lincoln or Maverick that?"

"No," I answer honestly, "but I also can't imagine wanting anyone but the four of them. But you are not me, my friend."

"This is insane, right?"

I take her hand and squeeze it. "The matters of the heart usually are, but my dad always said the heart will never lead you wrong, so walk down that path, no matter how dark it gets. Because there is always light in darkness."

"You are such a bed hog," Indi groans as I rip the sheets from her. "Why do you hate me?"

I can't help but laugh at her. My sunshine friend is all sparkles, except when she very first opens her eyes for the day. "I've been up for hours, been training with Luc and been for my run with Linc. I was barely in the bed to hog it."

I leave out how I was also training with Alex, and that I chewed his ass out about kissing her again. She doesn't know about his training with the Saints, which I also chewed him out about, especially if he's making moves on her. She deserves to know. I gave him until my birthday to decide if he wants this thing with her and if he does then to tell her, otherwise I'm going to tell her myself. It shouldn't come from me, but I'm not going to leave her in the dark.

"Yuh-huh." I shake my head at her grumbling and finish pulling on my uniform. "Smithy is back and making breakfast, so if you want a shower before school, you're going to need to get up now."

"Fine, fine!" She sighs as she dramatically throws herself from the bed, flicking her newly blue hair over her shoulder as she pads to the bathroom. I stifle the laughter that rises and grab my blazer before heading downstairs.

"That smells delicious." I practically drool as I enter the kitchen. "I didn't realize you'd be back already."

He turns and smiles at me, waving for me to sit at the counter. "With everything going on around here at the minute, I didn't want to be gone longer than necessary. Matthew had some business to deal with, so we went to see his family too, but his trip got extended and I decided to come back."

"You didn't need to do that." I frown at his back, hating that he's putting his life on hold for me. He's done that enough for my family over the years.

"Nonsense, Miss Octavia. I like being here with you. It's not exactly a hardship. Not like I could assist Matthew with his business anyway, whereas here I'm helpful. Useful. And I worry about you when I'm gone. Especially right now. This way, I can try and make sure you're at least safe." He looks at me, and I can see his worry and love reflected back at me.

"As long as being here, with me, isn't a burden to you." I wring out my hands, hating feeling like I'm keeping him from living properly, but I'm also clueless as to how I'd survive without him.

"You could never be a burden, Miss Octavia. You are like the daughter I never got to have. It is my pleasure to be here for you, to help you when I can."

I jump from the stool and wrap my arms around his waist. "You're my family too, Smithy. I don't think I'd have made it through the last year without you."

He wraps one arm around me and squeezes. "You'd have made it through. You're stronger than you give yourself credit for." He pauses, kissing the top of my head before patting my arm. "Now sit back down. These breakfast burritos are nearly done."

"Did you say breakfast burrito? Smithy, my man, you are a GOD." Indi bounces into the room all smiles and heads straight for the coffee pot. "Want some?"

"Is water wet?" I deadpan and she laughs, grabbing two cups from the shelf and pouring us both a drink.

I hop back into my seat as Indi brings the coffee over and Smithy serves up our breakfast burritos.

"So, how is your training going? Have you had any luck finding the information Harrison wants? Your deadline is soon, right?" Indi's chatter stops me as I lift my burrito to my lips, and I let out a sigh as I drop it back on my plate.

"Training is fine. Getting my ass kicked every damn day, but it's fine. As for the information, honestly, I haven't had a chance to really start looking between training, school, and sleeping. I have Bentley digging around, and I'm meeting him on Saturday to discuss what he's found so far, but yeah my deadline is next Saturday. My birthday."

"Happy freaking birthday to you." Indi sighs. "We need to do something to celebrate."

"I'm good with something low-key." I groan and take a bite of my burrito. "Holy shit this is good."

"How about a dinner here? Just family and friends," Smithy suggests like he didn't hear me.

Indi's eyes light up. "Yes! We could totally do that. As like, a prelude. Dinner, a night with the boys, and then girls' weekend. Just like we did at the start of the year."

"Oh yes! We could book something, all of the bells and whistles. Especially now you're both eighteen, it opens up places for us too."

They both get excited, carried away with details, and I let them. I'll let them down gently later about how I have exactly zero intentions of celebrating my birthday.

It's why I haven't focused on it much beyond it being the

date of my deadline with Harrison. Birthdays were about cherry chocolate sundaes and movies with my dad. This will be my first birthday without him, and I'm not exactly looking forward to it. But I'm not about to rain on their parade right now.

I check my phone, eyes wide. "We need to go, otherwise we're going to be late."

"Crap," Indi gasps, and Smithy jumps to his feet.

"Let me wrap those and you can eat on the way in."

He rushes around, taking our plates and wrapping the burritos in foil as we grab our bags, taking the burritos before rushing out to her Wrangler.

"If I'm late, my mom is going to kill me," Indi groans as she starts the car.

"We won't be late if you put your foot down." I grin, pulling my seatbelt on as she tears past the gate and out of the drive.

I laugh wildly as she breaks every speed limit through the Cove, tires screeching as we pull into the school lot. "Go, go, go!"

Eyes wide, she scrambles from the car, and if it wasn't for her panic, I'd just laugh the entire way in. The sound of the bell rings as we're rushing up the steps. We don't bother hitting our lockers, sliding into our seats in class just as the final bell sounds.

"That shit was close," she gasps, chest heaving. "Man, I need to work out more."

"I can think of a few guys who wouldn't mind helping you."

I wink at her, and she rolls her eyes.

"Do not give them ideas. Have you seen them? Ellis is the least active of them all and he's still lean as fuck. They'd kill me off. Nope. No thanks."

"Better than the training I'm doing." I sigh as Miss Summers walks into the room, closing the door behind her.

She turns to face us, the look on her face making me sit up a little straighter. Her gaze roams over the room, settling on me, and something inside of me sinks. "This is it. The start of the end."

SIXTEEN

FINLEY

"You've got to be kidding me." I sit with my spoon halfway to my mouth, balking at my dad. "Running for mayor? Why the fuck would you do that?"

"The mayor's term is up at the next election, and he's going to be announcing that he's stepping up into the big leagues. He's going to run for governor. Which leaves it open. The Conclave decided it would be best to have one of us in the position, one less person to manipulate. So I'm going to run. He'll stay in our pocket and having him in that position is good for us. I could go for that, but he has the political capital I don't, and, honestly, I have my hands full anyway."

Coming home this morning at my parents' request wasn't

something I was looking forward to, but I definitely wasn't expecting this. I glance at my mom who is beaming from ear to ear.

There is no way these monsters should be put in office, but it's not like I can say that out loud. "Why are you telling me? You never run this stuff past me."

My father quirks a brow at me as he finishes his mouthful, pointing his knife at me. "I'll need you to be around for the campaign. We're going to be getting started soon."

"What does that mean, exactly?" My gaze bounces between the two of them, I'm still not quite over the fact that she's even here, and my dad grips his knife tighter.

"Oh, Charles." My mom sighs, patting his arm. "Of course he has questions. Just answer him. I'm sure Finley will do what is needed. Isn't that right, dear?"

Her gaze turns back to me, but I'm not foolish. I know my mom is just as fucked up as my dad—maybe more so—so I say nothing and just stare at my father, waiting for him to answer me. The election is November, and I'm hoping to be far, far the fuck away from here for college by then.

"We don't need you for much. Just don't fuck up between now and then and be around for photo ops. If I need you for anything else, I expect you to come running." He grins maliciously at me, tilting his head, and my stomach drops in anticipation. "That also means distancing yourself from the Royal girl. Can't have my son seen to be fucking the town whore."

I grind my teeth together, dropping my spoon into my bowl and clenching my fists. "Fuck you. She isn't a whore, and I'm not distancing myself from her for you or anyone."

"What else do you call a bitch who gets on her back for the four of you? You're not fooling anyone by pretending otherwise. And you either distance yourself by choice, or we will arrange it for you."

"Do not threaten me, Father."

"I don't make threats, Finley. You know that." The twist of his lips makes my heart beat erratically. I'm fully aware of just how much my father doesn't bluff about this shit. Fuck.

I push my chair back and stand. "I've suddenly lost my appetite. I'll just grab some of my things, and then I'll be gone."

"Finley—" my mom calls, but I'm already storming from the dining room toward my bedroom. I grab a duffel from the bottom of my closet and throw most of the contents of my closet into it. If he thinks I'm coming back here after that, he has another thing coming.

We need eyes on Octavia.

Permanently.

We've all basically been living next door to her the last few weeks, and Mav has wrangled a few overnighters at her place, but I'm thinking we need to try and stay with her.

Once the duffel is bursting at the seams, I glance around the room. I should probably feel something about leaving this room, hopefully for the last time, but this place was tainted a long time ago. The whole fucking house, for that matter.

There is nothing but relief rolling around in my chest at the thought of never coming back here. Because even if my father does actually run for mayor, I'm not coming back. I was already set on it, but this… this confirmed it for me.

I might not be able to free myself from the Knights yet, but I can escape this toxicity. Until we find a way out that doesn't equal death for us all, this will have to be enough.

Closing the door to my childhood room, a weight lifts from my shoulders. It's not like I'm leaving the horrors behind, those are etched into both my mind and my flesh, but I don't have to see them, be ruled by them anymore.

Octavia taught me that much.

I stride out of the house, ignoring the shouts from my parents, feeling freer than I ever have in my life.

I might still be chained to the Knights, but the demons that kept me captive in this house… they're not going to hunt me anymore.

I climb into my car, reveling in the power beneath me as it purrs to life.

Today might just be the start of a new chapter, now I just need to work out where I go from here.

Mr. Collins, my AP Computer Science teacher, drones on at the front of the room, and I tune him out. Everything he's prattling on about is shit I taught myself years ago. I took this class because I knew it would be an easy win for me, and I'll need it for my degree access.

All of my college applications were submitted months ago. Even before I knew if I'd survive the year. Lincoln, Mav, and I all applied to the exact same schools. It wasn't necessary, we all know that the Knights can pull strings and put us in any school they or we want, but we wanted to do something normal.

I'm not sure if Octavia submitted any, what with everything she had going on, but submission deadlines aren't really a problem when you have money. Sounds crass, but it's true.

The bell finally rings, and I massage my temples before grabbing my shit and heading to my locker. I didn't get to see my girl before class this morning, but she dropped us a message to let us know her and Indi were just running late.

After the conversation with my parents, I need to see her, just to prove to myself that she's okay, that my father hasn't already fucked with her. Not seeing her this morning had us all on high alert, especially after I told the boys about what my dad had said.

I hate how they use her against us, but I wouldn't give her up for anything.

By the time I'm striding into the cafeteria, my nerves are on fucking edge. I grab a burger and fries with a soda and sit at our usual table. No one else is here yet, so I play with my foot, knee bouncing.

I don't breathe easy until she breezes into the room, Indi at her side, laughing about something. It's like a weight is lifted from my chest, and I can take in a full breath again.

Lincoln and Mav enter the room seconds later, but rather than joining the line, they head straight toward me.

"What's wrong?" I ask as they sit. Lincoln is stiff as a board. He glances over his shoulder at Octavia before leaning forward.

"Our fathers need to fucking die."

"What did Harrison do now?" Mav asks, sighing.

"He called me at the end of class. More threats about Georgia, but apparently East is pissing him off. Something about him snubbing the Conclave seat, but he told me if I don't secure the deal with Georgia, either East or Octavia will pay the price, and I'll get to pick which."

I grind my teeth together, pushing away the tray in front of me. I get why he didn't get food now. It's like a lead weight in my stomach. Mav steals the tray; him and his thing with food is well known between us, so I don't say a word about it.

"He wants you to actually marry her? Is he fucking insane?" I hiss, glancing back up at our girl laughing with her best friend like she has no cares in the world.

If only she knew the danger she was in now. "What about Stone's contract? Her taking the regency? It's like he's just forgotten about it."

"There is no way Harrison will give her that seat. I know

they spoke, he said that he offered to uphold the contract of her being out if that's what she wanted, and she agreed. I don't trust him, but she said the same thing, so I guess she's out. Just under constant threat because she's attached to us."

"Maybe since I now sit on the actual Conclave, I can keep her safe?" Mav interjects. I open my mouth to refute it, but then close it. Wives aren't always necessarily safe, but as long as they toe the line, they're usually left alone.

Much as I want to be the one who claims her like that, her being married to Mav might make her a little safer than she is right now.

"I hate to say that's a good idea—" I start, and Lincoln nods.

"I know. Same."

"She's coming," Maverick says before taking a bite of my burger, and we shut the fuck up. A silent agreement to come back to this later.

I smile as she slides into the seat beside me and kisses my cheek. "Hey, pretty girl. Good morning?"

"Not really, but I remain hopeful for the day. You guys okay? You all look so serious."

"Just Knight bullshit," Lincoln says, dismissing it. "Nothing major."

She watches him closely, but whatever she sees seems to convince her and she shrugs. "If you say so."

"Have you guys started getting your college acceptance letters yet?" Indi asks, and I grin.

"Acceptances?" Octavia gasps. "I haven't even applied yet."

"You've got time," I say to her, squeezing her thigh. "Where are you looking to apply?"

"Honestly, I haven't even decided. I might just apply to a dozen and go from there."

Mav grins at her from across the table. "That's what we did, but between your money and our connections, you can go wherever you want, princess. Don't sweat it."

"You say the sweetest things," Indi deadpans at him.

"Don't hate the player, Pixie. Hate the game." He winks at her, and I groan. Sometimes it's funny to watch these two battle it out, but my head already hurts with all of the bullshit from my dad and Harrison.

"Maybe I'll do both," she snarks at him. "But rather than talk about college, we have more important things to discuss. V's birthday."

"I told you, I don't want to celebrate," my girl says, glaring at Indi. "So let's not."

"Of course we're going to celebrate," Mav counters, and Lincoln barks out a laugh.

"Did you just agree with Indi?" he asks, and Mav's eyes go wide.

"I would never," he declares before smiling. "Or maybe just this once. What did you have in mind, Pixie?"

SEVENTEEN

OCTAVIA

"I hear you have tomorrow off school," Luc barks from across the sand ring he's been training me in. A shout from across the room as Artemis takes down Alex distracts me and I end up on my back, winded, seeing stars. "Pay attention, Octavia. You'll end up dead if you get distracted."

I groan as I sit up, bringing my knees up and resting my elbows on them while I catch my breath. "Yeah, yeah. I know. I'm trying."

"Try harder," he growls as he takes my hand and pulls me up to my feet. "How is your scavenger hunt coming along?"

I raise my eyebrows, surprised he's aware of what Harrison asked of me. "Harrison?"

He nods once, and I'm torn. He's close with Lincoln, but he's obviously under Harrison's thumb. "I'm working on it."

He looks disappointed, but that's not my problem. What *is* my problem is finding time to look through Dad's stuff. Which is exactly why I'm glad I don't have school tomorrow. I asked Smithy to get all of his boxes put up in the spare room. If I have to spend the whole weekend searching, it's what I'll do, because I can't let the guys down.

Not that I'm about to tell Luc that.

"Again," he barks and comes at me. These few days of training with him and Artemis have helped more than I thought they would. I dodge his fist before spinning a roundhouse kick at him, using his movement against him. He stumbles and I kick out again, planting my foot on his chest, making him fall backward.

As much as I want to do a happy dance, I pull the blade from my boot and pounce. But I'm too slow. He's already off the ground and grabs my wrist, sending a fist into my ribs while trying to disarm me. He tightens his grip and twists, causing me to cry out and drop the knife. He pushes on my shoulder while sweeping my ankle and I drop to the ground. Pissed and panting, I wrench myself away from him, rolling up into a crouch, flicking my hair back out of my face.

He smirks at me, and it stokes my anger.

I let it burn, but take on his advice from earlier. A parroting of my dad's from when he used to train me.

Let the anger fuel you, not rule you.

I take a deep breath and lunge for him again, except this time, I go full bitch. I fake a swing at his jaw, but bring my knee up to connect with his dick. As he gasps, I thread my fingers in his hair and lift my knee again, feeling the crunch of his nose before I fling him to the ground. I grab the blade from my other boot and dive onto him, bringing the blade to his throat. I feel a pinch in my side and hiss, looking down to see my blade from earlier pointed at my ribs.

"Better, but not good enough. Not yet." I roll off of him and he climbs to his feet, wiping at the blood running from his nose. "We're getting there though. Training with Artemis too is obviously working for you, so I'm going to leave her to deal with your hand-to-hand. I'm going to work on your shooting with you. Not tonight, you've been here long enough, but Saturday. Take tomorrow off, be fresh for Saturday, because that is going to test you."

I swallow the lump in my throat from the implication in his voice but nod. "Saturday, here?"

"I'll grab you in the morning. Be ready by six."

I blow out a breath. Don't these assholes understand the need for sleep? Goddamn. "Sure thing."

I start walking away from him, grabbing my phone, keys, and water bottle from the edge of the room where I left them, hearing Luc yell at Alex about being done, but I don't wait around to listen to them bitch. I haul ass out of the warehouse and to my car.

Checking my phone on the way out, I notice a message from Indi.

Indi:

<image> I'm holed up in your media room, it's such a hardship being your bestie and alibi. I'll be here when you get back.

I grin at the screen and let her know I'm heading back now before peeling away from the warehouse. I can't tell if it's because of my speed, or just because I'm getting used to the drive, but the journey home passes in a blink.

By the time I'm strolling into the media room, I'm hungry, in need of caffeine, and ready to drop.

"Wow, you look like shit."

I roll my eyes as I drop onto the couch next to her. "Thanks, sunshine. You're so good to me."

"That's what besties are for." She sticks her tongue out at me and I laugh, rubbing a hand down my face. "Long night?"

"Just exhausting. All of this is just so tiring. The secrets, the training, trying to keep up with the guys, school, not losing touch with my freaking life. I still haven't started looking for my dad's stash for Harrison, and I have no idea what I'm even looking for."

"Dude you need a break. Or to tell the guys what you did."

"I can't." I sigh. "That was part of the deal, remember? Plus, if they find out before it's a done deal, they'll find a way to undo it. They've done enough for me. It's my turn to do something to save them."

"I get the feeling they're going to try and find a way to reverse it regardless once they find out."

Pinching the bridge of my nose, I take a deep breath. She's not wrong. They're going to be angry. Especially Lincoln, even though he's the most likely to understand it. Probably *because* he'll understand.

"Maybe. But first, I need to find what Harrison wants. He already gave me one extension, I doubt I'll get another."

She nods, pulling her blanket tighter around her. "Truth. Do you need my help?"

"I wouldn't ask that of you."

She quirks a brow at me and I can't help but smirk. "Then I guess it's a good thing the question was just a formality. I'm helping."

"Would you girls like some refreshments?" Smithy asks as he climbs to his feet. We've been in the spare room going through all of my dad's boxes all freaking morning. So far, we've found sweet fuck all, but I refuse to give up. My guys' freedom rides on whatever my dad had hidden, and it has to be here *somewhere*.

"I'd kill for an iced coffee," Indi exclaims, wiping her brow. "All I've found so far that might lead to something are some random keys and a receipt for a locker in New York. Not sure what use that'll be."

"It's more than I've found. Come on, let's go get some java, have some lunch, and then we can dive back in after."

"Sounds perfect. Come, ladies. Let's fuel up, shall we?"

Smithy turns and heads out of the room, and I glance over at Indi. "You don't have to stick around for this."

"Shut up, bitch. I've got nothing else to do with my Saturday, so I'm here for as long as you need me. Even with the three of us, we've only made it through a quarter of the boxes in here, and we don't even know if what you're after is in here."

I scrape my hair into a messy bun on top of my head and nod. "I know, it's like looking for a needle in a stack of needles, with no idea what the needle looks like. Couldn't be as simple as a USB drive with a label saying 'Knight Shit,' could it?"

She laughs as she climbs to her feet, shaking her head. "If only life was that simple."

I watch as she worries her lip, and concern floods me. "What's wrong?"

"Alex." She starts and I curse him out in my head.

"What did the fuckwit do now?"

"He texted me, says he wants to talk."

Oh… I guess he took my advice. "You going to meet him?"

"I mean… I think so, but I was wondering if I could have

him come here. That way the guys don't see him around my place, and it's like neutral ground. Plus, I could use you in my corner."

"You know I got you. Mi Casa es su casa. and all that shit. Whatever you need, and if that means me kicking his ass, I can do that too." I grin as I stand, but worry that she's going to be pissed at me for not telling her about training with him. I'm sure she'll understand, but I hate that it'll be a thing between us.

"I love you."

"I love you too, now let's go eat before we come back to this mess."

We spend an hour or so eating, caffeinating, and just gossiping. Indi texts Alex to say she'd talk with him here, and he said he'd come over this afternoon, so at least their talk will be done. Once everything is agreed, we dive back into my dad's boxes.

We find a few extra random keys that I have no idea what they belong to, a few notes in one of his journals, but fuck all else.

"This was such a bust." I droop against the wall, feeling a little beaten. This is all of my dad's shit. Other than the locker in New York we found the receipt for, I have no idea where else he might have hidden something. I don't even know if he still has the locker, for fuck sake.

"We still have a week until your birthday, right? Maybe we'll find something else before then? Or we can fly up to New

York tomorrow afternoon and see what this locker is." Indi's optimism isn't as catching as I'd like, but that could be from the overwhelming urge to throw up.

"It's worth a try."

Her phone rings, and her eyes go wide when she looks at the screen. "Alex."

"Well, answer the phone."

The line goes dead, followed by mine starting to ring. I see his name on the screen and answer, putting it on speaker. "Baby Royal, I'm outside, as per my summons. Now, be a doll and buzz me in."

"Alexander, where are your manners?" I tease and Indi rolls her eyes.

"Saving them for the demon. Now, can I come in? Please?"

I look over at Indi who looks like she's going to vomit, but nods. I might need to find this information for Harrison, but considering we're getting nowhere on that front, I am here for this distraction.

"Opening the gate now." I end the call and open my app to unlock the gate. "I guess we should head back downstairs. Do you want to speak to him alone?"

"Yes, but no. Maybe wait outside the room or something? So you're not too far away?"

"Are you afraid of him?" I ask, surprise flooding me.

She shakes her head vehemently. "No, I'm afraid of this conversation though.'

"Well, I've got you. I'll do whatever you ask."

She takes my hand and squeezes it. "Then let's go face the music, shall we?"

You ever have one of those moments, where you'd just like to curl up in a ball and escape reality? Yeah, that's me right now. After a morning of being absolutely *schooled* by Luc in just how shit I am with a firearm—which I'm totally not, he's just a fucking jedi master or some shit—I'm waiting for Bentley to arrive and my guys keep messaging me.

I get it, I've been MIA, I've had to be with all this fucking training. But I just have one week left till my birthday. Next Saturday, I turn eighteen. My deal with Harrison will be complete—if I find these fucking documents—and they will be free. I can come clean with them and we can work out where we go from here. My biggest worry right now is East because he doesn't win with my deal. He's already out… and I don't want him to think that I didn't think of him when I made this deal, but I did. All I thought of was them.

The four of them will finally be able to exist outside of Harrison's reach, and *that* is what I get to gift to East. While I hope they don't hate me over it, I'm big enough to wear the consequences of my actions. So I'll shoulder whatever happens, even if it breaks me.

The upside to the long weekend so far is that Indi didn't hold the whole Alex thing against me. Though her shock at him becoming a Knight was… painful. I'm not sure how they'll make it work, but they seem to want to. In fact, they're flying off to New York this afternoon to look into the locker for me at Smithy's suggestion, and since she's from there, there was no real need for an excuse like I would've had to have. I trust Indi with my life and I trust Alex to not fuck me. He gets what he wants if Lincoln is released from the Knights, so it works in his favor not to screw me over.

Indi said she'd call me as soon as they found anything, so now it's a waiting game on her, and on Bentley to arrive. I'm hoping Bentley has good news, because fuck do I need some. I know he said he'd found something, but Lord only knows what that means.

So yes, curling up in a ball and escaping reality sounds really fun right now. But life isn't that simple, and running from my problems hasn't gotten me anywhere. So I'm taking control of what I can and dealing with the rest, even if running away sounds better.

My phone buzzes again, and I smile at the group text.

Mav:
Princess, stop ignoring us. Don't make me beg. We're trying to be good and give you space to catch up on your school work, but my dick misses you.

East:

Oh yeah, Romeo. That's really the way to woo her. Such sweet words you speak.

Mav:

Better than letting her think I've forgotten about her, ass sack.

East:

She knows I haven't forgotten about her. I've been busy with Chase.

East:

You know I've not forgotten about you, right Octavia?

Lincoln:

You lot keep simping like this, and the only dick she'll ride will be mine.

Finn:

Wouldn't be so sure about that, Linc.

East:

Octavia?

Mav:

Come on, princess. Come and play.

Linc:

Let the girl study. Jesus christ. I'd have muted your asses too.

Mav:

pouts You haven't muted us, right princess?

Finn:

Silence is pretty telling Mav. Come and work out with me. It will distract you.

Mav:

Fine, fine. I'm on my way.

Linc:

Thank you, maybe now I can focus too.

I cackle as I close out the message. I need to keep up my façade of school work, at least until Bentley is gone. Once I know what he knows, then I can reassess. I know they're all planning something for next weekend for my birthday, despite my protests, but I miss them. I know I've seen them, but still. This is the most closed off I've been from them since we decided to make this work.

I don't hold East's absence against him. I have no idea what he's doing, but I'm trying not to pry like a hypocrite. If anything, whatever is keeping him busy is working in my favor.

It's one less person to dodge and lie to. Though, barely seeing him the last two weeks hasn't been exactly fun either. I see the others at school, even with everything else we have going on, we have that.

I don't even have that with East. I just have to hope he doesn't hold that against me, too.

Blowing out a breath, I check the time again, wondering what is keeping Bentley when I see his car pull up in front of the gates. I hit the button in the app to allow his entry without waiting for him to buzz in.

"He's here," I call out to Smithy, who appears from the hall off the kitchen.

"It's about time. I've been looking into Kensington. He seems like someone we can trust. Whoever recommended him to you did a stellar job." He squeezes my shoulder as he moves past me to open the front door. I hear the murmur of their voices as Smithy lets him in, but can't make out their conversation. Probably Smithy being over-protective again.

I smile to myself as I turn on the coffee pot, and they enter the room. "Octavia, good to see you."

"You too. Coffee?" He nods as he sits at the counter while Smithy watches over him. I pour two mugs, knowing better than to offer Smithy any, and take a seat. "So what did you find?"

"Your dad is a pack rat. He has hidey holes all over the world," he starts, and I let out a sigh. That doesn't sound promising. "But I did find this."

He pulls an envelope from inside his jacket and upends it on the counter. A black USB drive falls from it and I raise an eyebrow at him. "What is it?"

"Whatever it is, it needs an encryption key. I've been scouring the hidey holes along the west coast searching for something that could help, but all I've found so far are stashes of newspaper clippings, a journal, some jewels, and some bearer bonds. I've got them here for you too." He motions toward the bag at his feet and my heart sinks.

"Thank you. I guess it was too much to hope this would be easy."

"I think that that USB file will be crucial, you just need to work out how to open it. I have a hacker friend, but I figured you wouldn't want anyone else looking at it. Your friend is a hacker right?"

I gulp and nod. He means Finn. "Yeah, but I don't want to involve him if I can help it either."

"I wouldn't blame you. I've learned a lot of things about your Knights while working for you, and I have to say, I'm not comfortable helping you join their ranks. They're just as likely to kill you off when you hand this over as they are to welcome you." He glances back at Smithy who is nodding. "I'll keep searching if you want, but some of these hidey holes are on the other side of the world. London, Paris, Sydney…"

He trails off but I hear what he's not saying. There isn't enough time to search them all. I take a deep breath and mull it over. "Keep searching, as much as you can. Cost isn't a problem. We have until Friday, so we need to do what we can before then."

"Okay. I can do that." He stands, grabbing his case and opening it for me. "This is for you."

I glance inside, wondering why my dad hid all of this. Maybe it was just a way to disguise whatever he was hiding in one of the others. "Smithy, would you mind?"

"Of course, Miss Octavia." He takes the case, closing it, before disappearing into his quarters. I know he'll arrange for it to be put where it should be. I wouldn't even know what to do with most of that stuff.

"Walk me out?" Bentley says, watching Smithy disappear.

"Umm, sure." I jump from the stool, noticing he didn't touch his coffee. We walk outside in silence, but when we reach his car, he takes hold of my arm, watching over my shoulder at the front door.

"Be careful who you trust, Miss Royal. The Knights reach might be wider than you think. I would suggest if you find what you're looking for, make a copy and keep it somewhere safe. Somewhere that isn't linked to you. These are dangerous waters you're playing in."

"I know," I say with a nod. "Can I really trust you?"

He smirks at me. "I would suggest trusting no one, but yes, I have nothing to do with your Knights. I have managed to stay unaffiliated, by some miracle, my entire life. Even from my own brother's reach. If you want me to keep a hold of the information you seek once we find it, just let me know."

"I'll think about it," I say, just as the front door opens behind me and Bentley takes a step back.

He puts his friendly mask back on and glances over my shoulder at Smithy, his brow furrowing so minutely I wonder if I imagined it. Weird. He looks back to me and warmth fills his eyes again as he opens the driver's side door to the car. "I'll let you know if I find anything else."

EIGHTEEN

OCTAVIA

"If you don't focus, he's going to pin you again," Finn barks, and I huff at how right he is. I might not have told these guys the truth of why I wanted to train with them, but they are kicking my ass for real.

"I'm trying." My words are sharp and terse. I thought hanging out with the guys would've taken the edge off of my meeting with Bentley earlier, but I'm still wound up so fucking tight. Add that to everything else I have going on and its not a surprise I'm a fucking mess.

I was hoping my training with Luc and Artemis would've helped me a bit more, but Maverick really is just a fucking lethal machine and I am useless compared to him.

Woe is fucking you, Octavia. This isn't the time for a tiny violin, buck the fuck up.

"Again." Finley's voice snaps my focus back to reality in time for me to see Maverick barreling toward me in the Octagon. I try to brace myself but I'm too slow as he slams into me, tackling me to the floor. I grapple with him, trying to bring my legs up to kick him off of me or flip him onto his back, but he smiles at me as his hands cage my wrists and uses his hips to pin me to the floor.

"I'm definitely not opposed to this position, princess," he growls as he grinds his dick against my core and I whimper beneath him at the touch.

Maybe that is exactly what I need to get rid of this humming beneath my skin.

So I lift up and press my lips to his, knowing that Finley is watching, hoping they both get the fucking hint.

"Hey, Finn, looks like our little fighter here is itching to get fucked." Mav's grin takes up half his face as he grinds his half-hard cock against my already-wet pussy.

Finn's heavy steps end behind my head, his eyes landing on me from above—the filthy glint in his eyes unmistakable.

"Looks like it." Cocking his head to the side, he adds, "Who are we to deny her?"

"Indeed." It's the only word Mav throws at me before I'm suddenly turned onto my hands and knees, my leggings gone right along with my panties.

Finn disappears for a heartbeat before he's back—a good length of rope in his hands—settling in front of me.

The scent of sweat quickly gives way to sex as he places the silky material around my throat, sliding it back and forth at the nape of my neck. All the while, Mav feasts on my pussy from behind, moaning and grunting as he goes deeper and deeper.

Crossing the ends of the rope at the base of my neck, Finn looks me straight in the eyes and grins.

"You look beautiful all tied up."

His words and Mav's expert tongue wreak havoc on my body, my nerve endings blazing with my rising need to come.

"She's almost there, Mav." Finn's gaze never leaves mine as he speaks.

"I know, she's fucking dripping wet."

Closing my eyes, I revel in the feel of Mav's tongue, now joined by his fingers, as he traces circles around my swollen clit. It's all exacerbated by the silky feel of the rope sliding over the skin of my neck—back and forth.

Mav pushes two fingers inside my pussy as his tongue slides over to my puckered hole, pushing and prodding, moaning his pleasure as he fucks both of my holes. I can't help it, the sensation is too much and my orgasm overtakes me without warning. The heat of it spreads throughout my body is almost overwhelming.

"Don't be a greedy bastard, Mav."

He curls his fingers inside me, ripping a cry from my throat with the pleasure of it. Gasping, I try to catch my breath but Finn tightens my ropes and the slight deprivation of air just makes my orgasm that much more potent.

"That's our good girl." Finn's words heat me from the inside but I don't have time to think about this newfound praise kink I may or may not have, because the next thing I know, I'm kneeling on the octagon—straddling Mav's cock as it juts up and teases my swollen lips. Pushing into me, he groans in my ear as Finn's rope is pulled taut around my neck, dragging my head down toward Finn's now-exposed cock. He slides it into my mouth and we both moan at the feel.

Two large hands push up my sports bra, exposing my already hard nipples to the air. Using his grip on me, Maverick fucks me slowly, deliberately, his fingers pinching my nipples every time he bottoms out. Alternating their movements, Mav pulls out just as Finn drives his cock deep inside my throat.

Mav thrusts once more, then twice, and on the third push he pulls me off and turns me around as if I weigh nothing.

With one hand in my hair, Mav presses my mouth onto his dick, deciding the speed and force with which I suck his dick. Behind me, Finn is impaling his cock inside me without any preamble. One hand on my hip the other on the rope that he uses as a leash.

It's demeaning—degrading even—and I love it.

"How do you taste on my cock, princess?"

I don't answer, obviously, but I moan and it's answer enough for him.

"Fucking delicious, aren't we?"

I moan again as he fucks my face, Finn behind me fucking my pussy with determined thrusts.

Again, Mav pulls out of my mouth, this time pulling my head up to his mouth and kissing me hard and fast, his tongue licking a hot path across my lips before his teeth bite into my bottom lip hard enough to break the skin. The tip of his tongue flicks over the drop of blood that pebbles where he broke skin.

"Like I said: fucking delicious."

I'm spun around once again, my mouth on Finn's dick, my pussy getting rammed by a very horny Maverick, whose curses and grunts echo throughout the gym.

This time I'm on my hands and knees, Mav's hands on my hips controlling the speed of his fucking, mindful that I'm also sucking off Finn and biting would be frowned upon.

I spend more time in this position, licking and sucking on Finn's dick, I taste myself all over his shaft, licking it all up right up to the slit sitting on top of his swollen head. Finn's control is slipping, his moans rivaling Mav's. Typically, he's more reserved, but even Finn has his limits.

He tightens the rope, pulling me closer just as I swallow him down at the back of my throat.

Mav reaches around and plays with my clit as he continues thrusting inside me, hard and fast.

"Fuck, Mav, I'm not going to last much longer."

I hollow my cheeks on his next thrust and I swear I feel him grow inside my mouth. Finn pushes my head down an extra inch with the rope tight around my neck, his girth feels restricted in my throat making us both tremble with how good it feels.

"Fuck!" Finn cries out as he pulls out quickly, his fingers squeezing the base of his cock. I was sure he was going to come.

Behind me, Mav drives into me once more before he pulls out and turns me on my back where he begins to eat me again—licking my slit and sucking on my clit. I look up at Finn, his eyes dark with lust and love as he bends over me and kisses my mouth deeply—lovingly.

It's weird how they can be so animalistic and caring all at the same time.

Finn's hands trail down to my tits where he places them both, big and warm, over them and massages hard enough to make the walls of my pussy spasm against Mav's prodding tongue.

"She's so wet, Finn. So fucking wet."

Finn inches around me, his mouth never leaving my skin as he peppers me with tender kisses on my jaw, my neck, my tit, and his hands never leaving my flesh as he slides them along my sides. His mouth settles on my nipple, his tongue flicking the hard peak before he sucks it deep into his mouth as his thumbs press against my hip bones.

Giving my other nipple the same attention, his tongue circles over and over again before he nips at the tender flesh, making me gasp from the pleasure and pain.

Finn's finger is now on my clit as he pulls me up to a sitting position, forcing Mav to lick me up one more time before he stops and they're both looking at me with lust written all over their features.

Without speaking, Mav moves away from my pussy and straddles my chest taking Finn's rope and wrapping the silk around the palm of his hand until I'm forced to take his cock in my mouth. Just as Mav bottoms out, Finn's cock spears my pussy with a force that almost causes damage to Maverick's beautiful cock.

"Watch it, Finn. I need my cock attached to my body."

Finn doesn't respond, only grunts as he grabs my thighs and tilts me back. Mav's hand is at the back of my head as he lowers us back down, never missing a beat.

One hand on the octagon, Mav holds his weight as the other wraps around my throat. He doesn't care about ropes or anything else. I know from experience that all he wants is to feel his cock as I swallow him whole.

Finn's thrusts are getting harder, faster as I suck Mav's cock with more and more gusto. A thumb grazes my clit and I swear I'm about to lose my mind all over again. I'm trying really fucking hard to keep up with their frenzied fucking—my hands fly up to Mav's naked chest, fingers digging into his hard abs, nails leaving a mark—as my climax erupts inside me. They leave me no choice but to take Mav's dick out of my mouth so I can scream out the ecstasy of it all.

The first spurt of Mav's cum lands on my chin, the next on my lips. The rest of his orgasm is in my mouth. I swallow just as Finn roars out his own climax, causing aftershocks to tremor through my body. I take it all inside me. Filled with their cum, I heave a deep breath, willing my heart to slow down.

"If this is how you train, princess, no wonder you need to practice."

Waking up in a puppy pile of my guys might be my favorite way to start the day. After my training fuckery with Mav and Finn yesterday, we came back home, and Linc and East joined us for a movie marathon before crashing here. It was a much needed night with them, and I could see it on them as well as feel it in myself. East still seemed a little distant, but that's probably just me projecting.

Mav is wrapped around me from behind, his face nuzzled in my neck; East has an arm draped over us both, his hand resting on my hip; Lincoln is in front of me, his legs intertwined with mine, my head on his chest; and Finn is on the other side of him, as if watching over us all.

I don't want to move, I'd happily stay here all day, but my bladder is about to burst.

Slipping out from the entanglement of limbs without

waking anyone feels impossible, but I do my best and slip into the bathroom. I freshen myself up once I'm done, wiping away the raccoon eyes that look back at me in the mirror, and run a brush through my hair.

"You okay?" Finn asks as he pops his head around the door. When he sees me standing in front of the mirror in my tank and boy shorts, he enters the room and shuts the door. I try not to drool over him as he stretches in front of me and he yawns, wearing even less than me. He pads sleepily over to me and pulls me against his chest. "I miss you," he breathes the words into my hair as I wrap my arms around him.

"I miss you, too," I say before pressing my lips to one of the scars that adorn his chest.

"We going to talk about these bruises of yours anytime soon?" he asks quietly, and I stiffen in his arms. "You don't have to tell me, the others might not have noticed, Mav is usually too distracted by you being half naked, and I'm guessing you've told the others they're from sparring with Maverick and me… but I see them, Octavia. Just tell me you're not in trouble."

I gulp down, blinking back tears from how reasonable he's being and how much of a bitch I feel. "I'm not in trouble. I'll explain soon, just… just give me some time?"

He pulls back and clasps my chin in his finger and thumb. "I can do that, and I won't mention it to the others either, but whatever is going on, we're with you. You can let us in."

"I will," I murmur, his eyes fixed on my lips as I run my

tongue over them. "I promise."

"That's all I ask." He captures my lips with his and I give myself over to his kiss. Letting him take everything he wants from me without question.

When he pulls back, letting me suck in some much needed oxygen, he holds me against his chest again. "I'm going back to Ocean Falls today to see my mom, if you want to try and see yours again?"

A shudder runs through me. I'm still waiting to hear back from Indi and Bentley, but maybe my mom might have an idea of where Dad might have hidden something. Assuming she'll see me this time anyway.

"Sure, maybe this time will be better."

"Let's hope so. Come on, I said I'd be there early." He takes my hand and pulls me from the bathroom. We find the others awake already, half dressed and sleepy eyed. "Breakfast, then Octavia and I are driving out to Ocean Falls."

Linc looks at me, as if checking that I'm okay, and I nod. It seems to appease him, cause he nods back.

We head downstairs and Smithy fusses around us all, sorting breakfast, and once we're fed, Finn ushers me next door to his car, and we make our way to Ocean Falls.

He keeps my hand clasped in his the entire way, leaving me to my thoughts in the way that he always does. It's why coming here with him is probably the least daunting it could be. I know he won't make me talk about everything that's swirling around in my head if I don't want to, but I also know he'd listen to me talk about it if I needed to.

His presence is enough to stop me falling in the well of anxiety though, even if I am teetering on the edge.

I'm not even sure if I want her to agree to see me, or if it'd be easier for her to just keep rejecting me. Rejecting me means I don't have to deal with the reality of her, of what happened to her, but that feels like running away from my problems. Again.

Except if she does want to see me, I still haven't figured out what the fuck I would even say to her.

We pull up out front again and the butterflies in my stomach start a riot.

"You've got this, pretty girl. Come on." Finn squeezes my hand before releasing me and climbing from the car. I take a deep breath and follow suit, rounding the car to join him at the door. He takes us to the receptionist, who smiles widely at him just like last time we were here.

"Mr. Knight, lovely to see you. Your mom checked back in last night, I assume you're here for her?"

"I am," he confirms to her, squeezing my hand again. "And Mrs. Royal."

Her smile drops a little. "I will see what I can do."

She disappears and we take a seat, waiting for her to return.

"It will be okay, whatever happens." Finn's reassurances barely break the surface of everything going on inside of me, but I lean into him and accept the comfort nonetheless. It's not until the receptionist reappears, looking wary.

"Your mom is waiting for you Mr. Knight."

"And Mrs. Royal?" he asks as I hold my breath.

"She agreed to see her daughter, albeit briefly. Though I must say, I don't know that this is a good idea." My heart pounds as her words sink in. I guess this is it, bad idea or not.

"Thank you Annie, we'll be fine I'm sure." Finn stands, pulling me up with him, and leads me through the frosted glass door we didn't make it through last time I was here. We walk down a sterile white hall in near-silence before he asks, "Do you want me to stay with you while you see your mom?"

"No, it's fine," I say, shaking my head. "It's probably better that I see her alone and you need to see your mom anyway, right?"

"I do, I need to talk to her about some stuff going on with Dad. I'll catch you up on that later, but even so, if you need me, I won't leave your side."

We pause in the hall outside of a door that says Emily Royal on the attached whiteboard. "I know, and I love you for it, but this is something I should do alone. Go, see your mom, do what you need to. I'll meet you at the car when we're done."

"Okay, but I have my phone if you need me."

I reach up and kiss him chastely before pushing him down the hall. "Go, I've got this." I smile at him, feeling like I look more confident than I actually feel. Once he turns the corner with a wave, I take a breath and knock on the door to my mom's room.

"Come in," her voice is quiet through the door, but clear enough to make out. Pushing on the door, I head inside, trying not to let her see how much my hands shake. I find her sitting on her bed, knees pulled up against her chest. Her dark hair is pulled back in a tight bun, she's wearing jeans and a white sweater, but they seem to hang from her thin frame. The glow I remember her having, the light in her eyes... none of that is present anymore. It's not surprising, but for some reason, I can't not see it. The woman looking back at me is a shadow of a human and less than a shadow of the woman I knew as my mother.

"What do you want, Octavia?" Her words are little more than a hiss as she sneers at me from across the room.

I pause in the middle of the room, not sure what to say. I clasp my hands in front of me, wringing them out, feeling like that little girl she left behind so long ago

"I said, what the fuck do you want, Octavia? Haven't you already done enough? Daddy's little princess ruining my life, three times over now. Have you come to fuck with me some more, demon spawn of mine? I don't know what I did to deserve a child like you, but if I could go back, I'd fucking abort you."

I suck in a breath at her tirade as tears spring in my eyes. "I didn't do anything to you! I thought you left us!"

She rolls her eyes at me and grabs a pack of cigarettes on the nightstand, lighting one up and sucking down the nicotine

281

before turning back to me. "I did leave, because your daddy loved you more than me. We were in danger, but he always put you first. Everything he ever did was for you. I left, and I was finally happy. Free. Free of you, the shit that followed him around… and then you came of age and he decided once again you were more important than the rest of us."

"I don't understand…" I trail off, clenching my fists at my sides. I might not have had much idea what coming here would be like, but I definitely didn't expect this.

"Of course you don't," she says, blowing out another lungful of smoke. "Lose one to save one. I don't know how many fucking times I heard that stupid ultimatum. Do you know what it means, Octavia?" Her sneer makes me take a step back as I shake my head. "It means that to keep you, I had to be lost. To buy your freedom, your dad sold mine. To that monster. I was caged, trapped, tortured, raped, all so you could escape the life your daddy originally had you for. Fucking bullshit. And now you stand there, looking at me like a lost fucking puppy, like I have the answers to save you. Well, fuck you, Octavia. I'm not saving you ever again. Stop coming here. I don't want to see you. You died to me a long time ago, just like I did for you. Let's keep it that way."

She takes another drag on her cigarette before glaring at me once more. "Get the fuck out of here, little girl, before I really make you regret your existence."

I gulp, blinking back the tears in my eyes, and leave without another word.

My dad sacrificed her to save me. Just another person lost so I wouldn't have to be a Knight. Am I really doing the right thing with this deal with Harrison? Going against everything they sacrificed for me?

I guess it's too late now. I don't look at anyone as I leave Ocean Falls, but once I'm outside I slide down the side of the car and pull my knees up to my chest, letting the tears fall as the wounds my mother just ripped open bleed out.

I guess I really am an orphan after all.

NINETEEN

OCTAVIA

"So there was nothing?" My heart drops as Indi tells me the bad news.

"Sorry, V. We looked. The locker was a bust. If there was anything in it, it's not there anymore. Your dad only had the locker for two weeks. That was eighteen months ago." She grabs our coffee order from the drive-thru window, handing them to me before pulling off toward school.

"It's fine. We knew it was a long shot. Was everything okay with you and Alex?"

She glances at me as we drive through the center of the cove, biting her lip. "Yeah, we talked through everything again on the flight, and now I need to talk to Ryker. I already spoke to

Dylan, he's chill, but before I do anything with Alex, the twins need to know. I'm not sure what it is between us, but there's something there… something about him that calls to a part of me that I didn't even know was there."

I nod, knowing exactly how she feels.

"How was visiting with your mom? Did she have any ideas about your dad's hidey holes?"

My stomach flips at the question, wishing I could just scrub that part of my weekend from my mind. "It was horrific."

She looks at me wide-eyed as we pull into school, and I give her the quick version of what happened, watching as she grows angrier on my behalf.

"Goddamn, what a bitch! Like, I know she's been through a lot, but it's hardly your fault. She's blaming you for the fuck ups of the people in your life. What an asshole."

I shrug as I unbuckle myself. "It is what it is, I guess. She doesn't want to see me, and I'm not going to make her. Finley said she'll likely live out the rest of her life in that place. She knows too much to be let out, for one, but also, due to her trauma, it won't be good for her to go back out in the real world. Not for a long time anyway. I'm sad she's suffered, but I have family now and if she doesn't want to be part of it, then that's her choice. She left me a long time ago."

The words taste like ash on my tongue. It's not a lie, but it's also not something I've fully accepted, despite what I'm saying. I thought she left me, but the possibility that we could've had a relationship has been skirting around the outside of my mind since the guys told me she was alive. That's no more than dust now and there's nothing that I can do about it.

I need to focus on what I can control.

Which is finding these fucking documents and unlocking this USB without asking Finn for help. I will if I have to, but I'd really rather not. I know he'll be pissed about everything and he'll try to stop me from doing what I'm determined to do.

"You and me, tonight. Girls night. Smithy can make us margs. Who gives a fuck that it's Monday? Media room, margs, and karaoke. That is what we need, my friend. Let's blow off some steam. It won't be the first time someone's gone to school with a hangover."

I match her grin and nod, "That sounds like perfection. But first, we must survive the day."

We climb from the car and find my guys, minus East, waiting for us. I try to shake off the sadness from thinking about my mom, and lose myself to the bickering of Mav and Indi and the predictability of school.

The day passes in a blur, and before I know it, Indi is bundling me back into her Wrangler after pulling me away from Linc—who told me we need to talk, not ominous at all—to get ready for girls night.

Being around Indi is like being around a whirlwind of energy. Her excitement is contagious and it's impossible not to get pulled in by her joy.

I officially have the best bestie in existence.

Once we're home, I follow her as she bounces inside, and I hear her squealing and laughing with Smithy as I take off my shoes and drop my bag.

"You're the best, Smithy!" she exclaims as she bounces back toward me. "Come on, you!" Grabbing my arm, she drags me toward the media room and I can't help but laugh at her.

"So what is the plan, oh sensei of joy?"

"There is no plan, *that* is the fun of it. Smithy is on pizza and marg duty. We may not be legal, but he's a big softie. As long as we keep it to three. That was the deal. And we just have some fun."

She pulls out the karaoke machine I'd forgotten was even in here and hooks it up to the big screen, "First, we need something cathartic. How about we go old school?"

She turns to the screen, flicking through the options, then glances at me over her shoulder, waging her brows at me. "Found it!"

The opening bars of *My Happy Ending* by Avril Lavigne start playing and I laugh at her. It is kind of perfect. She lifts one of the mics to her lips and starts singing as the lyrics appear on the screen, making a drama show of her performance, waving for me to join her. It takes me nearly a minute before I decide fuck it.

By the time Smithy appears with two margaritas and the biggest pepperoni pizza I've ever seen, my throat is scratchy from screaming at the top of my lungs, the old school pop-punk tunes being absolutely slayed, and not always in a good way.

I fall onto the couch, pulling a slice of the cheesy goodness, I take a bite while Indi finishes up *Bring Me to Life* by Evanescence.

"I might not be Amy Lee, but damn I love singing that song." Indi grins at me as she drops beside me, taking a sip of the icy drink, as *The Black Parade* starts playing in the background. "Goddamn that is good. Weak, but tasty regardless."

"Honestly, I'm surprised he put any alcohol in them at all." I shrug and grab another slice. Smithy makes the best damn pizza.

"Smithy is aware that teens are going to drink. He's a chill old guy. Any adult that thinks their kid doesn't drink is either stupid or delusional. Even the straight-A students kick back sometimes. I think he'd rather us drink here, where it's safe, than anywhere else."

I smirk at her, "God, could you imagine if someone like Mikayla's mom saw what I did on tour? She'd have a freaking conniption."

Indi bursts out laughing. "Oh my God, yes. I'd pay to see her face backstage at a show. Hell, just *at* a show. Did you see her when she came in to speak to Principal Evans after the whole, you-were-crowned-queen thing? Someone was *not* happy."

"No! Why on earth was she there about that?"

"Apparently, Mikayla was being bullied by you and Blair." She cackles before taking a slice of pizza. "Unfortunately for

Mikayla, enough people had witnessed her bullshit and came forward before it even got that far, and now she's been outcast as a snitch."

"Holy shit," I giggle. "Can you imagine if *that* was the worst part of our year? Being dethroned?"

"I think Mikayla would've perished at the first obstacle you faced, my friend." She raises her glass in a toast before taking a sip as *Face Down* by The Red Jumpsuit Apparatus starts playing. "Oh my God, I love this song!"

She drops the glass and her slice and starts dancing around the media room, not giving a fuck as I laugh at her antics. "Come on! Dance it off, shake it out! Meredith Grey says this shit is the best way to shake off a funk. If her and Swifty say it, it must be true."

I shake my head but stand with her, dancing as the playlist changes to *Miss Murder* by AFI. Now this is a fucking classic.

We sing at the top of our lungs once more and I thank God for my best friend. This night is exactly what I needed.

My phone buzzes on the couch, so I prance over and grab it, my smile dropping when I see the message on the screen.

Harrison:

Your time is nearly up, Miss Royal, which means our deal is about to expire. I already gave you one extension. Do not disappoint me. You might find it's the last thing you do.

After being dropped back to reality by Harrison's message last night, girls night turned somber, and Indi headed over to see the twins to try and talk to them about the whole Alex thing. She offered to stay with me, but there was no point.

Harrison effectively dropped a bomb on us and killed the mood.

So I decided to skip school today—after I messaged the guys in a group chat to let them know I was okay but wouldn't be around—and have spent the best part of my day reading through all of my dad's journals that I'd stashed down in the music room. I hadn't gone through them with Indi the other day, we had enough stuff, and older journals.

These journals are from more recently, so I'm hoping theres something in them that will help with this fucking USB drive. I don't even know if what I need is on the fucking drive, but it's all I've got, dammit. I even tried to open it on my laptop, but just like Bentley said, it asked for an encryption key.

"More coffee, Miss Octavia?" I look up and find Smithy hovering in the doorway of the music room, while I'm in the middle of a dozen open journals. I bet I don't even look crazy.

He already has a steaming mug in his hands, because he's freaking awesome like that. "You're a God, Smithy. Thank you."

"I wish I could be more help—"

"It's fine. This is something I need to do myself. Plus, I don't know that I'd feel okay with anyone else reading this stuff. It feels like an invasion of Dad's privacy enough, me reading them. At least I was there for a lot of this, even if this is like a window into his mind. But so far, there's just ramblings. Though," I pause, finding the journal I was reading earlier. "I've noticed these symbols reoccurring throughout the journals. Do you have any idea what they might be?"

He takes the journal, flicking through the pages at the lines and dots that make no sense to me. It's almost like a code, or shorthand, that I don't have the cypher for.

"I'm sorry, I don't know. I could keep looking if you like, but even as well as I knew your father, he always did like to play things close to the vest. They could be something, but they could be nothing but drunken scribbles."

"Don't I know it," I huff. "Thank you anyway. I texted Bentley earlier, so I'm hoping I hear from him soon. He flew out to Sydney after he left here on Saturday, then he was going to go from there to Prague, then Rome, Paris, and London. The last few he thought he could do in a day with how quick the flights are. So I'm just hoping he comes up with something."

He offers me the mug and sits down on the couch opposite me. "Would it be the worst thing if he didn't?"

I look at him wide eyed. "How can you—"

He cuts me off with a wave of his hand. "The Knights are no joke, Miss Octavia. You are free, and I can't imagine

292

Harrison wants to give up his power to you. If you don't find the documents, you remain free, yes? I know that means that the boys wouldn't be, but this is a life they are used to. Maybe it would be for the best. Anything that Harrison wants this badly… I can't imagine it would be good to give it to him."

I chew on my lip, because I know he's right about that last bit, I've thought about it a dozen times since I made the damn deal. "I know, but I can't leave them tied to the Knights. They've been through so much, and they've saved me time and again. They deserve to be free, to pick their own futures."

"I know they do, Miss Octavia, but sacrificing your own future probably isn't the best way to buy theirs. Along with whatever else is on those documents that Harrison wants."

I frown, feeling hopeless again. "I thought you were on board with my plan? You didn't say anything before."

"I will always support you, Miss Octavia. But I can't deny that I'm worried. I didn't want to be overbearing, you're nearly eighteen. It's not my place to try and tell you what to do. I just want to make sure that you've thought about all of the outcomes here."

"I have," I say, chewing the inside of my lip. "But when I asked Harrison for an extension, he said that if I don't find the documents… well, I might not be free anyway."

His brow furrows when I tell him what I've been holding back for the last week. "Show me."

I pull up the message from Harrison and show him my

phone. His face turns a deep shade of red as he reads the message. "That man—" he blows out a breath, like he's too angry to keep speaking. "—Well, I suggest you keep looking, and I'll try to work out a plan for just in case you don't find them. Maybe one for if you do."

He stands and leaves me sitting among the pages of the journals, coffee in hand, wondering if I've managed to disappoint everyone in my life with this deal I've made.

I keep reading, and find nothing but the weird code that might not be anything anyway. Regardless, I copy it from the pages to my notebook, in date order, in the hope that something makes sense or I find the cypher for it.

My phone buzzes, pulling me from my trance, and my stomach rumbles as I start paying attention to the world around me again.

Linc:

I'm heading over. You weren't at school and we still need to talk.

Me:

Okay, see you in a few.

I stand up, dusting down my leggings, straightening my sweater that falls off one shoulder, and make my way upstairs, running a hand through my hair as I go so I don't look a total freaking mess. Not that Lincoln would care, but I do.

I reach the kitchen just as Linc appears at the back door. He's still partially in his uniform, the arms of his shirt rolled up to his elbows, the top few buttons undone, and his hair looks like he's run his hands through it all day.

"Where were you?" He asks once he closes the door and moves toward me. He leans against the counter, arms folded, and I quirk a brow at him.

"Hi Linc. Yeah, I'm okay. Thanks for asking. How was your day? Oh, dull? I'm sorry to hear that." I deadpan, but he doesn't move an inch. I let out a sigh, running a hand through my hair again. "I was home all day. I just needed some alone time."

He continues to watch me as if looking for the lie. It wasn't one, not entirely, so he won't find it. My stomach churns once more at keeping stuff from him, but he nods once and then visibly loosens up.

"Sorry, I worry. And you never go MIA." I push myself up to sit on the edge of the counter, and he moves to stand between my legs. "I meant it yesterday when I said we needed to talk."

"I really hate that sentence," I tell him and he kisses me softly, like he's trying to make up for whatever it is he's going to say already.

When he pulls back, I already know I'm going to hate whatever falls out of his mouth next. He clamps his lips together when I sigh. "Just tell me."

"I have a date with Georgia at Harrison's insistence."

"I thought that shit was over with." I am going to give Harrison fucking *hell* about this. Lincoln is supposed to be free of that skank. He still looks like he's holding something back, something that I don't want to know. "When?"

"Friday," he tells me and I clench my fists. "It was supposed to be Saturday, but I refused. That's your day. Friday was the compromise."

I grind my teeth together, trying to keep a lid on my shit, because this is not Lincoln's fault. Fighting Harrison is like trying to ride a surfboard in a tsunami. Especially when he has to live with him. *This* is exactly why I made that fucking deal in the first place. Lincoln shouldn't be subjected to this bullshit.

Especially not by his fucking father.

"It's fine," I grind out and his shoulders stiffen under my fingers. "And yes I'm pissed, but not at you."

"Octavia—"

"You don't have to apologize, Linc. This isn't your fault. Am I furious? Of course I am, imagine if the roles were reversed and I was being forced to date, be engaged to, and fuck knows what else to someone."

His eyes darken to thunder clouds at my words. "I know, I'm working on getting out of it, it's just—"

"That your dad is a fucking psychopath? Yeah I know." I let out a deep breath, running my hands through the end of his hair. "We'll figure something out."

"I love you," he says, resting his forehead against mine.

"One day we'll be free, and when that day comes—"

I briefly press my lips to his then pull back. "Don't make promises, Lincoln. The Knights are unpredictable assholes. But we *will* deal with Georgia. Even if I have to do it my damn self."

TWENTY

OCTAVIA

"He found something?" Indi squeaks as I close my locker and pull my bag up on my shoulder. "Do you know what it is?"

"No, Bentley is all kinds of weird about talking over the phone. He reminds me of my dad a bit like that. Though, with everything I know now, my dad's aversion to technology is kind of understandable." I pull out my keys as we make our way out of school. "But he flew back this morning. He's coming straight to the house when he lands, so I need to haul ass home."

"Okay, call me when you know what it is, if it's what you need. And if it's not, we'll work out an emergency plan. I might not exactly be on board with you being a Knight, but I know doing this for the guys is important to you, so I'll support you no matter what."

"And that is why you're my best bitch." She grins before hugging me quickly then darting around to her Wrangler.

"Call me! Gotta go deal with Ryker fallout from yesterday!" She jumps in her Wrangler and I laugh as I slide into the Range Rover, waiting for her to reverse before I even start the car. I catch sight of my guys coming out of the door, and pull out of my space before they can question what I'm doing.

Just two more days until I can stop hiding shit from them.

I have no idea how they did it. Keeping secrets is fucking exhausting. Especially ones like this. All I want is to tell them the truth, but I'm also aware of the consequences of that.

I try not to think about it and turn up my sound system as *Street Lightning* by The Summer Set starts playing. Losing myself to music is always the answer when the voices in my head get too loud. And right now, there is so much going on that I've pushed aside to deal with later that the voices are more like a stadium full of angry fans.

It's *loud.*

Just not for much longer, I hope.

I come to a stop at the gate and see Bentley's car coming down the street, so I wait for him to pull up behind me before I tap the code in. I drive into the garage, darting into the house and opening the front door for him just as he's about to knock.

"Miss Royal," he says with a smile.

"Come in," I utter, waving him in the house and closing the door. "Do you want coffee?"

He nods, yawning at me. "Yes, please. The coffee on the flight from London was abysmal."

We head into the kitchen, finding Smithy already pouring coffee. That guy really is a saint.

"Miss Octavia, I have dinner in the oven warming already. You're welcome to join us, Mr. Kensington."

"Thank you, but after we're done here, I'm going home to sleep for three days."

Smithy nods as he slides a mug of coffee in front of us both. "Of course."

"Thank you." Bentley pulls a laptop out of his bag and boots it up as he reaches back down. "I found this in Sydney," he says, pushing a notebook across to me, and an envelope with my name on it. "Then I found this in Prague, and this in London." He produces another USB and what looks like a children's coding toy.

"What is all of this?"

"I didn't read the letter, that was obviously for you. But the journal is what seems like a log of someone's movements, maybe a few people. Part of it reads like a ledger. The USB I think is the encryption key, and the cypher... well I'm not sure what that's for yet, but let's have a look, shall we? Do you have the other USB I gave you?"

"I have it, let me go and retrieve it." Smithy heads off into his quarters, while I stare at the envelope with my name like it's trying to kill me.

I don't know what it says, but I'm fairly certain that whatever it is, I'm not ready to read it. I might make out like I've moved past my dad's death, but I'm very aware that I still haven't fully dealt with my grief. I've shoved it down since I got back to Echoes Cove and locked it in a box, put it on a shelf, and shut the door on the room I stored it in. Reading that letter is going to rip away all of the chains I locked around that door. My focus has been purely on dealing with everything that's been going on, and graduation.

Grief hasn't really factored into the last nine months.

I can't believe it's been nine months since he was taken from me.

I choke down that realization as Smithy reappears, USB in hand. "Here you are," he says, handing it over to Bentley. He puts the two drives into the slots on his laptop then hands it over to me.

"You should be the one to open the files," he says as I look at the screen. He reaches over and taps a few buttons and the screen whirrs to life, the encryption box popping up again. Then he clicks something else, the screen flashes, and a folder opens.

The top file, a video file, is titled 'Octavia', so I click on it, my heart in my mouth.

A window opens, and a small cry works up my throat as the screen comes to life and I see my dad's face staring back at me.

He's fiddling with the camera before taking a seat on the chair placed in front of it.

"Octavia," he starts, a sad smile on his face. "If you're watching this, I imagine that you're confused, pissed off, and probably crying." I hiccup a laugh as a tear runs down my cheek. Hearing his voice again rips me in two, but seeing his face... I hadn't realized that I'd forgotten his smile a little until now. "There's a lot I should have told you, but I wanted to keep you away from the darkness that has haunted our family for decades. If I'm dead, chances are you know about the Knights. I'm sure they've tried to reclaim you, I just hope that I did enough to prepare you for them. I tried everything I could think of to keep you out of their grasp, but I am just one man. Just remember that even within the pits of darkness, light is easily found. You, Bug, were that light for me. I hope that my death hasn't dimmed that light too much.

"I've spent years collecting the information on this drive, it's everything you need to ensure Harrison comes to heel. I don't know what will have transpired for you to find this, but trust your gut. You always had the best judgment. If you've ended up a part of them, I understand. If you found your mom, I'm sorry. I made the only decision I had at the time.

"I hope the boys have helped bring you into the loop, and always trust Smithy. He will lead you right while I can't. I trust him with your life, so even if you take no other advice from me, take that part. Trust him. Implicitly. I don't have much time, just know that I love you, Bug, whether I'm there with you or not, I'll never really leave you. I'm just sorry our time was cut short.

"And if you need help working out my codes, just remember raindrops."

He looks off screen, and I hear Mac's voice calling him for rehearsal, "I have to go, Bug. I love you. Always. Trust yourself, trust your friends, those boys will always look out for you, and trust Smithy. I hope everything I collected is enough to help."

The screen flickers to black as tears silently travel down my face as I stare at the black screen. I didn't expect that. Not at all. I thought the letter would be bad, but seeing his face…

I take a deep breath and shove it down to deal with later as I swipe the tears from my cheeks. "Let's look at these files shall we?" I don't look at either of them as I close the video window. If I see the pity or sadness on their faces, I'll break, and we don't have time for that.

I start opening the other files, and there is all sorts of information in here: videos, voice recordings, copies of emails, Shit that would bury Harrison, Charles, and God knows how many other Knights. There are names of senators and people in just about any other position of power there is in here. "Holy shit."

"Something like that," Bentley agrees. "This is definitely what he wants from you. What do you want to do with it?"

I chew on my lip and look at Smithy, remembering our conversation from the other day. "We should make a copy of it, in case Harrison reneges on his side of the deal. Or if anything should happen to me, because he's a dick like that."

Smithy nods, almost looking like he's proud.

"Will you hold the copy for me?" I ask Bentley. "No one around here knows you, or that you're linked to me."

"I'd be happy to." He smiles, glancing at Smithy. "And if something should happen, then what?"

"Then we release the documents to the press." I grin wickedly. "Burn them all to the fucking ground."

The car pulls up in front of the building where I met Harrison the last time he called on me. I take a deep breath and open the car door as it comes to a stop, making sure that the USB is in my pocket. Looking up at the building, a feeling of foreboding settles over me.

If Harrison works out I made copies, he'll kill me. Bentley assured me he wouldn't know, that he masked the copy, but my stomach still flips at the possibility.

The guys all knew something was off with me at school today, I told them I just didn't feel well, and they left me to myself, but I could tell they weren't fully buying it. They stopped questioning me though. I'm just glad that after this is final, I can tell them.

As of Saturday, I'm eighteen, I'll be the regent heir, and I get to tell them what's been going on. I'm both looking forward to it, and dreading it. I'll just be glad that there will be no more secrets. I'm so tired of secrets.

I make my way through the lobby to the private elevator in the back, hitting the button for the top floor. When the doors close, I relax a little, knowing that once they reopen, I'm going to have to be on edge the entire meeting, and probably for the entire time I'm associated with the Knights. Likely after too, but who knows what the hell life is going to look like then?

The number above the door ascends, and when the 'P' shows for the top floor, the *bing* sounds to tell me the doors are opening. I straighten my shoulders and find Harrison standing outside the elevator waiting for me.

"Nothing like sailing close to the wind, Miss Royal." He looks down at me, arms folded over his chest, and it takes all of my willpower to not roll my eyes at him.

"It wasn't the easiest of tasks. But I have what you want."

He purses his lips and looks me over. "Well, let's go check that shall we?"

He turns and heads toward the office we met in previously, expecting me to follow. The audacity of this guy. I follow, because I have no other option. He enters the office, leaving the door open for me, and I take the seat I occupied previously.

"Let me see the documents."

"First," I say, pulling an envelope from my bag. "I had a contract drawn up. To confirm everything we agreed to when we spoke last, including the freedom of Lincoln, Maverick, and Finley. I added Easton considering his newly discovered bloodline. Considering your unwillingness to stick to our agreement the last few weeks, and yes I am talking about Lincoln and Georgia, you haven't exactly instilled confidence in me that you'll keep your word." He scowls at me as I slide the papers across the desk at him. "Once you have signed, I'll show you what I found."

He grinds his teeth as he picks up the contract that Smithy and Chase helped me put together last night, and I try not to smile at his obvious anger.

"You'll note that I haven't amended any terms, just what we originally agreed to, including my limited time as a Knight. The only additions I made are that I get to tell the guys on Saturday, my birthday, myself. That if you break this deal, you give up your seat as Regent, effective immediately, but the four of them remain free regardless."

"I can see," he grinds out, flicking through the pages of the contract. He grabs a pen, and signs the document before slamming his pen on the desk.

I take the contract from him, tucking it back away, before I pull the USB drive from my pocket. "This is what you asked me to get." I say, sliding it across the desk. I deleted the video from my dad, Bentley ensured it wasn't retrievable, because that was for me, and Harrison can suck a dick.

Anyone would think I'd just pushed dog shit across the desk

from the look on his face. "What is that?"

"I just told you. It's what you asked for." He sneers at the drive before swiping it into the top drawer on his desk. "You don't want to check it?"

"I signed your contract, I know how much you want this deal, Miss Royal. I trust that what I wanted is on there. I'll go through it in my own time."

Well, that wasn't what I expected at all. "Very well, if that is all…" I trail off.

"Not quite. Lincoln will still need to go on his evening with Georgia tomorrow. I require it to finalize my deal with her father, but after that, he will be free from any responsibilities to me and the Knights."

"That wasn't our agreement." I clench my fists in my lap as he grins at me.

"No it wasn't but I have the drive now, Miss Royal. It's just one small term. And then you get what you wanted." I should've known he'd pull something. He didn't expect the contract, so this is his power play.

Asshole.

"Fine, but anything after this I will consider a breach of our contract, and I will go above you if needed." I push the chair back and stand, smoothing out my blazer as I do. "I'll see you on Saturday."

He grins at me as he relaxes back in his chair. "Yes, yes you will."

TWENTY ONE

LINCOLN

The tension in this car is fucking insane. So much has been going on that I haven't had much time to spend with Octavia, but since I told her about my so called date tonight, she's been pissed. I get it. Tomorrow is her birthday, we were supposed to be hanging out tonight, but my hands are tied. Harrison's threats against her have been ramping up, and I feel fucking sick.

The thought of breathing the same air as Georgia makes me want to suffocate.

My knuckles are white on the steering wheel from my vice grip on it. I'm trying not to be pissed that she's hung up on the Georgia thing again, but every time it comes up, it's like she doesn't trust me and *that* pisses me off.

I know the waves of tension aren't coming from just me.

Even yesterday, she said she felt sick, but I'm sure it was more than that. She's been so distant lately, and I know she's hiding something, but I can't work out what. She's never hidden stuff from us before which makes me terrified… but for some reason, with her, it comes out as anger.

"Are we going to talk about this?" she asks, the bite of her words not as bad as they were earlier.

I glance over at her, trying not to let my rage shine through. "What is there to talk about?"

"Don't give me your bullshit." She snaps. "I'm tired of this Lincoln, can we just get this night over with and deal with everything else tomorrow?"

That is fucking it. I swerve the car off the main road, pulling onto the dirt before turning and glaring at her. "My bullshit? You're the one who's angry. I thought this whole Georgia thing was clear between us!"

"So did I! You're the one who's been walking around like this is my fault all morning!" she yells before climbing out of my Cayenne and slamming the door.

Fuck me.

I am so sick of everything to do with Georgia, especially when it affects Octavia like this, but I'm pissed too. She leans back against the car and I climb out, slamming my door as well as I walk around the car toward her.

"This is fucking ridiculous. You're hiding something, and you're acting like you're pissed about Georgia to hide it. I know you, Octavia. You know I don't give a fuck about her, I fucking love *you*." The words fall from my lips so easily. The truth isn't always that easy for me, but telling her that is simple. I grab her blazer and pull her toward me a few steps, her hands pressing on my chest as my lips fall on hers, and I devour her. I walk her backward until she's pressed up against the car, trapped between me and it, not relinquishing the control I have over her breath. The power I have over her body.

When I pull back, she pants as I lean my forehead against hers.

"I love you too," she whispers as she closes her eyes. If my heart wasn't already like a stampede of wild horses, it sure as fuck is now.

Maybe I need to show her just how serious I am about the fact that she is it for me.

"When will you understand that there is no one else for me?" My fingers trail up the soft, supple skin of her thigh and slip under her skirt, teasing along the edges of her lace panties.

My dick twitches at the wet heat. Fuck I love when she's ready for me. I swear the fighting turns her on. "Maybe you need a quick reminder that you are mine."

"Maybe, I do."

I don't hesitate. My fingers are inside her before she finishes her last syllable, the word ending on a moan as I push deep into

313

her wet heat.

Stepping fully between her parted legs, I rub my already hardened cock over her naked thigh. "Feel that? You do this to me. You. *Only* fucking you." I punctuate my words with the curling of my fingers and revel in her gasp.

Her fucking mouth will be the death of me. Not able or willing to resist her plump lips, I'm on her in a heartbeat. My lips devouring, my tongue searching, my breath mingling with hers. I'm not being gentle. Fuck that. I'm fucking her mouth with the same determination my fingers are fucking her pussy.

"You're so fucking wet, Octavia. You like this, don't you? Making me fucking insane. You like to push me?" Her eyes flash as my fingers curl around her long tresses, angling her face so the only thing she can see is me. My lust, my need. My fucking love for her.

Retreating my fingers, I don't blink as I pull down the zipper of my slacks and pop off the button until my engorged dick is out and begging for her wet hole.

I push Octavia onto the hood of my car—my hips nestled between her legs—and admire the art that is her body. Fucking hell, she's perfect.

"Be careful, Octavia. Don't fuck up the paint job on my Porsche." I don't give two fucks about my car. I can buy ten more like it. But what I do like is giving her ultimatums. Giving her limits. Inevitably, she'll push the line and just the thought makes me harder than fucking steel.

"If you cared so much, you'd fuck me against that tree over there." Smart girl.

I'm done playing, though. I need to be inside her.

Flipping her uniform skirt over her hips, I scan her half naked form before zeroing in on the wet spot she's left on her panties. I can't help the smirk that creeps up the corners of my lips. I flick my gaze to hers and she just shrugs. She knows exactly what I'm looking at.

"You make me wet, Linc. Even when we fight. *Especially* when we fight. That shouldn't be a surprise to you." It's not, but I won't lie, it turns me the fuck on.

My hand lands on her panties and without preamble, I push them to the side—my other hand on my dick—and I sink inside her wet, hot, pussy.

I sigh at the feel of her walls squeezing my cock. I almost don't want to move, but the need to fuck her rules above all else.

Octavia's entire body bows at my intrusion. Her chest reaching for the sky while I push down on her hips and thrust twice inside her, hard enough to make her jolt.

"You know what I'm going to do?"

"I think you're already doing it." I can barely hear her words, they're so breathy.

"Not yet, but I'm about to." I plunge back inside her so hard, I think the actual fucking car may have moved an inch.

Again, I'm not gentle. I pull out slowly and then slam back into her, stealing her breath on every plunge.

"I'm going to…" grabbing the back of her thighs, I push them against her chest, giving me deeper access, "… make it crystal fucking clear…" I pull out, waiting for her whimper before I slam my dick back inside her again. "… that my cock is. Only. Yours." Every word is punctuated with a thrust so deep, I'm certain she can feel me inside her fucking soul. "Do. You. Fucking. Under. Stand?"

I don't realize I'm practically screaming until the silence falls all around and all I can hear is the sound of my dick plunging in and out of Octavia's hungry pussy. She doesn't answer—out of stubbornness or because her voice is caught in our rhythm, I have no fucking clue. It doesn't matter.

I bring my face close to hers so the only thing she can see is the truth in my eyes. Slowing down my thrusts, I place two fingers on her clit and torture her with slow circles while my dick leisurely fucks her, in and out. I want to see her come—watch as she completely falls apart in my arms—and then I want to destroy every doubt she's ever had about my love for her. My devotion to her.

"Feel that, Octavia?" My free hand tweaks one of her nipples beneath her button-down all the while keeping my rhythm on her clit. "Do you feel what you do to me?" She nods, her mouth open and breaths coming in small hiccups. I know that sound. It's my cue she's about to fucking come all over my dick.

Fuck, I love her.

Lifting my thumb to her mouth, I push it in. "Suck." No

hesitation, she wraps her pretty little lips around my digit and sucks like a fucking pro.

"Good girl."

And then I make her come with that same thumb on her swollen clit.

I don't slow as her torso lifts from the hood. In fact, I fuck her even harder. I go even deeper. Seeking out that place inside her that makes her scream my name.

Octavia's arms search out something—anything—to grab onto, but all she's got is her own clothes. I watch as her fingers reach for her shirt and in half a second, she's pulling—the buttons flying and bouncing off my new paint job. Fucking hell.

My name is spilling from her open mouth as my dick continues to fuck her, helping her come down from her very vocal orgasm. Her cum is coating my cock with every plunge inside her, testing my control.

When she finally settles back down, I decide to make it last just a little longer.

Pulling her back onto her feet, I slip out just the few seconds it takes me to turn her around and place her hands on the hood. Her panties are in my way again and instead of being a gentleman, I rip that shit right off before I slam back in from behind—my mouth at the shell of her ear.

"You're mine, Octavia."

I've got both hands on her tits and I'm fucking her raw, animal-like, grunting and growling every time I bottom out. I can't help the pride I feel when her breaths whoosh out of her lungs.

"But more importantly…" I slam one final time inside her and freeze as my entire body shudders—my legs trembling—with pure, unadulterated pleasure. My cum is filling her tight little pussy, coating her walls with my mark. My very existence.

"More importantly, I'm yours."

Reaching up, I place the palm of my hand on her jaw and turn her beautiful, satiated face toward me. I kiss her with every tender fiber in my soul. Mouths searching, tongues dancing, we seal this angry fuck into a promise.

"I'm yours, Octavia. Always."

Pacing the kitchen waiting for Harrison to deign me with his presence has me on edge. It's Octavia's birthday and I wanted to be over at her place already. Maverick and Finley are already out picking up the cake and dozen cupcakes we ordered for her. East is grabbing the gift from the jewelers, because the last part wasn't finished until last night.

All of it has me on edge.

I'm telling Harrison I'm done. I've tried to tell him a dozen times, but this time, I'm going to make him listen. I don't care what he threatens, or what manipulations he has tucked away, I am *done*.

I turn to pace back across the kitchen as Harrison walks down the hall toward me. Pausing, I wonder if the apocalypse is coming, because… Harrison is *smiling*.

"Good morning, son." He claps my shoulder as he strides past me and pours himself a cup of coffee.

What in the name of the pod people is this?

"You seem like you're in a good mood," I pry, moving to lean against the table as he sips on his drink.

"It's a beautiful morning, and my plans are finally coming to fruition. What's not to be happy about?"

This is weird as fuck. I run a hand through my hair, and figure if he's in a good mood, this is as good a time as any to broach the subject of Georgia. "Speaking of plans, I wanted to speak to you about Georgia."

"Yes, indeed. I set the wedding date with her father last night. Let the planning begin."

I fold my arms across my chest, mentally preparing myself for battle. "No."

"Oh?" He raises his brows at me, still smiling, and it's creepy as fuck. "You've decided you're done fighting for the Royal girl's life? If you don't care about hers, maybe I'll go after your bastard brother's? I'm sure you care for him. Which of them will it be? The girl or the brother? One of them will die should you chose to disobey me."

"Why are you so fucking twisted?" I hiss, my battle-ready walls crumbling.

He waves me off as he takes another mouthful of his coffee. "Oh, don't get so worked up, Lincoln. Your little girlfriend already went to war for you. The wedding is off. I spent last night finalizing the deal so you can scurry away with your dick fully owned by the Royal bitch."

I try to disguise my shock. "What do you mean?"

"It's good to see she's a woman of her word. The Royal girl came to me a month ago, bartering once that contract of Stone's came to light, and we reached an… agreement."

My stomach drops at the glee on his face. What the fuck did she do?

"What agreement?" I ask, my jaw clenched. Fucking Octavia, why would she hide this from us? From me?

"She bought your freedom. Yours and your friends'. As of today, you are free from the Knights. Your trust funds were released without condition on the day we made the agreement. You will benefit from everything, as you would've as a member, but you are free from us."

My stomach twists, because there's no way he'd let me go. Let us all go. What the fuck did Octavia offer him?

"What was the rest?"

His eyes sparkle with glee as he finishes his drink and places his mug down on the counter. "She offered up herself. Along with some other things of Stone's that I was after. She will be my heir apparent, and now… she's mine."

Without another word he strides past me, grinning from ear

to ear.

This doesn't make sense. She wouldn't.

Except she would.

Fucking woman is infuriating. She has no idea what the fuck she's done. Harrison doesn't stick to deals he makes unless they're entirely beneficial to him. Ever.

Rage pools in my stomach. She lied to us, kept secrets, after berating us, me, for doing that to her when she came back here.

Why wouldn't she speak to us first? We would have come up with another way.

Fuck.

I grip my hair, willing the pain to tug me back to reality, but anger rolls over me, creating a red haze over everything. Grabbing my keys, I storm from the house, going to the front gate without even really thinking.

Before I realize it, I'm standing in front of her gate, anger boiling over, when I see her appear in her front door. She waves at me and moves toward her car. The door opens and I lose sight of her as the engine starts.

That's when I feel the heat on my face, my ears ringing as I watch the flames engulf the black metal, the explosion knocking me to my knees as smoke billows into the sky. I blink, hoping, praying she wasn't in the car, or even near it, but I saw her open the door. She was right there. I tap in the code to the gate and my feet are moving before I can stop myself, but I'm stopped by a tackle from the side.

I try to fight them off, I need to get to her. I need to get to my girl. The world around me blurs in on itself, my focus solely on helping her.

"Master Saint." Smithy holds me down as I scream and struggle to get to the girl who holds my heart.

"Master Saint, you can't." His voice is firmer this time, and I turn to look at him, seeing the truth in his glassy eyes.

"Smithy, she… I…" The words just won't come out, everything good about the world has just… I can't even think it… I can't concentrate. My world is crumbling around me and I struggle to breathe. "She…"

His head hangs as he finally loosens his hold, sirens blaring in the distance. "I know, Master Saint. I know."

Octavia.

TWENTY TWO

MAVERICK

I smile at the girl in the bakery, flirting in the hopes that she moves a little faster so we can get back to our girl quicker. I wouldn't have agreed to this stupid little errand if V hadn't asked for the morning to herself. I've been wanting to go to her since midnight to wish her a happy birthday. Birthdays have always been her thing and I refuse to let this year be any different, even with the shit show we find ourselves in.

Sirens blare outside, followed by a fire truck, ambulance, and police cars flying down Main Street.

"What the fuck was that?"

Finn rolls his eyes at me as the woman behind the counter appears with our order. "I'm sure it's nothing. Come on, we need to get back. I want to see Octavia."

He pays for the cakes while I grab the boxes and we head outside to Linc's SUV. My Ducati and his Lamborghini were not suitable for the sheer amount of cake that Indi told us to order. I'm not sure how any of us are going to eat this much cake.

I lay the cakes out in the trunk and hop in the passenger seat, my knee bouncing with excitement as we head back toward Linc's place.

When we turn onto their road, the car rolls to a stop, a line of traffic halting us in place. "What the…?"

I see the smoke first and something inside me tells me to get the fuck out of the car.

"Mav?"

I ignore Finn as I bail. Panic has me in a choke hold and I start running up the road, through the traffic, not wanting to believe what I can see in front of me. The barrier around the Saint and Royal houses from the first responders aren't enough to keep me out.

Finn reaches me, and I realize he bailed too. I push through the crazed masses and find Lincoln standing with Smithy and East. The looks on their faces… I can't…

No, no, no.

"Where is she?" I ask as I run toward them. Lincoln doesn't even look my way, he's just looking through the gate to Octavia's house.

"Mav—" Finn starts, but I don't pay attention.

I move closer, looking in the direction of Linc's gaze and see the dying blaze, the burnt out car, and part of the Royal place is damaged, the smoke a light gray, but I still don't see her. My heart pounds, while my stomach twists.

"Where is she?!" My words are more of a bellow as I turn back to face them.

"Master Riley…"

I fall to my knees, my legs not able to keep me standing as something inside of me breaks.

Since Smithy moved us all away from the scene in front of the Royal house, I've been hammering on the punching bag in Lincoln's basement. My knuckles are split, my blood runs rivulets to the ground, but I feel nothing.

Nothing but rage.

She can't be gone.

I can't accept that.

Music blares through the speakers, blocking everyone out. I don't want to see any of them. They're too busy pretending they don't feel, too, looking into how this could have happened.

After Lincoln explained what happened, I left the table. Smithy is working with the morgue, or so he said when he came down to speak to me, but I wasn't in a talking mood.

I'm still not.

The only thing that is going to make this better is it not happening. Or bleeding out whoever is responsible. Slowly. Oh so slowly.

Until then, I'll make myself bleed for not being able to save her.

The music cuts out, and I turn to scream at whoever is trying to fuck with me. I find Indi standing at the bottom of the stairs. Her face is stained with tears, but I still don't let myself feel anything.

"What the fuck are you doing down here?"

"Don't start with me, Pixie."

I turn back to the bag and beat on it. I don't know who is responsible, but when I find out…

"Fuck you! You don't get to hide away and be an asshole right now."

"Indi," I growl. "I don't want to be an asshole to you right now, but asshole is all I've got, so back the fuck off."

"What is wrong with you?!" she screams at me, putting herself between me and the bag, pushing on my chest. "How can you just stand there, like she isn't gone? Like this wasn't so obviously Harrison? How are you not burning the entire fucking world down?"

She hits me, pushes me, and I let her. I deserve it. I should have protected her harder. I should have worked harder to make her leave. If she hadn't stayed, she wouldn't be…

Tears run down Indi's face as she whales on me, and I

take every hit without a word until she falls against me, sobs wracking though her. Only then do tears threaten to fall down my face.

I fight them, because I know if they fall, if I let myself feel, there won't be any coming back.

TWENTY THREE

FINLEY

It's been three days. Three days since our world was torn apart, and I've barely been able to function since then. Lincoln hasn't slept; he's been looking at every single possible lead as to who could have done this.

The list isn't that long—the Knights are our main focus, namely Harrison. After everything on Saturday... Lincoln told us about the deal she made with him. To free us. Apparently, Harrison is upholding his part of the deal even in her death. That alone is suspicious enough, but his joy at his son's devastation is sickening.

East... he's basically disappeared. He's been gone the last few weeks, so I don't know why I'm surprised, but it's also suspicious. He was the first of us to be on Team V, so why the fuck did he disappear, and why isn't he here now when we need him most? When Linc needs him most.

And Mav... well he's basically living at the fight club. I tried dragging him back here, but after Indi's visit... I'm not sure how to pull him out of the hole he's gone into. Especially when I'm in one of my own.

The body in the car was charred beyond recognition. If it hadn't been for Lincoln seeing her approach and unlock the car, I'd question if it was even her. But she has no reason to disappear. No reason to leave us behind. I get that she was keeping secrets, keeping her arrangement with Harrison from us, but I understand that.

Something like this... I just can't see her hiding from us.

Nothing about this makes sense. Harrison isn't really the blow-them-up kind of guy. He's usually more subtle, so as much as Lincoln is convinced that his father is behind this, I can't stop thinking about the guy who came to visit her while Evan had her held hostage.

Which is exactly why I've started trawling through Evan's past. My father didn't know how Evan came to be a Knight, and none of us know either. Just that he was one. My problem is that Evan doesn't seem to have existed until six months before the tour.

I'm not sure how no one noticed this before. I haven't looked into Evan before now, and admittedly without paying a lot of attention, it's not something you'd find, but still… the Knights are more thorough than that.

Unless the Knights gave him the new identity.

But that doesn't make sense either, and losing myself down this rabbit hole is exactly how I'm going to distract myself from the endless pit of despair that is calling my name.

I finish hacking into the local P.D. system and find the file on Octavia's case. There isn't much to go on other than a pipe bomb, triggered by a suspected pressure plate. But that doesn't line up with what Lincoln said… he said the engine started and then it blew. That suggests a trigger rather than pressure, unless it went off as she sat down.

I need to look at the car.

I slam my laptop closed and grab my keys. I'm going to find out what the fuck is going on. Between Evan's mysterious past, and East just being gone… nothing is adding up.

Grabbing my jacket, I head downstairs. The sound of bass from the basement means Maverick is likely back down there, beating himself up. I can't remember a time when a distance like this existed among us all.

"Where are you going?" I turn at Linc's words and find him leaning against the wall, hands in his pockets, looking a fucking mess. He's coming apart at the seams, and it's showing.

"I'm going to look at Octavia's car."

"What's the point? We know how she died. You should be helping me look at Harrison."

I take a deep breath, trying not to let his snappy bullshit get to me, but I am walking the end of my rope. "I'm sure you've got it covered, so I'm following my own suspicions."

"This is bullshit. Why do none of you give a fuck what happened to her? East is gone, Mav is out beating the fuck out of anything that moves rather than helping, and you're not even looking in the right direction."

"Fuck you, Linc," I snap. "Just because you think you're looking at the right thing, doesn't mean you are. Mav is coping in his own way. As for East, I don't have a clue what's going on with him, but he's probably working through his grief in his own way, too. Just like you are."

"Of course you'd stick up for him," he scoffs, rolling his eyes. "Just run along on your little scavenger hunt while I do the real work. Like always."

I clench my fist around my keys, the pain of the metal digging into me grounding me and stopping me from lashing out at him. I watch him deflate in front of me, not what I expected. I thought he'd fight back, get angry, something Linc like, but he just crumbles before my eyes, and that hurts almost as much as the wound of losing Octavia. He's hurting, we're all fucking hurting, so I swallow the words on the tip of my tongue that want him to fight back, to show him that there is more than anger, and instead I turn on my heel and leave the house.

I've got shit to do, and if I want to not fall into the darkness inside of myself, especially now I'm free, I need to find out the truth. Otherwise, everything Octavia arranged for us will be for nothing. I refuse to let her sacrifice mean nothing.

TWENTY FOUR

EAST

I never thought I'd regret my choices of the last two weeks…
but here I am, faced with the reality of where those decisions
have led.

Octavia is gone. It doesn't matter that it's been four days,
I'm still in shock. I'm in denial.

She can't be dead.

I can't have given up that last bit of time I should've been
with her willingly.

If only I'd made a different decision, maybe she'd still be
here.

I haven't been back to the Saint house since Saturday
morning. I can't be there. Not when every nook and cranny

of that place reminds me of her. Not when I can look out my window and see on to her property.

See the scorch marks on the ground.

I just can't.

The problem is, I'm letting them down—letting *her* down—by hiding away. I've spent most of the last few weeks here at Chase's, so it made sense that I'd escape here. Though I've barely left the room I've been staying in since I got back Saturday morning.

I can't get the sight of that charred SUV out of my mind.

I hit replay on the playlist she shared with me a few weeks ago, yet again. Wallowing in the thing she held closest is about all I've managed to do for four days. It's pathetic, yet I can't seem to make myself do anything else.

I should be there for Linc, for Mav, for Finn. I've always been the chill one… but I can't find it in myself to do much of anything.

A knock at the door has me lifting my head off of the pillow as Chase's face appears through the gap. "Morning, I'm getting ready to head down to the police station. I wondered if you wanted to come with me? I'm going to go and see Smithy too. Offer my condolences."

"I don't know if I can." God I'm such a woe is me asshole.

Chase sighs and enters the room fully. "I haven't been around for much of your life, Easton, but I get the feeling that you've never been one to run from your problems. Do you think

Octavia would want you to start now?"

"Octavia is dead." My voice sounds as hollow as I've been trying to feel.

"She is, but that doesn't mean that you died too. You need to keep living. Your brother, your friends, they all need you. I'm doing everything I can to ensure that her case is investigated properly, but I can't do that *and* worry that I'm going to find you dead when I come home. I'm not trying to be an insensitive dick, and I'm obviously not great at this parenting thing, but you need to be around the people who are hurting just as much as you are."

"Are you kicking me out?"

"Never," he sighs, running a hand down his face. "You always have a place here. I meant it when I said that, just like I meant it when I said I wouldn't officially claim you so you'd never be subject to the Knights' bullshit, but you need your brother, your friends. Hell, maybe even Smithy. These are the people who have always been there for you when you've fallen down. They'll be there for you now too, and they'll need you. Losing someone is never easy, but being around others who are grieving them as well can help."

I consider what he's saying. I'm not sure there's any way I can feel worse or any more guilty. Maybe being around the others, talking about her, will be good for me. For them.

Letting out a deep sigh, I sit up. "Fine, I'll just pull on some clothes and I'll head over to see them."

He smiles tightly, nodding once. "Okay, good. I'll check in with you later."

"Thank you," I say quietly and he strides across the room, putting a hand on my shoulder.

"Always, Easton. I missed enough, I don't intend on not being there for you ever again." He turns and leaves me alone with the sounds of *Lately* by Future Palace playing on my phone from her playlist.

He's right. She wouldn't want this. She dealt with all of the loss in her life like a fucking warrior. I'm not about to dishonor her by doing anything less.

I make my way home the long way round, purely so I don't have to pass her gate to get to ours. Pain rips through me as I enter the driveway, knowing that she should be just next door, but that she won't be there ever again.

Taking a few deep breaths, I pull myself together before shutting off the car and heading inside. It's quiet. Creepily so.

"Hello? Anyone here?" The deafening silence is all that greets me. It doesn't seem like even Mrs. Potts is here. Well this is a shit pile.

I head upstairs and change into sweats and a muscle top before going down to the basement, which is where I find Lincoln running on a treadmill, headphones in, like he's running from all of the demons that chase him.

He glares at me when he sees me, sneering as I approach. "So the prodigal son returns. Good of you to finally show your face."

"Fuck off, Linc. I've been dealing with all of this too."

He scoffs as he slams his hand down on the screen of the treadmill, bringing it to a stop. "Dealing? What the fuck have you ever dealt with in your life? You've never been the one with the weight of the world put on you. You got to fuck around with zero responsibilities, and the first time something happens that we actually need you for, you fucking disappear. You've barely been around for weeks, even before this. We all noticed. *She* noticed. So don't come back here like you're here to save the day. You're not the white knight here, brother."

Apparently he's hurting more than I could've imagined. That or he really has always been this much of a fucking asshole.

"Don't get all holier than thou, *brother,*" I sneer. "You're the one that was an asshole to her when she arrived. You tried to make her leave. You lost that time with her. A few weeks is nothing compared to that."

He charges at me, knocking me to the ground and winding me before bringing his fist down on my cheek. I fight back, and while I might not have the training he does, I'm not exactly a green eyed wonder.

I manage to pin him and get in a few shots of my own before he bests me once more. He rains down blows on my face and chest, before I hear shouts and he's ripped off of me.

"What the fuck is wrong with you two?" Finley roars as he holds Lincoln back. He struggles against his blond haired friend, but Finley has more bulk than Lincoln and holds him with relative ease as I try to suck in a breath.

"She's gone." Linc's voice is so quiet I almost miss it before his knees give way and he crumples to the ground. He looks up at me with glassy eyes, and the devastation reflecting back at me breaks another part of me. "She's really fucking gone."

He chokes on a sob as his pain rips through me worse than any of the blows he just landed. I don't think I've ever heard him so broken. So small. He's always been strong, stronger than any of us. I know how much he loved Octavia, but I'm not sure he's going to come back from losing her.

Finn drops down beside him, like they're propping each other up, and I watch my little brother break beside his best friend who breaks right along with him. Sobs wrack Linc's body, and something inside of me breaks with them.

I don't think I've ever seen Lincoln cry.

Groaning, I pull myself up and move to sit on his other side, supporting him in the only way I know he'll let me right now, and let my own tears spill down my cheeks.

She's really gone, and there's nothing any of us can do about it.

TWENTY FIVE

LINCOLN

After an emotional day yesterday, I called it quits on even attempting to keep up the pretense that I'm okay. I find myself sitting alone at the table in a baggy t-shirt and sweats. It's not that I've stopped giving a fuck, it's just that I've run into wall after wall trying to figure out what the fuck happened to Octavia, and there are only so many walls I can crash into before I admit that I need some help. That I admit I'm not coping and accept that she isn't coming back.

We got a message from Smithy last night to tell us that her funeral will be held in two days. Just something small. She didn't have many people left, so we wanted it to be the people she would've wanted there.

Acceptance seems like all I have left.

Except for revenge.

I'm still convinced it was Harrison. He made too many threats. Even that morning when he told me the deal he'd made with her, he was too fucking happy about it. I might not know everything, but I know Harrison. I know there is no way he'd be happy about being cornered into a deal with her. Releasing the three of us.

I just wish I knew what she gave him. Maybe then this would make more sense. It might give me a lead on what happened to her.

I'm not going to give up. Even if it takes my entire life, I will find out the truth.

I've already called in a dozen favors, having the Range and the remains of the device used for the explosion moved to a federal facility to have it looked over privately. My, well, I wouldn't call him a friend... but my contact there owes me a few times over, so he's looking over it himself.

The problem with fire that burns that hot is that it destroys everything in its path. There isn't much to go on, so it's more about looking at the components of the explosive, how it was built, to try and get a lead.

I've already been through all of the security feeds from here and Octavia's place, but they were scrubbed remotely. I have another contact trying to see if they can recover anything, but I've still heard jack shit.

Antsy isn't a good look on me, but neither is helpless.

I've been speaking to Artemis. After hearing about the explosion, she reached out to offer her condolences, told me about her training with Octavia, and offered her help. She knows people in some fucking seriously low places, so she's put out feelers too, to see if we can find if a contract was put out. If so, who took it up, and who the fuck hired them.

The problem with grief is that I know I'm missing something, but my brain is so fucking tripped up that I can't work out what it is. It doesn't help that I'm not sleeping. Every time I close my eyes, I see her smile before she got in that car. Then I feel the heat on my face again. In my nightmares I hear her screams, but I'm sure the only screams I heard that day were my own.

A buzz on the intercom has me glancing at my phone. Who the fuck could be here now?

"Hello?" I say into my phone, speaking to whoever is at the gate.

"Mr. Saint? This is Special Agent Carter. Can we come in?" I flick the app over to video and see the badge of the guy who's speaking, seeing another three agents with him.

"What is this about?"

"I'd rather discuss it once we're inside." I hit the button to open the gates and drop a message in the group chat for the guys to get their asses down here.

They all clamber down the stairs as I move to the front door.

"Feds are here," I say, their faces ranging from suspicion to surprise.

"At six in the morning? What the fuck?" Mav rubs at his eyes. This isn't exactly his favorite time of day.

"I guess we're about to find out," I say as a knock sounds on the door.

I step forward and open it, finding the four of them standing on the steps. "Mr. Saint?"

"Yes," I answer with a nod, wishing like fuck I was dressed like I was going to court instead of the gym. Something about being dressed like this makes me feel like I'm going in without my armor.

"We're looking for your father, is he home?" the agent asks as he glances over my shoulder and sees the others.

"I don't think he's left for the day yet," I tell them, still suspicious as fuck.

Agent Carter pushes past me, and him plus two of the others spread out throughout the house. "What the fuck is going on?"

The last agent stands at the door. "If the four of you will step outside. We have a warrant for Harrison Saint's arrest, and to search this property."

I look at him, slack jawed, seeing the other agents waiting at the gate. What the fuck is going on?

I take the warrant from the agent, scanning over it, when Finn curses behind me. He hands me his phone, open on his news app.

"Documents were leaked late last night regarding the

involvement of several prominent members of our community, involved in everything from fraud and money laundering to human and drug trafficking."

Oh shit.

A picture of my father, Edward, Charles, and a few of the other Knights flashes on the screen as the guys watch over my shoulder.

We move outside at the insistence of the agent as Harrison is dragged down the stairs, half dressed, handcuffed, and shouting blue fucking murder.

They pull him past us as he struggles against them, and for the first time in five days, a smile tugs at the edges of my lips.

Maybe this time, the king will actually fall.

After the arrests this morning and the news reports all day, an emergency Conclave meeting was called by Chase. Apparently the fact that we've been released from the Knights skipped the memo, so we've been summoned. Chase even called in East, since he's linked to all of the stuff that's going down.

We sit around the board room, everyone on edge as we wait for Chase to reappear. He's the most senior Knight left on the Conclave currently, which is kind of hilarious, but it is what it is.

"Do you have any idea what this is about?" Artemis hisses at me from across the table.

I shrug and pull down the sleeves of my shirt. "Considering everything else that happened today? We're probably about to get read the riot act and then be told to keep our mouths shut until we're told otherwise."

"This is such bullshit. How did your dad even let that sort of information leak out into the world?"

"Fucked if I know, maybe he really pissed someone off."

She eyes me, watching me like she's trying to see inside of me. "Did you do this?"

"Me? No, though I wish I had. You should've seen his face this morning."

She smirks at me, before her eyes turn sad. "You still think he's behind what happened to our favorite Royal?"

The whole room sucks in a breath at her question, and I nod once. "I do. And if he did, well he already had this coming, but he can go to hell for all I care. He made his bed."

She nods as the door opens and Chase strides into the room, moving toward his normal seat rather than taking the one my father usually occupies. "Thank you all for coming. This emergency meeting was called by the Archon, who will be here momentarily."

The room is blanketed in a heavy silence as I look at the others wide-eyed. Artemis sits a little taller, while her father looks like he's about to shit his pants.

"Keep your mouths shut, and do not speak unless spoken to, do you understand?" His gaze bounces between us all as we agree.

"Why is the Archon here?" I ask him, and the corners of his lips tilt up.

"You'll see. He won't be long."

We sit in a tense silence, voices approaching slowly up the hall. This is fucking ridiculous. I know we're supposed to be afraid of the Archon, he's the head of the entire fucking society, but still. Recent events have me feeling a little reckless. Maybe if I push his buttons, he'll punish Harrison some more.

I watch the clock, the second hand seeming to take way too long to tick over, but the voices outside get louder, though they're muffled by the closed door. After a few more seconds, the voices go quiet.

The door opens, and East pales as an older man enters the room. "Matthew?"

The man glances at my brother and nods, but the person who follows behind him is the one who makes me sit a little straighter.

"You have got to be fucking kidding me?" Anger and relief war inside of me. How is this possible? Did he betray her? Did she know all along?

Is he the reason that she's dead?

Smithy looks sadly at me before clearing his face to the cold mask all of us know how to wear. He walks to the front of the room, his presence commanding attention in a way I've never seen him do before and sits in Harrison's usual seat.

"Thank you all for coming tonight. I called this meeting because of recent events that I know you are all aware of. I'm sure my presence is something of a shock to some of you, but all of that will be explained in due course."

What the fuck is happening right now?

Smithy is the Archon?

What the fuck?

TWENTY SIX

STONE

I have been pacing up and down this office so much the carpet is starting to wear. I have done a lot of things in my life that I'd take back if I could, but one thing I will never regret is keeping my daughter safe. I might not be a good man, but I've made damn sure that I'm a good dad.

Even after Emily left and I lost my shit for a bit, I tried to be there for her as much as I could stand. Lying to my little girl isn't something I wanted to do, but I learned a long time ago that sometimes lying is the kinder path.

One day, I'll have to tell her the truth, but for now, she's too young. She's lost too much. This new opportunity I've been handed is the perfect excuse to get me away from here, from the legacy my great-great grandfather passed down to us ...

The Knights are not what they once were. Once they were loyal, working to help strengthen the power of each family. Keep our people safe.

But now? Now it has become something dark and twisted. Something so far from what it was intended to be, but once you're in, there's almost no way out other than death.

I refuse to accept that fate for her. My Octavia. She has been the ray of light in my life since the minute she came screaming into the world. There isn't anything I won't do to protect her. Even sacrificing her mother.

The deal I agreed to with Harrison was such fucking shit, but it's my only way out. I know the only reason he was willing to let me go is because he'll take over my seat as Regent.

If only it were so simple as filling the power vacuum. Making a deal with Harrison Saint is like making a deal with the devil himself. Especially when Fiona let him believe that she was fucking me instead of my pool guy. Nothing like that to add to the tension between us and make saving my daughter a little harder.

Each time I try to think of another way around this, stopping her initiation without giving up my seat, I see the impossibility. I don't want the seat—I don't want Harrison in it either—but my wants versus Octavia's needs are not an even match.

"Master Stone, there you are." I look up and find Smithy smiling at me. "Still debating if this is the right idea?"

I shake my head, running a hand through my hair. "I know it's the right decision, I just wish there was someone else."

"You and I both know that Harrison is the only one stupid enough to make the deal you want. He won't see past what it will do for him."

I drop onto the couch in my home office and he sits opposite me in the leather chair. "I know. I just wish I could save the boys too. We both know that taking her from them..."

"They will survive. I will make sure of it. They will suffer, the way we all have, but I cannot save them the same way I can save our Octavia. Their parents do not see the darkness that has taken over the organization, or if they do, they thrive in it. Between you and I, we will find a way to restore the Knights back to what they once were."

"You really think this will work?" This one part of our plan has plagued me since we came up with the idea of how to get what we both want with one action. What if I can't find what we need? What if it hurts him? Hurts Octavia?

None of it will be worth it if it hurts her. That's the one thing we agreed on.

"I do," he says, seeming far more confident than I feel right now. "I will keep residence at the house, ensure that you are kept apprised of everything that happens here, while looking out for the boys as much as I can. If I could stop the initiation, you know I would. Those boys already struggle. Master Lincoln the least, but the Knight boy... it's impossible not to see that he is

already haunted. We're not doing this just for us, we're doing it for all of them. The Knights cannot continue the way they have been. The other sects aren't exactly sunshine and roses, but this sect... under your father, too much changed. I know it wasn't all on him, but after everything... we need to fix what was broken."

I drop my head into my hands, trying not to think too much about my father and his bullshit. "Is it even possible? I know that you're the Archon. Is there no way that you can just stop all of this?"

"The Knights have evolved past that. It's something of a hydra. Even if everyone fears the supposed mythical person at the top of the ladder, they only do so because of lies and stories. I am but one man."

"So am I."

"But together, we can do this, Master Stone. I know that how we came to be aware of each other was not exactly the best start to a relationship, but your father, God rest his soul... well, he was a complex man beneath it all. With his illness—"

"His illness didn't make him a monster to me. He was that long before. And Emily's parents are going to be a fucking nightmare about me taking Octavia away from here. They've done nothing but argue with me since Emily left. They still blame me for her disappearance. They can never find out the truth."

Smithy lets out a sigh, giving me a sad smile. "Your father loved you, even if he struggled to show it. He was never the type to show emotion easily. Look at how he was with your mother before she passed."

My father was a shit to me, but he was worse to my mom. I think the only person he ever truly loved was the man sitting in front of me. "He showed you."

"Yes, but only in private, and hidden beneath enough secrets to break the world. And once his illness claimed him... well, I don't need to tell you about that."

No he doesn't. My father was a monster long before his illness, but with the loss of his mind, he became even worse. I refuse to become him or be the kind of father he was.

"This has to work," I say, swallowing my resolve. "For her. This cannot be her future. I won't allow it."

His smile grows and he nods. "Then let's get to work, Master Stone, because this deal... this is just the beginning."

TWENTY SEVEN

OCTAVIA

SIX DAYS AGO

I am exhausted. Between school, training, finding everything that Harrison wanted, and finally handing it over, I am fucked. The thought that in less than twenty four hours, I can tell the guys everything that has happened… that alone has me all kinds of giddy, but I know I still need to get through tonight without losing my shit over Lincoln having his final date with Georgia.

I can deal with just one more. Because then he is mine. They all are. As long as they don't hate me for signing myself over to the Knights. It's not forever, but I'm aware that what the Knights can make you do are things that will haunt you.

Panda was living proof of that. The things he did, that he witnessed, were enough to push him over the edge.

I'm aware that this probably wasn't my brightest idea, but I will not regret sacrificing for them. I know what I'm getting myself into. They had no choice. Now they do.

First, I just need to last until Saturday without spilling my guts.

I already told the guys they couldn't stay tonight, because I don't know how to keep seeing them and not tell them, so I told them I wanted tonight with Smithy, and first thing tomorrow I'm going to swing by and see Indi real quick before I lose myself in the four of them for the whole weekend.

A knock at the door disturbs me from just staring at the ceiling counting down the minutes until I know Lincoln leaves to be with her. I sit up and find Smithy already striding toward the door.

Weird. I didn't hear the buzzer.

"Smithy, good, you're here too." I blink at the sound of Luc's voice, turning to find him and Smithy heading toward me. "Octavia. We need to talk."

I sit up straight as he strides around the couch to stand in front of the TV, while Smithy stands to my side. "That sounds terrifying. What's wrong?"

"My fucking brother," he growls. "He contacted me tonight with a new task."

"For me?"

He grinds his teeth together. I don't know what Harrison did, but I know that Luc is pissed. "Not exactly." He looks over to Smithy before glancing back to me. "I assume he knows everything?"

"He does," I say with a nod. "Someone that would give a fuck had to know in case I disappeared. My deal only stated the guys couldn't know."

Luc nods, running a hand through his hair, tugging on the strands. "Fuck, this is so fucked."

"Why don't you sit? I'll get us all a drink and you can explain what exactly Harrison has done now."

Worry churns in my stomach while Luc paces in front of me. I don't think I've ever seen him so off-kilter. He's done a lot of things, so whatever Harrison has asked him to do must be fucking crazy to have him react like this.

"Should I be worried?" I ask as Smithy appears with a bottle of whiskey and two glasses, plus a steaming mug of coffee. He hands me the coffee and pours two fingers for Luc, who shoots the drink back in one go.

"Yes." Luc finally answers my question, and I put my mug of coffee on the table. "He wants me to kill you."

"I'm sorry, he what now?" I blink in shock up at Luc, trying to process what the fuck he just said.

"He wants me to kill you."

Smithy stands, hand gripping his whiskey glass so tight it looks like it might shatter. "Luc, sit down. There are some things we need to discuss."

"Smi—"

"Sit down, Lucas." My eyes go wide at Smithy's tone. It's like he became an entirely different person before my eyes. Luc shifts quickly to sit in the leather chair to my left while we wait for Smithy to speak. "There are some things that you need to know. Both of you. Some of this is going to seem outrageous, some of it ridiculous, but know, Miss Octavia, that I never wanted anything but your happiness. Some secrets had to be kept for everyone's safety, including my own."

I open my mouth to speak, but Smithy shakes his head, so I keep my comments to myself. Probably not helpful right now since I'm just low-key freaking out about the whole 'Harrison wants me dead' thing. It's not that surprising, but fuck me, it's different knowing it's a reality. I try to turn my focus back on Smithy because he looks deadly fucking serious.

"Something I learned very early on in life, one of the first things my father taught me... there are two parts of this world: one that most people don't see—where those with power revel— and they will do anything, anything to keep it. The other part lives in an ignorant kind of bliss. Walking through their lives without even a hint of the darkness that lurks around them. But that darkness..." He pauses, turning to face me again. "It is why who I am has always been guarded."

"You're talking in riddles, old man," Luc grumbles, and Smithy shoots him a glare.

"How's this for a riddle? I am the Archon."

Luc's eyes go wide, and I rack my mind for why that sounds familiar to me. "Oh shit, wait—"

"Yes, Miss Octavia. I am the one who arranged the contract with your father for your freedom."

Luc stands, moving behind the chair, before bracing himself on it. "If you're the Archon, how the fuck are you here as a house manager?"

"That is a long story." Smithy sighs, motioning for Luc to take a seat as he sits in the leather chair to my right. I haven't said much yet, because holy shit, this is a lot to process. First, Harrison wants me dead, and second, Smithy is the head of the Knights.

Mind blown doesn't quite cover how I feel right now.

"Well, we have time, considering we need to come up with a way to save not just Octavia's life, but mine and Alex's too. If Harrison finds out I'm here, or if she doesn't die tomorrow morning, we're fucked."

I blow out a deep breath and lean forward. Holy shit this is a lot. "He wants me to die tomorrow? He really never intended on keeping his part in the deal, did he?"

"We will find an answer to all of this, Miss Octavia. But first, let me tell you about how I ended up here, and how I worked with your father. Then I think we should call Mr. Kensington."

Right. Bentley. He has my copy of the documents I gave to Harrison.

"Okay," I say with a nod, trying to process, knowing that there's still so much more to come.

Smithy leans forward and pats my knee. "Well, I guess I should start with how I ended up working for your family. That all started with your grandfather… that man was the love of my life."

Happy freaking birthday to me…

Today is the day I die. I've barely slept, even after I was up until the fucking ass crack of dawn with Smithy, Luc, and Bentley, I couldn't sleep once I finally crawled into bed.

Is this really my life now? I survived so much for this to be the way everything ends? We came up with a plan, but I'm not sure it will work. It's not that I don't trust Luc, I mean, he didn't have to come here. He put a lot at risk by coming here and speaking to us, but there are so many things that could go wrong.

The only upside to last night was that I was definitely distracted from Lincoln's date with Georgia and the fact that Dad won't be here for my birthday. Can't say Indi's sunshine disposition isn't rubbing off on me if I can find an upside to someone trying to kill me.

Again.

I shower once my alarm goes off, preparing for my day,

wherever it's going to lead me. I take extra time doing my hair and makeup, snapping a picture and sending it to the group chat I have with the guys with the caption, Happy Birthday to Me.

If I'm going to die, at least they got to see me smile.

I pull on a pair of leggings and a hoodie, because birthdays are for comfort, before heading downstairs. There's no sign of Luc, but Bentley is sitting at the kitchen counter, sipping on a mug of coffee, while Smithy stands at the stove. He turns to face me with a tight smile before striding toward me and wrapping me up in a hug. "Happy Birthday, Miss Octavia."

I hug him back so tight that my arms almost ache. It was definitely a shock hearing his truths last night, but I've learned recently that secrets are the currency of Knights. I'm past holding it against anyone. Especially with the secrets I hold myself.

"Are you ready for today?" Bentley asks as Smithy releases me and pushes me onto a stool at the counter opposite him.

"Not even a little." I grimace. "But I guess I better just put on my big girl pants right?"

"Indeed," he says, the corners of his lips tilting up. "Trust me, Miss Royal, this isn't my first rodeo. We will get out of here in one piece as long as you follow my instruction."

I let out another deep breath, shaking my arms out. "Okay, so run me through it once more. You know, so I don't actually end up dead by accident."

He smiles at me while Smithy scoffs at the stove. "I can do that. Let's get some caffeine in you so you're alert. Even one misstep could mess with everything. I need you to stay focused."

I nod, the seriousness of all of this very much apparent.

"I mean it, Miss Royal. It will only take one distraction on your part for this all to go to hell."

TWENTY EIGHT

LINCOLN

James Smith is the Archon.

Harrison and Charles are in jail.

Octavia is dead.

My world has officially blown the fuck up, and I'm not sure I give a fuck anymore. About anything. The only upside to any of this is that my trust fund is free and clear from Harrison's bullshit. So I don't *have* to care. I can get the hell away from here and never look back.

There isn't much of anything here for me anymore. The guys are all hurting just as bad as I am, and they're the only reason I'd stay. Pretty sure they'd be more than willing to leave. If she was still here, I'd probably be pissed beyond recognition about the fact that she sacrificed her freedom for ours, but she's not. So I just have to swallow that anger.

Our freedom cost her life, and that's something we'll have to carry for the rest of our lives, but I won't waste what she gave me. No matter how much I want to climb into a hole and never resurface.

I wait in the lobby of the Knights' meeting place as per Smithy's request before the end of the meeting. Not sure why he wants to see me on my own, but despite my freedom, I know how much he meant to her, so I stay.

After much persuasion, Finn, Mav, and East went home. We each have our own devices for coping right now, focusing on anything that isn't Octavia being gone is mine.

I put my headphones in while I wait for them and torture myself some more with the playlist she made for me, putting on *As You Leave* by Canaan Cox. The lyrics rip me apart, shredding me into little pieces, but the hurt is better than the numb feeling that's been threatening to swallow me whole.

Smithy has placed Matthew as temporary Regent while he sorts out the mess that is happening around us. He's made it very apparent that he intends on changing things up, including freeing anyone that wants out. I'm glad that he's making changes, apparently bringing the Knights back to what the Knights were meant to be, but I'm not foolish enough to think everything is going to change.

Change like this takes time.

It took time to corrupt the Knights, bringing them back from the pits of hell isn't going to be any quicker. If anything, it's going to take longer.

I've been trying to focus on all of this, and who killed Octavia, to try and stave off the reality that she isn't coming back. I'm not ready to accept it yet.

I'm not sure I ever will be. They say time heals everything, but whoever the fuck they are never had Octavia Royal in their life.

Movement brings me back to reality, and I tug out my AirPods, putting them away as Smithy approaches. He motions for me to follow him into the office Harrison used to keep and turns, not waiting for me. I let loose a deep breath and stand, following him without a word.

Closing the door behind me, I take a seat on the opposite side of the desk, and wait for him to speak.

"This must be quite a shock for you, Master Lincoln." I look up at him, trying to reconcile the man I thought I knew with the myth I've always heard about. Smithy being the Archon wasn't something I ever expected, but I have questions. So many fucking questions.

"Did you orchestrate Octavia's kidnapping?" He leans back in the chair, watching me closely.

"Not what I expected your first question to be."

"Your name was on the trail for who paid Dranas. We figured it was a set up, because you would never hurt her. But it seems like maybe we didn't know you after all."

He takes a deep breath, fiddling with the cufflinks on his shirt before answering me. "Yes, I was aware of it. Evan is… was, Matthew's son. We didn't realize just how unhinged he'd become. He did not follow the plan we had set out. Once we found him, Matthew went in to ensure she was okay. Once we knew what had happened, I was working on an extraction, but then you found her instead."

Anger flares in me at his confession, even if I had suspected once I saw him tonight. Evan being Matthew's son barely registers on my radar because of the surprises being thrown around tonight. "East nearly died."

"I'm aware. I ensured he had the best possible care once I was made aware. As I said, Evan went off script. No one was meant to get hurt. Not your brother, and certainly not Miss Octavia."

"Are you the reason she is dead?"

He shakes his head, resting his chin on steepled fingers. "No, that bombing lies at Harrison's feet. It's why I have pulled any and all support from him, and if I discover anyone helping him… well, I am the Archon after all." His smile is darker than I've ever seen, but despite everything, I know he loved Octavia like a daughter.

"Good."

I wait for him to continue, knowing that he didn't pull me in here just to talk about Evan and my father.

"As I said in the meeting before, I am going to honor the deal Octavia made. You boys are free of any binds that have been placed on you. I am just sorry I couldn't prevent everything you have been through up to this point." He pauses, as if waiting for a response, but I don't have one for him. "I have made the arrangements for the funeral, it will take place in two days. If there is anything any of you boys need, please, just ask. I know you didn't know who I truly was, but I still care for you all very much."

I try to swallow around the lump in my throat at the thought of her funeral. I can't cope with all of this. Smithy was always the warm father figure, even if we didn't see him often. He always made cake for our birthdays, helped us bandage ourselves up, or just allowed us to stay at the Royal place if we needed to escape. Reconciling that version of him with this one is just... it's fucking hard.

"Thank you," I croak as I stand. "Was there anything else?"

He pauses as he examines me, and I know he can see how raw I am. I hurt too much to hide it. "No, nothing. You can go."

He smiles sadly as I turn to leave, one thought piercing my mind as I do. Turning back to him as I open the door, I smile cruelly. "I want my father dead."

Finding out that Harrison truly is responsible for Octavia's death has lit a fire in me that burns so hot that I should probably be worried that I'll emerge from the ashes a different person, but losing her has already changed me irrevocably.

"I still can't believe Smithy is the Archon," Finn says, rubbing at his temples. The four of us are sitting around my kitchen table, talking through everything we found out last night. "And somehow, I'm less surprised that Harrison is behind everything else."

Maverick snorts, shaking his head, while East sits clenching his fists.

"I knew it was him, I just couldn't find out the details." I take a drink from my bottle of water, my skin feeling too fucking tight. I need to punch something or make someone bleed.

I'm turning into fucking Maverick.

"I want him dead. I told Smithy as much, and he didn't dissuade me. Just told me to speak to Luc," I tell them, having already filled them in on the rest of the conversation I had last night.

"That's weird... why would you speak to Luc?" East asks, looking as confused as I feel about that little bit.

"I'm guessing he has contacts that can get the job done. It's not like there's any love lost between the two of them." I shrug, leaning back in my chair. "I asked him to come over later anyway."

I push the chair back and stand, needing to get out some of this tightness in my chest. "I'm heading to the basement. I've got someone watching Harrison's movements, but he's not the guy to end him. Right now, I just need to not think."

They all stand up and follow me down into the basement. Apparently I'm not the only one who needed to not think.

I crank up the speakers, *Hell and Back* by Self Deception blares through as I make my way to the treadmill. East heads straight for the free weights while Finn and Mav move to the mats in the middle of the room to spar.

I run until sweat streams down my spine in thick rivulets, trying not to think about how I won't be doing my morning runs with Octavia anymore. I push myself so far past when I should stop that by the time I get off the machine, my legs are shaking.

"I figured if I followed the music, I'd find you boys." Looking up, I find Luc approaching me. "You asked me to come over, how are you holding up, kid?"

He wraps me in a hug and I lean on him for a minute. His hugs make me remember that I'm only eighteen and my life shouldn't be this fucking complicated and broken. I let myself take solace just for a moment before I break the hug. The music shuts off and the others join us, each of them saying hello before I move on to why I asked him to head over.

"I figure you've heard the news about Smithy?" A trace of something shadows his eyes before it disappears again.

"Yeah, the Knights might be a secret organization, but fuck me do these people gossip worse than a bunch of women in the salon."

"Yeah, though I'm sure Smithy will put a stop to that soon enough. Anyway, I met with him last night, and he told me to get in touch with you about how to deal with Harrison." A bolt of hatred spears me just thinking of my sperm donor and everything he's done to fuck with my life.

"What do you mean, deal with him?" He eyes me closely, but I know he already knows.

"I mean, he killed Octavia. I want him dead. I wanted him dead before and there wasn't anything I could do about it. With everything that's happened, now there is. I'd rather do it myself, but Smithy seemed to think that was a bad idea."

I'm still not sure why he was so opposed to it. Even if I got caught, it's not really a problem anymore. Not for me anyway.

"And he told you to call me?" Luc asks and I nod, even when he frowns.

"I guess he figured you'd know a way to get it done without us getting caught. I have someone watching him already, I just don't have anyone I trust to do the job. But I have money."

His frown deepens, but I push past him and head back upstairs. Everyone follows, just like they always have. It's how I know Luc will get this done. It's why I know that the others might not agree, but they won't stop me.

I grab another bottle of water from the fridge and lean against the counter as they make their way into the room. Looking at Luc, I see when he notices my resolve. He might not want to help me, but that doesn't mean I won't get it done. I have resources, so even if I don't know someone in prison, it doesn't mean I won't find someone. The Knights deal with enough people that I'll find someone. Hell, Ryker probably knows someone, and considering his issues with Harrison, I know he won't say no. Even if he did, all it would take is a word to Indi about Harrison being responsible and he'd be on board. I should've just gone to them first. Luc is family, but that's probably a reason not to involve him this time.

"You're sure about this?" Luc asks, and I nod.

"I am, and if you don't want to help, it's fine. I just came up with another option."

He shakes his head, scrubbing a hand down his face. "No way, kid. Your dad has been an ass my entire life, I'm not giving that kill to anyone else. It might just take a minute."

I nod before finishing the rest of the bottle. "Just make sure it doesn't take too long."

My phone buzzes in my pocket, and I grind my teeth when I see the message. "It'll be easier now anyway."

"What do you mean?" Finn asks from across the room.

I look up at them all, trying to tamper down my rage. "I mean, Harrison apparently had a federal judge in his pocket because he just made bail."

TWENTY NINE

MAVERICK

I can't believe this day is here. I've spent the last week in denial, trying to break everything around me, bleeding people out, fighting at the club every night, but nothing has made the hole in my chest feel any smaller.

I'm at the point where I'm so broken, I don't even want to break anything anymore. I just want to fall into the abyss over the edge of the cliff where I've been living since I saw the smoke rising into the sky on the day she was taken from us.

Today feels like nothing more than going through the motions. I'm not ready to say goodbye to her. I'd rather join her than let her go. I'm only going to the funeral because I know that the others won't understand.

They've never understood the knife edge I've lived on. She was my safety net, the light in the never-ending darkness. My dad made me a monster, but she loved the monster inside of me. She liked to play with it, and I loved her so fucking much for it. She was the only place I've ever called home, and now that's gone.

I've spent a week trying to break everything else, just to try and feel *something*. Anything.

It didn't work.

I'm not sure it ever will again.

I step out of the shower, my dark hair dripping wet, the purple rings under my eyes an obvious sign that I've barely slept since that day. Every time I sleep, I dream of her, and waking without her hurts too fucking much to keep torturing myself like that.

I towel off, pulling on the black shirt and trousers that Mrs. Potts laid out for me. She's officially tried to take over as our live-in-mom since we all moved in here, and while she's been good about giving us all space this week, she's been hovering around the edges of existence, trying to make sure that we don't lose ourselves to the anger we all feel.

The only one dealing with our loss in a somewhat normal way is East, I think. But then again, he was always the least broken of us. I'm almost jealous of how he's dealing with it. Don't get me wrong, he seems like he's hurting, but on the outside at least, he doesn't look like he'd rather die than live without her.

Which means he's already doing better than I am.

Once I have the shirt and slacks on, I put the tie around my neck before throwing it back on the bed. Fuck a tie. I'm not that guy, and Octavia would never ask me to pretend to be anything that I'm not.

Fuck, I miss her.

So fucking bad.

The pain claws through my chest and I crouch down, trying to suck in breath. Being without her is literally like trying to survive without oxygen.

It's fucking impossible.

I struggle to breathe, pain tearing my insides to ribbons as I try to fight off the tears that threaten to overwhelm me. Images of her flash through my mind, her smile, hair a mess, dressed in my t-shirt; flicking to me having her pinned against the wall at school, my knife pressing into her skin, the smile on her face before she kissed me, even when she was angry at me. Especially when she was angry at me. The soft smile she'd give me when she first woke up. The feel of her in my arms as we'd fall asleep.

Fuck.

I'm not going to survive this.

Maybe I'll kill Harrison my fucking self. It sounds like a worthy way to die.

"Mav," Finn calls out, knocking at my locked door. I open

my mouth to answer him, but nothing comes out. He knocks again, trying the handle, and I wrestle every fucking emotion in me back down, knowing that I can't break.

Not yet.

Not until Harrison is dead.

My resolve in place, I take a breath and stand, grabbing my suit jacket and yanking the bedroom door open. "I'm ready."

My voice is laced with venom, thoughts of ending Harrison before joining my girl are all that's on my mind.

I follow him downstairs, finding Linc and East waiting for us. We're all matching in our black shirts, pants, shoes, and jackets. Without a word, Linc heads outside and down the drive to where the car is waiting for us outside of the gates.

We've barely reached the car when I spot Smithy approaching us. "Boys, before you go. We need to talk."

Pausing at his words, the gate to the Royal house opens and we head back up the drive. I stuff my hands in my pockets wanting this day to be fucking over with.

We meet him at the front door, and he looks about as shitty as I feel.

"What is it?" Lincoln asks, his patience apparently as thin as mine.

Smithy smiles sadly at us, and opens the door to the house. "I need you all to come inside for a moment."

THIRTY

OCTAVIA

I hold my breath, waiting for one of them to speak. To move. Just do anything. I know they must be angry, shocked, hurt.

I never wanted to hurt them, but there's a lot that's happened the last three weeks.

They all stand there, dressed for the funeral they no longer have to attend. They look like something out of a magazine shoot. All in black suits, black shirts, and skinny black ties, except for Mav who never wears a tie. It's enough to make a girl's mouth water.

Also makes me wish I was dressed in something more than jeans, a crop top, and a shirt hanging over my shoulders.

Lincoln steps toward me and then pauses, emotions running

over his face, but he locks it down quickly, his cold mask slipping back into place, and I stand, captured in his gray eyes that look like ice cold metal.

"Fuck this," Maverick says, rushing toward me and wrapping me up in his arms, lifting me off the ground. "Don't think I'm not happy to see you, princess, but what the fuck?"

He places me back down on my feet, and East steps in, taking his place. He holds me like he can't believe I'm here.

I get it. I didn't want to keep everything from them, and God knows there's still a lot to say between us, but when Maverick grips my chin and pulls my attention back to him, all thoughts of words disappear. He pulls me from East's arms and presses his lips against mine as East presses against my back.

He kisses me until I struggle to breathe and as I pull back, he grips my hair so tight, my scalp stings. "I'm not letting you out of my sight again, princess."

I smile up at him, a hand on his chest as I lean back onto East. "Understood, but I think we should talk first."

I glance over to where Lincoln and Finley haven't moved. I can't tell if they're more pissed or hurt, but I do know that Finn is likely to soften first. Extracting myself from East and Mav, I move toward them, brushing my hand against Linc's as I put my hand on Finn's chest. Linc stiffens but doesn't move. I knew he'd be the biggest hurdle. The one who would find it hardest to forgive me. We said no secrets, and then I held back more than a few truths.

"I'm sorry."

Finn's blue eyes look down at me and I can feel his heart race beneath my palm. "We thought—"

"I know. I wanted to tell you guys, but until it was done, I had no choice."

"You could have trusted us," Linc hisses, drawing my attention back to him. "You could have trusted me." I wince at his roar and try to find the words, though I know none will erase what they've been through this last week.

"There's so much that you still don't know," I sigh, exhausted from my earlier conversation with Smithy, my mind still reeling from everything I've learned this last week, but I need to do this with them now. Make them see.

"Then tell us." Linc's demand makes my spine stiffen, his cold, detached bark reminding me of the way things were a year ago.

"Lincoln, don't be such an asshole." Mav mutters as he and East crowd around me.

Linc glares at him. "We thought she was dead! Fucking *dead!*"

"But she's not," Finn says softly, his eyes roaming over me like he thinks I might disappear at any moment.

"I'm not going anywhere. Not ever again," I say, looking at Lincoln, but I'm talking to them all.

Lincoln's growl reverberates through me as he steps forward and claims me with a bruising kiss. When I feel heat at my back, arms wrapping around my waist, I pull back to take a breath, leaning my head back and looking up into Finley's eyes. I press my lips to his as Lincoln kisses down my throat. "I thought we lost you," he whispers against my lips. "There was so much darkness."

My heart clenches at the pain in his voice. I hate that I put it there. The others give us a little space, and I realize that for whatever reason, my being gone is going to haunt him the longest. I reach up and cup his cheek with my hand. "I won't leave. Ever again. I promise.

He closes his eyes and rests his forehead against mine, just holding me, breathing me in, as if convincing himself this is real. My eyes flutter closed, and I squeak when he bends and lifts me against his chest. He strides up the stairs to my room, the other three close behind us.

Once we're all in the room, East closes the door and flicks the lock. I guess no one wants any interruptions. Finn puts me on my feet and steps back, the four of them standing before me with my bed at my back.

"I missed you. All of you. I'm sorry I didn't reach out, but there was too much at stake. I hate that I hurt you—"

"Later," Mav growls, as he strides forward and grips my throat. "First, we're going to punish you for leaving."

"Then we're going to reward you for taking it so well," East adds.

"Then you get to explain everything,." Lincoln finishes. I

glance over to Finn who just nods. My four kings stand before me, waiting for me to say something, anything. Instead, I drop to my knees, and look up at them.

"I am yours to do with as you wish."

My gaze travels to all four of the guys, pausing at each of them like we're having our own little conversations. Like I'm begging for forgiveness with just one long, apologetic look.

They all grunt at my immediate submission, and a tremor runs through me at the sound, making me wet within seconds.

Four gorgeous, lethal, hurting men standing in front of me and I have no idea who to go to first.

True to his character, Mav steps forward first, one hand already making quick work of his belt while the other holds my throat at the perfect angle for his taking.

"You're lucky I'm more thankful than seething right now, or I'd make you bleed for what you did." He scoffs at himself and then adds, "Hell, I still might."

His words are deathly quiet, like he's speaking only to me. The enormity of the moment isn't lost on me. He wants my blood. As a punishment or to release some of his pent-up pain? Either way, I won't deny him what he needs. I hold out my arms and tell him, "I'm yours. Do what you must, Maverick."

The pressure at my throat increases under the pads of his fingers and the look on his face darkens. "I'll decide when and where you bleed, you've made enough decisions about us lately."

My breath catches at his words and by the tiny smile that creeps up one corner of his mouth, I'm guessing he felt that at the tips of his fingers. I bet he's hard as a rock behind that zipper.

I give a longing look at the bulge that's right in front of my face and then raise my gaze to find his hard stare. I already know it's going to take time to earn their forgiveness, but I'm willing to work at it. I'll make it up to them. Eventually.

In my periphery, I see Lincoln languidly make his way over to my small couch where he makes himself at home.

"Get up." Mav gives me the order, bringing my focus back to him but he doesn't wait for me to rise on my own. His forearm bulges as he pulls me up by my throat until I'm face to face with him. Our mouths are so close I can feel his breath on my lips, his heat on my skin—the anger that's simmering just below the surface of his touch.

This is my atonement—and I happily accept it—which is why I don't even flinch when he pushes me back onto the bed. I accept it because the look in his eyes tells me an entirely different story. His relief at me being here with him is stronger than any anger or deep-rooted agony he may have felt thinking I was dead. I can't imagine having to survive the death of any of them, and the guilt has weighed on me heavily this last week, but there really was no other way.

"Clothes off." I don't hesitate, and before I get the chance to slide my panties off, Mav curls his fingers around the soft fabric and rips them off of me, letting them drop at his feet.

Four pairs of eyes are roaming different parts of my body and never in my life have I felt more alive, and more on edge, than this very moment.

"When I think how you made us believe that we'd lost you. Lost this... angry doesn't even begin to cover it, princess." My teeth sink into the flesh of my bottom lip as I try my best not to justify my actions.

Mav kneels at the foot of the bed and, with his big hands on my thighs, pulls me to the very edge of the mattress, a millisecond before his mouth is on my pussy. Licking, sucking, and biting every inch of the skin between my legs. The cries fall from between my lips, but Finn kneels behind me, resting my head on his thighs and slaps his hand over my mouth.

"This isn't about you, V." His words are harsh, but his finger caressing the underside of my chin tells me a whole different story. It's punishment, no doubt, but it's also so much more.

Mav hits a magic spot that makes my hips spring from the mattress, the pleasure taking over my body without warning.

"He feels good, doesn't he?" Finn whispers from above, the pressure against my mouth increasing and the bulge of his hardening cock pressing against my temple.

Movement has my gaze swing over to East, then Linc. They are both sitting on their own ends of the couch, flies open, hands stroking their cocks, hungry eyes on us.

I lick my lips as the scene before me sinks in. Here I am, getting my pussy thoroughly fucked by Mav's tongue while

Finn effectively shuts me up and the Saint brothers jack off to the sight of it.

My thoughts are brought back to the bed as Mav tweaks my nipple and Finn snaps, "Focus, pretty girl."

I almost narrow my eyes at them both but the reminder of my penance is in his eyes, so I take everything they have like the sinner that I am.

Two fingers sink inside my pussy while Mav continues to worship my clit.

"Fuck," I hear Finn above me. Raising my gaze to his, I see his hard exterior melt into red-hot lust. It's heady and Mav licks up my reaction to it.

"Goddamn, she's fucking delicious," he groans as grunts sound all around.

My hips buck when Mav pushes in two fingers again, curling them just right and making my entire body shake.

Finn replaces his hand with his mouth, his lips almost imitating Mav's as he bends over me. I'm so hyper aware of them that it's difficult to keep any sort of rhythm going. I'm bucking at Mav and moaning into Finn's mouth as his tongue sweeps in and out from between my lips.

My hands are at my sides, my fingers curling around the sheets beneath me as I get devoured from either end. I know better than to touch either of them without permission.

It doesn't take long to bring me to orgasm again, the stimulation is almost overwhelming. When it does come, though, I'm a quivering mess. Finn doesn't let up, his mouth is hot on mine. Lips gliding over lips. We swallow each other's moans while Mav fucks my pussy with two, maybe three fingers, pummeling the same spot over and over again. It's when he squeezes my clit with his teeth that I lose my fucking mind. My hands reach out, trying to grab at anything, begging to be tethered to something, but Finn holds me down, his fingers cuffing my wrists and pushing me down against the mattress without once lifting his mouth from mine.

The orgasm flies through my body like a tornado, wreaking havoc with my nerve endings.

And still, they won't let me touch them.

Heaving and fighting for every breath, Finn licks a path at the seam of my mouth before he releases me and Mav comes into my line of vision. "I think Finn needs to sink into your pussy."

My tongue darts out, licking my swollen lips at the suggestion. I'm aware that while they love me, right now, I'm their toy, and I'll take the position willingly.

They trade places and as I'm looking up at the evil glint in Maverick's eyes, I smile up at him. He may be a psychopath but he's *my* psychopath, and I wouldn't want him any other way.

I gasp when Finn kneels on the mattress between my legs and, without warning, plunges inside me to the fucking hilt. The burn from the stretch of him is enough to make my eyes water. When I open my eyes, Mav's glint turns into a blinding grin that takes my breath away.

"Finn was right. This isn't about you, princess. This is for us." He rises on his knees and straddles my face, his balls dancing over my lips.

I get it. They need to let go of the images of my death in their minds. I'm being punished in the most delicious of ways and I'm okay with that.

"Lick."

My mouth opens at Mav's command and my tongue searches out the fragile ball sack as he slowly jacks himself off above my face. But my attention is on Finn as he grunts with every thrust. His fingers press hard into my thighs, the jerk of his cock brutal on my core. Mav moans at the feel of my tongue when I flutter the tip over the seam between his two balls.

"That's it, princess, make me come all over your face." What does it say about me that his words make me even wetter than I am?

"Do it," Lincoln commands from across the space between us, the deep rumble of his lust-filled voice makes my hips buck just as Finn takes my hand and places it on my clit.

"Play with yourself," Finn orders and I don't hesitate, not even for a second. Being back with them has me all kinds of needy.

My senses are on full alert with the sounds of Mav stroking himself harder and faster as Finn's thrusts inside of me increase in tempo. Bottoming out with every plunge to the hilt. My fingers are soaked as I stroke myself.

"That's it, V. Yeah, fuck, I'm gonna come." Finn's movements become less controlled and wild like the man himself as his stare pierces me, his intentions clear.

See my hurt.

See my pain.

See the shell you would have left had you really been dead.

My chest aches at the truth of his what he says to me wordlessly, his walls completely broken down as he pulls my thighs into him and buries his dick so deep inside me I swear to fuck I can feel him in every molecule of my being.

Finn roars out his orgasm, his pain echoing against the four walls of my room before it hits me with its force and I come all over his cock.

"Fuuuuuuck!" Mav moves so quickly I barely have time to understand what he's doing.

On instinct, I open my mouth and while my own orgasm is still rushing through me, I swallow every drop of Mav's cum as he spurts down my throat.

"Good girl. Now, go suck Linc's dick before he embarrasses himself." Mav wipes a drop of his cum from the corner of my mouth, pushing his finger between my lips before helping me up.

Finn drops a kiss on my navel, his eyes on me and his words clear in my head as though he's saying them out loud.

Thank you for coming home.

If only he knew…

On shaky legs, I stand, but Linc is having none of it.

"Crawl to me, Octavia."

Oh yeah, he's pissed off. There's no doubt about that. But I do as he commands, dropping to my hands and knees.

Without taking my eyes off his hard stare, I slowly make my way to him, watching in fascination as he slides his pants off and lets them drop to his ankles before kicking them—and his dress shoes—to the side. Despite the anger that's rolling off of him in turbulent waves, his dick is hard and thick lying proudly against his lower abs. He's magnificent at any time of day, but when he exudes power and control… he's simply breathtaking.

I dare a look at East, who's been quiet this whole time, probably ruminating in his own head, wondering where he went wrong. Possibly even blaming himself somehow for not being able to protect me, even if from myself and my decisions.

Like his brother, East has placed his mask on, making it impossible for me to read him.

Once I reach Lincoln, I kneel in front of him and wait, palms flat on my naked thighs, for my next instruction.

And I wait.

What feels like endless seconds turn to minutes before Lincoln wraps his palm around his cock and begins to stroke himself in front of me. His hard stare is penetrating, irises cold as steel, plump lips drawn in a straight, unforgiving line.

I'm almost afraid as I look at him that he may never forgive me. Of the four, Lincoln was the biggest gamble, but it doesn't matter. I stand behind my actions, even if I have to live without one of the men I love. Knowing they are all safe is enough for me.

It has to be.

"Suck." He strokes his cock twice more before adding, "my." Twice more with a swift glide of his thumb across the tip. "Cock."

He lets go of his dick and sits on the couch like a king on a throne—arms resting on the back, eyes sending daggers that pierce my heart with every glare.

And still, I don't hesitate. I move to grab onto his shaft but I don't have time to before I'm flying in the air, an arm banded around my stomach.

I gasp when I find myself kneeling between Linc and East, my mouth on Linc's cock and my ass ready for the taking by East.

I have no idea how I ended up like this but I'm pretty sure East didn't feel like watching this time.

Linc doesn't touch me, but East runs a large hand over the globes of my naked ass. Fingers probing my pussy, circling my clit then sliding back up to my ass before starting the process over and over again.

I think I feel his lips on my flesh, but I'm concentrating on Linc's thick cock and trying my best not to choke on it.

Apparently, I'm not sucking hard enough because Linc

finally touches me with one hand in my hair—pulling tight against my scalp—as he takes control of the blowjob and starts to fuck my face.

He pushes my head down until he can feel me choking, my saliva dripping freely all over his dick. I might be humiliated if I wasn't so fucking turned on.

"Jesus Christ, she's soaked. Her pussy lips and her thighs are dripping." East's groan does nothing but make me needier.

"You like sucking on my cock, Octavia? Huh? You like knowing you're about to make me come when you don't get to?" I try to reply, but Linc doesn't let me and I realize he's not seeking out an answer. He's pissed off and feeling betrayed to the depths of his soul, and making me gag on his cock is his way of proving I'm still here.

Alive.

East shifts behind me and just as I'm pulled almost off Linc's cock, East thumbs my clit and thrusts his tongue inside my pussy, fucking it the way Lincoln fucks my mouth.

I feel him eating every inch of me, licking one side then the other, and it's fucking with my rhythm on Linc's cock.

If I weren't so afraid they'd stop, I'd tell him to stop distracting me.

I'm not that stupid though. I give them the upper hand, the control they lost this last week. It's the least I owe them after how they've been suffering.

Linc's dick swells under my tongue as I feel an orgasm wash

over me, the telling tremors running through my entire body.

"Goddammit!" One word and Linc screams it out like he's angry that I've made him come in my mouth.

But I lick it all up, swallowing every drop. Trying to ignore my own orgasm, I take everything he has to give all while East feasts on me like he's been deprived of food for weeks.

All too soon, I'm pulled away from Linc's cock and I think he'll discard me when, instead, he roughly takes my mouth, no doubt tasting himself on my lips.

His kiss is hard and unforgiving. It's angry and devoid of tenderness.

But that's okay. The fact that he's kissing me gives me hope, and right now, I'll take it.

I know the exact moment that Linc is done with me. His lust-filled eyes turn to ice, his walls firmly back in place, as he hands me over to his brother.

I feel the loss of his heat but don't have time to linger on my hurt before I'm straddling East, his forehead resting against mine, my soaked pussy gliding easily down his waiting cock.

We both sigh once I'm fully seated on him and he begins to whisper. His breath bathes my lips with every "Thank God you're here" that falls from his mouth. I revel in the heat of his body, in the hardness of his chest and the welcome in his embrace. I'm thankful too, so I tell him as much.

"I love you, East. So much." Large hands travel from my thighs to my waist and up and around to my shoulder blades where he tightens his hold on me. Finally, our lips meet, our mouths crashing together with a clash of teeth and hurried tongues. Frantically, I begin fucking him, rolling my hips, trying to show him just how much I mean everything I've said, all the while our kiss lingers.

He's giving me as good as I'm giving him, meeting me halfway with his thrusts from below—his palms on the balls of my shoulders as he controls the rhythm. It almost hurts, this pace, this frantic need we have to feel each other.

"Come again, V. I need to feel you all over my dick." He's practically begging, but we're hidden behind a curtain of my hair, in our own little world where he doesn't have to hate me and I don't have to beg for forgiveness.

"I can't, East. I c—"

"You will. You'll fucking come for me, V." I concentrate on the friction of his groin against my aching clit. On the intensity of his kiss. I visualize every movement, every dirty thing he's doing to me, and just when I think it's just not possible, I explode.

My head falls back and as quickly as it comes it fades away, but I don't care because East is filling me, giving me everything he's got.

When we both catch our breaths, East kisses me again before he takes my hips and rises from the couch like I weigh next to nothing.

Slowly, he walks me to the bed where he reverently places me on top of the comforter, legs spread, chest heaving, and looks at me in awe.

They're all there, standing around me. Watching me, each of them painted with a different emotion. But I know them, and I know we'll be okay once they've forgiven me.

Mav, as always, is the first to move. Placing his hand on my chin, he kisses me hard and fast before turning me back on my stomach and hitching up my ass so he can, unceremoniously, thrust inside me from behind.

I gasp and so do the other three men standing around watching as Mav fucks his anger out on me.

I know it all will be okay when his hands land on my tits and he flicks at my nipples before leaning down and biting my shoulder as he begins a punishing rhythm that rips every breath out of my lungs when he plunges to the hilt.

Mav is often the volatile one of the group, but right now he's calculated and in control, which means I'll have hell to pay later.

It doesn't take him long to slam into me and hold me in place as he empties himself inside of me, his cries filling the large space of my bedroom.

"Fuck yeah!"

Gasping for air, my breaths erratic and short, I let myself fall onto the mattress once more and smile when I realize they've all fucked me except for Linc.

He can't refuse or else they'll have something he doesn't and he's never going to let that happen.

With the ace up my proverbial sleeve, I use every ounce of strength I have left to heft myself up and turn around to face him.

"Show me your cunt, Octavia." With a grin that feels like it might rip my face open, I spread my legs and show him just how battered I am and still… I'm ready for more. For him.

"Christ, she's fucking beautiful." That's East, who is now settling behind me as Finn and Mav lie down on either side of me—hands and mouths roaming across my skin.

"Fuck." That's Lincoln's resigned sigh, because we are all bonded and there's no fucking way he can walk away from me.

At least I fucking hope not.

The bed sinks under his weight as he lifts my ass up and sinks deep inside me. I gasp into East's mouth as Mav licks at my nipple and Finn leaves tiny bites across my other tit. I've got four pairs of hands on me, three mouths worshipping, and one huge fucking dick pounding me into my next existence.

Even if it's the last time, it's fucking worth it.

Lincoln doesn't take long before he pulls out and comes all over my stomach, his cum falling in spurts of white thick liquid, marking me as visibly as Finn and Mav's bite marks.

Holy fuck.

I suck in a breath, trying to make my lungs work properly again.

Linc looks down at me, the warmth that flickers in his eyes disappears again as quick as it appeared. "Now, you need to tell us what the fuck happened."

THIRTY ONE

OCTAVIA

ONE DAY AGO

*O*ne part of me feels guilty about the breaking of the worlds that's happening in the media right now. The secrets that are coming out, especially for the innocent parties that are being swept up in the tidal wave, but I'm not sure that anyone associated with the Knights is truly innocent.

There might be some children affected by parents being caught up in the storm, but while this might suck for them, I guarantee it's better than a future with the Knights. Even if they won't see it that way. Some stains on the soul are impossible to get rid of.

I pace around the safe house that Bentley holed me away

in after rushing me from the inferno of my dad's Range. I don't have all the details as to how he, Smithy, and Luc faked my death, all I know is it was really fucking good. All I have to do is put on the news to see that.

My biggest regret is that the guys and Indi don't know I'm alive, but Smithy and Luc hammered home the importance of no one knowing the truth until Smithy had things in line on his end. My head hurt as he tried to explain the many moving parts of his chessboard, but I trust that he'll get what needs to be done, done quickly so I can go home.

He and Bentley told me the risks of coming back, the fact that I would be in danger purely because of who I am, because of the people I was going to hurt by releasing some of the documents Dad had stashed away, but there's too much in the Cove for me to disappear under a new identity.

That was their original plan. Then the boys would be free, because Smithy would ensure it, but so would I. I could live anywhere, do anything, be anyone I wanted to be, but as I told them... I wouldn't get to be the me I want to be without the people in my life that I hold dearest.

A knock at the door has me readying my gun before I check the peephole. I let out a breath when I see Luc's face. I didn't know he knew I was here, but I guess it makes sense that he would. He is one of the four people who know I'm still alive after all. I unlock the million locks Bentley had me engage when he left this morning, and let Luc in, keeping the safety off my gun *until he's inside and the locks are back in place.*

"Good to see you in one piece," Luc says with a tight smile, checking out the windows of the remote cabin I'm stashed in. "Keeping yourself sane?"

"As sane as I can be, having been on my own for a week while everyone I love thinks I'm dead. How are they?" I can't help but ask, I know he'll have seen them, and by the twist of his lips, I already know it's not good.

"They're in a bad way. East is just about holding it together, but Linc... he's even colder than normal, frantically chasing down every lead for your killer. Mav is beating the shit out of everything that moves—and some things that don't... and Finn. Well, he's gone inward again. Like he did when you left."

I nod, swallowing down the rising emotions. I knew it would be bad, it's why I wanted to tell them what was really going on, but they had to think I was dead for Harrison and the others to buy it. If those four weren't so raw, then people would be suspicious. Just because I see the merit in it, doesn't mean I agree with it.

"How much longer do I have to stay here?"

"Not my decision," he responds and my heart sinks. I knew it would be his answer, it's exactly what Bentley said, but fuck my life. "I'm here because Linc has put a hit out on Harrison."

"Shit," I sigh, running a hand through my hair. I knew it was a possibility that he'd work it out and do something like this. It's Linc. If anything I'm surprised it took this long.

"Something like that. As much as I'd like to see my brother dead for everything he's done, I don't want it on Linc. He might feel like there's no redemption for himself, but some things you can't come back from."

I nod, because I thought something very similar myself already. "What are we going to do?"

"He asked me to take care of it, but I have a feeling if I don't do it, he has a back up plan."

I bark out a laugh. "Of course he does. He's Lincoln Saint."

There's another knock on the door, which has us both on high alert and me reaching for my gun again. Luc motions for me to stay hidden as he answers the door. Bentley strides in, nodding to Luc as he does before turning his gaze to me.

He drops a passport on the table before folding his arms. "It's decision time. That there is your ticket to a whole new life. I've arranged access to money, and there is no way for you to be traced back to this one. It would be the much safer option."

I stare at the passport on the table like it might burn me, before turning my gaze to Bentley. "Safe doesn't mean happy. Nothing worth doing comes without risk."

This day has been exhausting. Amazing, but exhausting. And it's not over yet. Having explained everything to the guys after taking my punishment, and then taking it all over again, my body is sore in the best of ways. I ache every time I move, but my day isn't over yet.

There's one more person I need to see, and I'm kind of terrified about it.

My bestie might be sunshine and puppies embodied in a human, but she's a spitfire, and she's going to kick my ass.

I'm not sure what Smithy said to ensure she wasn't at the funeral earlier, all he said was that he had invited her this evening, which is why I'm sitting curled up in a ball on the couch, waiting anxiously for her to arrive.

We haven't announced that I'm not dead yet, Smithy is handling all of that, but it means not using my phone, so I can't even text her and tell her to hurry her ass up. My knee bounces as my nerves get the better of me.

Somehow, facing Indi is scarier than the guys. She was there for me from the second I stepped into the Cove. She is my ride or die. It's very probable that she is going to be the angriest of anyone because I didn't tell her.

Smithy strides into the room from the kitchen, patting my shoulder as he moves to the front door, and my heart races as he opens it.

"Hey, Smithy," she says quietly, hugging him as he greets her. "What did you want me to come over for? Are you okay?"

It hurts me so bad that her sparkle is dulled right now. I can't see her, she's hidden behind Smithy, but I can hear it in her voice. I get up quietly, moving to the other side of the couch, feeling nervous as fuck.

"Yes, Miss Indi. I have something I need to tell you." He moves to one side and my gaze lands on my best friend who screams and then crumbles to the floor, sobbing.

My heart breaks as I rush across the room, dropping to the floor and hugging the walking rainbow that I hurt so much. "I'm so sorry, Indi."

She holds me tight while she cries. Smithy leaves us while I cry for the bestie I broke so badly.

"I can't believe you're really here," she whispers shakily. "What happened? When Maverick called me... I thought he was fucking around. But then I saw the news, I saw Maverick... You were dead."

"I know," I sigh, running a hand through my hair to try and ground myself a little. "So much happened, and it all happened so freaking quickly. There wasn't time, and it wasn't safe for anyone to know the truth."

"But it's okay now?" she asks and then her eyes go wide. "Oh shit, it was you wasn't it? That leaked all of that information! It can't be safe for you to be here already, surely?"

"Smithy says I'll be fine. I was hidden at first, but he's been working tirelessly this week to ensure that I'm protected better than the freaking president. Plus, after this, I doubt the guys are going to leave my side much."

She laughs, then gazes around the room. "Where are they?"

"Smithy forced them to go next door while I spoke to you.

There was a lot of angry testosterone up in here about an hour ago, my friend."

"Yeah I bet." She tucks her hair behind her ear, looking at me like she has more questions.

"What?" I ask, worried that the relief of me being alive is running out, and that the anger I left is going to rear its head any minute.

"I get why you didn't tell me, didn't tell anyone, but I want more details on how this all came about and where the hell you've been. And I'm still kinda pissed you didn't tell me. It's unreasonable, but I never said I made any sense."

"It's not unreasonable," I sigh. "I'd be pissed too." I stand up, offering her a hand, and we go and curl up on the couch in the media room while I tell her everything. About Luc coming here that night, and everything that happened since then. I can't answer every question, because I have some questions myself, but I tell her everything I know.

Even some things I probably shouldn't, but the same way I didn't keep secrets from the guys, I won't keep them from her either. I've had enough secrets to last a fucking lifetime.

"Does Blair know you're not dead?" she asks, shocking me.

"No, why?"

She presses her lips together and then shrugs. "I can't believe I'm even saying these words, but she was pretty torn up when the news broke. You should probably tell her."

Well shit, I definitely wasn't expecting that. I nod, taking it on board. "Okay, I'll reach out to her tomorrow. Today has been a long ass day."

"Yeah I get that, so what happens next?"

"Honestly?" I blow out a breath, trying to loosen the tightness in my chest. "I have no fucking idea."

When Indi leaves, I'm exhausted, so I pad back to the kitchen to say goodnight to Smithy and find him on the phone. Now that I know who he is, the fact that he only stayed here for me, even though he could've been living life very differently, it's weird.

On the one hand, I can't help but wonder why he stuck around here, but on the other, it makes me feel loved.

But whatever he's talking about can't be good, not by the look on his face. He holds up a finger, signaling he'll just be a minute, waving at me to sit down, so I grab a bottle of water from the refrigerator and take a seat, waiting for him to finish his call.

"I don't care what you need to do, just fix it," he growls and ends the call. "I swear, people that require micromanagement shouldn't be involved in complex matters. Sorry, I just wanted to get that sorted, but there's something we need to discuss."

Butterflies take flight in my stomach at his words. "That doesn't sound ominous at all."

He smirks at me as he makes a cup of tea before sitting

down with me. "It's not too ominous, we just need to talk about the Knights, and about Harrison."

"Yeah, not ominous at all, old man," I tease and he scoffs at me, making me laugh.

"I'm not sure if Lincoln or the others mentioned that Harrison managed to weasel his way out of prison?"

I shake my head, chewing on the inside of my lip.

"Well, that makes sense, I imagine that they were more focused on you being alive. Well, this has caused a slight hiccup, in that he has to reside at home. So I've invited the boys to move in here until we can deal with Harrison."

I just blink at him, processing that little nugget.

"This means that I don't really want you back at school yet. I won't stop you going back to your life. It might just mean I put extra security on you when you're away from the house. I've already arranged for extra security here. They will stay out of the way, but they will be here before you wake up tomorrow."

"Okay. That's a lot, but okay. I appreciate the security, but I really do just want to get life back to normal. I can deal with the extra security if I get my life back."

He nods, smiling as he takes a sip of his tea. "I'm glad you're being rational about it. Though I must say, I had a whole speech prepared to persuade you why it was necessary."

I stick my tongue out at him. "I can be an adult ya know. Sometimes."

"Oh, I know, Miss Octavia. The way you have handled all

of this... I couldn't be more proud of you." He reaches over and pats my hand, squeezing it tight. "Now, for the next thing I need to speak to you about. The Knights and your Regency."

He pauses and I just kind of stare at him. I am way too tired for him to keep dropping these bombs. It has been a day, but I promised myself while I was gone that I was going to try and not just react to stuff, that I'd try and think it out before I do anything. So I take a deep breath and center myself.

"What about it?"

He interlinks his fingers on the counter as he watches me, myriad emotions flit across his face so quickly that I can't really catch what he's feeling.

"Well, technically the Regency is yours, what I need to know is if you still want it."

I open my mouth to respond with a resounding hell no, but he cuts me off before I can start. "Let me finish. I do not want the Knights to be what they are. That isn't the legacy I want, and it's going to take time, and people I trust to get to where I want it to be. Some things can't be left to chance, it's why the Knights were created in the first place, but I don't want the guns or the drugs. The flesh trading. The use of children. All of that just turns my stomach.

"Other sects don't do any of these things, and that's exactly why I stayed here when I discovered the truth of this place. It's why your father agreed to collect the information for me, he was in a better position, he had an 'in' with all the people we needed to connect with that I didn't. It didn't play out how I wanted, and for that I am truly sorry, but I think between the two of us, we can make this sect what it was meant to be."

"That is… Wow."

He smiles sadly at me. "I know, and I don't expect you to answer right away. I just wanted you to know what I'm thinking, but if you say no, I will understand."

We sit and talk for another hour about what me taking the Regency would mean, the reality of what that would mean for my life, and it's a lot to take on board.

"Just think on it. Please. It's getting late, so sleep on it, and if you have any questions, please don't hesitate to ask." He gets up, moving around the counter and kisses the top of my head. "I'm going to retire to my rooms, but I'll introduce you to the security team in the morning. Goodnight, Miss Octavia."

I blow out a breath and watch him walk away, trying to process everything. "Night, Smithy."

THIRTY TWO

OCTAVIA

"I still can't believe you're really here," Linc murmurs, kissing me softly before tucking my hair behind my ear. He snuck in here a few minutes ago after I finally decided to crash. Turns out Harrison fled the country after his release, so the guys didn't have to move here, but it has me a little on edge that no one can find him.

The last week since I've been back in the Cove, and come back to life… well, if I said it had been insane, that would be an understatement. I still haven't given an answer to Smithy about the Regency, because I have no idea what to do. There have been many heated conversations between me and the guys about it.

Linc pulls me against his chest, kissing the top of my head. To say he's been mercurial since everything happened is an understatement. Sometimes he looks at me like he wants to kill me himself, and others… he looks at me like this.

I hate how much I hurt him—hurt them all. It's going to take a long time to make it up to them, I'm acutely aware of that, but I'm willing to do whatever it takes.

"I'm here, and I'm not going anywhere. Ever again," I murmur, my lips brushing against his.

His hand moves from my cheek to my throat, and he wraps his fingers around it, squeezing until it feels like I can't breathe. "If you ever…" he growls and my heart races, my pulse fluttering under his fingertips.

He releases me, pushing me away from him, making me stumble. "Strip."

There is no tenderness in the word. None in his face, or in the rigid set of his shoulders. "Linc—"

"I told you to strip, Octavia. Do not make me tell you again."

A shiver runs down my spine as his eyes narrow at me, his heated stare burning my skin. His is a fire I will happily burn in until the end of time.

I step back as he moves to sit on the end of my bed, his eyes never leaving me. I grasp the bottom of my sweater, lifting it over my head, my nipples pebbling against the lace of my red bra.

"Now your jeans," he orders and a shiver runs down my

spine. I love Linc when he's like this. Not that I haven't enjoyed the softer side of him, but this… well hot damn.

I unbutton my jeans, pulling the zipper down slowly, pushing them down my legs, turning so my ass is in his face as I do, before kicking them off, glancing back at him over my shoulder. In a blink, he's standing behind me, his chest pressed to my back, and he pushes me up against the wall. "I might have punished you once already, but I don't think you've been punished enough."

I bite down on my lip, eyes on his as I nod. This might be punishment to him, but I'm definitely not complaining.

I'm trapped between the cold surface of the wall and the burning heat of Linc's chest pressed against my bare back. They say the opposite of love is indifference and from the steel rod peeking between the open flaps of his zipper, there is nothing indifferent about Linc. I imagine he's still struggling with what happened so when he pushes his pants down just enough to free his cock completely, and when he bends just slightly at the knees to align his head with my soaked pussy, I ache with the need for him.

When he sinks his teeth into the fleshy part of my collarbone as he slowly buries his cock inside my pussy, I moan for him.

When he grunts my name as soon as his cock is completely enveloped by my heat, I tell him I love him.

I know he hears me because those three little words awaken the beast in him. The angry force inside him that hasn't quite forgiven me for causing him more pain than he ever thought he could handle.

He pulls out and spins me around before pushing me back up against the wall. He wraps his long fingers around my outer thighs and grips me like he's afraid I'll disappear. I wonder how long it'll take for him to realize that I'll never leave him again.

I barely finish that thought when I feel the first punishing thrust as my back and head slam against the wall. It feels fucking amazing, but it's how he punctuates each thrust with his feelings that make me melt into him.

"I am so fucking angry."

He thrusts again, this time his mouth latches onto the flesh just below my jaw before he reveals a little more.

"You hurt me."

Slowly, he pulls out and plunges right back in before I can get my next breath causing, me to rasp out a soundless "Yes!"

"I was dead inside." The pain in his voice makes my throat thick with emotion as tears prick my eyes. I slam my own head against the wall, the desperation pouring from him making my heart cry out. "I'm so sorry."

With his cock completely sheathed by the walls of my pussy, he secures his hold on me and carries me back to the bed, before kneeling then gently placing me on the soft covers.

The look in his eyes is pure and unshielded. He's completely open, vulnerable once again, telling me his truth as best he can. As much as I love it, because he never does that, I know this is going to hurt.

"You didn't trust me enough to tell me your plan."

He sounds like the boy who needed to control his entire world and like it or not, I've been his entire world since we were kids. And then I broke him because I left. Again.

"Linc–"

His gaze shutters and I don't have time to utter another word before he's fucking me like he's punishing me all over again. I can feel every hard ridge of his abs as he slides up and down my body with every unyielding thrust of his hips. We're both quiet now, but our bodies are saying everything we don't. The chaotic sound of skin against skin, our sweat mingling and creating more heat between us.

My breathing becomes harder to control as Linc continues to fuck me without mercy.

I lose myself in him as my hands glide up his back, the glean of sweat making it harder to latch onto him until I dig my nails into his shoulders and push him harder into me, the heels of my feet locking him in place, begging him for more.

And he doesn't disappoint.

With every deliberate plunge inside me, we both grunt out our pleasure. He gives me everything he's got, and I lay myself bare to him, letting him take whatever he needs.

I'm dizzy with it, loving every fucking second of it, but nothing compares to the moment he roars out my name and slams his mouth onto mine on the last syllable, just as he grinds against my aching clit.

My orgasm is swift and all-consuming. It shatters me into a million pieces as I feel it bloom in the base of my stomach and run a fiery course throughout my bloodstream and every nerve ending in my entire body.

It's electric and I know Linc feels it too.

Our kiss is messy—all tongues and teeth and slipping lips—but it's real. It's everything we are and will ever be.

As Linc spills inside of me and kisses the life right back into me, I know we'll be okay. At least I hope so, because I can't give him up.

Even if it leads to my demise.

I curl into East on the couch in the media room while Maverick has my feet in his lap. Finn and Linc are on the couch behind us, the lights turned down as the movie credits start rolling. This entire day has been so relaxing, exactly what I needed after the whirlwind of the last week.

Coming back to life is exhausting.

But this day with the four of them is exactly what I needed before we head back to the chaos of school tomorrow. Prom is coming, exams are coming, decisions about our future are coming, and it all feels really overwhelming.

We've barely had room to breathe this year, and I'm so

ready for summer. We haven't talked about what everyone's plans are, especially now that they're free, but this last week has been more about me being alive than what the future holds.

But we need to talk, especially since I haven't told them about Smithy's proposal yet.

"You okay?" East murmurs into my hair, his arms squeezing me tightly against his hard chest, making me feel all kinds of safe and loved.

I clear my throat before grabbing the tablet that controls the room to stop the movie and turn the lights up. "I'm good, there's just something I need to tell you guys."

Linc and Finn move instantly, standing before me. I pull myself up to sitting, taking my feet from Mav's lap and planting them on the floor. Linc looks stoney already, and I haven't even told him what's going on. Not that I'm surprised. He's the unpredictable one of the group. "What is it?"

He folds his arms over his chest, the black sweater hugging every chiseled inch of him. My gaze slides to Finn, who looks about as happy as Linc right now, and I let out a sigh. "Smithy wants me to take the Regency seat."

Surprisingly, East is the first to speak. "Are you fucking kidding me?" He springs up from the couch and starts pacing. "I thought after all of this you'd be free and clear."

I look to Mav, who is somehow the calmest one of the four. Have I stepped into the Twilight Zone?

"What are you thinking?" Finn asks quietly. So I tell them

everything Smithy said to me last week, giving them all of the information I have because this isn't a decision I should make on my own. If we're going to work, we need to start working as a unit. My time away gave me a lot of alone time to think and reflect. I came to the stark realization that I need to change my mindset if this thing between us is going to work.

I don't have to do everything alone.

"So he really wants change?" East asks skeptically.

"It makes sense," Linc adds. "Smithy is a good man. In his position, that sort of power can corrupt people, but it hasn't with him. That much is obvious in just how he has looked after us all."

"You think she should do it, don't you?" Finn asks him.

Linc's gaze slides to mine and he nods.

"I do. But I think if you're Regent, then we should take our seats too."

"Nothing like keeping it in the family," Maverick laughs.

"Do you think Smithy would be open to that?" East asks me, and I nod.

"I do. Plus, I'll be Regent, so I'd get that say anyway. I want to keep Artemis too, she's a force to be reckoned with, but I think the Mitchell kid needs to go. He isn't the brightest bulb in the box from what I can make out."

"I second that," Linc scoffs. "He's about as useful as a knitted condom."

Maverick snorts a laugh beside me before pulling me onto

426

his lap. "What we're basically saying, is we support whatever choice you want to make and we'll be by your side every step of the way."

I kiss his cheek and smile. "Thank you." I turn to the others too. "I mean it, thank you for always being there. But if we do this, what does this mean for college?"

"We can cross that bridge when we get there. We should speak to Smithy, see what he thinks about it all," East says, squeezing my hand. "But wherever you are, we'll be there too."

"I love you guys," I say wistfully. I really don't know what I'd do without them.

"We love you too, pretty girl," Finn says with a smile.

I check my watch, noticing the time. "Shit, Blair is supposed to be coming over in twenty minutes. I'd totally forgotten."

"What does she want?" Linc asks, eyebrows raised.

I shrug. "She just wanted to come and talk. I'm guessing about Nate. I haven't really paid attention to everything that's been going on with them, but Indi told me that Blair was pretty broken up while I was gone, and this last week, she's actually been nice."

"Yeah, I noticed," Finn smirks. "It's weird as fuck."

"She's only nice to you though, she's still a bitch to everyone else," Mav adds.

"Blair is who she is. She's unapologetic about it, and I'm kind of starting to love that about her."

"Of course you are," Linc responds, rolling his eyes. "Well

if she's heading over, we'll go home. I'm waiting on a call about Harrison anyway, so hopefully we'll have some answers about his whereabouts by tomorrow."

"That will be good, I hate feeling like he's out there unchecked."

"We won't let him hurt you," Maverick says, squeezing me tightly before kissing me. "Never again."

They leave after an extended goodbye, and I barely shut the door when the buzzer to the gate sounds. *That'll be Blair.*

I blow out a deep breath, trying to psych myself up for this. I know Indi said she'd turned a corner when I was 'dead,' but still…I have flashbacks to when I first came back to the Cove, and just how shit she was to me. It's hard to reconcile that version of her with this new one, but I want to give her the benefit of the doubt, and not just assume that she's playing me.

She didn't know I wasn't dead, and I trust Indi when she says that there was a change. I mean, I've seen glimpses of it, but at school, she's still Blair.

I open the front door, finding my blonde cousin standing there waiting for me, looking almost nervous. "Hey."

I smile at her before stepping back to let her in the house, but she launches herself at me and hugs me. I freeze, shocked for a second before I hug her back. "You okay, Blair?"

"Shut up, let me just be happy you're not dead." I can't help but chuckle at the very Blair thing that falls from her lips before she releases me. "I know I've still been a bit of a bitch at school, but if those assholes sense even a millimeter of weakness, the sharks will circle. I really was devastated when I thought you died."

She tucks her hair behind her ear and I close the door before leading her to the couches. "Thank you?" I say, a little unsure. We had a weird truce before my 'death' but that doesn't make this feel any less weird.

"Don't be weird," she says, flicking her hair over her shoulder as she sits down. " I just wanted to talk about everything that happened before. You being 'dead' made me look at myself in a way I never have before. I felt responsible, even though I didn't do it. Like, what if something I had done or said sent you down the path that led to that moment. I hated myself for what I did to you."

"Blair—" I start, not sure what to say but she cuts me off.

"No, don't. I just wanted to come and clear the air. Properly. I know we had a sort of truce before, but I don't want our entire relationship to be some sort of weird alliance. You're family, and God knows we don't have much of that left. I want you to know I'm sorry, and if you'll give me another chance, I'll show you that I'm more than a raging, jealous bitch."

She stands, brushing down her skirt, while I sit there trying to find words.

"I don't expect you to forgive me instantly, but I'm willing to show you that I've changed."

I smile at her, everything she's saying slowly registering.

"I'd like for us to try to be friends, Blair."

"Good," she says with a nod. "I've got to go, Mom is meeting with Chase, and I want to be there, but I'll text you later."

Without another word, she breezes from the house like she didn't just rock my world. I sit there in shock, trying to process the new version of Blair I just witnessed, hoping that it's not just a blip.

After Blair's visit, I head back to the kitchen and find Smithy making supper. "You need any help?"

"Miss Octavia, you know better than trying to mess with my kitchen," he teases.

"I'm going to need to learn to cook one day, ya know."

He waves the wooden spoon in his hand at me. "That is very true, but today is not that day, and not in my kitchen."

"Fine, fine. What are you making?" I ask, grabbing a can of soda from the fridge before sitting on the counter.

"Chicken Alfredo with garlic bread."

"Yes," I groan, my stomach rumbling at the thought. "You're too good to me, Smithy."

"Hardly, Miss Octavia. I love you like my daughter, and I like seeing you happy. Food makes you happy, and I love to cook."

He turns back to the stove and I bite the inside of my lip, trying to think of how to start the conversation I know I need to have with him. Except, there isn't really a guidebook for weird conversations with your surrogate dad.

"I spoke to the guys about the Regency thing," I blurt out, because well, in for a penny, in for a pound.

"Oh? Have you come to a decision?" he asks as he starts plating the meal. I jump down from the counter and take the plates from him as he pulls the garlic bread from the oven.

"I have," I respond as he sits opposite me. "We have some questions about what the future will look like, but I want to accept the chair. I think it's what Dad would've want. I know he was a Knight, and that he obviously wanted more—his deal with you shows as much—but I want to be a part of the change."

He beams a smile at me, clapping his hands together once. "Oh, Miss Octavia. I'm so glad. This will be great for us both. It's rare to be able to trust people as much as I trust you."

"I agree, but the guys would like their seats on the Conclave back too. East included."

His eyes go wide momentarily as he takes in my words. I pick up my fork and take a mouthful of the creamy deliciousness on my plate, not wanting to rush him.

"I think that is a great idea. Your Conclave should be comprised of people you can trust. What about the other current members?"

"I'd like to keep Artemis if she wants to stay, but the

Mitchell kid can go."

He nods as he swallows his mouthful. "Very good decision."

"I was also thinking…" I pause, hoping this is a good idea, but it just feels right. "I know we all need a second chair. I figure Alex and Linc can take the Saint seats, Mav and Finn we can work on, Chase and East will have theirs, but for my second seat… I was thinking of inviting Blair into the fold. I know Aunt Vi and Uncle Nate have always been pretty awful to me, but Blair and I have grown closer since Nate's arrest."

He quirks a brow at me, his surprise obvious. "Now that, I was not expecting. You really think that's a good idea?"

"Blair is cold and calculating, but she's also very good at looking at the big picture. How to break things down and build them up. She's all kinds of ruthless. I think she'll be a good second, and it's not like we won't keep her in check. Plus, it evens out the male-female number a little better. Artemis and I are a little outnumbered currently."

He chuckles softly as he takes a sip from his glass of water. "You're not wrong there, Miss Octavia. It is entirely your decision who you have as your second, and I will support you regardless. You're a good judge of character, always have been."

"Thank you."

"What about Miss Indi?" he asks, and I twist my lips.

"I had thought of her, but I didn't know if we could offer her a seat, or if she'd even want it. Especially with Ryker and the boys being part of the Kings."

He smiles at me and winks. "There are always new partnerships to be made, Miss Octavia. But I think Indi and her gentlemen would be a good addition, as long as they're open to our new ways."

I nod, mulling it over. I guess I have a lot to consider before I make any decisions.

"What would this mean for college?"

"You would still be going, Miss Octavia. Your education is of the utmost importance to me, your career path can be whatever you want it to be, you will just have extra responsibilities on top of college parties and your studies."

I laugh softly. "Okay, that's good to know. I'll have a think on it all and let you know."

"That sounds perfect. Have you thought about your college options? I know you haven't applied to any, but your status gives you an advantage where that isn't really a problem. We should probably still get it sorted for you quickly."

I smile at him, thankful to have him in my life. "I have a few ideas…"

THIRTY THREE

OCTAVIA

"I can't believe we're actually here," Indi grins at me from the mirror across the room. "We made it to the end of the year, prom is tomorrow, exams are about to begin, and college is calling our names. Freedom, my friend. I can almost taste it."

I laugh at her. She's been so excited the last two weeks since I rose from the dead. Everything has been about prom, summer trip planning, and college. Though I still don't know if I'm going straight to college. I have to graduate first, and if I called this last year rocky, it'd be the understatement of the century.

"Well, we'll be going to prom if we ever decide on dresses," I giggle and she glares at me.

"You can't rush perfection." She sticks her tongue out at

me and twists and turns to take in the sight of the floor-length midnight-blue dress she's wearing. It's unlike anything I've ever seen her wear, but it's perfection.

It looks like the night sky, the sewn-in beads and gems like a blanket of stars on the inky material. Her newly dyed hair is black, making her pale skin glow even more than usual. The dress adds to it, but my compliments have fallen on deaf ears.

"You really think this is the one?"

"Indi, you've tried on thirty two dresses in three hours. You've put this one back on four times. It's stunning. So I think you already know the answer to that."

She sticks her tongue out at me before looking back at the dress. "Not all of us decide as quickly as you did."

I laugh because she's not wrong. When I put my dress on this morning, it was the first one I picked, but the way Maverick's eyes lit up when I walked out of the dressing room sold me on it instantly.

The blood-red number made me look so vampy, and the halter neck did all sorts of things to my girls. I was sold. He snapped a picture, and then ducked out when he knew it was the one I was getting to go to his tux fitting with the guys.

Even East is coming to prom, and I'm so excited to be able to experience it with all of them. It's the next step to the rest of our lives.

I still need to talk to Indi about the Knights, and if that's something that she'd want. I've been meaning to bring it up all week, but I haven't worked out how yet. Especially since Ryker is still well and truly pissed at me.

Making his girl cry put me on his shit list, and I get it. Alex hasn't exactly been sunshine and rainbows with me either, though Ellis and Dylan were a little more understanding. No real surprises there. I was more shocked to find Alex there with the rest of them when I went to get Indi this morning.

Apparently my death brought them together, so it's not all a bad thing. Even if I am still sorry about it all.

"Okay, I'm buying the dress!" Indi announces, and I beam at her.

"Good! Let's get this thing paid for and then I demand lunch. I'm starving over here."

"Oh yeah, you're absolutely wasting away," she deadpans, and I bark out a laugh.

"Fuck you. Come on, you know you want a big cheesy slice from Tony's." I grin wider as she looks like she's about to drool all over her dress.

"Fine, yes, you know I can't say no to cheese. Unzip me?"

I stand and help her out of the dress, then head to the checkout while she dresses. I buy her the matching drop earrings too, and wait for the woman to box it up. "Are you okay to deliver it?"

"Yes, Miss Royal. Absolutely," the girl behind the counter responds, a little flustered. She was the same way when we came in at first too, and Indi and Mav teased me about it. Apparently she was a big Stone Royal fan. I give her Indi's address since her guys are all going with her to this dance

"You didn't have to do that, you know." Indi sighs as she finds me at the counter, motioning to the box.

"I know, but I wanted to. Gift giving is my love language, just let me love you."

"Fine," she grins, rolling her eyes at me. "But lunch is on me."

"If you say so," I tease, looping my arm through hers. We exit the store and head two blocks over to the new pizza place, which has been jam packed since it opened a week ago. We enter, finding Scout at the hostess station.

"Hey you guys!" She waves at us excitedly. "Just the two of you?"

"Yes, please," I say with a smile. She looks so much like Ryker and Ellis, she could easily be their triplet. "Busy morning?"

"Yeah, who would've thought so many people wanted pizza for breakfast?" She laughs as she grabs the menus. She hugs Indi quickly before leading us to an empty booth in the back of the place.

"Drinks?" Scout asks as she hands us our menus.

"I'll take a coke please," I say, and Indi has the same. Scout skips off behind the serving counter to grab our drinks.

"How are the guys dealing with her working here?" I ask Indi, smirking. 'Cause I'd put money on them stressing the fuck out.

"They're not," she giggles, pointing to a guy sitting at the far end of the counter. "That's one of Ryker's guys. The argument about her having a babysitter was earsplitting, but obviously, Ryker is a stubborn asshole. So she's been messing with Karl all week."

I take the guy in. He's tall, even curled over the counter the way he is, it's impossible to miss. So are the tattoos that cover every visible inch of his skin. The seat beside him is empty, and I can't tell if that's due to Scout or the sheer menacing aura he's projected. His eyes never leave Scout as she flits around the place, and there's a reverence in the way he looks at her that makes me smirk. "I think Ryker might have more trouble on his hands than he thought he would."

Indi cackles, nodding. "You saw that too, huh? The boys are oblivious to it, and I'm not about to say anything. I'm not sure how she feels about him, but I'm not about to rain on her parade."

I high five her across the table. "We should invite her on our girls weekend."

"Yes!" she exclaims, her eyes shining. "That'd be amazing."

"What would?" Scout asks as she appears with our drinks.

"V was just saying you should join us on our girls trip the weekend after prom." Scout turns to me, eyes wide.

"Really? I'd love that!"

"Then consider it done. We'll grab you after school on Friday," I tell her, making a mental note to adjust the booking I made yesterday when Indi and I decided on a belated birthday trip. The guys weren't exactly happy about me going away without them, but I reminded them that we have all summer, and the road trip we have planned is all kinds of epic. It quieted them down for the time being at least.

"You guys rock! Thank you! And since I'm with you guys, I can ditch the babysitter!"

"Only if you want to," I wink at her, and she smirks at me, flicking her dark hair over her shoulder.

"I think it'll be good for him to realize I don't need him." Her eyes sparkle with mischief and I can't help but laugh. I haven't spent much time with Scout, but I know she's good people from what Indi has said about her, and that's all I need to know.

I grin at her, nodding. "Got to keep them guessing."

Prom is finally here. I've spent all day primping and preening. Gracie came over and removed my extensions, cut my hair since it's mostly grown back now, and put it up for me. Butterflies flutter in my stomach at the thought of the dance. I know things have changed dramatically since homecoming, but illogical fears are just that.

The limo collected us from the house about ten minutes ago, and we're heading to the hotel the ECP prom committee picked for this year's prom. The theme is red carpet, so I'm sure it's going to be all kinds of glam, but I can't really think much past the guys right now.

They look good enough to fucking eat. You'd think with the amount of fucking we've been doing since I got back that my appetite would be satiated, yet… apparently I'm a greedy bitch, because I want more. All of them in their black-on-black suits is fucking mouthwatering.

"Hungry, pretty girl?" Finn murmurs in my ear, his fingers playing with the bare skin on my back. The material of the back only just covers the top of my ass, and the thigh-high splits in the skirt make this dress possibly the most risqué I've ever worn, but when I saw Mav's face in the store, I knew this was the dress to have.

I glance at him, nodding, and he pats his lap.

The other three are talking, not paying too much attention to the two of us. Even as I glance at them, I can tell that whatever they're debating has them distracted for the moment. Not a surprise with everything we have going on now that everyone's back on board with the Knights, and we had our first Conclave meeting this week about how to fix the sect, but that's for later. Right now, Finn has my attention on him, and I'm debating if I'm going to do as he asked.

Fuck it.

I climb into Finley's lap, thankful for the thigh slits as I straddle him. His hands clasp my hips as I lean forward, kissing him and rolling my hips against him.

"Looks like our princess is putting on a show," Maverick calls out from behind me. "I am always here for that."

Fucking Mav. Such a voyeur. Not going to lie that it makes me hotter though.

Finn moves one hand from my hip and through the slit of my skirt, hissing when he realizes I have no panties on. He runs one finger through my slick and groans. "She's fucking soaking."

I whimper at his touch as he gently teases me, trying to roll my hips again as I search for more friction.

"Fuck our girl, Finn. Give her what she wants." Linc's words are like a sharp sting across my back as Finley plunges two fingers inside of me.

"Can't deny her anything," he murmurs as I move to unzip his pants. I palm his already hard dick, loving his groans as I work my hand over the tip of him. Lifting up, I move my dress aside and line him up with my pussy as he withdraws his fingers. He pushes them into my mouth as I slide down onto him, tasting myself on his fingers as I burn at the stretch of him.

As soon as he's buried to the hilt, my head falls back with pure ecstasy and satisfaction at being this full. Finn's large palm is right between my shoulder blades, holding me steady as the limo takes us to our final destination.

"Fuck, she looks fucking delicious." Mav's words are dancing in my ears, but it's Linc's command that sends shivers down my spine.

"East, I think our girl is hungry. Feed her your cock, keep

her quiet." With my eyes closed, I moan out my approval.

East gets into a kneeling position and, careful of my hair, curls his fingers around the nape of my neck and pushes my mouth down onto his steel-hard dick.

Behind me, I hear the shifting of fabric and the thought that Mav and Linc are both jacking themselves off as they watch me fuck and suck in the back of this limo amps up my growing need. I'm flustered and horny and my body is aching for more.

Finn places a hand at the small of my back with his other firmly on my thigh as he fucks me like he's trying to ruin me—I've never been more willing to be ruined—all while East fucks my mouth until I'm gagging on the head every time he slams it to the back of my throat.

"Fucking hell."

Linc's groan makes me feel like a filthy princess as my pussy and mouth get a hard pounding.

"We're almost there." Finn's words are my undoing. I moan around the thick flesh of East's dick as he fucks my face with abandon just as my orgasm builds up from the friction on my clit. Finn grunts, my name falling from between his lips as he spills inside of me.

East lets out a roar as he buries my nose in his groin and feeds me his cum right down my throat before pulling out and kissing me with panting breaths.

I'm a fucking mess as the limo pulls up to the curb and the engine shuts off.

"I don't know whether to let you step out looking like a hot mess who's just been fucked to within an inch of her life, or allow you fix your filthy mouth." Linc grins like he already knows the answer.

Fucker.

He hands me my clutch that was lost in my fuckery and I take a minute to sort my face. Thank God for unsmearable lip stain! I retouch my eyeliner, my hair has barely moved despite everything, so it only takes about thirty seconds for me to put myself back together.

"Perfection," Finn utters as he turns my head back to him, kissing me gently. "Ready, pretty girl?"

A flash of what happened at homecoming sears my mind, but I push it away. I'm not that girl anymore. "Let's do this."

I sway in East's arms as *I'll Be* by Edwin McCain plays over the sound system. I grin over at Indi who is slow dancing next to us with Alex. As the song finishes, I extract myself from East, kissing him softly before moving over to Indi.

"Can I steal my girl?" I ask, but not really asking as I take her hand as *Shivers* by Ed Sheeran starts playing. I'm not sure who chose the DJ, but I'm here for it. He's been laying down some absolute jams tonight.

We laugh as we dance to the beat like loons, loving that we

don't take ourselves too seriously. We dance through the next four songs, laughing as we do, our guys all huddled around one table. Apparently my 'death' brought a lot of people together.

Maybe asking Indi and the guys to join the Knights is a good idea. Sunday, when Indi and I go out to lunch, I'm going to ask. It's decided.

"Ladies and gentlemen, it's time to declare our prom king and queen!" Blair's voice sounds across the room. She's standing on the raised platform where the DJ booth is in a shimmering, spaghetti strap silver dress that hugs every inch of her. She looks amazing.

Everyone turns to face her as Indi drags me from the dance floor to where our guys are sitting, waiting for us.

"And our prom king is... Maverick Riley!" My jaw drops at the announcement of Mav's name, who looks as shocked as I am that Blair just called his name. The spotlight moves to our table as cheers and applause fill the room.

"I don't know which of you fuckers did this, but revenge will be sweet," he threatens as he stands and heads toward the stage. Blair places the crown on his head and he stares menacingly out at the school body. My giggles erupt as he glares at me across the room.

"And our prom queen is..." Blair pauses for effect, winking at me before she opens her mouth. "Indigo Montoya!"

"What the fuck?" Indi groans and I laugh.

"Not so nice getting the crown, is it?" I tease. Feels all the sweeter after the shit she gave me about homecoming. "Now go rock the shit out of that crown."

"You're always a queen to me, Sunshine," Ryker says to her, kissing her before pushing her toward the stage. The cheers and applause greet her too as Blair gives her the sash and crown.

"Now for the Royal Dance!"

I burst out laughing, and Finley snickers next to me. "Those two dancing is going to be hilarious."

While Indi and Mav have come pretty far the last few weeks, they still bicker like siblings, but he takes her hand and leads her to the dance floor.

"If he touches her ass…" Ryker starts, but Ellis punches his arm.

"Don't be a dick, it's Mav. He's not going to do a damn thing."

I smile at Ellis. It's so nice that everyone is finally getting along. It's the start of something promising. While I hate what we had to go through to get here, I'll never regret the outcome of it. The photographer for the night snaps shots of them as they dance like fools to *Stay* by Justin Bieber and The Kid Laroi. They wave for us all to join them, so I coax the rest of the table up, and once we're all there dancing, everyone else joins in too.

This night is everything I wanted it to be. The cheese of prom and one of the better memories from our senior year. We all deserved a night like tonight, just something fun after the craziness of this year.

I dance and laugh with each of my guys, with Alex and Indi, and lose myself to the laughter of it all. A year ago I thought I wanted nothing less than to come back to Echoes Cove. That there was nothing here for me... and despite the reasons for my return, my new found family are more than I could've ever hoped for.

THIRTY FOUR

OCTAVIA

I walk into the back yard, heading for the pool. The sun is finally hot enough for a day on the sun loungers, and while I intend to swim some too, I am overdue a day of lying by the pool and reading, so that's exactly my plan. I have the house to myself after practically shoving Smithy out the door with Matthew this morning, making Matthew promise to make Smithy have a good weekend.

He deserves some rest. I'm not the only one who's been through the wringer lately. Plus, my feet still hurt from dancing all night last night, so a day of chill is exactly what the doctor ordered.

Sitting on the lounger, I pop my Kindle and phone on the

table before rubbing in my lotion, aviators in place so I can actually see for the time being. Once I've finished my lotion, I grab my Kindle and move to lie back when my phone buzzes.

Mav:

Remember the conversation we had about your punishment? And your safe word?

I suck in a breath and bite my lip, instantly fucking wet just from that message.

Me:

Yes.

Mav:

Run.

Holy fuck.

I glance around, not seeing him, but I feel his eyes on me. My breath hitches in anticipation as I scramble to my feet. Movement in my peripheral makes me run toward the back door. I know I agreed to this, I just didn't think it would be so fucking hot, while being so fucking terrifying.

Being hunted by my very own psychopath, knowing he intends on ruining me and making me bleed shouldn't make me this hot. Yet, I almost don't want to run.

But that's half of the game.

Bringing the predator out in him.

When I reach out for the door handle, it doesn't turn all the way. It's fucking locked. I don't remember locking it.

Shit.

Flattening my back against the wood, I frantically look right then left and try to think of another path to take, another entrance into the house.

The garage.

I don't see him anywhere, but I know he's here, his presence is palpable along every hair on my body.

Just as I'm about to make a run for the other side of the house, I stop dead in my tracks at the sound of whistling coming from the far end of the property. Close enough to hear, far away enough that I can't make out where, exactly.

A few weeks before my fake death, Mav and I binged on the Kill Bill movies and, like a fucking idiot, I told him the whistle they used was creepy and made my entire body shiver with fear.

The motherfucker is whistling that exact song right now and I've never been surer of his psychotic tendencies than at this very moment.

"You're evil," I mutter the words but I wouldn't be surprised if he heard them.

There's no time to figure out where he is, I need to run if I want any hope of winning this game. This very sinister and fucked up game that's making me wetter by the second.

Maybe I've got some psychopathic tendencies, too.

I make a run for it, heading straight for the side door to the garage and I'm a little wary that it's not locked. Then again, he couldn't have planned this, right? He hasn't been anywhere around here today.

Grateful, I rush inside, closing and locking the door behind me. With a panicked three-sixty I try to find a good hiding spot just in case this is a set-up. The garage is big and he can't just read my mind.

Then it hits me.

The panic room.

Dad built it to look like the continuation of the wall, said it would be my secret hiding place if ever I needed to feel safe.

I turn to the side and run on the balls of my feet to avoid making too much noise. The coast is clear, the hand drawn flower on the wall my clue to where the opening would be.

The thought of going into a small, confined space of my own accord makes my skin crawl as panic begins to rise, but I remind myself that this is my punishment and no matter what, I'm safe.

I'm always safe with Mav, even if the fear spike makes my heart race.

Breathing heavily, I open the door by pushing in the mechanism and quickly shut myself inside, fighting the urge to double over and hyperventilate.

Except, I don't have time to react because I don't bump into a wall.

Not even close.

"Getting brave, aren't we?"

I gasp so loudly at the low and dark tone of his voice that I nearly pee myself a little.

I'm about to tell him he scared the fuck out of me when his hand clamps down on my mouth and pulls me back against his chest. His dick is so hard, I'm not sure what I'm most afraid of right now. The dark or his huge cock.

How did he get here before me? He was out there whistling like a fucking maniac when I ran in here.

I want to ask him a million questions but they all die on my hitched breaths when I feel the cold, hard steel of what I'm pretty fucking sure is a blade pressing against my flesh.

Needless to say, this is not ideal. Trapped in a small space in complete and utter darkness, at the mercy of a man who has serious blurred vision about the line between what is right and wrong. Who is currently sliding a knife up the inside of my thigh.

It should be a huge fucking red flag. And yet...

On instinct, I fight him. I try to get myself free of him, crying into the palm of his hand as he clamps down harder and puts more pressure on the knife that has almost reached my pussy.

My wet as fuck and treacherous pussy.

"You should know by now, princess, that you can run..." he slides the knife to the small piece of fabric that holds my bathing suit together and slices it right off. "But you can never fucking hide from me."

I freeze as the lines between fantasy and real life fucking fear blur in my mind. The darkness is making things fuzzy, almost giving me the feeling that this is all in my head. That it's a dream or a nightmare, despite all of my senses being on high alert.

He moves the knife upward, slicing off the strings of my top and I'm suddenly completely naked in this fucking black hole.

Panic spikes in me again when I hear his breathy voice at my ear, the sultry sound running through my nerve endings like a small electric pulse.

"When I release your mouth, the only sounds I want to hear from you are your grunts while I fuck you hard enough to bruise your pretty little skin."

I shake my head no but what I really want to say is "Yes! God yes!"

But telling him no, fighting him, is like a red flag to a bull. So of course, I do whatever it takes to make him slam his dick inside my empty, wanting pussy.

I shake my head in a show of no consent, pretending to fight him and smile when he moans his approval.

"Tough fucking shit, princess. I said yes."

When I try to bite down on his hand, I clench my thighs at the filthy curses that pass through his lips, the breath landing on the column of my neck. I am so fucking turned on right now. I know we discussed playing out this whole non-consent thing, but fuck me it's hotter than I thought it would be.

When I start to fight him harder, turning and twisting and trying to grab at him on one side and the other, I almost sigh in relief when he grabs my forearms and pins them at the small of my back.

That's when he releases my mouth and pushes the side of my face against the wall.

I scream, my lungs filling with air and then releasing a screech like my life depends on it.

"Fuck, I love the way you cry." At first I'm confused when I hear him, but when he buries his fingers in my hair—holding me tight against the wall—and he licks a path up my cheek, taking his time to go from my jaw to my eye, I realize tears are falling freely and he's licking them up like they're his favorite meal.

I can't see him and he can't see me, but somehow he knows I'm crying before even I do.

With my hands secured behind me, and my legs kicked apart enough for his big body to nudge in between my thighs, he plunges inside me in one hard, quick move.

We both groan at the feel of us joined once more. At the fight that led us here. At the fantasy that he made a reality.

"This pussy will always be mine. Day, night, any hour. When I want it, when I crave it."

He's probably right.

But agreeing with him is not part of the fantasy.

Fighting him off? Yeah, that's what it's all about.

I push my ass toward him and try to free my hands, but almost weep when his dick slides out of me.

The next thing I know, my wrists are tied with whatever it is he'd had on hand.

"I thought you might disagree, so I made sure to be prepared."

Fucker.

I think that's all he's going to do but that was my first mistake.

Never underestimate a man with no limits.

Mav turns me around and in one smooth move, he's got my arms up over my head, the rope secured somewhere above me.

Fucking hell, how did he do that?

I'm guessing he put a lot of thought into this and for that alone, I want to kiss him. Hard and long.

Hiking my thighs up with his hands, he slams back inside me, but this time, he shuts me up with his tongue.

His kiss is demanding and invading. We're all lips and tongues and curses as he fucks with the force of a tsunami on the shores of an island. He's the power of the waves and I'm the sand that submits to his will.

"You think you can lead this dance, princess?"

"Fuck you." I spit the words out and cringe at the thought that I may have actually spit on his mouth.

"Hmm, is that your way of begging me for more?"

God, I love this man.

There are no words that I could say that would be as filthy and dubious as I want, so I say nothing as he pummels my pussy without a care in the world.

Our sweat mingles and our muscles are tight as he pistons in and out of me, making sure to grind against my clit every time he's at the hilt.

"Get off me!" I scream at him, feeding the fantasy, and I feel him grin as he bites down on my shoulder, making me cry out again.

I'm so close.

So fucking close but I don't dare say anything to him.

"Do it, princess. Come all over my dick."

He thrusts in once more, then again, and by the time he's slammed in the third time, I go off like a fucking volcano.

I scream again, this time his name falling from my mouth like a prayer. I repeat it over and over again as the shaking subsides and the warmth of my climax washes over me.

Blinking my euphoria away, I whimper as he continues to pound into me. He hasn't come yet.

"Mav?"

My arms are suddenly freed and his hand in my hair pushes me down to my knees as he slides out of my pussy.

"Open your mouth."

Fuck yes.

I do as I'm told and without waiting for a command or

permission, I take his balls into my hand and swallow his cock all the way to the back of my throat.

He tastes like me and him together and it makes me fucking hot all over again.

"Fuck yes. That's it, princess. Take my cock down your throat. Suck on it like a good girl."

God, his filthy mouth does things to me.

Placing both of his hands on the sides of my face, he rears back and fucks my face without abandon.

"I'm going to come so fucking hard down your throat. Come with me, princess. Play with your clit and come with me."

I move quickly at his demand and in the time it takes him to thrust three or four more times inside my mouth, we both let go.

Of every fucking thing.

I come all over my thighs and he jets his cum straight down my throat and I swallow every fucking drop he has to give me.

He roars in the small space before pulling out of my mouth. I fall back from my knees to sit back on my legs, spent and exhausted.

Mav picks me up and cradles me in his arms as he opens the door and leads me straight to my bathroom where there's already a steaming bubble bath waiting for me. He sits me on the counter while he strips out of his clothes, then picks me up again and carries me into the tub, sitting us down, shifting me so I can lie back against him.

"I love you, princess," he murmurs, his hands rubbing

circles on my thighs.

I let out a contented sigh and lean my head back so I can look up at him. "I love you too, Mav."

"Surprise!"

I startle at the shouts as I walk into the private room of the restaurant with Indi, grinning from ear to ear as I take in everyone here. Smithy and Matthew, my guys, Bentley and Luc. Indi's guys. Jenna and the Midnight Blue girls, plus Mac and some of the others from the tour.

"Happy belated birthday, V," Indi says, squeezing me. "And while I'd like to take all the credit for this, Smithy and the guys did most of the hard work. I have plans for next weekend though" She wags her brows at me and I laugh, hugging her back before making my way around the room, saying hello to everyone here.

Even Ryker hugs me, which shocks the shit out of me.

I sit down at the head of the table, Lincoln to my left, Indi to my right, and I try not to cry at just how happy I am to have everyone I love in one room. Seeing my past and present collide is kind of overwhelming in the best of ways.

I take a deep breath, trying to wrangle the emotions flooding me as I grin at Smithy, who is sitting opposite me at the end of the table, tucked between Matthew and Luc. I never thought I'd have a huge family, but I've learned family isn't blood. It's the people that show up for you, even when you don't ask them to.

These people right here are my family.

Smithy looks to me, then glances at Indi and back, and I can see the question in his gaze. Did I ask her yet? I shake my head, letting him know I didn't, and he gives me a quick nod. He knows I was going to ask her today, but I was going to ask her over food.

I wasn't expecting any of this, so I haven't had the chance.

"Thank you for all of this," I murmur to Lincoln, who takes my hand and squeezes it.

"Anything for you, Octavia. We had plans for your birthday before Harrison ruined them. This is just the start of what we have planned." He winks at me and I swear to God my pussy flutters at the sight of it.

Down girl.

"Any news on Harrison?" I ask, and he shakes his head.

"No, we know he's back in the States, but he's been very fucking clever about disguising his movements. We will find him though, and he will be dealt with." His eyes darken with rage, before he shakes it off. "But we can worry about that tomorrow, let's just enjoy today."

He kisses me quickly before my attention is pulled across the room to where Jenna and East are mid laughing fit. All I hear is the word tequila sunrise and I groan. "Jenna, whyyyyyyy?"

"Oh come on, Summertime Starlight. You know it's a good

story." I flip her the finger, and she tells the story about my first ever drunken episode on tour. The dancing on table tops, thinking I was living my best *Coyote Ugly* life, singing at the top of my lungs like I was Mariah freaking Carey.

The whole room is just love and laughter, and I feel so blessed.

The servers filter into the room to get everyone's drink orders. Once they move further down the table, East pulls me to one side, where there's a gift table, and pulls a small jewelry box from his back pocket.

"Happy Birthday, V."

I smile up at him, taking the box from his outstretched hand. "You totally didn't have to get me anything."

"Shh," he says, putting a finger over my mouth. "Just open the damn box."

I roll my eyes at him and remove his hand. I look down at the sparkly infinity charm, lined with black crystals. "East—"

"Forever. That's what I want with you, Octavia. That's what this is. I don't know where life is going to take us, but I am going be at your side for all of it." He cups my cheeks in his hands, looking at me like I'm the center of his universe, before he kisses me. He pours so much love into the action that my heart feels like it's going to explode.

"I love you," I whisper against his lips.

"I love you too." He pulls back, lifting my hand, and undoing my bracelet before slipping the new charm on and reattaching it to my wrist.

"Come on you two, it's time to order!" Mav hollers and my stomach gurgles as if in response. East chuckles at me as he leads me back to the table.

Hours pass in a blur of laughter, drinking, and food. I wasn't sure how we were being served alcohol until Matthew mentions that he owns this place. A few more things made sense after that.

I try to stifle a yawn, but Finn catches me, smirking at me as he moves to my chair. He stands me up, sits in my seat then puts me back in his lap. "Tired, pretty girl."

"Yeah," I nod, "but I also don't want to leave."

He kisses down my neck and shoulder, making me gasp as my eyes flutter closed.

"Well, isn't this just cozy?" The entire place goes silent as my eyes fly open and I see Harrison standing across the room, a gun raised, pointed in my direction. "I should've known I'd find your little whore in the arms of another man, Lincoln."

"Harrison," Lincoln starts, as Smithy stands facing off with the mad man holding a gun.

"What the fuck are you playing at, Harrison?" he hisses, and quicker than anyone can react, Harrison brings up his arm and smashes the gun into Smithy's temple. He drops to the ground like nothing, and I let out a scream. Matthew dives for him, but I can already see he's unconscious.

"Who would've thought the little Royal slut could cause so much damage? I should've killed you along with your daddy," he snarls at me. Finn is up and out of our chair, standing in front of me in a second, as Harrison moves toward us, one gun trained on me before pulling a second and keeping it on the rest of the room.

Lincoln stands, coming to stand in front of Finn, blocking Harrison's way. "Get out of my way, Lincoln. I don't want to kill you, but I will. She's ruined enough lives. I am here to put things back to rights."

"I don't fucking think so," Maverick yells, charging at Harrison with East. They tackle him and I scream, as the entire room bursts into movement. The gun pops three times, and screams erupt from in here and in the restaurant. I freeze, trying to look for my guys, when I hear Harrison's voice, and find him face to face with Lincoln, guns trained on him and on Mav. Finn holds me in place as I struggle against him, trying to get to East who is bleeding on the ground. I know he's not the only one hurt, the whimpers in the room from Indi and Matthew fill my ears.

"I told you not so long ago you'd have to pick between your brother and your slut. I guess you made your choice."

My ears ring at the next pop, a scream pierces the air as my knees go weak and the world goes dark.

EPILOGUE

FINLEY

ONE YEAR LATER

I sit in the sand, watching the lights from the pier illuminate the night sky. The sounds of the waves fill my ears, calming me despite the hubbub of voices and rides from the pier. It's weird being back in The Cove after being away for so long.

I've never been away from my home town for this long, and it was almost impossible to come back.

So much has changed in the last year. It's hard to wrap my head around it all. There was so much pain, so much anger, that we all got a little lost for a while after Octavia's surprise party. Blame was passed around from pillar to post, but that didn't get us anywhere.

The last time I was here, in this spot, I was comforting Octavia as she cried.

Fuck me, that feels like a few lifetimes ago.

"Finley, is that you?" I look up and find Indi hand-in-hand with Ryker, Ellis and Alex not far behind them.

"Hey, Indi. You got here early."

"Yeah, I wanted to walk the beach before we did this. Remember the good times, ya know?"

I nod as she smiles wistfully at me. "Yeah I know, it's why I came out here on my own too. The others shouldn't be long though."

"Yeah, Dylan is meeting us here, he had to help his dad finish up in the garage before he could head over." The other three say hello as they sit in the sand with me, filling me in on what's happened to them since we all left here at the start of last summer.

About twenty minutes later, Dylan lopes up on the beach, a giant grin on his face. "Look who I found in the parking lot!"

Octavia laughs from her perch on his back before squealing as he drops to sit with her still attached to him, her arms around his neck, and legs around his waist. "You're such an ass, Dylan!"

I press my lips together, trying not to laugh too hard at her fake outrage. It's so good to see her smile. There was a minute back there when I wondered if she'd ever smile again.

She's been through so much, but my girl is a fighter, and she's made it through the darkness that tried to take her from me.

Indi leaps on her once she detaches herself from Dylan and

the two of them laugh, catching up like they didn't FaceTime on the flight home earlier. I sit quietly, listening to their conversation as they talk like they don't talk to each other every single day.

I know it's not the same since we're on opposite sides of the country from her bestie now, but you'd never know there was a day that they'd been apart to look at them.

Thick as thieves.

Have been since day one.

It makes me so fucking happy that she had a friend like that through everything that happened senior year. After everything we went through, I think it would take the armies of Hell to separate those two, and even then, my bet's on the girls.

A figure drops down beside me, and I turn to find Mav sitting there, East dropping beside him in the next second. "Took you long enough."

Mav pushes me with his shoulder, making me rock into our girl who slides onto my lap. "Hey, pretty girl."

She leans in to kiss me, then moves to Mav and East, doing the same with them.

"Are we doing this thing?" Ryker asks, impatient as ever. Some things will never change.

"Let me just grab my bag. I put my stuff in there, since the gorilla man carried me down the beach," V smiles, moving back to where Indi is sitting next to her back pack.

She pulls out the box we put together earlier today while Mav and Ellis go and gather wood to start the fire.

"You sure you're ready for this?" I ask her, and she nods.

"Yeah, it's time. I'll never fully let him go, but I need to be able to move forward, and this seems like the best way to do that."

Indi smiles sadly at her, taking her hand and squeezing it. As much as I know Octavia loves us, and needs us, I'm not sure she'd have survived the last two years without her walking rainbow of a friend.

It doesn't take long for Dylan to get the bonfire lit, the flames crawling higher into the sky as the heat increases.

"Getting started without us?" I turn and smile as Lincoln, Smithy, and Matthew find us. V runs to them, wrapping each of them in a hug, leaving Linc for last. He scoops her into his arms and kisses her before joining the rest of us.

After Harrison was shot in the restaurant last year, a lot of things fell apart. Lincoln lost himself a little to a black hole, despite his hatred for his dad, it was still his dad, and he was covered in brain matter from the police officer's shot.

The fact that we nearly lost East and Smithy at his hands after losing so many others, including Stone... Linc took on the full force of guilt for his father's actions. It took our entire summer road trip before he fully came back to himself.

Thankfully, spending our freshman year together at Saints U in New York has been a breath of fresh air. I never thought I'd like the cold of the East Coast, and despite missing the sunshine of California, we all loved it there in our shared house.

V moves forward, pulling her dad's journals from the box and moves toward the fire. "I miss you, Dad, each and every day, but I know you wouldn't want me to keep looking back. So I'm doing this for you, as well as for me."

She holds the journals in shaking hands, so I move to stand at her back, my hands enclosing hers. "It's okay, pretty girl. You can do this." I help her as she drops the journals into the fire, purging the bad memories along with the words she's read endlessly the last year as she clung to his memory once her personal nightmare was over.

Each person steps forward, casting the memories they want to let go of into the fire too, taking a seat in the sand once they're done.

There is a peace as I let go of the last pieces of my parents, a weight lifting from me as I drop their pictures into the fire. The house that they ruined me in burned down last summer, by Maverick's swift hand, and that was how we got the idea for our little burn party. A way to cleanse the shadows on our souls.

Octavia drops back into my lap, leaning her head back on my shoulder. "It feels good to be home," she murmurs before turning her attention to Indi, and I smile as I press a kiss into her hair.

I never thought I'd agree with her, but she's right.

It is good to be home, and my home is wherever she is.

The End

ACKNOWLEDGMENTS

I can't believe we here, at the end of this book, the close of the series. It has been the wildest ride and there are so many people I need to thank.

First, thank you to KC for getting me past the finish line on this one. It was a hard bloody slog at the end there, but we made it!

Rose, you know you're my wifey, thank you for the FaceTimes at all times of day to keep my mental health on track so I could get to this point.

Nikki, for keeping my shit in line while I've been squirreling really freaking hard with this book. I appreciate the hell out of you, thank you so much for everything you do.

David, you sparkly unicorn you, thank you for everything, including the hilarious laughs when you should 100% be asleep! Thank you for loving these guys, and calling me out when it's needed. For making the words shine and well, for being my social butterfly bitch aha.

Eva, thank you for always being there when I need to gripe, and for well, all the things. If I listed it all I'd be here all damn day ahaha.

To my alpha & beta teams, you guys are freaking rockstars. Lisa, Zoe, Megan, Kiera, Jeni, Liberty, Kyla, Sam, Jessi & Nicole. Thank you for your priceless feedback, and for loving these characters as much as I do.

Thank you to Sarah and Sam for making sure the words shine by the time I'm done fucking around with them, and for letting me corrupt you aha.

Finally, to you the reader, thank you. For taking a chance on an author you've probably never heard of. For picking up a new book. For running the gauntlet with us. Just thank you.

Here's looking forward what comes next!

Peace out

xoxo

ABOUT THE AUTHOR

Lily is a writer, dreamer, fur mom and serial killer, crime documentary addict.

She loves to write dark, reverse harem romance and characters who will shatter your heart. Characters who enjoy stomping on the pieces and then laugh before putting you back together again. And she definitely doesn't enjoy readers tears. Nope. Not even a little.

If you want to keep up to date with all things Lily, including where her next book is out, please find join her reader group, Lily's Wild Hearts, on Facebook.

ALSO BY LILY WILDHART

THE KNIGHTS OF ECHOES COVE

(Dark, Bully, High School Reverse Harem Romance)

Tormented Royal

Lost Royal

Caged Royal

Forever Royal

THE SAINTS OF SERENTIY FALLS

(Dark, Bully, Step Brother, College, Reverse Harem Romance)

Burn

Lightning Source UK Ltd.
Milton Keynes UK
UKHW010053120822
407175UK00001B/14